THE
VERDICT

BOOKS BY

HILDEGARD KNEF

•

THE GIFT HORSE

THE VERDICT

THE
VERDICT

·

Hildegard
Knef

TRANSLATED FROM THE GERMAN BY

DAVID ANTHONY PALASTANGA

Farrar, Straus and Giroux · *New York*

Library of Congress Cataloging in Publication Data

Knef, Hildegard.

The verdict.

Translation of Das Urteil.

I.   Title.

PZ4.N38Ve3 [PT2674.E36]   833'.9'14   75-34174

The events described in this book are based on personal experience. But the characters portrayed, together with their actions and statements, are freely interpreted and not intended precisely to depict actual persons.

THE

VERDICT

1

·

The windows of my hospital rooms are almost invariably on the right when looking from the bed, and seem to delight in enticing me into the forbidden and often impossible act of rolling over on my side. So I turn just my head toward the glass oblong, which is usually shut, and measure hope and desperation against its prosaic presentation which, depending on weather and the time of year, offers scant variety. Some three months ago it had been a chestnut tree, in the Swiss hospital; I had seen its candle-like cones blossom whitely and yellow-grayly die, had endured the daily songs sung in its praise by all the day, night, and special-duty nurses until, grown weary, I came to regard it as a stoical, inexorably observing censurer, and pronounced it guilty of spying and delighting in others' misfortunes, saw it as a gross parasite parading its health and strength, using its long arms to feast on the scenes of life and slow violent death it saw in all the isolation and intensive-care departments, the cancer wards, stretching its suckers down to the thermographic, mammographic stations, cobalt, and X-ray rooms in the cellar, until finally, after many weeks, I began to apprehend the analogy of our situations: it would never again leave the gray square of its courtyard, nor I the white of my room.

At that time I had no inkling of the verdict. Life seems to arrange itself into a Before and an After. Since yesterday I shall think in terms of pre-verdict and post-verdict.

Before the chestnut tree, it had been a palm and the roof of a garage. It was a flaccid palm, its leaves the color of eggplant and smeared with oil; only once, during a storm, did they heave themselves angrily to and fro before drooping back again into their apathy, sagging wanly over the pineapple-like trunk. Long before this, a courtyard in Berlin, with flaking walls and faded traces of bullet holes and an apron hung out to dry over the elaborate rusty iron balustrade of a turn-of-the-century balcony that also harbored an untenanted bird cage and a pot of chives; a man in a gray-white undershirt who stretched his bones between muslin drapes at six-ten in the morning, scratched his old man's chest, and looked disgustedly across at the rows of hospital windows, turned and disappeared until the next morning. Then a window in London, and multipotted chimneystacks against a yellow-green sky; a cared-for, finicky lawn seen through the soundproofed windows of a Zurich clinic, its green smooth, with no patches, as though it had been shampooed, brushed, and vacuumed, in short, perfect; a garden in Hamburg with narrow, timorously fenced-in flower beds. There were New York's fire escapes and vertical tunnels of light, St. Moritz's snow-swept airport, Vienna's locked and sealed but still drafty double windows, and then, near Munich, a weeping willow and May's freshness at the edges of the glass oblong, there where the verdict first sensed the opportunity it was later to use so effectively.

Now it's Salzburg: a blue-white sky behind green plastic venetian blinds. Heat-wave sky. I can see the windows of the gynecological wing, a corner of the Fischer von Erlach Church as wide as my thumb, and the frayed crown of a walnut tree. I can't see the flower beds beneath my window, or the parking lot with the license plates of the doctors. I know that they're there. On the evening before the operation I had stood at the window while two nurses smoothed the sheets, slapped the pillows, and rubbed the washbasin. That was the day before yesterday. Pre-verdict.

These are the windows of the last years.

•

The faces above the bakers' aprons had been sour. But really sour, almost up in arms. Even so, they still reminded me of those small-part actors who appear briefly on the stage and bring the tragic news so vital to the plot: "It's . . ." said one, and promptly blew the rest—after having waited calmly through the first and second acts, he fell headlong into that gaping bourn of memory from which no traveler returns. "It's . . ." he said again valiantly, arousing general sympathy, but I, as the anxious but masterful leading lady exclaimed, "The truth, I demand to know the truth!" I overdid the "demand" a little. They now nodded as though I'd sprung into the breach for the sleeping prompter, given the signal, closed the level crossing, shifted the points of memory. "The biopsy was suspect." This came easily, on safe ground. "I went down to the lab, the last test confirmed it," said a second. Yet another cleared his throat raspingly and followed up with a long-drawn "Yeees . . . it's a carcinoma, about the size of a cherry." The cherry is growing bigger and bigger—doesn't it ring a frivolous note? Isn't it full of hope? Warm from the summer sun, deep red, vibrant?—"Great God Almighty," the first one said, but it was lame, had no conviction, didn't suit the part. The visit to the badly directed dress rehearsal seemed at an end.

The verdict had been spoken. "This is getting ridiculous," I'd said. And hadn't their worried, closed faces opened up? Hadn't they suddenly smoothed out, brightened up, grown younger, shown signs of surprise and gratitude? They were wearing crisp, starched, steam-pressed aprons. Bakers' aprons. White. And the way they stood there—from the tops of their heads to their toes they might well have been members of that worthy profession on the annual outing, lined up self-consciously for the obligatory photo. No sign of the familiar sexy green of the Swiss hospitals, with the chic high collars nestling against the curls at the neck, always looking as though they'd been casually thrown on, more as a precaution than a necessity, playing down the gravity of the situation. The *"haute couture"* look of the surgeons' masks and nurses' caps had allowed me to forget my driftwood condition for a few seconds before my fifty-fourth—or was it the fifty-fifth?—operation; driftwood, washed up by the tide, battened down to the table, seared with anesthetic.

But now the Viennese gentleman, present address Salzburg, spoke, or rather announced his intention of doing so by clearing his throat. He stood there in his baker's apron and looked at me with astonished eyes, and this in itself was astonishing because the eyes of people standing looking at people lying nearly always take on an expression of arrogance and superiority. He must have had red hair as a child, a few wisps are still poking out from his round skull, the backs of his hands too are full of brick-red fluff, as though he'd been cavorting on a lamb's wool carpet with wet hands. I hoped for a second that he'd whisper a comfy, motherly "You do lead us a dance, you know." He said, "Do we have a free hand?" and, as though French might lend precision, *"carte blanche?"* I nodded quickly, mistrustingly, unaccustomed to being asked in hospitals. The fluffy hand reached for mine, covered it briefly, and withdrew.

Immediately all four walls start to scream TERMINAL. "Dignity," I hear it babbling behind my leaden brows. "Why me?" it wails and flaps. "Why not me?" it echoes with a leer. Words and visions sense a free-for-all and pour in, admittance no longer prohibited.

It's August 10, 1973. Yesterday, on the ninth, they operated, took their sample. Yesterday belongs to pre-verdict. They were certain. I was certain. Not a word about verdict. In two hours they will fetch me again, for the fifty-sixth operation. Sometime before, the anesthetist will inject Dolantin with a well-meaning "This'll make you sleepy," then the saliva-damming atropine, perhaps a little strophantin for the narcotic-weary heart. The chief doctor will come in, the same one who yesterday said, "With two or three more semesters you could become a bad-to-average country quack." Curly thick hair he has, and a sunny young face, with soft, very blue eyes. "What's your birth sign?" I'd asked.

"I don't know."

"When were you born?"

"Forty-six."

"Which day?"

He rears back, then hesitantly, "Fourth of July."

"Then you're Cancer."

He goes red and looks at the Fischer von Erlach Church as though hoping that the bells might start ringing and carry the word away. They remain silent, only the blind creaks softly, regularly, like an old man's denture.

In one and a half hours they'll take off their jackets, trousers, shirts, change their shoes, come clattering in on their Swedish clogs, wash their hands for five minutes, pull on the thin, sterilized rubber gloves with the help of a nurse. A man in a white apron will push me into the white-tiled room next door; I'll watch as the thick needle nudges through to the vein and the pentothal seeps in. I'll watch until I see no more, feel nothing. They will stroke my lashes, test the reflexes of the lids, then shoot curare—no, they won't, they only use that on belly operations, so that the intestines won't jump out at them like ten hungry rattlesnakes. The surgeon will murmur his "Can I start?" and the anesthetist will nod, or even say yes. They will sterilize the skin, cut around fat and muscles, cleave the tissue, still the blood, dissect the glands and fat up to the large muscle, then lift out the whole. At some stage the surgeon will say, "It was high time I worked with amateurs again," or, "If even only one of you would wake up I'd be thrilled," and then, of course, "When I say scalpel I always mean clamp, you know that." And if the needle is too big, the gagged conversation will query the presence of a rhinoceros. They won't go into the "fat women" routine, bovine comparisons, nor will there be any jokes on the "economic miracle"; one of them might just tell of a nocturnal adventure, enlarge on her various qualities. They'll sigh as they are careful with the nerves, take away the lymphatic nodules, watch out for the main arteries, cauterize small hemorrhages with the electric-powered knife, take great pains to avoid hematoma, or blood effusions; they'll sew with catgut, put in the suction tubes, drain off the persistent last trickles of blood. The first assistant will come forward with two surgical pincers, sew the skin with silk, spray the wound, bandage it with sterile gauze, adjust the transfusion bottle. Then they'll drink coffee in the adjacent room, smoke a cigarette, wait for the next one.

For the moment they're still lingering at my bed, all three, the surgeon, the gynecologist, the anesthetist. One of them sniffs impatiently, angrily, but doesn't say whether it's the heat or the verdict that causes him to do so. He was a submarine commander during the war and had been in an English prison camp near Singapore. This much I know already. He's taken me this far into his confidence. A desire to discuss something other than the body in need, which is mine, gave rise to the occasion. In the Swiss hospitals it had been considered a matter of decency not to mention it, the Second World War. There it had taken on an air of deep-frozen aggression, even frustration, truncated adventure, dead but won't lie down, belonging neither to the present nor to the past. German nurses would take great trouble to camouflage their nationality, reminding me of the immigrants in America, 1947. Only one, Trude, the East German girl who'd escaped with only her handbag, didn't give a hoot. Even so, it was rumored that a Swiss nurse had barked at her in the canteen just as she was removing fat and skin from the midday wurst: "You'd have given a lot for that when you were still over there, wouldn't you?" "According to her, everywhere's 'over there,'" Trude told me in her purest, toe-curling Saxon accent, which, riding on the newly learned Baden singsong lilt, had acquired a most original if, sadly, not more pleasant slant. Soft hands she had, hands one was thankful for when the body waxed violent, when it showed its susceptibility to pain and torture. I'd even grown fond of her back-combed hair, ghastly as it was. It towered over her already immense head like a beehive, fragile and endangered whenever she made an incautious movement with her head, threatening to collapse in the faintest breeze, carrying the head and the neck with it to the depths. She kept her cap in her apron pocket—the ensuing rows with the head nurse were part of the daily routine.

My submarine commander says, "We have lots of time, we'll make our preparations at leisure." He takes his time intoning "leisure," as though he wants to hypnotize me with the timbre of his deep voice, let me take part in this wonderful leisure. I immediately hope for a pardon, a reprieve, an annulment of the verdict. My eyelids seem to be gaining independence; they're stretching down to the jaw, I fear. The grain of hope dissolves in the dry foam that's spooking through my veins and backbone, swallowing my spittle, blossoming on my tongue like yeast. "Till then," the three say and move off irresolutely, each giving the other priority and thereby delaying the exit in a comic-helpless way, one step forward, one step back, hands pointing futilely in the direction of the door. "Till then," as though we'd meet for a coffee, a walk, take the sun on the banks of the Salzach River.

The blanket is coiling and uncoiling, swimming, as though under water. The linen sheet is sticking to my shins, and the sweat's dripping from the backs of my knees as from a garden hose; fresh scars, old scars, brand-new scars whistle and scratch like all the sweaters of my childhood. The heat billows up the spinach green of the curtains, over the washbasin, the thermometer glass, around the oxygen cylinder and the electrocardiograph, which looks like a homemade radio; my hair is like drive-in spaghetti, wet and smelling sour, the craving for a deodorant becomes manic, all the TV commercials I've ever seen come back. Salzburg's August sky beams at me. How I long for the soothing, humanely pain-relieving drugs of my first operations, when all the hospitals stank of Lysol disinfectant and one retched after the ether. How I long for the divine days and nights when one could trade squalor and panic for a violet-colored pillow to fly painlessly away on, the time when Spasmo-Inalgon, Fortral, Valium, and Novalgin infusions, and all the other expensive, worthless junk of the pharmaceutical industry still lay dormant, unfermented in macabre brains, when no one dreamed of injecting nerve-racking, neck-breaking, allergy-inducing abominations, when pain was never allowed to know to what limits it could go, when the mention of Eukodal or Klyradon or morphine didn't conjure a knowing smile on the nurse's lips, knowing about the wicked pleasures of addiction, or prompt the hale and bodily still-unscarred doctor to paroxysms of pseudo-sage admonishment, when the rattle of keys to the narcotics cupboard was an innocent, heavenly sound, and the millions of monkeys on teenage backs had still cast no pall over the concept of charity.

•

Liverish and morose the awakening. I'm lying trussed up like a bale of freight. Coils, brown with whitish knobs, dangle between me and the electrocardiograph sentry. An infusion is trickling, draggingly, stubbornly, as though the yield of each tiny drop cost it painful decision.

"How long have I got?" I ask. She's as round as a rubber ball with dark-brown button eyes in a round face. The black thin hair is drawn back to a bun which sticks out from under the crackling stiff cap like a pigeon's egg. She's jolly, she's content. "My days are full," she says, and, "I'm always on top of the world, don't know why, I certainly haven't deserved it." Twenty years she's stood in the operating theater and assisted, admiring "her" professor, criticizing the others' clumsy paws; she drools over the comparison, "her" professor soars to unparalleled heights.

Her name is Erasta. Erasta says, "You mustn't think that way," and her voice, at other times clear and vigorously accentuated by the South Austrian accent, rattles with excitement, for fear that the pauses between the sporadic, post-narcotic sentences could become shorter, give way to a conversation. "I know many, a great many who've lived with it for years, lived to a ripe old age," she says emphatically. I, grumpy, looking for a fight, singed by anesthesia and Inalgon: "What does 'with it' mean? Why so squeamish?" She chooses not to hear, sticks to her "A ripe old age, you mark my words." She sits down on the chair next to my bed, jumps up again immediately, and hurries to the window just as the bells of the Erlach Church start to clamor. Voices in the hospital grounds, until now drawling and soporific, awaken sullenly, raspingly. Cries crackle and croak, car doors slam violently, as though the clamor were demanding an answer, a point of view, a letting off of steam. Erastra plucks at the plastic slats of the venetian blind which usually flutter and clatter constantly, but which are now inaudible. She then hastens to the washbasin, checks glasses and towels, rubs the tap and the mirror. Her quick movements are more indolent now, worn down by the day, even peaceful compared with the way she bursts into the room in the morning; propelled by her internal sponge-rubber combustion, she hurtles in at such a pace that I always fear she'll go straight through and out the window, land in the parking lot, and march back up the stairs, repeat the procedure endlessly until someone pins her down, harnesses her energy to the operating theater, calls halt to the wild self-destruction. "The professor threw a tantrum this morning in the operating room 'cause it was so hot," she yells over the clamor. " 'If you gentlemen were to eat less at breakfast and not drink so much coffee, you wouldn't sweat so much,' I said to 'em. Ooh, you should have seen the way those gentlemen looked at me." Her last words synchronize perfectly with the death rattle of the final bell. "You in pain?" she asks abruptly, and two fat tears are sitting in front of the dark-brown buttons. They squat there fixedly, without running down, covering the buttons like gelatin. "It's always the others who die," I say, still grumpy-refractory. "You must be big" shoots through a head that's apparently mine. It seems to be lying next to my shoulder, my beheaded head, rather like the silly ad in which the frilled gent is carrying his grinning face under his arm. Through this, my head then, shoots the idea of being big, which suggests as little to me now as the pre-operative "dignity" did then. Still it helps. First lesson for internees: Don't think further ahead than sixty seconds. The minute is important, it could carry you to the next. What is more banal? Addiction to life, or to abandoning hope?

"The incision will hurt for three or four days," Erasta says. She sits down again. "You must believe it; it's gone, out, they found it, everything's going to be all right." She smooths the sheet, is delighted to find a stain on it, hurries to the cupboard, changes it, fetches alcohol, and massages the pale, disgustingly slack calves that have been parked, deposited, forgotten about. "There was nothing in the lymphs," she says, still bending over my legs.

The sky is dark red, as though a town were burning, a country; a white-gray jet streak marks the red, crumbles to balls of fluff; the red assimilates them, eradicates all signs of the jet and the streak. They'll still be swimming, splashing about, sailing, rolling on the banks, lolling in the grass, still taking possession of Wallersee, Mondsee, Wolfgangsee, Traunsee, and all the other lakes surrounding Salzburg. Their skin will still be hot from the sun, with the first glass of Kalterer wine they'll become giggly or morose. Later, limp from the theater, the opera, a concert, they'll charge to the green tablecloths of the Goldener Hirsch restaurant, swallow boiled beef and Leberknödel, torte, first murmur, then scream their criticism of the evening's show, count their calories, order the last carafe.

"Do you go to the concerts sometimes?" I ask her. She looks up, thunderstruck. "Me?" she cries, as though convinced I must mean someone else; "No," she says, shaking her head wonderingly, and sits down, the bottle of alcohol still in her hand. She laughs in astonishment, trying to picture a life outside the clinic. She has the same expression people have when they see themselves on the screen for the first time, or hear themselves on tape. "I go for walks sometimes on the Mönchsberg, sit on the bank there in my free hour." She blushes as if confessing to a fault, as if the discrepancy between her hospital Salzburg and the festival town Salzburg were due to some failure of hers. "I'll get the shot, then you can sleep." She gets up quickly and disappears.

My Salzburg had been free of hospitals, as free as a tourist's itinerary. A hot afternoon, twenty years ago, a performance of *Everyman*, with Mother. And then Wilhelm Backhaus; like an outraged eagle he swept the audience, looking for prey, made out a woman with a child on her arm in the act of getting up, nailed her to her seat with a scalding look, and moved his attention back to the keys and Beethoven, beak and claws ever at the alert. And *Don Giovanni*, memories of delightful chuckles: a walk-on appearing in a costume quite wrong for the period, the stage manager's hand beckoning desperately from the wings, the shock on the walk-on's face as he grasped his dire mistake, tried to make his about-turn as elegant as possible; on the way out he seemed to shrink and shrink until he finally scuttled off on all fours. —And I, convulsed and under heavy fire from my hissing neighbors, exiting in much the same manner. Salzburg in November: a town with hunched shoulders, on foggy black days the narrow streets like their counterparts in Venice, huddled together, as though the high-rise buildings on the outskirts wanted to take over, shove aside the ancient object of summer tourists' praise. Rainy, happy days in Sankt Gilgen. Later the one-night honeymoon in Fuschl, chugging around the lake in an electric boat the next morning. Which of us said, "We should live here," at that time? He or I? In Gmunden it was. Then Mondsee, I was very pregnant, corpulently content, fat as a hippopotamus; lapping ice cream at Tomaselli's in the evening, strolling through the Getreidegasse, gazing down at the Salzach River. Only three days ago, *Idomeneo*, with its ridiculous libretto, the drafty festival hall, a conductor who made one forget everything else. Salzburg, a festival town as in a storybook, as it should be; I'd always been a fan.

•

What is different since the verdict? Nothing is different. Everything is different. No, nothing. What would I do if they were to come in now and say, "We made a mistake"? Scream for joy? Hardly. Cry thankfully? Perhaps. Cuddle up to a furry, pink security? Yes. And then? The dread had always been present, at hand. —Is it only since the tank clambered over the line of prisoners, or had it already been there before? Since the tank rolled by and I lay in the ditch and felt the blow on the jaw, pushed the loose teeth around with my tongue. Since then I've always had the feeling of living on credit, hurriedly, furtively, shoulders always tensed, one arm raised even in sleep, as though I expected a clout, a thick ear . . . With the doctors I rattle off my rhyme, as at a cross-examination. I'm their captive, their personal prisoner, but there's cunning skulking in the background somewhere and with its help I'll steal a march on him, my murderer. How can one get him by the throat, where does one set the trap, where's the bridle, the scruff of the neck? The tyrant jailer becomes a go-between, going between still existing and not existing.

They're not of one mind, the go-betweens. They grate their teeth, gaze goofily, even the scalpel has question marks. Rather than whimper, they make a dignified suggestion: cobalt rays. Even here they'll debate, come to no agreement, the house senior will have his way. In between, more harmless proposals: milk, lots of it, walk, sleep, don't think about it, ignore it. —Ignore your murderer? A murderer needs a stooge just as a king needs courtiers to bow before him. Why am I shaking? Am I incapable of living with the one sole guarantee, that I'm still here? Am I afraid of living because I fear death? Afraid of success because I fear failure. Fear old age. —Ah no, not that, not me. If only I'll be allowed to experience it . . . Humility as a hiding place. Good boy, good boy, sit, bring your bone, even if we are vegetarians. Live modestly, die modestly. Good, good, back to your kennel. Crumbs of hope, shortcake . . . The darkness is killing me—no, not the darkness, you idiot. I'll call up Emergencies and say, I'm in an emergency. I am going to die. Don't tell me you're going to die too, because you don't know your murderer. Not yet. I know mine. Who'd want to be alone in the dark with his murderer, be stared at, pawed about by the single cell, many cells? I'll tell the man at Emergencies, I have a child. She doesn't even go to school yet and it looks as if the Caesarean sold us both—both, you understand?—down the river. Where is the fellow human being? Why isn't he called the anti-human being? A world full of anti-human beings, and the reformers look uglier than the comedians . . . I'm standing on a station platform—even though I hate trains, I'm standing on a platform and waving. Tell me how to die decently. Nobody tells you how to live decently, perhaps somebody knows how to die decently. I am, according to my income tax returns, a "natural person," and want to know how one dies decently. Embarrassing, embarrassing, they'll say, and take up physical exercises, go off for a rest cure, tread water, do push-ups, procrastinate. Fate has a bone to pick with us, a gigantic insurgent bone. The gentle, shaky, Valium-addicted nurse in the Swiss hospital had said, "Most of all I like to work in the cancer ward. The people are so grateful."

Erasta prods my hipbone, injects into the muscle, puts down the syringe. "I'll stay until you fall asleep." She sits down, places her hands next to each other, and looks at them. "They're awfully red," she says vexedly, then, "Did you often come to Salzburg?"

"The first time was during the war."

"My cousin Karli liked it, the music, I mean; he played the piano, lovely he played." The gelatin is covering the buttons again. "They'd just got engaged, him and my friend, Gertie her name was. The war was on and he'd been called up to the combat fighters or whatever they were called. And Gertie and me were in the nurses' holiday camp, and then they bring a telegram, Karli's been shot down." The gelatin finds the spot and splashes down over her cheeks, trickles like country rain. She rubs her chin, neck, and eyes with a handkerchief, the trickle won't stop. Her voice is clear and dry. "That night I sat outside with Gertie, in front of the nurses' home. The bench was on top of a little cliff and down below was a patch of concrete which was going to be a parking lot one day, and then she asks me if I believe that we'll be joined with our loved ones after death. 'Yes,' I said, 'yes, I do believe that.' She stood straight up and jumped. I don't remember anything else, only her body on the concrete, the twisted head and her long hair. I screamed and screamed. —I shouldn't be telling you this." She tugs at her belt. "I'm so fat, if only I knew why I get so fat." She gets up, puts the chair in a corner, stands at the end of the bed, and puffs her cheeks, like a child blowing bubbles. "I shouldn't have said that and I shouldn't have told you. Go to sleep now, forget all about it, you know what I mean, we've found it and everything's going to be all right." At the door she says, "I'm on night duty tonight, I'll drop by again."

The drug seeps in. My thoughts seem to have been dipped in

egg, egg and flour, glutinous goo, ready for the pan. A white-hot pain shoots through me, taut like a piano string. —What happened to my protest march? The Veterans Crippled by War and Physicians march, what became of it? I groveled and bootlicked at the great commercial shrine of youth plus health equals success with the rest of them, God forbid you have to have a tooth pulled—you're getting on, dearie, coming apart at the seams.

I could weep bitter tears when I think of my lovely protest getting classified under "stress" and "psychosomatic" by the herds of town and country specialists I've been crawling to for help over the past five years. The verdict went to work with a gleeful vengeance, in the knowledge that green grass grows just as juicily over psychosomatics.

I'd like to see autumn reds again, November fogs, snow too, although I can't really stand it any more after living so long in the Swiss Alps; it pins you down and calls your bluff, the chalk-white addles the pate, it's stolid, like tropical blue. I'd like to see the green of spring again, the next quince-yellow, honey-blond summer. Passion certainly doesn't wither. If it's true that only the aged love life, then I was ancient at eighteen. "Only do the things you really enjoy during the next couple of trial years," the one with the fluffy red hands said. Have I ever learned to do the things I enjoy? I've learned to do. Period. Did I enjoy the doing? I don't know, I really don't. —And then, "You insisted on hearing the truth. You're the first one we've told it to since a woman threw herself out of the window. We could have cured her too."

We are given very little by way of preparation for the first part of our lives, hardly anything for the second, and for death none at all. What are we prepared for? —Oh, and another thing: "Don't ever get excited." I shall call Martin, my friend Martin. I'll say, "You're a priest, a most reverend. Say something. Help me. My escape routes are all as slippery as eels, like clay after rain." In America they tell you. Coolly, bluntly, shockingly, no messing around. Not here. Here they shuffle their feet.

How gratefully everyone laps up those breathtaking tales of adventure and endurance, they make you feel you've dealt death a mortal blow yourself. The Indians don't have a word for "tomorrow." I'm a tomorrow person, this cloyed negation of life revolts me, the coquetry with death and terror. Let's show what horrors man is capable of! wide screen, stereo, maybe pretty it up a little so the whole family can go; no, let's show it all, let's waken the latent maniacs, you too can enjoy the luxury of a private bloodbath right here in your own home. Let's show it, so the sick will never forget it, fill them with panic-stricken dread of their fellow human beings for all time. And there they are, scenes of satanic torture on afternoon TV, with a lazy sardonic commentary. How proud we are of the brutalization, of our love of allegiance, which is just as insane as a love of truth. Then I'd rather have the soft sell, please keep your straight-from-the-shoulder truth that must be a lunatic lie. From barbarity to decadence and back again in one deep breath of a single generation. "We certainly saw life," they say, when their life was full of survived horror. They talk and talk about the cruel world, trends and developments of society; only of death, of dying, do you never talk. You shy away, as you used to at the mention of pornography. The ever-ready verbal flood stutters to a halt, appears to be indisposed, sensitive, and mutters on the way out, "Did you ever?"

Even the hospitals have coined an esoteric term. "We had an *exitus*," they say, crease their brows, not in their line of business, *exitus*. A little earlier a confused priest plods along the lines of beds, is devoured by the sunken eyes and their loneliness, is the only one to confront himself with taboo death. When did I have the vision of us all sitting on plastic chairs in a vast airport waiting for our flight to be called? I don't want sympathy. I do want it, but not yours, perhaps my own; even if we did happen to be of the same opinion, it would be for different reasons.

No, I'm not a hypochondriac. Not any more. I went from hospital to hospital, they got to be milestones. "At the time after Hamburg," or "That was between Los Angeles and Zurich," or "That was before Munich." What was meant were the operations, doctors, bills. That's how it is. —I refuse to ac-

· 17 ·

cept "that's how it is." Not yet anyway, I'll keep on kicking. There were always two of them, two operations, one right after the other. Always the same monotonous surprise on the doctors' faces, and on mine. Something always went wrong with the first one, or some complication cropped up; in between I worked —is there an excuse for liking work, being as busy as a bumble-bee? In between I worked, and had many a numskulled inter-view: "What is the meaning of life?" and the smug smile that oozes insipidity.

Our roof will be completed in four weeks, we'll celebrate with the workers, drink to our first own house—not just rented, really ours; after thirty years on the run and ten years searching for the right one, in the course of which I've seen more sites, countries, and houses than Caesar's centurions.

•

"Why aren't you asleep?" Erasta asks. Part concern, part rebuke.

"When can I leave?"

Her lips go as round as her eyes. After two sharp sucks of breath: "Did you ever hear the like? Talks of leaving."

"What else?"

"Don't you like it here with us?" As though she's running a hotel. "I'll have you know we have to throw most of them out. Always think of something, they do. 'Herr Professor, the pain's down here now and will you have a look at this.'" She throws up her hands and chuckles merrily, then slaps her hand to her mouth guiltily. "No, but really, they're mad about hos-pitals, they really are, always ringing the bell when there's ab-solutely nothing wrong." She takes my hand as though wanting to say good morning or goodbye, holds it, reluctant to let it go. It's firm, her hand, firm and chubby, like a child's. Pain, anger, uproar recede in her presence, slither off, give way to ease and exhaustion. "I'll bring you up a TV set, your show's on tomor-row," she says. "It's such a long time ago," I hear myself say, feel myself slipping down between the bandages, tubes, and pillows, seem to become invisible, break up into teeny-weeny prisms like in a child's kaleidoscope, making ever-new patterns.

The morning is bad. It's the crackling crisp noises that freshly bathed, rested people make, the expectant irregular rush of their footsteps in the hall, the subdued greetings that suddenly bubble over, the click of door handles, the rattle of breakfast trolleys. The head nurse comes in. The white of her cap and apron suits her dark-blond hair and wide gray eyes. Her movements are slow and considered. "Did you sleep a little?" she asks. I know I mustn't answer, know I'll start crying if I do, blubber like a cry-baby that I can't face the day, the night, the verdict, the certainty. "Pain?" "Not bad." "You'll pull through," she says, almost inaudibly. Awkwardly I pick up my powder compact from the night table and throw it at the wall. It cracks and falls to the gleaming linoleum in a cloud of powder. We both look at it in astonishment, as though it had done it all by itself. She bends down and gathers the splinters, lays them carefully on the edge of the washbasin, takes my head in her hands, and presses it to her shoulder. "You mustn't get excited," she repeats over and over again, pushes my head carefully back into the pillows, sits down beside me, screws up her eyes, tries to dodge the lemon-yellow ray of sunlight that's blinding her.

My U-boat commander comes by in the evening. He is pale and sweaty; on his nose there's a red mark where the surgical mask has cut into it. "Just finished operating," he says and thumps down into a chair. "Don't know if she'll come through. For weeks she's been running to some damnfool doctor and he's been pumping her full of morphine and what has she got? A belly full of pus I've never seen the likes of. And when does she come? At night, of course. It's enough to drive you round the bend. I ought to sue the doctor, get him behind bars where he belongs, the orangutan, and who'll take the rap if she kicks the bucket? We will, that you can depend on. We both need a whiskey now." He strides to the door as though he were wading through knee-high grass, strides back with a bottle and one glass, pours the Scotch, lets me take a sip, gulps a lot himself, and groans with relish. "I walked by the river for half an hour this afternoon; I tell you, you have to step between the writhing bodies, the ground was covered with semen . . ." He shakes his head disapprovingly, then adds, "It's enough to turn you green with envy. —In ten days we'll remove the stitches, then you can get out of here, out of the heat and sweat. Does it still hurt much?" "Medium rare." "You're not a Viennese. If you tell a Viennese lady she's looking splendid, she'll say, 'Yes, but my feet hurt.' "

•

It's Sunday, hospital Sunday, leathery, grumpy, oppressive. Red Fluff breaks the tedium. "I've been flying," he announces and strokes his hairless head exactly as people with great shocks of hair do when waging battle with the wind. "Just a little round trip, did me a world of good." His right hand is stretched out toward the sky. He stops and looks around as though trying to remember what brought him here, then starts meandering; he fidgets back and forth, describes first a curve and then a circle, two figure eights and a square. "I've been flying for years," he continues, stretching the years to at least a century. The attempt to imagine him as a pilot is a flop, I see him mixing up knobs and levers, mishearing radio commands; I'm sure all his reserves of self-discipline have been spent at the operating table. He seems to read my thoughts. "It's my hobby," he says, shrugging his shoulders. "Everybody has his quirks." He stretches up proudly, like a man who's pulled off a ticklish repair job even though he's been blessed with a handful of thumbs. "You want to live in Austria?" he asks abruptly and presses his lips together. "Mainly live," I answer. He shoots off as though an alarm bell had sounded. "You will," he cries. "Austria'll do you good. We've been through everything the others are only just starting in on. Quite a comfort. Got enough guts for the stitches?" "Ready when you are." "Well, not if you're not keen, let's leave it for today. Let's just talk a little, it's through talking that people come together." "Ready steady go!" I yell. He flings the door open and the chief nurse is standing there beside a trolley laden with tweezers scalpels scissors tubes rubber gloves. "We're a little behind the times," he says, unwrapping me like a parcel, "but perhaps it's better than being too advanced at a time when they're all standing on the edge of Hades." He selects a scalpel and a pair of tweezers, bends forward, and murmurs, "People ought to be banned, taken out of circulation." A black thread dangles before my eyes, disappears. "We got the first one," I hear, and "You didn't miss much at the festival, I've never seen such a muddle on a stage as there was in the Shakespeare production; if we were to carry on like that, we'd end up operating on everything in sight except the patients. Now, we've got six out and thirty more to go. Do we go on?" The yes I manage to squeeze out discourages him. "Oh no, not if it hurts that bad, we don't." "It won't hurt any less tomorrow," I say. He turns to the nurse and makes eyes at her. "D'you think we'll get 'extenuating circumstances'?" She stares at him aghast, horrified, then yelps, "Really, Herr Professor!" realizes she's gone too far, and adds a little chuckle to make amends.

"I once knew a lady doctor out in the country," I tell him. "She was called out one night to the local village tyrant. He said, 'Please, Doctor, you've got to help me, I don't want to die.' 'Enough now,' she answered, 'you've done nothing but make people miserable the whole of your life, now go on and die.'" He laughs in gushes, it comes spurting out like water from a rusty tap; he stands there with his rubber-gloved hands stretched out in front of him as though he were being excruciatingly tickled, then bends forward again composedly, eyes the scar and the stitches, resumes snipping. Grunting, "Now then" and "Got you," at regular intervals, he launches into a monologue designed to distract. "Everybody's wrapped up in politics today; even if they only learn how to treat bunions, they treat them politically. But just you wait and see; Heraclitus says everything's got to change, but then along comes Parmenides and says not a damn thing will ever change, and we all know that cold can be generated by heat and that nothing ever is as bad as it seems— except when pulling stitches—and if we carry on the way we're going and your gynecologist doesn't have other ideas, I see no reason why you shouldn't go home today." He straightens up, looks down, and enjoys my speechlessness. The verdict starts to crack, break up, lose its weight and authority in the face of the onslaught of rapture that glimpses a glimmer of amnesty behind the sudden inexplicable turn of events, transforms the hospital into an immense stronghold, and interprets the regained freedom as a synonym of a clean bill of health. Before he can change his mind, I get up. "Not so fast," squeals the nurse and waves gauze and rolls of tape. Shakily, I feel my way along the bed. My incisions seem to gasp, screech like a sawmill at break of day, cut rapture down to size, set snares along the escape route. I thank him hurriedly, pump his hand, and embrace the nurse; she's fighting two tears as she says, "Careful, careful," and "I've called your home," and "Don't lie in the sun, come and see the professor in ten days." She warns me all the way to the door.

Outside there's a car. Standing beside it, my husband. For a second I see him as I saw him fifteen years ago. It was at an airport. He stood there towering above the crowd, smiling uncertainly, thin, frangibly young in a flapping shirt and creased trousers. It's the smile that's reminding me, the same now as then. He drives off slowly, swerves around a Volkswagen bus that comes hurtling out of a side street, swerves nonchalantly, assuredly. The profile betrays no gentleness now; now it's bold, brash, measuring the odds. I see myself falling, blindly running into fear, intractable, raw fear; fear of being excluded, of being incapable of rehabilitating into a world of fearless diffidents, fear of the drawbridge that's up, separating me from those who know nothing of pain. It's fear's poison, fear's pride, desperation raising Cain.

His right hand closes over my left. It draws me back into the serene bright day, into the myriad greens and the tepid light-hearted wind that's bowling through beeches and birches, tickling wriggling poplars. The beauty hits me like an unexpected blow. It caresses and clobbers at the same time. The sticky hot sick room had been made for pain; the beauty is mocking, cooing cruelly, is irritated by the verdict, by me.

•

Ten days later a white lacquered monster descends on me. It howls just once, stridently, then looks at me with its single red-rimmed eye. I'm lying on a narrow bench in a large cellar chewing on my lower and upper lips, trying to swallow, but there's nothing there; I can see two fluorescent lights, four windows, one of which is open, gray linoleum, a crucifix above a metal table, an opening in a wall, through the opening, two steel doors. Twenty minutes ago my U-boat commander, Red Fluff, and I had picked our way stealthily through the subterranean corridors of the hospital, climbed stairs and ramps, sped past piles of bedsteads, bookcases full of files, mattresses, and beaten-up teddy bears until we came to a sign bearing the legend: COBALT ROOM, and, standing beside it, an upright blond-gray man who was introduced to me as the Primarius. We had decided on the devious route in the hope of avoiding recognition and being able to read all about it in the press the next day. As we went through the door, I had instantly begun to start shivering as though I were standing on a conveyor belt. "We'll put these twenty sessions behind us too," Red Fluff had said. "We want to take every possible precaution, like wearing suspenders and a belt, you might say." As he said this, he had gone through every pocket on his person as if searching for a written confirmation. My U-boat commander had laid his heavy arm around my shoulders, intent no doubt on keeping my feet on the ground. Then they hurried out and peered in at me through the glass slit in the control room; four eyes bobbed up and down as they nodded, seeming to say, "Chin up, nothing to it, routine job." Then the howl. The nurse with the beehive hair in the Swiss clinic had told of her father: "Ah well, he's had a prostate carcinoma, but he's quite content again, drinks his beer and smokes his cigarillos." I'd rather kill myself, I'd thought at the time.

Suddenly a smell, just like the one behind the brewery in Berlin-Schöneberg. As a child I'd always run down the road as fast as I could to escape the bitter-sickly smell. My eyes are riveted to the hanging head of Christ. There's a heavy click as one of the steel doors opens, the single eye snaps shut, the monster retreats. The Primarius skips in lightly, he's in good shape, well preserved, trim from sports and diets and from living in fear of the monster; his smile is taut and adamant; day in, day out, he smiles at them, those with and those without hope, the enlightened and the unwitting. It's much like the reserved smile one meets at a dentist's door: Do come in, won't you, pain is a thing of the past. "Was it awful?" he asks, anticipating the answer. "No," I say, as expected. He turns me this way and that, raises the monster and then me, says, "Three minutes is a long time when one has to keep still," and disappears behind the wall. Again it howls, again it's silent. I'll paint, I'll take thick dripping brushes and paint red green yellow love letters, avowals of love of life. I'll say thank you for a morning, for a day, for a night, thank you for now.

After the fourth howl I'm an old hand, blasé; I grow sleepy, doze off, awake with a start as the eye snaps shut and the Primarius skips through the opening. "Till the day after tomorrow," he says, pulling off his apron and taking a small meter from the pocket. He examines it and says, "If we get exposed to too many rays, we have to take a vacation." His smile grows warmer, asks my pardon.

2

·

I get dizzy in the car, roller-coaster dizzy. There's a white mist over the lake at Sankt Wolfgang, it drips from the leaves like rain. We drive down the soggy lane to the terrifying temporary quarters we've rented until we can finally move into our own house. The rented one has a ghost, thirty uninhabitable rooms, no central heating, but very picturesque rococo stoves that fill the rooms with smoke the minute you light them, and that musty sour smell that goes with tombs, slimy ramparts, and mushroom cellars. The walls are cracked and laden with antlers, the horns of great stags and delicate deer jut out into every dark passageway, cast crisscross shadows under the gloomy antler lamps; buffaloes dating from the turn of the century stare down in the awesome living room; among the leather chairs that are split open and have slanting seats that tip you to the floor, there are man-sized elephant tusks and carefully arranged stuffed swans and guinea fowls, some standing and some hanging, ruffling their feathers when there's a draft, as though about to take off. There are piles of magazines from the years 1919–30 on the coffinlike black sideboard, and a mildewed guest book that bears witness to Kaiser Franz Josef's elaborate gratitude is lying on a green-baize card table that the moths must have abandoned at about the same time.

Andreas clomps up the passage. His dyed black hair nods around his lined grouser's face; the archaic, dark-green servant's apron flaps around his trouser legs. As always he's muttering to himself, and after a long string of unintelligible oaths he suddenly cries, "We're a socialist state now and it's forbidden to work as much as we used to; I don't need to work any more, not at my age, and sure as hell not for people with no title." He belongs to the terrifying side of the house, along with the cupboards that are stuffed full of disintegrating linen, chipped Meissen and Dresden china, antique silver, and whole flotillas of sauceboats. Andreas sometimes doesn't emerge from the moldy lair he calls his room for days on end. Our suggestion that he move to an airier, less moldy one was greeted with an icy stare designed to restrain commoners with the wrong shade of blood in their veins from meddling. Then he does emerge, grabs his basket, goes off, reappears when you least expect or need him, and is gone again.

In addition to the usual musty smell, there's one of burning today, of scorching. Andreas has lit his stove. It's smoldering. The grating is shut tight. Andreas has decided on murder. Even Juliane, standing in full glory at the top of the stairs, can do nothing to alleviate the endless gloom of this house. Juliane is buxom, full-bosomed, bright blonde, man-crazy, sixty years old, and from time to time radiates an excess of *joie de vivre* and vitality. At the moment she's radiating. "The snake!" she roars. The swans ruffle their feathers, the antlers creak, and the floor begins to sway like a hammock. "The divine child has seen that hideous loathsome snake." She rolls her eyes and shakes her head, slaps her forehead with enough force to cleave it in two. The "divine child" waves, calls out, "Mama," and turns back again, eager not to miss a second of Juliane's act. "What shall we do, what shall we do?" she bellows dementedly, tearing at her pony tail. A thirty-watt bulb illuminates her high cheekbones and short straight nose. Her skin is smooth and rosy. "I had all the wrinkles and folds amputated, zick zack and they'd had it," she'd announced after we had known her for some five minutes, and proudly shown us the scars behind her ears. She's now standing there, snorting like a Wagnerian heroine at the final curtain, holding a spade in her hands. "I went after it with this here." She raises it and, rotten like everything else in the house, the spade takes leave of its handle and clatters down the stairs. "Oh, God, oh, God, what a life, what a house," she wails. As though this were their cue, two bats swoop in and begin to circle around Juliane's blond hair. Her bloodcurdling scream sends me shooting up the stairs, we cower there pitifully, trying to protect the child and our heads with our hands as we used to when the fighters flew low over the town, machine-gunning. "Did your ladyship call?" says a squeaky voice from the ground floor. Andreas is cackling senilely and looking at Juliane, who, as the sole aristocrat—she's a baroness—among the paying guests, is worthy of his attention. She wags a hand as though swatting a fly and whispers in my ear, "He's a boozer. I smelled it right away, nobody fools me on that one." Gasping, she gets up and pulls her jacket over her head, clicks the faulty light switch several times without success, and disappears into our bedroom. I hear things crashing to the floor, hear exclamations of fury and then helpless golloping laughter; she reappears with her great breasts heaving and announces rapturously that the bat squadron has turned tail.

She came to us three months ago. "My name is Juliane," she'd said. "I'm an alcoholic. Dry for five years now." She'd beamed at me as though I'd done something to help. "Why do you say 'I am' if you've been off it for five years?" I'd asked innocently. "Because that's the way it is," she'd howled mournfully and wrung her hands in despair, "an alcoholic's an alcoholic whether he drinks or not. I'm a member of AA, they saved me." I'd gone through all the abbreviations I knew in my mind, foreign airlines, automobile and sporting clubs, but none seemed to fit. Seeing my baffled expression, she'd taken three pamphlets with ALCOHOLICS ANONYMOUS printed on them from her patent-leather bag and pointed to the ground. "They picked me up out of the gutter." She'd repeated, "Out of the gutter," and tightly shut her eyes, as though still seeing filthy curbstones and drains. But then she'd given a short laugh and dabbed at her face with a lace handkerchief that looked ridiculous in her large hand. "I don't need money," she'd continued, throwing her head back, "what I need is work and a full day." And so she stayed. We have to bear with her odd schedule, which has her getting up at four in the morning and collapsing at eight at night, with her frenetic passion for crochet work, which has supplied us with enough scarves and table mats for life, also her periods of wild sap rising, which she gives signal to by saying, "I feel dissolute today," and which suddenly turn into lurching depressions without warning. Odd too, and in this she has one thing in common with Andreas, is her insistence on living in the worst possible room in the house, as though she must do penance; and then, in each new town we visit, the panic-stricken search for the AA office, the breathless inquiries as to when and where the fellowship meet, last but not least her manic need to own a power scooter, on which she drives several ferocious ear-splitting laps every day. She seldom talks about her life, but when she does she begins hesitantly: "I was rich, I was beautiful, I had everything one could wish for. A husband, a child, good health. Then the war came, the vile war, and took everything. After eight years in a prison camp, eight years in Poland and Siberia, I started to drink . . ." Her day begins with an AA slogan: "I have to do some good every day. I ask God to give me strength. I mustn't say I'll never drink again, I can only say I won't drink today." Her descriptions of life in the gutter are curiously objective, as though she were talking of a casual acquaintance; only on "dissolute" days does she identify herself with Juliane the dipsomaniac. Then she laughs contemptuously, tugs at imaginary rings on her fingers, and flings them grandly at the feet of an invisible assembly. "Take them, take it all," she cries. A little later, without reducing the volume of her ever-present transistor radio and regardless of what it's playing, she will launch into a many-stanzaed hymn which, on better days, only sounds incongruous as it fills the kitchen and adjacent rooms, but which, on the bad ones, is like a cry from the depths. She sits with her swollen, bandaged legs propped up on a chair, singing ardently, the intensity subsiding toward the end of the hymn as she takes up her cellophane-wrapped cook book. The book is beautifully kept and spotless, except that every recipe prescribing even a teaspoonful of alcohol has been savagely crossed through and rendered illegible. "One drop and I'm in hell," she says; "an alcoholic can't stop until he's lying in the gutter," and again underlines the proximity by pointing emphatically at the floor. She always refers to alcoholics as "he," never "she," as though masculine genes were to blame for the whole thing. If the hymn doesn't have the right purgative effect, she'll spring up, throwing cushions around like tennis balls, run to the window, and call in a tormented voice, "I need Ahmed." Ahmed is a crucial stage in the procedure and it's better to steer her off the subject as soon as possible, since the mere mention of Ahmed can summon depressions that last for days. Ahmed is an Arab who lives in Pittsburgh and is, as far as one can tell from the yellow, dog-eared photos, a kindly looking gentleman of indeterminate age. "I loved him," Juliane whispers, pressing the photos to her massive bosom. "Five long years I loved him, I cooked for him day and night. He got fat." Her expression becomes slack and glazed, and after a long silence she replaces Ahmed in the side pocket of the patent-leather bag. "Fat," she says disgustedly, staring at the bag, and begins to rock her head from side to side, slowly at first, then faster and faster, moving palely and unsteadily to the window as she does so, murmuring the first of a long series of breathy "Ahmeds."

At the moment Juliane is standing controlled and in charge of the situation in front of the bedroom door, saying reverently, "The window's closed, the bats outside, and you must go to bed." Mother and daughter follow her meekly, although the thought of the bone-hard mattresses with the ditches in the middle fills them with dread; this plus the awareness that the hour is at hand when the feudal former hunting lodge will commence its own eerie activities. The spooky aspect, laughable by daylight, takes on enervating and sleep-robbing dimensions as dusk approaches. Tottering, and doomed to dereliction, the house runs amok at night, builds from unsettling but ambiguous movements to a veritable tumult. Doors open grindingly of their own volition; curtains billow, although the windows are closed and there's no breath of wind; door handles move up and down; and on the uppermost floor, which has been untenanted for generations, there's moaning and groaning and hammering. The suspicion that Andreas, who's a cunning critter at the best of times, might be playing nocturnal pranks proved groundless, and our assumption peeved him greatly; the experts we called in to hunt out rats or similar rodents drew a blank. The mailman—an incurable alcoholic, according to Juliane—refuses to set foot in the door even at midday and in glorious sunshine, and informs us indignantly, standing at a respectable distance with one hand raised, that everyone knows all about it down in the village, and not only there.

"Where was the snake?" I ask, slithering into the clammy sheets. Her eyes are drawn to a cigarette smoldering in the ashtray. "Implements of the devil! The work of Satan!" she cries in horror, fluttering her short black lashes, and sweeps the ashtray, cigarettes, and matches into her apron pocket. After a short humiliating pause, she sags down onto the edge of the bed, mutters, "Snake, snake," and gazes remotely at her broad knees. "There's a meeting at AA. I won't be back until the day after tomorrow," she says haltingly, as though reading an unclear text. She gets up heavily, stares vacantly, sightlessly, over my head and says, "It was in the living room, two meters long it is. What could it want in the living room? Andreas said it lives in the garden."

Two days later she hammers on the door, rushes in, chortles, "Fabulous, fabulous, next to me there was a professor, ten relapses in three years he's had, he'll make it this time. A new day, a new life, Juliane's feeling dissolute," and starts heaving enormous saucepans, ramming the feeble chair legs with a mop, peeling vegetables; she goes into her hymn, storms out, and throws herself onto her spluttering scooter, her buttocks protruding on both sides like well-stocked saddle bags, skids through puddles and slush, orders Andreas to mount the tiny passenger seat, and hurtles around the garbage cans, with Andreas squealing like a stuck pig. In the evening she appears in a frilled negligee, staggers in, and asks if she may telephone. "A private plane, if you don't mind!" she roars grandiosely, and a piece of the receiver flies off as she whacks it back on the hook; then she lies huddled on her disarrayed bed moaning grievously.

A thin elderly lady gets out of the ramshackle Volkswagen and says, "I've come to fetch her, I belong to AA." Juliane, with swollen eyes and scratches on her hands and arms, throws her bags, dresses, shoes, and balls of wool down the stairs and sings, "I need love, just a little bit of love," bangs her head against an antler, and follows the lady docilely, a bottle of gin in her arm. She looks very frail as she clambers into the car and presses her tearstained face to the window. We watch until the bobbing taillights disappear from view, then pack our bags, take leave of the house, Andreas, and the spooks.

•

We move into a small motel. The bowling alley is in full swing, and a German tourist guide is conducting a group of Swedes as they sing, "Oh, My Papa." There's a smell of garlic, of rancid fat and cheap oil. The toilet next to our room has been gushing for hours. At three in the morning the German guides his Swedes up stairways and down passageways as they joyously dance the conga.

In the evening the monster and his keeper are waiting. "During the treatment you should live as peacefully as possible," the Primarius-keeper says, and turns me over to his ward.

Arriving back at the motel, we see two women standing beside the gasoline pumps; the smaller of the two is wearing a scarf of mine, both of them are shaking their fists threateningly. "The dragons," my husband and I say simultaneously. The "dragons" are casing the joint, beating the jungle drums, fanning their fire of grievance against us, feeling their way along the rocky path of blackmail. Scum, I think to myself, and am surprised by my own fury, my vulgarity.

I had always wanted success, wanted the "painted bird" whose plumage evokes mistrust, envy, and malice, the bird that cries out for enmity and extinction; he's so suspect, and exploitable, remunerative and top-heavy, both the idol and the prey. "You have haunted eyes," Tennessee Williams had told me in

Chicago. Haunted eyes. Haunted by what, by whom? In front of the filling station, hard to beat in its stark reality, the surroundings I had hardly noticed till now suddenly waft away, become unreal, intangible; the pumps, the neon sign, the dusty rubber plant behind the dirt-streaked window turn into a picture bursting its frame, with a cacophonous soundtrack. Faces contort and blur, but in a comic way, not at all frightening. And for a moment I seem to step outside myself, drop out of my existence and time, feel as I'd felt on leaving the hospital, blinded, removed, incapable of picking up the threads.

My tensed shoulders relax, the ever-present Angst switches itself off, and I step into a light curious world without force, drift toward a buoyant gaiety from which I look down at my Angst, Angst in general, even the verdict, with interest but with no emotion. But then, after leaving the car, climbing the back stairs, and reaching our room, I stumble over the rut of habit, fall headlong down the beaten path again.

3

.

On a Sunday, which also happened to be the first of January 1973, the dragons shuffled into our life. With them began the year of the verdict, the year of the chestnut tree, the year without Bertha; for Bertha, our cook, housekeeper, Mother Confessor, nanny to our child in its cradle years, our Bertha, an integral and almost permanent part of the family for nearly two decades, had left us. For the second time. There had already been a sharp difference of opinion in the year 1965, and Bertha had absented herself for three years. Now again. The storm had been brewing for some time, and after a row, we came home one day to find a penciled note and chaos. Motherless, sold down the river, in short, desperate, we wailed: Where's Bertha? And Bertha doesn't leave without dire consequences. She'd hardly left for an "address unknown" when the dam burst and the agents of dark powers swept into the secluded chambers of the august St. Moritz apartment we were renting at the time.

The dragons shuffled into our life just as they'd shuffled into the lives of many before us, presumably; only this time, I imagine, the prey seemed fatter, slowed down by illness, incapable of defending itself, and just right for the caldron. Our acquaintanceship dated back to my childhood—they had been vague friends of my mother's—and was flavored by a fateful, good-old-days intimacy that led me to the idea of forming a sort of commune, although the world at large was just abandoning the idea as unworkable, and although I well knew that they belonged to the legions who live on the fringe of artistic professions, cadging here and wheedling there, never ever really doing anything except complaining of their bad luck. However, we were Berthaless and had no better idea. They shuffled in.

There was Libby: large, heavy-boned, hair like a horse's. Her legs are like stovepipes and seem to want to thrust her weird feet into the ground. The soles of her shoes are shaped like a desk blotter or the runners of a rocking chair, quite contrary to the conventional concept of a foot's needs, so that even when she's standing quite still, her toes and heels are turned up, leaving the convex arches to bear the whole, not inconsiderable burden. Most of her soles are of crepe rubber two fingers thick, and Libby is shuffling her way through her fifties on them. Her slowness inspires confidence, and her huge, clublike hands arouse sympathy, and even though she does in fact sometimes offer to help with the housework, muttering and grumbling so that one hardly understands her, she wouldn't dream of really doing so. She did once carry a teapot from the kitchen table to the sink, right at the beginning of our association, and we never again wanted to hear that shrill scream of anguish as the teapot shattered. She uses the scream to vivid effect, then puckers up her mouth like a naughty child and lets great whooping, gurgling sobs come up from the depths of her barrel-like body, mops up the floods flowing from her eyes and nose with the man's handkerchief she always carries up the sleeve of her jacket, rubs and scours her face and forehead, even the cropped horse's hair, as though she's been out in a storm. Finally finished, she stuffs the soggy rag back up her sleeve and looks positively excoriated as she glowers at the bowed heads of her stricken public. She'll accept condolences, but has you know, by screwing up her brows and peering out from under them, that no sympathy, however heartfelt, will ever go the distance with her capacity for suffering.

When they arrived she immediately sat down at the kitchen table and impassively watched the preparations for our first meal together. She sat with her legs spread as widely as possible, her unaccustomed skirt—she probably thought it *de rigueur* for a lady traveling—bunched up over her thighs as though she were about to gather apples. The excitement and her first cognac-and-water had caused a flush that had crept up as far as her left ear, turning it pink, but hadn't affected the right one, still a yellowish white. Her ears were altogether astounding: they were extremely large and appeared to be joined to the head only by a loose thread, so that they flapped fascinatingly whenever she moved. My inquiry as to her health was answered with a loud Ha and a flap. Neither augured well. Her big hand closed around the glass and raised it to her mouth. I'd expected her to empty it in one long masculine draught, but no, Libby sipped, she always sipped; she'd form a kiss-mouth, swallow a little, and then listen, with bated breath, as though expecting a cramp, a stitch, a pain, some immediate sign of poisoning. Releasing the pent-up breath and nodding approvingly, she put down the glass and began to search the pockets of her tweed sports coat. In the third one she found what she was looking for, horn-rimmed glasses and a pack of cards held together with a rubber band. She shuffled expertly and drew three cards, placing them faceup on the table: nine of clubs, jack of clubs, ace of spades. She stared at them and said, "Can't get much worse than that." Her solid face widened into a dark smile. Lighting a cigarillo, she grunted, "What the hell, if we lived through the raid on Dresden, we'll cope with St. Moritz too. By the way, how are you going to arrange it with Samson?" "Who's Samson?" "Our canary," she answered. "That it's not going to work with your tomcat here is pretty clear."

At this point Bibba marched into the kitchen. Bibba doesn't walk, she doesn't skip, she marches, briskly and resolutely, as if in time to an Italian brass band. Bibba is small, muscular, short-legged, and easily excitable in a manner that indicates a particularly unpleasant phase of the menopause. Her heart-shaped face is attractive in an old-fashioned way; the slightly protruding eyes are the dominant feature, and the whole gives the impression of those gamin damsels of the early twenties. From the front. From the side, Bibba's profile reminds one of a predatory bird, sharp, aggressive, ready to swoop. She was still wearing a lilac beret over her thin, permanently waved hair; it was made of toweling and looked like a bathing cap. Still present too was the dark-lilac cape she'd worn as she descended from the train and delayed its progress by many minutes as she handed down cardboard tubes, cartons, kit bags, eiderdowns tied with string, and a canary in a cage.

Bibba's name is no more Bibba that Libby's is Libby. Bibba is Hannelore and Libby is Erna. At the beginning of their long association, they'd bestowed these nicknames upon each other. Libby, this much I know, is derived from Libelle, which means dragonfly; Bibba's origin is no longer clear and my conjectures as to whether it might come from *"bibbern,"* which means to shiver, or maybe *"Biber,"* beaver, were not encouraged.

Bibba's martial entrance was accompanied by a high-pitched "Did you get a look at the mountains? They sure are majestic." Libby lifted her head wearily and got up slowly, pushing the table away with her heavy thighs. "Who're you telling? I first came to the Engadine when I was a kid, we spent our summers at the Palace Hotel," she growled and then stomped to the icebox on her seven-league stovepipes. Bibba's eyes widened adoringly, as though she were hearing something new. The profile swooped at me. "Our Libby," she gushed ecstatically, "she could have been a millionaire if her relatives hadn't done her out of it. She was born rich, she's got it in her blood. She needn't have lifted a finger ever again—while we are on the subject, how many servants have you got?" "None." She looked at me in sheer amazement. When this had subsided, she said studiedly and very precisely, "And another thing, this furniture won't do at all. I mean, I imagine you'll be getting better stuff for the house in Austria when it's finished, but really . . . What is that sickly looking wood anyway?" "It's a pine that grows only at this height." Libby grunted disdainfully and sniffed up whatever was loose in her nose. Bibba turned quickly to the door and froze, listening to a strange series of squeals and hissings. Ludwig the tomcat appeared in the doorway, licking his chops and looking very pleased. Feathers were clinging to his fur. "I left the door open!" Bibba screamed and threw herself down beside the empty cage. Libby broke out some ice, plopped it into her glass, took several sips, and looked at me. Her eyes narrowed to slits as she deliberated. "The question is," she said with an expression designed to combine wisdom with cynicism, "is the world run by forces of good or forces of evil?" and shuffled out.

I tried to still the sickly flutterings in my stomach which were frantically signaling, "It's going to be a disaster," by thinking back on what had happened the last time Bertha had left us. Her first successor had been a nimble, capable woman who was a good cook but who was physically not very strong and had soon persuaded us to hire her ex-husband as man-about-the-house. We agreed to give it a try, and a fat, sleepy-looking man duly arrived and spent his days sitting between an atlas and an encyclopedia working on crossword puzzles, giving interviews on what it was like to serve prominent people, making transatlantic telephone calls, and sleeping. When we timidly called his attention to his duties, he snapped, "If you don't like it, I'll go, but I'm taking her with me." Next came a bright young thing who, as it turned out, couldn't stand the sight of kitchens and was a kleptomaniac to boot. Then, a ray of hope, a dear old girl with roguish eyes who instantly revived our courage and confidence; she had a thing about fish, however, went into epileptic spasms at the sight of it, and left foaming at the mouth and screaming curses. We then decided on a real butler and employed a man who'd been seventh or eighth manservant to a German duke all his life. He looked awfully emaciated but was pleasant and willing and wanted to cook but couldn't; he went off enthusiastically to a nearby school to learn, but soon came back with first-degree burns on his hands and feet. We nursed him and he enjoyed my husband's cooking, began putting on a lot of weight, but suddenly became very ill with hepatitis. We found the reason why in his room: he'd been hoarding food under his bed, and he confessed to us that he'd been fed only the leftovers of the leftovers at the duke's and had learned to fend for himself in this way. We were all very sad. He was followed by a politically inclined young lady who was so tired from reading the history of Communism all night that she couldn't get up in the morning. Then another married couple as fresh as daisies but very reticent and accompanied by two murderous-looking mastiffs; they were indignant that the TV set in their room was black-and-white instead of color, which they were accustomed to, and trotted off again with their dogs. We tried managing with just a daily woman coming in for a few hours, and found a merry widow in the neighborhood who had a novel method of dealing with dirty dishes, she just let them drop; then a punctilious Fräulein who came straight from a housekeeping school, wore elastic stockings, and played the recorder, but proved to be obsessed by the idea of marriage and liked to interview candidates in our guest-house bed. Turned out by her family, a sweet seventeen-year-old spent the final months of her first pregnancy with us, but her condition prevented her from being much help, of course.

Discouraged and at the end of our innate tolerance, we spent the months of my pregnancy alone. After the birth, we engaged a state-certified nurse to help the ripe but inexperienced mother. She kept detergents in empty baby-food jars on the same shelf with the jars full of baby food and got them mixed up one day, almost poisoning the child that had only just survived five weeks' solitary confinement in an incubator. The next one, stately and certified in every sense but the one she should have been, used baking instead of soap powder. I'll admit that I was becoming rabid by this time, and it sufficed when the third left an open safety pin in Christina's diapers for me to show her the door with outstretched, shaky arm.

Then Bertha had come back. After three years. She had stood there holding a bag with a plastic window through which one could see her tomcat, David, turning frantic somersaults and mewing furiously; behind her stood four red suitcases and the framed watercolor portrait of Bertha peering bleakly I'd painted in 1964. Bertha, born in the wooded hills of Thuringia, had been thin when she came to us eighteen years ago, now she's more than well covered, and rheumatic; she commences each new task with "So," ends it with "So," starts and finishes everything she does with "So," says each evening, as she winds up her watch and gazes around the assembly, "Time for the high road," and one more "So." The way she walks, on still slim, well-formed legs, is a reliable indication of what weather to expect; if she waddles like an albatross, the forecast is miserable. If she's light-footed and gliding, one has one's hopes.

"Well, well," she said, and of course, "So," and attacked the kitchen. She emptied drawers, filled garbage cans to overflowing, threw out all the artificial powders and culinary shortcuts that had accumulated in her absence, shook her smart, freshly set locks, and said, "So," again, as though she'd just got back from a short but exhausting trip, and took her place beside the cot. We sighed deeply; order was restored. But now, four and a half years later, after a low trough of unalleviated albatross depression, another bust-up, tears and departure, the prospect of new horrors, old chaos. Now Bibba, now Libby, and this dreadful squeamish fluttering that's howling, "Where's Bertha?"

Bibba and Libby take possession, spread themselves out, and make good use of the empty cage; it stands there accusingly on prominent display, looming like an epitaph. The sprawling apartment, with its many small rooms, begins to shake from the marching and shuffling. Half-emptied suitcases barricade the long narrow passageway, so that we feel we're back on tour again; red and lilac veils have been draped over the lampshades, casting a nightclub atmosphere on the "sickly" paneling, tables and shelves jammed full of pill and medicine bottles and piles of well-thumbed guides to good health bear evidence of an intensive do-it-yourself cure. The mornings are convulsive, the cooking of a warm midday meal being the predominant and seemingly insurmountably complicated neuralgic point of our daily existence, the afternoons damned to silence and taciturn pacing. They're relaxing, gathering strength, letting us stew in our own juice, since we have flatly refused to fulfill several demands they've made: (a) a cleaning woman, (b) a second car for them, (c) subscriptions to every German magazine (they're legion), (d) worldwide photographic rights to the family, in particular, the industrious mother, who, thanks to a number of prominent professions, such as acting, singing, and writing, had become public property for the press, especially the small-format, rainbow-colored house-wives' pamphlets that are produced en masse in Germany; Libby was to create the photographic works of art with her idiot-proof camera. This, plus cash salary, in return for the frenetic midday meal.

Crises escalate and trip over each other in the regularity of their occurrence; the joyfully promulgated independence of a professional woman becomes pure fiction. During these depressing melancholic days, my spine decides it's high time to remind me of what it went through in the war. Without much hope I renew my search for help and find Professor H., an orthopedic specialist and surgeon who, after having grown up in Paris and studied at the Sorbonne, had spent years in clinics in Rome and Boston, and had now returned home to the land of mountains and ski accidents.

Professor H. is tall, young, broad in the beam, nearsighted, inept at manipulating his own bones, and, considering he's Swiss, loquacious in a delightful manner. Entering the apartment, he throws his overcoat on the floor, shakes his gray-blond mane as though freeing it from cobwebs, and starts galloping about. "The land of the Etruscans," he roars, looking irately out the window, "bony, hideous Etruscans among bony, hideous mountains. They used to bury their dead standing up." He straightens and bangs his head against the low door frame, shows me what it must be like to be buried standing up. The door frame has taken the edge off his rage. "Even their sun is wooden," he adds, grinning self-consciously and bowing his head. He whisks the Libby-Bibba veils from the lamps, takes off the shades, moves one nearer to me. "You'll have to undress," he says and bares his teeth at the mountaintops as though planning something violent. Keeping as far away as possible, he starts pacing around me and suddenly springs back against the wall, pushing up against it, trying to gain more space. "I hope you don't think I was born here," he cries strickenly and tears his glasses from his nose. He rubs them on his sleeve, holds them up to the light, and examines the possibility that medical prowess might depend on one's place of birth. Nodding and puffing relievedly, he continues his pacing, jogging now and then, with his hands behind his back and his head inclined to one side, as though expecting to hear telltale creakings from the malformed backbone. Standing behind me, he suddenly claps his hands. "Your left buttock's lower than the right!" he pours out in a torrent. He leaps into view, comes so close that I think we're going to rub noses, and asks, "Did you ever have polio?"

"Yes."

"There you are!" he cries, spreading his arms and tumbling backward, falling against the wall. Coiled like a spring, he creeps forward again as though close to solving the mystery of a brilliantly planned crime. His questions fly at me like ping-pong balls.

"When did you have it?"

"As a child."

"Were you X-rayed?"

"Several times."

"Did they find anything?"

"No."

"And the buttock?"

"What?"

"Didn't anybody see that one buttock's lower?"

"No."

"That one leg is shorter?"

"No, never."

"One wouldn't believe it." He covers his face with both hands and turns to the window, gives the mountains a withering look through his fingers, and murmurs, "Don't let them X-ray you any more, your hair will turn green." He drops his hands and gallops to the door, grabs his coat, and thrusts his right arm into the left sleeve, gets tangled in the lining, finds his way into the coat but not out of the apartment. Running down the passage, he opens the doors to the kitchen, the toilet, the broom closet, laughing uproariously, obviously used to apartments with no exit, finally finds it with my help, and falls down the stairs yelling, "Come to my clinic in the morning."

His office is a disinfected junk room full of tables, chairs, telephones, shelves, books, and magazines. He stalks about, each step impeded by a piece of furniture or a wall, reminding me of a choleric crane in its zoo-prison. He looks disgustedly at the mountain that blocks all view of the sky from his window and asks, "Would you like my house? I'll give it to you. I have to get away from here, away from the Etruscans." He yanks the window open. The wind spits in snowflakes, billows the curtains, pushes prescription pads across the desk, threatens to create havoc. He slams the window shut and snarls, "That's what I mean." After one of the many telephones has rung four times, he picks it up gingerly and, with an expression of absolute mistrust, listens for a while without saying a word and then barks, "Well, of course," and drops it like a hot coal, wrinkling his nose. Pushing his finger through the puddles the snowflakes have made on his desk, he says, "Do you have time for a little test?"

"What sort of test?"

"I'd like to see whether a nerve's being squashed." He raises his shoulders and waves his arms, looks over the edge of his glasses innocently.

"How long will it take?"

"An hour."

"What's the time?"

He looks up in surprise, feels his wrist and then his elbow, says, "I've forgotten my watch," digs around among the pads and piles of papers, finds a small gold clock, shakes and taps it, says, "And this one has stopped." He sticks his fingers between his teeth and asks me warmly, "Do you forget to put your watch on too?"

"I don't own one, I prefer to ask."

He throws back his head and roars with laughter. "Splendid," he chortles and nods at me, delighted at finding a fellow scatterbrain. He unfolds himself and takes me by the arm, leading me through the door and along the rubber-planted clinic corridor.

A frail, very youthful-looking doctor with an Italian accent and a matching name gets up, listens to Professor H. as he expounds my case in Schweizerdeutsch, positions me next to an electronic enormity, and says softly, smiling gently, "A little prick, later it will tickle." He sticks two needles which look as big as those used in knitting into my neck, turns a knob, pulls a lever, the enormity grates and whistles and begins churning out a roll of paper with crisscross curves on it. Mild jabs of electric current course through me at regular intervals, making me bob up and down like a yo-yo. I roll my eyes in all directions, but no one takes any notice. After what seems like a very long time, he pulls the needles out, tapes the spots, and dismisses me. Professor H. lolls against the wall, immersed in his study of the roll of paper, finally whispers, "It's all poppycock really; what you need is a shoe with an elevated heel and later a new hip."

4

•

June 29, 1974

The present is in a turmoil, I can't deal with the past today. There's a new symptom, I'm to be X-rayed, day after tomorrow. They did all that before, in Switzerland. Pre-verdict. And didn't find a thing, not even on the fourth set of pictures. Three months later in Salzburg they played their hunch, forgot about the pictures, and used the knife. Now the same thing again, no mention of the knife as yet, they're just playing safe, keeping cool, X-ray.

The hepatitis doesn't help either. It smolders tetchily, has done so since the war; it never really healed, my colorless yellow jaundice, but it objects to drugs, raises dozy protest, slyly needles the liver, gets sentenced to bread and water. One more thing: the belly. There's an adhesion kicking up somewhere, bunging up the works. Ileus, they call it.

I walk through my own house and say, "This is my own house."

I went to a party and looked around thinking, Is there anyone else here with a verdict?

I fear the thought of another anesthetic, another operation; my veins are so scarred they can never get the needle in; the pain, the atropine. Will I wake up the next time?

Sleep gets shallower by the day, or night; I jump up, sit on Christina's bed, fall in the barrel of pitch. She asks sleepily, "Are you in pain?" She knows about infirmities, has one herself, thanks to the man in the merry month of May.

I'll know the day after tomorrow whether I'm to have the fifty-seventh operation.

July 2, 1974

I decided to underplay it; I pulled off the eternal jeans and sweater and donned a Balmain robe. Afterward I hammed it up, fairly threw myself at my U-boat commander. I am not in the habit of throwing myself at anybody, but with him I did, my go-between. The X-ray man was watching, it embarrassed him. "That's nothing to worry about, we'll take another look in three or four months' time. But the intestine, that's something different. We won't touch it this year but we'll have to sometime. I'm not at all eager to open that belly for the sixth time, believe me, but otherwise you'll be brought in one night and that's as amusing as a hole in the head. That knot's going to refuse to untie itself one day."

What did my friend Ludwig Marcuse use to say? There are illnesses that are elegant and others that are not: bowel, not. Hemorrhoids, not. Nearsightedness, yes; deafness, no. TB, not bad; appendix, fine; cancer, not.

Then I went to the other specialist. He leafed through the results of my liver tests like a grocer searching for change in the till, muttering darkly, "Let's see, bilirubin—well, not that bad, the transaminases almost, well, but the phosphate..." He clicked his tongue as though he'd asked for sweet but got sour. "And the potassium, well, I ask myself, I'd almost say there were, well, thymol density, oh, my God, gamma . . ." He raised a hand to his ear, looked right through me, and then went on, "Electrophorese, well, that's more like it, that we don't mind at all. Now you come back in two weeks' time, and you can relax the diet a little, otherwise you'll be slipping down drainholes, a glass of wine in the evening, one has to have a little joy now and then, even with hepatitis."

They make it easier on you here, there's less of the parade-ground atmosphere: lie still, hold your tongue in the presence of Great God Professor. I skipped across the hospital grounds as though it were my home away from home. Erasta was there, she'd spent about a third of her morning energy. "Well now, what do you think? I'm getting fatter than ever, what on earth shall I do? Come and see us, but not to stay, if you don't mind."

Gift-horse world, gift-horse town, gift-horse day. The Americans have occupied Salzburg; they all look so beaten up, wrecked, deigning to be impressed. The very fattest wear white pants and their rouge reminds me of scarlet fever. They're still wearing veils, and those silver and gold shimmering jackets on their old backs, and there are always a couple of younger ones who've been schlepped along; their expressions say, Who the hell needs it? But they bought my book and praised it lavishly; I'm corruptible, more corruptible than ever on this, my gift-horse day. I could fall in love with their hats and pants and cameras, maybe even their voices.

Now I can get on with the past again. Pre-verdict.

5

.

There was a hopeless snarl on one of the hairpin curves halfway up the Suvretta; the maharani's white Rolls had skidded on the ice and stood straight across the road, its nose and tail nudging the high walls of snow, looking like a stranded whale. Behind it two Bentleys, four Cadillacs, six Mercedes, a Porsche, two more Rollses, and several Fiats slithered and churned indignantly. The whoops from the open windows were naturally *comme il faut;* to get angry or show signs of common irk on the threshold of the evening's entertainment would have been boorish, beneath one's dignity, betrayed some glaring defect in one's background. The second, more socially oriented part of the season had begun, and almost all those waiting here composedly belonged to the elite, the exclusive club whose members were either boundlessly rich, of blue blood, rich or not, or of renowned beauty.

The door of the whale opened and a chubby young man let his white-clad legs dangle out, stepped charily onto the glittering ice, and fell in an ungracious heap, his arms waving. The ankle-length mink that had been around his shoulders slid away, gathering speed as it schussed down the hill past the Bentleys. The man struggled up, and by the glare of the headlights, one saw that he was wearing an open shirt knotted at his navel and wide chains around his neck, with diamonds the size of plums bouncing against his naked chest. He steadied himself with the aid of a post at the side of the road and stretched a hand full of rings toward the open door. The petite maharani, covered in silk and rubies, got out and smiled, raised her hand in majestic salute, and went up the hill, supported by two chauffeurs. One by one, the others now left their cozy carriages and pattered in their silk or velvet slippers toward a barnlike building that an eccentric Englishwoman had erected some fifty years ago and that had served her as a teahouse in summer. Although the evening's hostess, Marina Agallo, wife to one of Italy's richest industrialists, had a sumptuous chalet close by, it would have been deemed unoriginal to celebrate her husband's fifty-fifth birthday in the comfort and accessibility of their own home.

Signora Agallo stood at the door of the wood-paneled room that was overheated to the point of suffocation and greeted her guests, their frolicsome nonchalance a sharp contrast to her own mercurial tension. Her face was beautiful, regardless of its lines and wrinkles, but it was marred this evening by a general puffiness and swellings about the eyes, and the contours of her well-proportioned, long body were masked in unbecoming red and blue chiffon. Signor Agallo wasn't there. In spite of the squadron of Boeings, Lears, and helicopters that stood at his disposal, no one would ever have accused Signor Agallo of being punctual, and from the harassed manner in which he greeted, ate, drank, and spoke when he finally did arrive anywhere, it was clear that he was long overdue somewhere else.

Signora Agallo turned suddenly from the door, spilling the contents of her glass as she did so, and called out, "He'll arrive any minute," as though fearing they might get up and go if he didn't. A French banker sporting a coat of arms on the breast pocket of his blazer inspected her with hooded lids, performed his annual checkup. "She's grown old," he murmured. The others followed suit. Now everyone compared notes, carefully analyzing changes of appearance in others, always in the firm belief that they themselves were unchanged, and attributed the improvements that were to be found in nearly every case to the wonders of cosmetic surgery; Signora Agallo had apparently not availed herself of its uplifting benefits and had become the victim of a natural if regrettable decline.

Sitting in a dark corner, with his short legs stuck out in front of him and a martini glass in his small, childlike hand, was the remarkably articulate American writer H.P., who was a particular favorite of the elite, since they had never read his books; his broad face, incongruent with the diminutive, elegant body, had become wizened, as though it had abruptly decided to give up the fight and resigned itself to looking like the faces of all the other middle-age writers that have ever lived. The strong vertical lines between the brows were cockling the surrounding skin and muscles into fine furrows, like ripples in the sand, and bore early witness to the contraction and dehydration writers are heir to. They seem to wear it like a membership badge, this parchment mask, identifying them as warriors committed to do battle in total isolation with phantom contenders: the writer and the thought, the writer and the word, the writer and the page plus typewriter, the writer and the writer; the face gets drained, squeezed, screwed up, chewed, until nothing is left but a square feeding on itself, growing ever more alien to the grand sweeping landscapes of painters' faces. Even the younger writers, stocky, with bristling mustaches, soon retire behind their whiskers, and though their bellies may swell, the face will contract into fine etchings of total absorption.

"It's the last time I'm coming here," H.P. said broadly, in an alarmingly high nasal voice, as he disinterestedly watched the relentless flood of guests streaming in. "The altitude's not my cup of tea any more." With a faint nod he greeted an Austrian princess whose face, thanks to countless cosmetic operations, had achieved absolute immobility. Squinting at the spirals of cigarette smoke, he went on, "Hardly anyone smokes in New York any more. I stopped too. Kicking it was sheer hell, I've hardly written a thing since."

A celebrated racing driver entered, stood his ground silently against a circle of braying guests, and stared fixedly at some distant point with eyes so close-set one would have thought him incapable of seeing anything beyond his nose. Peals of affable but rather mirthless laughter issuing from Prince von S., the chairman of the pukka local ski club, rolled over the heads of the guests at regular intervals. It came to sound like a station identification, brought in every now and then, for no special reason. Equally often, he bowed his small head with its receding hair over the hands of the ladies, raising their fingers almost to his lips but never quite, then letting them fall again. The clothes of most of those present were downright tatty in comparison to the luxury of their cars: pop shirts, patched-up jeans, dresses the baker's wife wouldn't have been seen dead in at the local ball. Against the upholstery of their Rollses and Cadillacs they looked like high-school graduates hitching a ride.

The large majority of the now seemingly complete company was of Italian origin. Even at this Olympian height of the elite and despite the fact that one was cosmopolitan and able to conduct small talk in several languages, birds of a national feather still stuck together. Only the Germans preferred the company of the English or the French to that of their own countrymen. One Rhineland industrialist's wife, whose accent set Frenchmen's teeth chattering, went so far that she even answered the telephone with "*Qui est là?*" and this in the German-speaking Engadine.

"I hear she has cancer," said Béla, a Hungarian interior designer from New York who had disfigured countless lovely houses around the world, and looked disdainfully at the unsettlingly animated Signora Agallo. "She was in the Mayo clinic," he added, raising his discreetly made-up eyelids and looking at the ceiling, grabbing a Scotch-on-the-rocks from a passing waiter, then biting on one of the large ice cubes. "Guido's been causing her a lot of worry," he said, munching the ice as though it were celery, "but then he always did." His laugh implied that he knew a lot more than he was prepared to admit to. "When I come to think of it, I can't stand these annual rendezvous," he went on, darting a piercing glance at a young hungry-looking Italian with white-blond hair swirling softly around his narrow shoulders. He was leaning against a wall, and from each of his studied gestures it was clear that he'd decided to expend as little energy on life as possible. "One plays the same shallow drawing-room *comédie* year after year, I'm beginning to feel like my own stand-in," said Béla. He drained his glass, laughed coyly, to make clear that one should never take him too seriously, and drew a gold cigarette case from the pocket of his tight velvet trousers. "One ought to ban change," he continued, placing his thick fingers against an imaginary wall. "It's the same with the cities, they should stay the way they are, I wish to be able to orient myself by them, annul the other changes going on." His eyes wandered casually back to the blond youth and rested on the tender profile. "In other words, I demand a cease-fire," he said, louder than necessary, and clumsily lit a gold cigarette.

André came lolloping through the bedlam, out of breath as ever. He rolled his bright-blue eyes and mooed, "Ooh, what a boring season, not one single scandal. Even the Shah said at the *déjeuner* today—" He threw up his arms as though he were about to sink, launched himself at a spindly countess in out-of-place gold lamé, screamed, "*Ah, ma chère amie,*" dropped her like a hot potato, and turned back to ogle the languid blond youth. "Isn't he delicious, and so reserved," he whispered.

"He's not reserved, he just doesn't have anything to say," Béla spluttered.

André threw back his head and laughed breathlessly, showing his magnificent white teeth and the two clips that held them together. André, a Viennese of impoverished but esteemed aristocratic descent, dabbed his cheeks, which were, as always, glowing from excitement, drew a hand over his immaculately coiffeured white hair, and said in guarded tones, "No, but really, where on earth did Marina get that hideous *rouge* rag she's wearing, she looks as though she were standing at a well-frequented corner of the Via Veneto, and as if that weren't enough, she's supposed to have you know what . . ."

Béla lifted a glass from another passing tray. "In that case she should wear black," he said.

"And you are a *petit con,*" André cooed delightedly and continued making little waves at the blond youth, who was ignoring him completely. "Isn't that the one you took all those sleeping pills over?" he asked, grinning wickedly.

Béla pressed his lips together, and the sharp creases running from his nostrils to the corners of his mouth deepened, but then he smiled again, only the eyes kept their offer of trouble standing. "The reason for suicide is uninteresting, whether it's a *succès* is the thing that matters."

"And yours fell flat on its fanny, thank God," André purred, and widened his eyes benevolently.

Béla let his half-smoked cigarette fall to the floor, allowed André to grind it out for him in penance, then said, "Youth will go out of fashion, just as age went out of fashion, just as everything will go out of fashion at some time, even you and I." He sucked in his cheeks, lowered his eyes, and shrugged.

André waggled his fingers, as if loosening up, and called out, "Youth? I can't even remember mine. I spent it in a Gestapo prison, there were still heroes in those days."

He belted out the word "heroes" so loudly that even the American pop painter, who until now had been dozing on his feet a few yards away, woke up. He lifted his impassive chalk-white face for a few seconds; the slow, aimless way he turned his head led one to believe that the eyes behind the dark glasses were blind, but then something else warned that he couldn't be quite as vulnerable and helpless as he apparently wanted to be taken for. One sensed ambition lurking there, and toughness, hiding behind phlegm and lethargy. The clue as to which extraordinary original was here being counterfeited lay in the blasé naïveté, and after a few moments' conjecture, it became clear that not just one but a whole epoch of chosen people celebrating their sensitivity had served as a model: the very successful and thoroughly American artist was the Hollywood version of *fin de siècle* Paris, Proust's and Gide's country cousin.

"Can somebody tell me why we came to this infernal barn?" asked Béla, wiping the sweat dripping from his neck.

"They're terrified of paparazzi and strikes," André whispered, looking carefully over his shoulder. "Poor Guido doesn't dare go to a restaurant any more; one spoonful of caviar and they scream 'Capitalist!' "

Béla said, "*Dégoutant.* Only when we attain affluence do we realize how poor we are."

"You stole that from Shaw," André cried and tapped Béla's chest with an accusing finger.

"Who else?" Béla said, and stifled a yawn. He suddenly screwed up his eyes and thrust his chin toward the door. "As if we aren't suffering enough already," he sighed.

It was Lala's entrance. To invite Lala was to invite her entrance too. It was always excellently timed but might just have misfired on this evening had she not kept her nerve and remained standing in the door until every last head had turned to see where the icy draft was coming from. A triumph, and she enjoyed it immensely. Last season she had always seemed to me to be rather like the wife of a provincial playhouse manager, feared and sneered at, but still playing the ingenues, thanks to her influential marriage. She had invariably worn skin-tight, glittering silver creations with black feathers that had covered her five-foot-three-inch body like eczema, and the deep tan make-up and igneous hair had made even the most exquisite jewelry she wore look fake and vulgar. Now, since a courteous shy young man from Italy had entered her life, things had changed. Her hair was white-blond and cut short, simply; the once-round brown face had become lean and nobly pale, and the perfectly tailored black pantsuit she was wearing, adorned by a single enormous sapphire brooch, was a welcome relief from the rags and tatters so prevalent on this evening. Nothing in her appearance betrayed the fact that she had turned sixty-five, had survived four suicide attempts, and had buried her sixth husband only eighteen months ago.

Lala, alias Selma Kladtke, had come a long way. There was little she enjoyed more than a good gossip, and quite early in life she had come to realize that this one addiction was dangerous enough on its own and had decided never to touch another drop. One evening, however, and it's possible that my Berlin accent touched it off, she coolly reached for the bottle of Dom

Pérignon, followed it with six double brandies, and told me the following story: Lala was not, as generally supposed, the outcome of a noble relationship between two august families in Bern and Luxembourg, not a word of it; Selma Kladtke had been born illegitimately in Rangsdorf, near Berlin, and hadn't had a penny to her name; even worse, her looks were unprepossessing, if not to say ordinary. Thus equipped, Selma had set off on her triumphal path. She got a job ironing in a milliner's shop in the Spittelmarkt in the center of Berlin. After several disappointing months spent sweating over a hot iron in a sunless corner, she met an elderly vaudeville entertainer, and always having had a soft spot for music, she decided to put herself in his hands. He taught her a number of things, among others how to put over a popular song with a few elementary chords on the accordion, and the success of her first appearances at employee outings in beer gardens and on excursion boats persuaded her to try her luck at one of the many tiny cabarets in Berlin. The echo was annihilating. They now pooled their resources, that is to say, she got the entertainer to part with his savings, and she opened a hat shop of her own, resulting in the speedy loss of both the shop and the entertainer. Hard-pressed, Selma now went through a variety of occupations, some of which she described to me, and at a time when she was recuperating from an abortion, war broke out. As soon as she was well enough, she bought an accordion and joined the troops at the many fronts. She entertained them from Narvik to North Africa, from Italy to southern Russia, until, at the end of 1944, a voice told her that the alarming reduction in the size of her circuit, the number of towns and countries that had been struck from the list, boded no good. And so Selma Kladtke, artist, born in Rangsdorf near Berlin, tramped over the Swiss border in May 1945, carrying only a cardboard suitcase, immediately married a mature but willing citizen of the land, learned the native tongue, and became, shortly after obtaining her Swiss passport, a widow for the first time. Her name was now Lala, and, for a limited period, Wäggeli. A well-to-do banker took the bereaved under his wing, made her his spouse and sole heir, and died the same year. His successor was a South American billionaire—tin mines—after whose untimely death Selma resolved to stick with South American billionaires. The accumulated inheritance, immeasurable in its scope, with properties and holdings from Rio to New York, Zurich, Cannes, London, and Hong Kong, demanded careful management and total application from the ill-starred heiress. Lawyers who might have been lured to fraudulent thoughts at the sight of such a young widow soon had to admit that they didn't stand a chance against Selma's nimble business brain. "They'd have to start getting up much earlier to get their knife in me; we Berliners don't like being taken for a ride, do we?" she'd said, draining her third snifterful of brandy. "Only one gave it a real try, the nurse that looked after my last one." The memory transformed her jolly heart-shaped mouth to a grim thin line. "I showed her where to get off. She had the old man worked up into such a state that he didn't know whether he was coming or going." She went on to relate that he'd gone as far as to call the attorneys with a view to changing his will, whereupon Selma had had to stage a dramatic suicide attempt. Eventually she got the bitch out of the house, although the old guy hollered blue murder, and replaced her with a solid seventy-year-old dear who had no interest in material things. Selma-Lala had made little crosses on the immaculate white tablecloth with her long, perfectly manicured nails and said, "They all died on me," looking up with helpless astonishment in her cornflower-blue eyes, until a lusty gale of heartfelt laughter elbowed the helplessness away. It was a laugh from the dark doorways of the Spittelmarkt, from the drab dressing rooms of one-night stands at the front, a laugh to relieve the enforced celibacy of men in field gray. Her laughter had developed into a bout of hiccups, and between the hics she had spluttered, "Up till now they always paid, now it's my turn," and thumped the table with her fist. She had then leaned forward so low that her chin almost touched the tablecloth and whispered viciously, "But I never used tricks like they do here, the high society. I mean, letting their old men think the children are theirs. There are at least two in this room tonight who are raising the produce of alien seed, I mean, that's going too far." She had brushed away crumbs with the expression of an indignant, orderly housewife and punished the waiter with a meaningful sidelong glance as he tardily hurried over. Unlike most of her no-less-wealthy friends who lived in their own chalets for the thirty-day annual season in order to avoid travel groups and general unreliability, Lala lived in a hotel. She liked to see herself in the role of an unfettered globe-trotter, always on the move, prepared to attend business meetings in any corner of the earth; a predilection which had no doubt found its roots in her touring days. "I've never been back to Berlin, not even to Germany, why should I?" she said, shrugging her shoulders, and then, resuming the foreigner's accent she had assumed for her masquerade, "Intrigues prevented me from marrying the one great true love of my life. He was a prince." She went on with her narrative, unctuously now, stammering at times, like the heroine of a historical novel, humble in the face of royalty. She pouted her lips and gazed at herself in a large wall mirror, inspected herself to her apparent satisfaction, studied Selma, whom fate had not allowed to end life as a princess. She stood up with a rueful grimace, thanked the headwaiter with a tiny nod of the head, severed Selma from Lala in the twinkling of an eye, crossed the imposing hotel lobby, asked for her key and a call in the morning in convincing Schweizerdeutsch, discussed the weather and skiing conditions for a moment with the concierge in perfect French, stepped into the elevator, and was gone, leaving her confession far behind.

She had told me this story the year before. Now, on the evening of Guido Agallo's fifty-fifth birthday, Lala moved to the center of the room and announced, her blue eyes gleaming as she looked at her shy young Italian, that she had consented to marriage, her seventh wedding to be consecrated in a church. The moderate jubilation that followed coincided with Guido Agallo's entrance. He shot through the door with such vehemence that one half expected to see bloodhounds snapping at his heels, shook a few hands, grabbed a glass, turning his head this way and that so that no one be denied a glimpse of his bold profile. He was of the happy theatrical self-assurance one usually finds only in amateurs. He had nothing in common with the majority of magnates I have known, who are uneasy outside their own conference rooms, inconspicuous to a point of self-effacement. Guido enjoyed the yearning admiration of the women, the envious disregard of the men, and his constant agitation seemed to be part of this enjoyment and not, as one might have assumed, the gratifying confirmation that vast wealth brings vast frustration. Apart from his casual clothes, he resembled an aging matinee idol who still commands a following at smaller provincial houses. Undoubtedly, it was the knowledge of his power that persuaded one to believe oneself in the presence of charm and personality; without this knowledge, the cocky attitudinizing would surely have caused only tight smiles.

The momentary enthusiasm that greeted his appearance this evening was due to the fact that it meant that one could eat. He was still drinking, with his arm resting easily around the waist of a girl who had appeared out of the blue and was definitely not a member of the clique; in short, she'd been smuggled in. Her famished, this-is-my-big-chance, here's-where-the-bread-is look identified her as being a member of the swarm that camp-follows the super-rich, like groupies on the rock circuit. Her aproned dress, the thick wedge sandals, the modish eye make-up, with white lids and a black line under the lower lashes, the violet-red lipstick and fingernails were too influenced by magazines to pass muster by clique standards. Marina Agallo knew that she was under observation and that her reaction would make the rounds tomorrow. She ruined all hopes that she would furnish a scandal to spice the dreary season by standing up, walking a little unsteadily but smilingly to the center of the room, and announcing dinner.

The very ancient principessa was the first to take her place. She flopped down where she'd been standing, picked up the red-and-white-gingham napkin from the red-and-white-gingham tablecloth, stuffed its tip into the band of her skirt, and settled into a crouching comatose position, waiting for the first course. In a stranger who had had no opportunity to get used to the sight of her, she must have awakened the impression of a shattering case of invalidism. Loose yellow folds of skin hung from the face that had lost all contours in the course of its phenomenal longevity, making it impossible to judge whether the expression be one of wisdom or of plain exhaustion, of good or of evil; the face had outlived all forms of comparison and recognition. Nevertheless, the pitiful impression she made was insidious. She belonged to the season just as did the mountains, the snow, the low-oxygen air, the lunches and dinners. Her long thin neck seemed to be held as in a cast by a pearl necklace as wide as a man's hand; even so, it contracted at each swallow and slid out again each time she raised her fork, like a turtle's. Between swallows she opened her wide gray lids and looked around her, as though to assure herself that nothing had changed, that there was nothing new she hadn't seen or experienced. Watching her, one came to think that she probably got more out of life, restricted as it was to eating, drinking, and the annual winter sojourn, than the whole bevy of beautiful people who pitied her put together.

The abundance of her jowls and folds had an unsettling effect on another of the Agallos' guests. He was a cosmetic surgeon from South America. After one look at her he was sunk. Couldn't take his eyes off her. He sat opposite her the whole evening and allowed his interest to wander from the principessa only once. Catching sight of a French bank president's wife as she wolfed her third helping of crepes suzette, he cried, "Look at that, I removed whole mountains of fat from her ass, she's going to bust the stitches the way she's stuffing herself," and returned to his ardent study of the folds. After a series of deep soft belches, the principessa announced in a tremulous but quite audible voice, "This is my last season here. The cold is dreadful." Only the camp follower reacted and squeaked, "Awful," since she couldn't know that the principessa had been saying the same thing for the past fifteen years. Although her absence wouldn't exactly have harmed anybody, it was considered treacherous to stay at home or go to another resort, perish the thought.

To her right sat an Austrian duke who had not uttered a word during the whole meal but who now suddenly launched into a laudation of vegetarian food and abstinence in general, always excepting—and this he stressed in several languages—sex. One let him have his head, nodding tolerantly as one does when an otherwise pleasing child has to work off its aggressions. With an expression of sheer repugnance, he lifted the piece of veal from his plate and deposited it in his salad bowl, where it lay like something the cat had brought in.

He was the only person in the room, if one didn't include the camp follower, who worked as an employee. He was a buyer in a Frankfurt department store. He was singular too in his travel habits; he came by train and not in a private jet. He, who had no choice, suddenly roared, "Where on earth can one live today? New York is poison, Paris is suffocating, Rome certain death, and London—" Here he took pause, with a start, no doubt remembering his distant cousins at Buckingham Palace, folded his rough little hands soberly, and stuck out his chin. Nobody had taken the slightest notice. Nobody except Françoise, wife of a celebrated psychoanalyst. She threw her waist-length blond hair over her shoulders, unbuttoned her shirt, emptied a glass of red wine over her splendid bare bosom, and took the duke's head in her hands, drawing him down, rubbing her red breasts with his silver-gray tie. "*Je t'aime*," she moaned irresistibly and then threw him back into his seat. "Fabulous, fabulous," André whinnied from the other end of the table and flapped his arms like a chicken. "Where the devil's our Greek?" said Françoise, ignoring the applause. "I know him, I know him," the camp follower squealed, saw that enthusiasm was quite out of place in this company, screwed up her nose, and added, "He's a dwarf." "Not when he's standing on his money he's not," the South American surgeon murmured and grinned at the principessa, who was now enjoying forty winks after the heavy meal.

A loud report that might have been an explosion stopped all conversation. They all sat completely still and Herr Börti, who was acting as *maître d'* in honor of the occasion, leaped to the door. Börti was the mayor and ran the best restaurant in the village; he was also a master of karate and jujitsu, a colonel in the Swiss Army, and during the war, if one were to believe the rumors, had been a spy whom the Gestapo had tried desperately but unavailingly to capture. Börti's leap brought life to the proceedings. Benches fell over, the duke stalked with an expression of fearlessness to the window, André went pale and dived for his pillbox, the old cognac-king Bonato chuckled senilely and excitedly shook the battery of his hearing aid; even the principessa, nodding out of her snooze, cleared her throat noisily and said loudly, with a voice that sounded like a dented gong, "One's not safe in one's own home any longer."

Guido Agallo took advantage of the uproar and changed tables, pulled up a chair beside the camp follower, and placed his hand casually around the back of her neck. Marina immediately raised her arms and began to clap the fandango. Two waiters nodded startledly and hurried out, returning with a trio of musicians in ponchos. They slouched bad-temperedly into the suffocating room, tuned their guitars while hissing curses, took their positions, bared their teeth like baited gorillas, and launched into something Spanish with the appropriate howling and trampling. "Olé," cried Françoise, stamping her heels so hard that the floor shook. The ear-splitting din appeared to be a prearranged signal to let one's hair down, for Béla now ran his hands over the blond Italian's back, the master of the house chewed the camp follower's willing neck, and the principessa began digging in her teeth with a golden pick, making little attempt to mask her efforts behind her napkin. Herr Börti returned and raised his hand as he announced, "Everything's in order, some local teenagers had some rockets left over from New Year's." The Mexican trio apparently understood German, for as the applause at Herr Börti's reassuring news subsided, they took up the jubilant number exactly where they'd been interrupted, howled through to the end, and then, with the same grumpy expressions they'd had as they came in, slouched out again, lighting up cigarettes.

Dr. Mario Albertini now entered. He looked down the lines of his patients, let his fur coat slide from his shoulders, and cried joyously, "Viva." His long bony face was already showing the effects of alcohol. Marina ran over to him and threw her arms around his neck; together they went into a gavotte, stepping through the room until they were confronted with a waiter holding a tray of cheese; they stopped, holding each other tight and fighting for breath, then stuffed a large amount of bread and cheese into their mouths, Dr. Albertini winding up the snack with a large Scotch. "Cheese, my friends," he said, raising his index finger, "is as necessary to man as the lust for life, a love of lust, the rays of the sun." The rapturous reception these lines got was interrupted by the duke, who started to complain angrily at the cup of peppermint tea one had brought him; it had a teabag floating in it and this he considered an insult. Dr. Albertini took no notice of this rude interruption. He'd taken his second glass of Scotch and was now moving on to his favorite topic. "Our friend Börti," he proclaimed, "is as tough as nails. It doesn't do to cross swords with him. Even the Germans knew they couldn't take us, were scared to death of us. We'd have shot all suspects, blown up our passes, left our houses, and fought. Napoleon himself said, 'One has to admire these Schweizer.'" He was just warming to his subject when the refreshed trio launched their second onslaught. The illustrious guests on the long wooden benches all crossed their arms and joined hands and began to sing and heave themselves from side to side in a most un-Mexican manner. It took a few seconds until they were all heaving in the same direction, the trio increased the tempo, and the heaving became more and more frenetic until the people at the ends of the benches fell off and landed on the floor in a heap. The wife of a shipowner climbed up onto the table, which was quickly cleared for her, lifted her midiskirt to her waist, and danced a polka, ending her heartily welcomed act by falling headlong into the outstretched arms of a cackling English lord and screaming shrilly. The whole rustic room seemed to go off the rails now, alcohol, the heat, and the moment of anxiety swelled over the dams of deportment, and the surge of excitement that followed was of pubescent abandon but strangely affected, joyless, and labored, as though one wanted to show this permissive age a thing or two, come hell or high water. The fun and games of the mighty became as clammy and banal as a Saturday-night game of poker, striptease in the kitchen, sing-along in the club. And striptease time was here. "Rumba," a weather-worn, middle-aged tippler whose solid Bern personality and the slant-eyed incalculable expression he affected were sadly overtaxed by this frivolous nickname, put his masculinity to the test each year by hurtling down the Cresta run on a tiny skeleton sled. He opened his trousers, albeit hesitantly, and displayed a badly mangled stomach, saying, "I got that on my winning run," and illustrated the speed with which he'd gone into the hairpin curve with a wave of his hand. Dr. Albertini looked impressed, muttered, "Hard as nails, those boys," and reached for the cheese and the bottle of Chivas Regal. A publisher's wife weaved out of the corner, let the straps of her low-cut dress fall from her shoulders, revealing her large, firm white breasts lacerated at the sides with tiny red scars, and babbled at the South American surgeon, "He's an angel, he's a genius, he made me like a seventeen-year-old again. I can stand comparison with the best of them now, even the little whore this one"—grabbing her husband by the arm and yanking him to her as she repeated —"yes, this one, sleeps with twice a week. She's twenty-nine and I can take her on any day. Forty thousand dollars and I had my youth again." The publisher started at the words "forty thousand dollars," as though he'd been lashed with a cat-o'-nine-tails. His wife said, "You can kiss my ass," and pushed him onto the dance floor. "But look at this," she whispered confidentially and pulled back the hair behind her ears, revealing more red scars, "this he doesn't know about. I look about twenty, don't I?"

Françoise took hold of Dr. Albertini's arm, drank the remains of his whiskey, and cried, with mascara-blackened tears in her beautiful eyes, "Tell me what life is. Tell me what it means, is there a reason? I often think about it." "We're going to the club, we're going to the club," more and more guests began to chant. "The club" was the discotheque in the village; its decor and lighting reminded one of an Air India waiting room where the fuse had blown, and its disc jockeys were two languid, dough-white English maids who played rock records at maximum volume. Using doormats as sleds, the clique shot off singly or in pairs down the steep Suvretta road; at the third bend their lusty whoops suddenly ended and gave way to anxious shouts for a doctor. Dr. Albertini grabbed his coat and bag and hastened down the road. The Hungarian countess was lying at the foot of a tree with a bloody face and a dislocated shoulder. Swearing garrulously, Dr. Albertini set to work. Those still back at the house showed mild concern; Guido Agallo and his stowaway were nowhere to be seen; the trio were still plucking away, but disconsolately now, and they soon packed their guitars and ponchos, muffled themselves in furs, and set off. The tone had sobered and one was planning for the coming summer; invitations were issued with expressions of absolute sincerity in the assurance that those invited were initiated into this ritual and would never dream of coming, the wording was carefully vague, just in case someone present might not know the ropes: "You simply must visit us in Greece," or "We'll be waiting for you on the Côte," or "Now swear solemnly that you'll come to Sardinia." The ambulance siren interrupted the restored *Gemütlichkeit* for a few seconds; they said, *"Quel dommage,"* listened as the howl faded down the mountainside, and then decided it was high time to join the others at the club. Béla, leaning against the door of his Mercedes, shouted, "I'm going to spend the summer near Salzburg, I can't stand your filthy oceans any longer." The Austrian duchess hurried over to him, saying in her shrill voice, which always sounded as though she were about to bite someone, "You can have my house, it's lovely and right in the middle of the forest." "How much?" Béla shouted. "What?" she snapped, as though she hadn't heard right. "How much?" Béla repeated and grinned. Digging into her pearl-embroidered evening bag, she giggled like an oboe and said, "You really are impossible." But Béla stood his ground and aggressively asked once more, "Come on, how much?" "Six thousand a month," she answered with her nose pointing high over his shoulder. "Six thousand what? Zloty, dinar, schillings?" "D-marks, naturally," she cried, her temper flaring. Béla tipped his head back and his breath rose from his open mouth in a steep column as he roared like a stag and slapped his thigh. "You're still squeezing every drop you can out of the commoners, aren't you? You've just changed the methods, that's all," he chortled. She looked around wildly as though seeking help, then turned so abruptly on her heel that she almost lost her balance, climbed behind the wheel of her Fiat, and went crashing through the gears down the hill.

Marina stood at the door illuminated by the dying light of the torches stuck in the snow around the porch. Her face was sharp and drawn, glassy like a sago pudding; it looked for the moment older than the principessa's. Later, in front of the bathroom mirror, her tension and her deportment would slacken, she would be alone with her illness and her numbered days, the knowledge that they would be spent exiled from society. She would trace the deepening lines and wrinkles with her long fingers, admit to a small degree of self-pity, and add one or two sleeping pills to the normal dose. She might even realize with surprise or bitterness that the social circle had never really existed at all, that even a circle formed of common need will break in common affluence and prove to be nothing but a loose line, ever ready to move one step up, reform itself, proscribe infirmity, protect its own hide.

6

·

"You seem to have had a good time," Libby barked. She was crouched over a glass of whiskey and appeared wide awake in her sullen way. She had no doubt waited up in order to broach the subject of her discontent at a moment when we were dog-tired and longing to get to bed. Bibba emerged too, swathed in violet nylon and cackling in a dogmatic manner that presaged a lengthy harangue. In the apparent conviction that some of the Italian hosts' wealth must have rubbed off on their guests, they began their attack, constantly interrupting each other and then devotedly backing down. "We've come to the conclusion that we need a contract, witnessed by a lawyer; in other words"— this first was said in perfect high German but their normal Berlin slang soon asserted itself—"to put it in a nutshell, we want a proper deal, in writing, setting us up for life." I listened to the familiar hometown accent and for a moment I was unable to relate it to the infamy of what was being said and hoped that the threat would be mellowed by the language of my childhood, make it cheery and gay. But not for long. "And another thing, we ought to get danger money here. You ought to take that into consideration too. There were a couple of anonymous phone calls again, and somebody was scratching at the front door around midnight, must've been a burglar. Earlier on a fellow named Peter came, said he's a friend, wanted to wait. One of your hangers-on, no doubt, we got rid of him double quick."

Hangers-on can't fool hangers-on, they defend their territory as whores defend their beat or a dog its bone, confront the invaders with outraged indignity. "So what do you say?" Libby asked, slapping her stovepipes together and pouring the last of the whiskey into her glass. "One doesn't make lifelong contracts for cooking," I said. "It's exploitation, that's what it is, if you've got nothing you get played for a sucker," Libby countered and rubbed her spectacles with vehemence, making her kiss-mouth. The storm was about to break. "Welfare state!" she roared, shaking with bitterness, "and not a penny did they pay me in war reparations, not a penny!" The case for the prosecution became broader, embracing the socialists and the conservatives, the American intelligence service and the Russian secret police, even the West German banks stood accused of corruption. Bibba wrung her hands, rubbed the palms and the backs of them as though trying to get rid of tar stains, the avian profile darting backward and forward looking for worms; they exchanged one final hangdog look and stood up simultaneously, sniffing in perfect harmony, and left the room.

Their cunning clung to them like a morning mist, they symbolized perfectly the frighteningly large number of people who unite in hate and intrigue to chew the cud of what they call their bad luck, throwing monkey wrenches into the works where they can. They draw their information exclusively from illustrated newspapers and magazines and are malleable and highly dangerous; without them no fascist system could ever function. The dragons suckled senilely at the breast of their glorious past, which, although a figment of their fantasy, had become the fountain of their gripe; reveling in martyrdom, they were of the unshakable conviction that they were "good" and the world "bad." They reminded me of many of the agents it was my misfortune to meet during the years when I was a film actress, who are good for a laugh in retrospect but who, at the time, were anything but a joke.

•

I had an appointment with Dr. Mario Albertini the next afternoon. He wasn't there. Ski accidents, hangovers, broken hearts, influenzas of every type and convivial tête-à-têtes over a Scotch or a gin-and-tonic prevented him from ever showing up on time. Two cranes were at work in front of the window of his consulting room, a bulldozer roared intermittently, and the cries of the Italian workers bordered on hysteria in their fight for comprehension. His office resembled a lawyer's rather than a doctor's; an English clock, six photos in silver frames displaying horses' heads, and a large brass tray overflowing with invitation cards adorned the heavy renaissance table. Nothing betrayed the landlord as being a physician. Dr. Mario Albertini loved horses, social gatherings, his profession—so he said—and the thought of having a large family. He apparently cherished the thought more than the family itself, because above all he loved women, beautiful women, with boyish figures and Eurasian blood by preference. He loved them resolutely, like a student, and although his passion seemed to flame within platonic limits, it was still a heavy cross to bear for his wife, who had grown prematurely sharp and cantankerous. After twenty-five years of marriage, she'd reached the leathery and unrelentingly bitter point where she would give vent to her discontent by correcting him on little things. "On Thursday last week . . ." he'd say, and she would cut in like a rapier with, "It was Friday, your memory's not what it was, is it, dear?" His long and often magniloquent anecdotes conjured nothing but a joyless, almost nauseated smile to her lips, and she lit up whenever he was obliged to converse in his very faulty English. Sometimes her eyes were swollen and her austere lips loose and quivering, and on these occasions she would excuse herself graciously and leave the supervision of the evening to her husband and the two grim butlers who served dinner in white gloves that were several sizes too large for them, making them look like clowns without make-up. Even so, one accepted invitations to the Albertinis' gladly; their house was old-fashioned, large and solid, and furnished with typical Swiss modesty; wobbly lampshades, faded slipcovers, and rickety chairs seem imperative there, to parade one's wealth doesn't do at all—"I'd love to have a chauffeur," one old banker told me one day as he got behind the wheel of his Opel, "but what would the neighbors think? They'd think I was trying to impress."

Doors slamming and a long fit of coughing announced Dr. Albertini's arrival. He was one hour late. As always, he spread his arms, and as always, he was dressed as though on his way to a London club, rather than to the practice of a doctor residing in a carnivalesque skiing resort. After trumpeting "*Viva*" and "Hello," he let his arms drop and also his smile; it disappeared simultaneously as though somehow his face muscles were directly linked to his arms. A web of fine horizontal lines now showed on the brown face, transforming the jovial expression into one of caustic intolerance. Sighing deeply, he sat down and asked, "How are we today?" The word "we" set off a negative mechanism in me and I had to bite back the tart rejoinder that I had suffered enough of this degrading twaddle in hospitals. "I've been running a temperature for weeks and my stomach has been hurting for weeks," I said instead. His astonished but doubting reaction to this came not unexpectedly, but it still alarmed me because I could read the thought "psychosomatic" written all over it, could see him ticking off my professions and their inherent neuroses, and drawing his conclusions; "hysterical" was well in the running too. The astonishment turned into amused professional benevolence, which he strengthened with a soothing "Now, now, now," and the unsettling feeling of isolation that had befallen me in front of so many doctors' desks welled up inside me. The extraordinary fact is that the judgment of many highly intelligent and otherwise shrewd people proves to be buried under a heap of dusty cliché associations when there's mention of "artists" or "actors" or "singers," and they'll readily pop members of these professions into their mental pigeonholes labeled *Unstable, Intemperate, Dissolute, Given to Histrionics.*

Dr. Albertini's initial evaluation of my briefly stated symptoms was, "Now, now, now, it can't be as bad as all that." My "It is" irritated him, and he withdrew his benevolence. "That crane," he grumbled bitterly and rubbed a long ear, "they've been building for weeks now." He swiveled around to look at the crane and the bulldozer, said above the din, "Stress, my dear girl, stress is the malaise of our times. An infallible clue to the state of one's physical health lies in one's hair. And yours is glorious. Sign of good breeding." "It's not my hair, it's my stomach," I croaked, hoping to master the tears mounting from my throat.

He took out the instrument for measuring blood pressure from an alligator case, unrolled it slowly, pressed the little black ball until the tube swelled tightly around my arm, pursed his lips, and said, "Low, very low, but then that's excellent, you'll never die of a stroke." "There are a lot of other things I could die of." "Depression, nothing but depression. Go for walks, breathe in our splendid clear air. Enjoy life, that's the thing, that's what one has to learn. Your temperature? Who hasn't got a temperature? It's just a little virus infection that's running around. I'll keep an eye on the intestinal flora. B_{12} will build you up, Sympatrol for your blood pressure, Euphren for the brain, and sugar water by your bed at night if you're restless. In four weeks we'll be as right as rain."

In a beautiful Swiss city that would be hard to beat for its atmosphere of security and well-being, there lives an agile and amiable doctor; he's a professor and is head of the children's clinic there. We had gone to him when our child, our only daughter, who had been born behind windows framed by May's fresh greenery, was approaching her second birthday and still made no attempt to walk, couldn't even stand up, and the various German professors we'd consulted had said, "Sweet and lazy," "She'd rather be carried by her father," "You wouldn't believe how cunning they are at that age already," "Give her time, don't get nervous"; had, in other words, dispensed small comfort and large bills and sent us on our way to continue the search. "You should have come before," the Swiss professor said. "It's due to oxygen deficiency at birth. It'll take years; she should have been diagnosed and given treatment long ago. Physical therapy's what she needs, every day." She had begun her life in the solitude of an incubator and now, at the end of her second year, she was thrust into the hands of well-meaning but hectic therapists.

After my unsatisfactory consultation with Dr. Albertini, I called the professor. "You must go to a specialist," he said. "The best one is here, Professor M. First of all you should have your kidneys checked. For that you should go to Professor Z."

Professor Z. was very young and very sleepy. It was 7:30 a.m., the clinic was rattling with the high-powered activity peculiar to clinics in the early morning. Staring desperately at a bare white wall, he listened to my roster of infirmities and symptoms, got up looking depressed, gently pushed me into a dark room, and turned me over to his Swedish assistant, who liked my songs a lot, my scarred veins less. After many gruesome attempts, he finally got the needle in, and the colored liquid flowed through my vein and into my kidneys, delineating them sharply for the subsequent X-ray. A wide inflatable strap bore down on my Caesarean scar until I finally begged for mercy; the howling of the X-ray machines and the shrill commands of a vociferous nurse lent a chilling aspect to the otherwise painless procedure.

"A double kidney, on the left," said Professor Z., yawning, "but nothing else. Your urine test is miserable. We'll try a switch therapy. Ten days Chloromycetyn, ten days Negram, ten days Chloro—" He raised his hand as though he couldn't bear the monotony of his prescriptions any longer. "Come back in three weeks."

One town farther on: Professor M. When he's sitting down he's the personification of ease; when on his feet he's a man pursued. Everywhere and nowhere at the same time, he streaks soundlessly through the corridors of his clinic like the tormented hero of an Edgar Allan Poe thriller. His students call him Kaiser P. They're scared stiff of their master, who operates in the twinkling of an eye, is out of the room before one realizes he's got up, rocks them on their heels with a solitary glance. He is short, slender, and has hair like a much-used brush. The eyes behind the rimless glasses are alert, mocking, don't miss a thing. His hands are very small and sinewy, delicate and infinitely respectful of the violability of the patient. Like all gynecological surgeons, he has to suffer the drooling adoration of the pregnant and sick women who, after conquering the initial feeling of shame, lie on his table and inevitably experience an erotic awareness during the examination, however carefully and detachedly he may conduct it. Kaiser P. suffers shyly, one feels like commiserating with him. In the monosyllabic professionalism of the operating theater he awakens to authority, so that even his sorely tried assistants abandon their grudgingly accorded respect and idolize him with the shining humility of an elementary-school class. His personality and ability seemed to miss the nurses altogether, however. They, in the masochistic fervor of their bland pedantry, more receptive to the despotic airs so many of his less-able colleagues are given to, misinterpreting his haste and reticence as signs of weakness, exclude him from their favor, work off their displeasure on the patients, and openly mourn the vulgar pranks, even the towering rages of his predecessors. Kaiser P. is totally unaware of this sisterly duplicity and malice and so endangers his work in the operating room, which is to a large degree dependent on the good will and initiative of the green-capped gaggle, in that he unwaveringly believes in their ability to make decisions and take responsibility. Under his gentle guidance, almost every one of them turns into a fighting cock, and the feathers fly around the sore bellies of the newly operated on.

For the moment I am still ignorant of the intrigues at the Swiss court. I lie on his table trying to relax and am grateful for the delicacy of his hands, which seem to know so much about pain that they succeed in avoiding it altogether, am grateful for a gentle gentleman in a brutalizing profession, in which horror is a matter of course. Perching himself on his minute desk, he whispers, as though wanting to thwart an eavesdropper, "You must be in great pain, there's an abscess, we should drain it today. When did you eat last?" "Seven hours ago." He shoots into the room next door, mutters at his secretary, shoots back again, and perches now on the radiator, clutching its ribs so that his knuckles turn white. "In two or three weeks at the latest

I'd like to remove the uterus. You should rest in the meantime."

A constantly smiling, dark-skinned man—Spanish, Portuguese, Italian?—introduces himself as the anesthetist. I walk to the operating room, undress in a cubicle, pull on the apronlike shirt with strings at the back, swing myself up onto the narrow table with studied nonchalance, surrender my left arm to the smiler, deliberate a nickname for him to distract myself from the jab, and have just come up with "Happy Olive" when a sound like a shot from a small-caliber gun startles me; with positive jubilance, as though he'd just invented something, he shows me a small chrome tube which is, in fact, an air-pressure instrument that shoots a hole in the skin and vein, enabling him to insert the needle easily and painlessly and couple it to the infusion bottle, which gurgles and quickly empties. "D'you feel anything?" he asks with his dark harsh voice; his strong-on-consonants accent brings back fond memories of Count Orlovsky performances. "Not yet," I answer, and feeling obliged to offer apologies, I add, "This is my fifty-first anesthetic." His smile grows patronizing, as though he'd been expecting wild flights of fantasy with the advent of the drug.

The room is as green as Upper Austrian meadows, and the green of the walls blends with the green of their smocks, masks, and caps so that they stand there bodiless, half-faced, and scalped to boot, waiting for the patient to go to sleep. Kaiser P. joins them. The table I'm lying on has been raised very high, so that he appears ridiculously small. Without the brush and without his nose and mouth, his eyes are more benign, like those of a friendly, bright child. The unusual time of day—it's seven in the evening—seems to lend an air of adventure to the operation. I begin to feel well, I feel comfortable and confident, surrounded by soothing, patient eyes, safe behind the broad green back of a nurse arranging her instruments at a table; even the tinkling sounds they make are warming, like a saucepan full of coffee water coming to the boil over an open log fire. I've escaped from the "stress" and "psychosomatic" scoffers, I think to myself. Here they make decisions and go to work; my fever will sink, the pain will go away, I'm on my way to a fever-free, painless life.

For want of something better, I say, "Is the anesthetic in the transfusion?" and get all the syllables mixed up; slurred and blurred, they slobber from my mouth. The paralysis restricts itself to my tongue and speech center as yet; I can still think clearly and without delay, but I'm unable to communicate familiar thoughts in the familiar way. Agitation swarms over me like a herd of ants, scratching and biting. I feel I'm slipping out of the belts that are binding me to the table, I tumble gradually but relentlessly into a void growing void of color, gray-green wisps of mist swirl away as I fall, slower now; a brake is being applied and I swing back and forth between fear and indifference, accompanied by a smile that belongs neither to Happy Olive nor to Kaiser P. The smile stays close to me, it belongs to no one and nothing. A pleasant anesthetic, I think, soaring up once more, I must make a note of what it's called, preparing myself for further series of narcotics even here.

A fluorescent light is hurting my eyes. It goes out, and now the uneven yellow light from my bedside lamp illuminates a hand with stubby fingers and the girlish mouth that is Happy Olive's. "Back from the threshold of death," the harsh voice says. "Narcotics are the threshold of death." The hand is holding a syringe, it moves toward my right bicep and strikes lightly. He studies me, his eyes are amber-colored and pale yellow, mastiff eyes. His skull is broad and the hair black, each wave has been carefully managed with a fine-tooth comb. Without the green smock he could be a singing teacher, junior high school in a provincial town, or the owner of a flourishing waterfront café. "Why in the arm?" I ask, tripping over my tongue, "it's so much pleasanter in the buttock." Here too benevolence is given only in return for obedience and worship. The mastiff eyes look dangerous, that squawk will have to be paid for. Absolute subordination is the price on the ticket to charity; otherwise, as with divine infallibility, it may turn to terrible remonstrance. So I say, "I'm sorry," as pleasantly as I can. "It's your job, not mine." The sparks of aggravation die slowly over his humorless smile as he weighs my compliance. "It was an excellent anesthetic," I add, trying anew to bury the hatchet, but his mastiff eye remains glazed and critical. The small radio communications instrument he carries in his breast pocket starts to bleep, calling him to the nearest phone. "There's no peace anywhere," he sighs, switching off the bleeper, and seems glad to be able to prove his indispensability. I doze off, still blissfully unaware that I am soon to rename him from Happy Olive to Grand Inquisitor.

"Your doctor at home can pull the stitches," says Kaiser P. as he takes his usual seat on the radiator. He huddles up as though wanting to make himself invisible, as though he'd rather jump out of the window behind him than face a wide-awake, undrugged patient. The early hour seems to intensify his need for privacy to such a degree that each confrontation causes him physical pain. He bends forward so that I think his gall bladder is kicking up, straightens up again, and offers me his hand, his arm stretched out as far as possible. I do likewise and his eyebrows shoot up in surprise, the brush waggles, he fears I'm parodying him. Reassured that this is not the case, his surprise broadens to a sheepish, self-ironical grin. Our handshake seals a pact: ambiguous gestures are not to be interpreted as signs of animosity; our wish to separate from each other as soon as possible is natural and welcome to both parties under the present circumstances. He hurries after me with his head bowed and whispers, "Before you leave us, there's a lump I'd like to check, I noticed it yesterday. I'll be expecting you in three weeks' time for the hysterectomy."

The X-ray rooms are in the basement, together with the mammographic and thermographic departments. Dr. W. is waiting for me under the rows of hot-water pipes in the dim corridor. He is burly and blustering, and his voice is strained and hoarse, like a fairground barker's. "We don't whet knives down here," it rasps from the walls to the ceiling in a sizable echo. He puts his arm around my shoulder and leads me into a large square room in which stands a delicate woman who looks as if she's been scoured with cleansing powder. She introduces herself as his assistant and tells me she's Canadian. Together they push me from one apparatus to the next; I hobble, hindered by the new incisions, carry out their instructions, smile dutifully at his often outrageous attempts to be humorous, and am thankful for the enjoy-it-while-you-can atmosphere he creates. "What I see, what I see is nothing but a silly little cyst," he roars deliriously, smacks me on the back, and trots into the developing room. The Canadian girl takes advantage of his brief absence to tell me the story of her life. With red blotches on her neck and eyes wide with horror, she suddenly blurts out, "I've been through hell," as though she's had to wait years for this opportunity to impart the information and expects to be interrupted at any second; "I was in Anchorage, Alaska, when the great earthquake happened, my child was born right in the middle of it, the earth split wide open, the walls fell in, and the people screamed, I was hurt and my child too, my husband has left me, the scars, you know, the scars have mutilated my body and I'm a stranger here and all alone." Her hands claw my arm and she looks at me imploringly, as if I could erase the memory, bring her husband back, render the scars invisible. "You understand," she says adjuringly; her face is yellowish white and the skin drawn tightly as though it's being screwed up from the back of her head, "You understand, I've been through hell, you were in the war, you were often sick, you know about pain; only those who've seen horror and cruelty can understand and grasp it, nobody understands here, they're all so well off." She says this surprisedly and without reproof, as if in awe of heaven's mysterious dispensations. Dr. W.'s loud laughter echoes through the passageway, the door is thrown open, and his eyes sweep to the woman's blank disturbed face, a deep vertical line forming between his thick blond eyebrows. She raises her shoulders defensively and goes out quickly. Two doctors run down the passage with their bleepers bleeping, summoning them to the next phone, the next patient. They run as if trying to escape from the unwavering penetrating tone that accompanies them through the day and night shifts and has taken an unwelcome place in their lives, like the whistling of a pierced eardrum.

"Nothing to worry about," Dr. W. rasps and brings me to a large elevator in which there's an empty bed and a shivering nurse. The glass reception office is humming and ringing as I pass by it, two male faces come to the window, greet me courteously, and immediately pitch back into the row they were having. I stand in the courtyard and it's suddenly filled to bursting with the malicious howling of an ambulance. A highly pregnant woman is taken out on a stretcher, she stares at the gray sky; it will be succeeded by the gray corridor ceiling, the white of her room, and finally by the green of the operating theater. She seems very young and scarcely equipped for the ordeal awaiting her.

●

Once more I am in Dr. Mario Albertini's consulting room. He removes the stitches, niggles and nags, grumbles about surgeons "who always have to operate," complains of his lot as a seasonal practitioner. "At three in the morning and again at five in the morning I was called to the same ex-empress," he says, waving the pincers; "she had a bellyache, so I left her a suppository and told her to use it immediately. Two hours later she calls again, the pain has got worse. I go back and she tells me she never wants one of those dreadful suppositories again, she's never known such agony. It turns out that she's pushed it up her royal anus without removing the silver paper, she didn't know one had to." He clucks his tongue and sighs, "I've never known such a season . . . but we'll get through somehow, one has to be tough as nails."

It's midday. The crane is resting with its claw in the air, as though the man at the controls had been mowed down by machine-gun bullets in the middle of a grab. The streets of St. Moritz are empty, the steel shutters of the furriers' and jewelers' shops have been rolled down, ghost town. There's a smell of Maggi soup and burned onions. Now and then one hears the crunch of a ski boot on the crusty ice. The English clock on Dr. Albertini's desk tinkles a thin F sharp. I feel as if I'm standing on a conveyor belt that's rolling backward, drawing me away from the familiar surroundings, I'm positive I'm seeing the mountains, the lake, the streets for the last time. "That wasn't all," I say loudly. He looks up disapprovingly and his pincers pluck at a piece of raw skin, the sharp pain startles me. "What did you say?" he asks. "I think it was just the beginning," I answer. He looks at me as though I were the ex-empress's twin sister. A transparent fright overcomes me, a fright I can't express, even if I were able to find the words, give it a valid name. "Professor M. says he must do a hysterectomy," I say. "That's quite an undertaking," he says, "but for a specialist like him, it's a bagatelle."

I'll never see this place again, I'll never see this doctor again, I'll never see anything again; I'll die. It's the same transparent fright I had once before, in an ambulance one sunny May morning. Through the rear window I had seen the roof of our house and had known that I would meet death, pain, and horror. "I'm in danger," I want to say but don't. I can already see Dr. Albertini's cynical ire between half-closed lids and can't face it; nor can I face the dope-filled vaults of the psychiatric clinic. Dr. Albertini washes his hands, scrubs them thoroughly, each fingertip and each nail, picks up his alligator case, hurries to the door, and says, "I'll see you at the gala." "I don't think you will." "Now, now, now, fresh air, enjoy life and love," he chants like a litany.

I stand at the frosted, sun-streaked window and am convinced in a ridiculous but unconceited way that I am the only one who has noticed that the solid ground we are all walking on so resolutely is nothing but a thin, brittle layer of ice and that it's going to crack at the next firm footfall, that the ice is everywhere, that it's milky and opaque and not at all reliable, that the solid ground is illusory, the ice reality.

7
.

SHE, on whom SHE herself as well as others often cannot lay hands, SHE, outwardly alert and composed but who deep down inside—where in God is that? In the heart, the lungs, the liver, the spleen, the colon, or the small intestine? In the gall bladder, the kidneys, the arterial riverbeds, or is it farther up, there where the industrious glands are, the tough thyroid? All right: Knowing, or better, assuming, that there's a phantom relay system, a mobile control tower wandering through the unexplored wastelands of the brain, and assuming that it sends impulses, transmits Morse signals and scrambled dispatches which SHE, a receiver from the top to the bottom of her five-foot-six-inch, 120-pound body, diligently notes and interprets, SHE, deep down inside, is filled with terror and lying rolled up in a huddle on the back seat of a car eleven days later.

Through one half-open eye SHE sees the back of her husband's head and the snow thick as porridge building up around the steadily ticking windshield wipers. The snowstorm seems to rage on three parallel levels; it whistles and swirls over mountain peaks, over the roofs, spits under the doors of the small-windowed houses that are crouching as though they've been expecting the terrible death-dealing avalanche for centuries now, the final incarceration, the endless immeasurable cold. The wind slaps and tickles, giggles around us; the car heater hums gently as though wanting to prove that man can parry force with peace.

At the top of the pass demons are whipping a grayly foaming spiral like a top; it dances and hovers, swoops and doubles back, leaving a wispy trail, crumples to the ground. They drive silently, the man and SHE. Below the pass the porridge grows thinner, watery. The snow begins to trickle with the same slow regularity as the blood seeping from her body.

SHE, or I, welded together to a plucky, timorous bundle, welcomed the temporary separation and release; we let me experience the five-hour ride as SHE, and after initial difficulties, SHE mobilized the furies of our will to live, which had been intensively and expertly trained in the art of survival, thanks to animal reflexes, and then reverted to me with renewed virulence. None of the coquetry of stepping aside, retiring sedately behind a new name, none of your modesty-preaching self-effacement. I stepped into line the moment we reached Kaiser P.'s hospital town at 5:05 p.m.

The parking lot in the gray forecourt was empty except for three bicycles chained to the railings and two middle-class cars. In the reception glasshouse a face unknown to me announced a room number and also that they were expecting me. They were changing shifts as I walked down the corridor, doors crashed into their locks and the hollow tom-tom booms of wooden sandals echoed above the crisper click of high heels. The unbridled uproar gave no indication of the presence of sick, recently operated-on women. A clump of patients in livid dressing gowns hobbled along the ground floor, blocking the way; they craned their necks into every open door, tittered as a doctor hurried past, behaved like an unruly bunch of extras coming up for the finale of an operetta.

My room was on the second floor; the light from a weak lamp over the washbasin showed a bed, a table, and a chair. The beefy nurse seemed out of sorts. "So you finally made it, how much longer were we supposed to wait?" she said. "There was a snowstorm," I replied. "So what," she countered and pushed back the left sleeve of my coat. The needle lodged beside the vein in my forearm; after slapping my wrist with the palm of her hand and assuring herself there was no blood to be had there, she pulled the needle out again, flickered a we'll-see-about-that look at me, and thrust it into the crook of my arm. Here too, although she slapped again and dug the needle around in all directions, she was out of luck. At the third attempt, which drew a short gasp from me, her grim countenance lit up, fairly radiated; delightedly she noted the vulnerability of the new patient and almost started hopping as the first drop of blood now appeared. It had hardly begun to flow when it dried up again, the vein refused its yield; she gripped my arm, thrusting the crook forward, chopped at my pulse with the side of her hand, but drew nothing this time, not even a whimper. The round face, especially the forehead and the flaring nostrils, began to shine greasily; the one eye I could see started to swivel in alarm. "The night nurse could have done this, I should have been off long ago," she blistered, ramming a new needle into my right arm and beckoning with her free hand to a young nurse who had appeared in the doorway. The young one bent over, picked up some tubes and glass slides from her trolley, and sprang into the room as though she'd been awaiting this invitation for hours, took my hand feverishly and without a word, and stabbed two of my fingers with a razor blade. I saw myself in a medieval chamber with vixens swarming over me, teaming up in doubles to perpetrate their unspeakable deeds at the dictates of a diabolical rationalist. When the beefy one had three tubes full of blood, she ran out bellowing, "Don't bother to unpack, after the operation you'll be in the intensive-care station." She stopped at the door, gave the room one last going-over, checking its tidiness, and went, slamming the door behind her with her foot. The young one balanced a tray on her hip, whined, "The laboratory will have to do overtime because of you," and left too.

I stood in front of the washbasin and broke out into unaccustomed tears. Looking into the mirror, I hoped to find something laughable, but pain and the dread of what was about to happen to me spoiled self-irony's chances. I quickly got undressed, fought my way into the tight sheets, and looked at three white walls and a large window, behind which I could make out the dim outlines of a courtyard and the crown of a chestnut tree.

With Happy Olive hard on his heels, my husband came in carrying a bottle of wine. "The doctor says you should drink a glass before you get the injection and the infusion. They're not going to operate till the morning." Happy Olive smiled charitably. "I will do a very good anesthetic," he said, "without the tubes in the lungs, so you needn't worry about damaging your vocal cords." "Without tubes?" I asked worriedly; I'd never been operated on without them. He looked at the ceiling, smirked. "It's my invention, my secret." Only now did I notice that his right eye was a good deal lower than his left one. It seemed to have slipped down between the cheekbone and the bridge of the nose, and the left one gave the impression of looking down on it; since the eyes were also very wide-set, I had the feeling that I was looking at two separate face halves, each well formed in its own way, that had bumped into each other by pure accident and decided to stick together. On closer inspection, his hairline too and the corners of the mouth proved to conform to the expressionistic display of anomaly. The lower right eye was the ingratiating one, the one that had inspired the Happy Olive title, whereas the higher left one was cool and distant, almost disdainful; one looked rather into the auspicious right window of his soul than the censuring left.

The odd concoction bent over me and said with a right-sided, homely smile, "It'll do you good," and, to the offer of a glass of wine, "I never drink alcohol." The homeliness mingled with the sour pride of blameless character. "It helps," I said, emptying my glass. A syringe appeared in his hand as if by magic and he struck swiftly, again in the region of my right bicep. With a short challenging glance, he assured me that he hadn't forgotten my recent complaint. "Luminal," he said, raising his eyebrows, the left eye widening. "You will sleep now." I felt him hook me up to an infusion; then the pictures started falling over each other, edging away, only the laughing eyes of my daughter remained in the foreground, growing more and more serious until they too receded.

I awake to the tune of "What do I hear about you from the doctor? Consuming alcohol before the operation?" The day-shift bloodsucker is spraying poison. "How can he be expected to anesthetize if you drink alcohol the night before?"

"He recommended it," I say.

"That's impossible, he never drinks."

"I didn't say he did. I did."

"Exactly. You shouldn't have."

"He recommended it."

Her look insinuates mendacity and insubordination, but above all dissipation. "We've only got forty minutes," she barks. "We've still got to shave you, change your gown, prepare everything." She initiates the preparations with the desperation of a trapped wasp.

"Where are you from?" I ask her.

"What?" she screams, momentarily thrown.

"You're not Swiss," I say.

She stands perplexed, stares, and gasps for breath two or three times. "I was born in Cottbus," she grates defiantly and sticks out her chin.

I start to chuckle, at first softly, muffled by the Luminal, then progressively more uncontrolled, insultingly. "I didn't mean to . . ." I splutter and am rocked by another gale of hilarity. "I didn't mean to hurt you, but I saw a film once with Wolfgang Neuss; in the movie his father comes home from the Russian prison camp he's been in for years, and Neuss looks up and sees his father totter in in rags and says, 'Have a good time in Cottbus?' The prison camp was in Cottbus, you see? And when you said that, the association just . . ." I stop. She's looking down at me inanely, her face locked and barred, the mouth clamped to a thin line.

The heavy quiet is broken by a young white-blond doctor whose height, walk, and the way he holds his head remind me of a giraffe. He stalks up to my bed and whispers, "I have to take down your details, previous illnesses and operations, and so on." The bloodsucker springs to life again; at first her movements are jumpy and uncoordinated, but the sight of a doctor helps her rise to the occasion. "Good morning, Doctor," she says, does an awkward about-turn, and marches out.

"Is it absolutely necessary?" I ask.

"What?" the doctor replies.

"To give the lifelong misery the once-over."

"What does 'give the once-over' mean?" he asks, leafing through his pad concernedly.

"In this case it means remembering the illnesses, recalling them, listing them, counting them up, and so on." With great strain he stares into the crown of the chestnut tree and nods ponderously.

"Are you a captain?" I ask him.

His head whips around as though a horse had kicked him. "Yes, I am," he gasps. "How did you know?"

"I did a little calculating: your age, your profession, Swiss citizen. Knowing you all serve in the army, I came up with captain."

"Is that possible? Good gracious." The Giraffe folds himself up, slides down in his chair, and looks at me intensely, surely hoping to make out a crystal ball under the blanket.

"May I smoke?" I ask.

He wrinkles his forehead and looks uneasily into the court-yard. "Two puffs," he says thoughtfully and pulls a pack of American cigarettes from his smock pocket. He sniffs the smoke with obvious pleasure, pats his pad, and says, "Where did we get to?"

"We got to giving it the once-over," I answer.

This amuses him and he now gets down to business. "Which illnesses have you had and have you had surgery before?"

"If you want them all, we'll have to postpone the operation." His knowing smile seems to want to inform me that he's spent time in the psychiatric ward. After filling two sides of his pad in shorthand, he lets it sink and stretches his giraffe neck. "That's really dreadful. My word," he says. "You're a war victim and a doctor victim to boot."

"The Hippocratic oath is a victim of bad pay," I reply. He applauds with his neck. "And most doctors never recover from the penury of the first years, even after they're established."

The neck stiffens and overlong fingers tug at an overlong

earlobe. "There are doctors with whom it's advisable to stay healthy," he says wistfully, and it only gradually dawns on him what he's said. He unfolds himself and stalks from one corner of the room to the other, grinning.

The door slams and startles us both. The Cottbus bloodsucker is standing there, rooted to the spot, trembling with rage. "Smoking," she spits and rams a short fat arm into her hip. "It's all right," the Giraffe murmurs placatingly and holds the cigarette end under the tap. She marches toward me mouthing silent words and stabs me in the thigh with a syringe. "Atropine?" I ask sweetly, as though totally immune to pain. She stares at me in dismay. "She knows the procedure," the Giraffe says quietly. He sits down and fidgets worriedly, says, "We ought to hurry."

"The patient still has to be shaved," the Cottbus lady says and glares down at me sullenly.

"The hour before the operation is never very edifying," I say.

She raises her shoulders and her neck crinkles into four rolls of fat. "That I can't judge. I've never been ill," she answers in a tone that implies that it's all a matter of character, and her chest swells as though she were expecting to have a medal pinned on it.

"Could we go into that at some other . . ." the Giraffe sighs.

"Never ill in my life," she repeats adamantly and seems to retire into herself, listening to the purr of her perfectly tuned motor.

"I have to examine the patient as well," the Giraffe says. He's impatient now.

But Cottbus won't surrender; she fusses around the room, moves a glass, moves a table, polishes the mirror, and gabbles, "All the rest were weaklings in my family, only me, I was the only one who was never sick, that's because I'm from good stock—"

"Apparently not, the stock seems to be rotten," says the Giraffe.

"How do you mean?" she asks astonishedly, biting her lips.

"If all the others were weaklings, then the stock must have been rotten," he says in distaste.

"Well, I never had anything," she insists stentoriously and wades to the door.

I rattle off the rest of my medical history elliptically, his head sinks deeper and deeper, silently he writes it all down, silently he closes his pad, stands up, and prods and knocks on me daintily. "You have green eyes," he says, studying my belly.

"Is that a bad sign?"

He laughs like a child, unpracticed, as though he hasn't laughed aloud for years. "Captain," he murmurs, and "See you at the operation."

8

·

September 1974

The authoress would like to admit, not too loudly but still clearly, so there's no mistake about it, that she's been hedging. She's been hedging around the present. She's been stealing around it, dawdling, postponing it, rattling down the beaten track, explaining this and exposing that; in other words, she's been swindling, because she's known all along that, having decided to make these diarylike forays into the present, she'd have to follow it through. Admittedly, she was never as rawly self-assured as the world at large seems to think her, as her critics delight in crowing when she puts a foot wrong, no, very much the contrary, she's dependent, dubious, even prim at times, then again coarse and aggressive, rather like a suicidal hare who bolts in a straight line at the first scent of danger instead of zigzagging as he's been taught to. Should she happen to decide to get things off her chest and cuss, then she'll explain the cussing, discuss the necessity of cussing, because she doesn't seem to be able to get along without a modicum of support and sympathy. She's a conglomeration of incompatible ingredients and she gave up trying to court their favor long ago; well aware of the disharmony, she spends a great deal of her life futilely patching things up, futile in that the patches come unstuck at the slightest pressure. And so she falls back on her predilection to prattle, not to talk away the loggerhead components of her still-there existence, but to talk them together. This doesn't work either. But it makes for huge telephone bills.

She presents herself to her immediate surroundings as a dynamo subject to alternating currents; the trouble is that so many know all about this faulty mechanism, even clever strangers see it with half an eye, they know about the futile patches and her dithering efforts to get the works to gel, are well informed of the delicate corset she dons sporadically and calls self-discipline. In her worst, courageless, terrified moments she holds on to a person, her house, an object, holds on to the next minute. And although she's living with a verdict, a lot of things have undergone only a minimal change, which is incredible. Her warring ingredients haven't changed an iota; she still gives the impression of breathing in but never out. She still becomes wide-awake and completely immobile when the dwarflike daemon registered under A, meaning Angst plus aggression, makes his entrance. Her components' habits appear to be unimpeachable, immune to shock. She puts up a weak show of resistance from time to time by resorting to the pessimistic "same to you with brass knobs on" type of humor which is a Berliner's trademark; otherwise, what she calls her vulnerability, or skinlessness, rules the roost. Her garrulity is prompted by a dread of weighty pauses, of empty or inquisitive eyes. Of course, she's quick to enthuse and is endangered and dangerous too, like all enthusiasts when they're disappointed. She spits and fumes, gets niggardly and embittered, hones her dull desire to do murder, forgets it. She switches her roles from the witness to the accused, from the judge to the unanimously condemned prisoner. Not much more than thirteen months ago she was convinced that her duo-trio-quartet would gang up against the verdict invader; as far as she was able to plan at all, this seemed to be imperative for survival. But the plan never took on any real form, because the reflexes of the second-third-fourth egos didn't dream of bowing to the gravity of the situation, they went their vituperative ways as ever and let it be emphatically known that they were rabid anarchists and didn't give a hoot for survival.

She knows that thoughts are things. Not just the seed that

results in the thing, but the thing itself. Her attempts to bridle her thought/things are disappointing; the third ego sniggers provocatively, the second rejects all suggestion of discipline, and yet another touches off a series of underground avalanches that shatter her wish for an ordered stream and turn it into an uncontrollable delta. As a result, she has formed a habit of pushing various facets of the weaker traits of her character into the realms of mysticism, or, if it happens to suit her purpose better, into the machinations of the unilluminable subconscious. Admittedly again, she does have bursts of courage, but she always keeps a letter of pardon up her sleeve.

People tell her she "emanates." How she does it she doesn't know. Her emanating, not to be mistaken for vivacity or limitless cheer, takes the form of an unintentionally vibrant presence, a sort of ignore-me-if-you're-man-enough clarion call, when the emanating's behaving well. Whenever she enters the ring as an actress or a singer, it's a great help, it transforms her into a shimmering lion tamer, but at home and in non-professional privacy, it's like having body odor. It disturbs, gives offense, outrages. Whatever she feels about people and what they say communicates itself to them without her opening her mouth. If her family says, "You look as though you've—" then they're damned upset about something. So there she sits on her vibrancy like an insect on a DDT spray can and sends her surroundings reeling with a squirt from her poisonous nozzle. What is she to do about the emanating when she doesn't know who's behind it? Is it Hildegard I or II or III? Which one of the daemons who are so handy on the stage but sheer hell at home? She does nothing. She runs around as transparent as a pane of glass and waits for the first stone. In self-critical moments she puts aside the daemons and parapsychological first-aid kits and substitutes schizoid ossification, reasons that the translucent quality of her feelings is a logical and disciplined outcome of her extrovert professions, but her heart's not in the reasoning, she knows that it's a slack hypothesis, light-years from cognition and truth.

She first came to realize her capacity for emanating at the tender age of eight and a half on a sunlit school playground in

Berlin-Wilmersdorf. A woman teacher had commanded the children to form lines of four in the harsh barking tone prevalent during those Nazi years and had driven the sandwich-munching class before her like a herd of donkeys. "Dumb," the authoress-to-be had thought to herself. Nota bene: had thought, not murmured or hissed through her teeth to her best friend, just thought. Before she could add "crazy" or "stupid cow" to her initial thought, she felt a blow on her head. "I won't have that!" the teacher announced, her voice full of hatred. She didn't define what she meant by "that." A short while later, the emanating earned her a thick ear from her grandfather, who was usually so gentle and peace-loving. So she began to try to confine the informative aspect of her vibrancy, radiation, or whatever by lowering her eyelids or gazing at anything but the person talking to her. But then everyone accused her of shiftiness and lack of moral fiber since "she can't look you in the eyes"; with the expediency children are blessed with in order to get a foothold and advance into the adult world, she upped the lids again and bored into the pupils of anything that crossed her path. This wasn't right either. She was impertinent, unladylike, and should have been ashamed of herself. The whole period of honest-to-goodness baleful staring brought her nothing but trouble; the fact that her irises were green with a black line around them gave even dear friends the idea of associating her with medieval witchhunts and bonfires. When one of them said, "Not too long ago they'd have burned you at the stake," she went into a goose-pimply despond and laid the first foundations for her later anxieties and neuroses.

Without a doubt, the emanating was a downright nuisance until she was about sixteen. Then she had an idea which, as time told, was not at all bad; she became an actress, and lo and behold, in this context the anomalous and ostracized radiation proved a godsend, turned out to be a prerequisite tool of the trade, became useful and profitable, and was soon blessed with a whole series of new, if indeterminate, connotations. Her business associates described her as being "talented," said, "She's got something" or "She comes across" (the footlights) or "She exudes" (this worried her at first). Even the more articulate of her mentors, all of whom were susceptible to the exuding, seemed oddly vague in their choice of terminology until she had her first big successes; then they settled for a common title and named her: a personality. Even then, they agreed that any definition was no better than a feeble attempt to express the inexplicable, the "it" that Klee and Faulkner, Salinger, Miller, Kafka, and even Arnold Toynbee discuss. And so they stuck to "it," to exuding and personality, and were content with the woolly characterization, content with not knowing and not wanting to know, left the unexplored unexplored.

But to get back to the emanating authoress: she'd hardly taken leave of her childhood when, as nature will have it, the opposite sex entered the fray and mistook the radiation for libidinous angling, bold and saucy provocation, and deplored the lack of wistful frailty that typifies the feminine gender. Her radiations, so welcome in her profession, soon caused chaotic circumstances in her private life. She tried to storm the biased male barricades by behaving in a chummy, comradely fashion, which exposed her first to a barrage of boorish insolence and later to long periods of wary isolation. Professional recognition seemed to widen her radius of emanation, whereas negative publicity pared it down again; during the frequent spells of inactivity all actors are subjected to, it would boomerang on her and squirt her full of her own black ink. It reached the height of its powers whenever the utmost tips of her feelings were touched, when she was head over heels in love, say, or floundering in a well of depression. In the course of her nomadic existence, she was to meet a great many people who had made careers in public professions and she noticed that they were all, to a greater or lesser degree, emanators. It also became all too clear that emanating was no indication of character, its owners were as often choleric as they were peace-loving, but it did appear to feel most at home in neurotics and hairy lone wolves.

The authoress is sometimes overcome by fits of janitorlike curiosity; one day she decided to get to the bottom of the enigma and went to Belgrave Square, London, S.W.1., to the home of

the British Spiritualists' Association. It was a well-ordered estab-
lishment; each floor housed its own special group of spiritualists.
Her first thought, as she stood at the reception desk, was "spiritual
supermarket"; she formulated her thought in German, but even
so the British receptionist shot her a stinging glance. She decided
to watch her step. The receptionist led her past a row of waiting
people and into a sparely furnished room. A few moments later
a tiny man came in and looked at her fixedly for a long time;
then his eyes traveled around her as though she were standing
in front of an important notice he wanted to read. He held his
hands up to her face without touching it and immediately freed
her of an allergy that had been giving her pain and resisting
treatment for weeks and told her she was pregnant. As she was
only in the sixth week, it was unlikely that signs of swelling could
have influenced his diagnosis. She remained cool and tried not
to be too impressed for fear of hurtling headlong into a tangle
of naïve belief in something she knew nothing about until he
suddenly spoke of the "aura." "Exceptionally wide beam," the
man said matter-of-factly, as though he'd measured it with a
yardstick; "and red is predominant," he added. The word "aura"
startled her. Although she was well acquainted with it and knew
that it was bandied about with a dozen other vague terms in
connection with parapsychology, here it had a professional ring
about it, an authority and accuracy. The man inferred from her
aura that she'd had an unhappy childhood, that she was prone
to illness, that she had a vile temper—uncontrolled and self-
destructive, not British at all—and that the breadth of her aura
was astounding, even for a jaded aura reader. Then she was dismissed. As she left the house she was extremely agitated and
only later noticed that she'd been given a book written by the
head of the association.

From the first page the book was written with a lucid certainty
that brushed away the mumbo-jumbo cobwebs, explained the
hitherto unfathomable, spoke of reincarnation as a proven fact,
citing Hippocrates, and maintained that we comfortably reach
for the word "phenomenon" whenever confronted with something we don't immediately understand. She learned that the

paranormal would become easily graspable once we were able to relate it to those regions of the mind that are still a closed book according to the scientific authorities. A long section of the book dealt with spiritual healing and here the writer made clear that the success of this method was not dependent on raping nature's laws; on the contrary, it could only succeed by restoring harmony between the physical and the spiritual bodies common to all living things. This last gave her an unpleasant jolt, since it coincided with the maxims of those diagnosticians who crowed "psychosomatic" to everything and construed physical illness as a manifestation of psychic disorder, and it was from this group that she'd been hoping to escape.

Nevertheless, she was filled with insight and enthusiasm and made an appointment to see the writer. His name was Bertrand B. He was in his early forties, had red-brown eyes, titian-red hair and matching beard, and limped dreadfully. "It's the result of a war wound plus a stroke," he said, looking past and around her in the same manner the little man in Belgrave Square had done. The hall and passageway of his ground-floor apartment were dark and meandering and empty, except for a Chinese settee. He showed her into a room as big as a dance hall which was furnished with one frayed armchair, two rickety rococo chairs, and a glowing electric heater on a stand. He gestured for her to be seated opposite him and pulled his chair so close that it took them some embarrassed moments to arrange their legs; they now sat there in the large empty room like two actors on a deserted stage. He closed his eyes and began to feel her head carefully. There was no sound except Bertrand B.'s heavy breathing and an occasional cheep from the heater. She felt more and more uncomfortable and tense and exposed, as though all her woes and afflictions were crawling out of their holes, until suddenly a cool indifference settled over her, which in turn gave way to a feeling of absolute well-being and repose. When he lowered his hands, she had lost all sense of time, was unable to judge how long the sitting had lasted. He began to talk easily and casually, and what he told her corresponded with the little man's findings, only Bertrand B.'s diagnosis went deeper and added a few disturbing reports on the state of her spine and nervous system. His face, or what one could see of it through the bushy beard, showed distinct signs of exhaustion. He gazed wearily at the uneven parquet floor, absently offered her a squashed cigarette, and stuck one himself in the hole between his mustache and beard, leaned back so slowly and heavily that she feared the dainty chair back would collapse, and then smiled at her in a manner she interpreted as encouraging. Tapping their ashes into the empty cigarette pack, they agreed it was time for an unspiritual whiskey.

Mutual sympathy and above all her unquenchable thirst for exhaustive information on all subjects that take her fancy turned this strange interlude into an even more unusual friendship; it flowered sporadically and then lay fallow for months at a time, due partly to the considerable distance between their places of residence and partly to a common distaste for letter writing, and so was limited to telephone calls, experiments in telepathic linkups, and short turbulent visits.

The happening at Bertrand B.'s hadn't satisfied her curiosity by any means; that same evening she went to a public healing demonstration in a London suburb.

The high narrow room was ice cold, two dusty naked bulbs dangled from the ceiling, and the wooden benches were crowded with old men and women whose clothing and hopeless-looking faces reminded her of Berlin at the end of the war. The man next to her was wrapped up in several woolen scarves and kept turning the pages of a very large newspaper, folded and smoothed it, immediately turned and folded it again, never got around to reading a word for all the folding and turning. Next to him a woman was knitting something indefinable in gray wool. All the others sat completely still. Somewhere in the background a door slammed, but no one reacted. An anemic woman of indeterminate age stole onto the podium on tiptoe, as though afraid of waking somebody, and sighed. The sigh could have meant anything from despair to anticipation, excitement even. She licked her blue-and-white lips several times and went into her announcement at breakneck speed, apparently urged on by a fear of losing the thread. The congregation listened to her proclamation without altering its lethargic demeanor. A young Negro sprang lightly onto the podium like a dancer and requested the sick to come up and join him. A few old ladies got up timidly, shuffled down the aisle, and stood in line in front of the platform as though waiting for a bus. The Negro stretched, threw his head back, closed his eyes, and began to breathe deeply. Then he bent forward, raised his arms toward the first old lady, laid his hands on her shoulders, let one slide down over her back, let it rest between her shoulder blades, then pressed and squeezed, felt her neck and skull. The anemic woman stood beside an old harmonium dabbing her nose with a handkerchief as she followed the proceedings. The Negro shook his hands, turned the old lady around, and pushed her away. Without any visible signs of change, she left the podium and slid back onto her seat, pulled a woolen beret over her thin hair, fumbled with her coat buttons and her shopping bag, cleared her throat, and settled down again. When the Negro had finished squeezing all the applicants, the anemic woman lent him her arm and led him from the stage. The audience applauded his exit thinly and now sat up as though expecting the evening's star attraction. An unattractive youth appeared and set about erecting a tattered screen and a 16mm film projector. Even though it took him several attempts before he was able to adjust the film correctly, the audience waited patiently and attentively and let out a warm "ahh" as the black-and-white picture finally flimmered on the screen. After panning shakily over fields and bushes, the camera wobbled up to the sky, remained focused on the unrelieved grayness of clouds for several minutes, then jerked onto a chubby-cheeked man shielding his eyes either from the camera or the sun, cut to an empty chair, and dwelt on its beauty for what seemed an eternity; finally something that seemed to be a fat dog crawled up onto it and lay down panting; then the camera dithered back to the cherubic man and rolling fields of wheat. The anemic woman came back again and announced that the cherub, who was a revered former leader of the spiritual circle now living in retirement, had sent his dear friends this delightful film in place of a greeting card. The film recapitulated its record of wheat, meadows, the chair, and the dog, and shivered to a halt. The youth rewound the film; specks of dust drifted through the white beam of light as the audience applauded respectfully. After dismantling the projector and the screen, the youth seated himself at the harmonium. The man who had folded his newspaper sang fervently; he fairly belted out the hymn, whereas the rest of the congregation seemed none too sure of the words and dragged behind him with trembling voices. The hymn at an end, the members of the circle gathered up their knitting things, shopping bags, and scarves and drifted into a grubby back room where herb tea and biscuits were being served. They discussed the film excitedly as though they'd just come from a glittering premiere, then gradually wandered out into the night and waited on the rainy, windy street while the anemic woman turned out the light, locked the door, and joined them with the can of film under her arm; then they all moved off to the bus stop.

Needless to say, the authoress was disappointed. Undaunted and spurred on by her own special brand of optimism, which can cope with all manner of absurdities, she attended a "spiritual operation" the next night. It took place in the East End of London and she arrived an hour late—the street signs were badly placed and the houses in that neighborhood rarely bore numbers. She knocked timidly on what she hoped was the right door, and an amiable, expansive woman with a black patch over her left eye opened it, put a finger to her lips, and drew her into a red-lit hall. "Our medium has established contact," she whispered, waddled heavily over the creaking floorboards, and led the authoress into a small room full of Japanese bric-a-brac and plastic flowers. A big blonde woman in a baby-blue knitted dress was standing next to the sofa with her arms outstretched and her eyelids tightly shut but flickering, like a child feigning sleep. "We've made a link with a German surgeon," the one with the eyepatch whispered excitedly. Her clothes smelled of incense, moth balls, and pine deodorant. "He's from Heidelberg," she continued. "Don't say anything to her, only talk when she asks you something."

"*Wer ist?*" the blonde called out in a strangled Santa Claus voice. "*Gut Mensch?*" The medium's German seemed to issue from an English fourth form rather than from a Heidelberg professor.

"Good man," Eyepatch echoed and nodded affirmatively.

"*Jojo*," boomed the bass voice out of the blonde, "*Hinlegen, wir machen Operation.*"

Two elderly ladies hurried in, carrying kitchen towels and enamel bowls full of water. The authoress said no and sent them all into a tizzy. "Don't talk, or she'll get a heart attack," the trio squeaked. "No need to worry, no harm'll come to you, she's only going to operate the aura, only the aura." Five eyes peered at her anxiously. The blonde still looked as though she were playing blindman's buff and had begun to snort. "Only the aura," the choir chanted and pushed the author onto the lopsided sofa full of cushions. "You've got a terrible pain," the bass voice said in a perfect cockney accent. This was true. The blonde bent forward and her fingers fumbled at something about six inches above the region of the authoress's gall bladder, then moved up and concentrated on the right eye. "*Nix gutt,*" she burbled, relapsing into the German Santa Claus number, and began to describe circles and crosses in front of her face; she then placed her hands in one of the washbasins, let out a thundering old man's laugh, and exclaimed, "She vill haf child." This again was true. "*Einen Jungen*—boy, boy." This proved to be wrong. Eyepatch took the authoress's hand and said, "You can get up now, the operation was successful."

Since the authoress needed somebody to let steam off on, she called Bertrand B., told him about the amateur dramatics, and upbraided him violently; told him that she had been degraded from unconditional belief to wounded cynicism and heard a chuckle at the other end of the line which soon exploded into a bellow of laughter. "What on earth took you there?" He giggled. "You don't go to a blacksmith when you've a tooth that needs looking at." "Who's to tell me which are the blacksmiths and which the dentists?" she cried. "I will," said Bertrand B. and told her to lie down and think of nothing. Still bubbling with anger, she did as she was told and tried to concentrate on the telepathic link; colored sails and screens grew behind her closed eyes, dirty at first, then growing clearer and more luminous until they became transparent, with Bertrand B.'s face looking through them. She fell asleep and woke up again with the testy thought that she'd found a thread, though very flimsy, but that she didn't know who was holding it or where it would lead her or whether the other end was bound to anything at all; perhaps it was loose, just swaying in the wind, just pretending to be a sign.

9
.

May 1973

The Giraffe has hardly gone out when Kaiser P. shoots in. The Cottbus lady is right behind him, dealing glances like dagger thrusts in all directions; she comes to attention and yells, "The professor is here!" Kaiser P. twitches at each syllable. With his brush-head bowed, he races over to the window and is visibly disconcerted to find his beloved radiator encased in a cage with a large shelf on top of it; he pulls himself disgustedly up onto the ledge and huddles there with his arms crossed over his chest, each hand holding a shoulder. Cottbus bawls, "The patient still has to be shaved." Kaiser P. begins to swing his legs, slowly at first, then quicker and quicker, stops abruptly, and places them neatly alongside each other as he whispers, "This is earlier than we planned. I'm sorry that we have to rush things." His brush bobs up and down and his eyes inadvertently bump into the Cottbus lady's. He twitches again and looks at the toes of his shoes. "When did the hemorrhage begin?" he asks, almost inaudibly.

"The day before yesterday," I whisper, trying to match his volume.

"Fever?"

"Yesterday." Brushing all anxieties aside, I ask, "Since you have to hack me open anyway, could you tidy up all the other scars on my belly while you're about it? I look as if I've been on a chopping block."

He rubs his left ear with his right hand and feels his brush. "I'll have to ask the cosmetic surgeon, we'll see what can be done. It depends on what else we find in—" A clog clatters through the open inner door all by itself; hard on its heel a long-toothed albino nurse hops in, whinnying asininely, and looks like a malicious piebald nag that's lost its shoe. Her cap has slipped down over her forehead. She holds on to the door and stares at Kaiser P. Bubbles swell out of the corners of her mouth, then she opens it as though someone had ordered her to show her tongue. "It slipped off, ran away," she snickers inanely, drops to her knees, and fishes under the bed, still whinnying, finds her shoe, and scuttles out under heavy fire from Cottbus. Kaiser P. changes his position laboriously and stares desperately at the big clock in the courtyard. "See you soon," he whispers and runs out, rubbing his ear.

A nervous young nurse comes in right away; she's holding a razor in her rubber-gloved right hand and begins to scratch away awkwardly at my pubic hair. "Get a move on," Cottbus shouts and yanks my bed toward the door. The corridor is in its usual uproar. Three carefree, nattering women in hideous dressing gowns are leaning against the wall; they interrupt their chat to get a good look at the scalpel's next victim. Cottbus shoots me around the corner, taps the floor impatiently with her toe as we wait for the elevator, and bawls at a passing nurse, "Are you finished with 14?" The nurse doesn't hear; she hurries by and collides head-on with another who's carrying a bedpan. It falls to the floor with a clatter and gives off an unlovely odor. Three other nurses holding syringes emerge from a doorway and set off in different directions; another trundles an infusion stand up the corridor, yet another is smashing trays onto a trolley. They yell at each other over my head, "Busy day, today." "D-day." "Once more into the breach!" The noise hammers through my brain, pounds at my ears. "The atropine's beginning to work, I feel awful," I gasp. The bed rumbles into the elevator, Cottbus looks up contemptuously at the fluorescent light, her wide nostrils widen even further and seem to look at me like two close-set eyes. With one last spirited shove, she propels me into the operating theater.

The gay meadow-green has grown murky, muddy, moldy, slimy; it washes over me like seaweed, clinging, sucking me in. I'm lying next to a swing door that creaks and slams irregularly, I seem to have been forgotten, I have no part in the taut activity prevailing here; there's no uproar, the voices I hear are terse, toneless, subdued, it's like hearing a considerate neighbor's late-night radio. The easy hospitality I'd experienced that evening two weeks ago has gone, I'm a cog in the well-oiled machinery of the morning treadmill of major operations. Four hands lift me onto the narrow table, broad leather straps are fastened around my ankles and right wrist, someone raises my left arm, behind it I catch a glimpse of Happy Olive's eyes. Neither the cool left nor the ingratiating right one impart anything; dispassionately they regard something beyond my field of vision. There's a loud metallic pop and the needle slides into my vein. I search among the eyes hurrying by for Kaiser P.'s but can't find them; I get desperate, he should be here by now, perhaps there's a mix-up and I'll be operated on by another surgeon by mistake—the green rushes down on me, scoops me up, and swallows me abruptly, there's no gentle slide this time, slap bang pow terror, black-tinged green, then coal-black night, Happy Olive's threshold of death.

●

I can't breathe. Something's rustling beside me. My belly is burning brightly. There's a plate of lead lying on it, squashing my pelvis, my ribs. Somebody whispers. The whispering incites the fire, it roars like a furnace, singeing, searing. The pain spins like a saw and chops through the leaden plate and the ribs and the belly. A clammy cold hand feels my hip and I feel the sting of a needle. A white face emerges from the green and a pale mouth murmurs, "You're in the intensive-care room." Intensive green hell. Hell whose walls dispense pains in every known variety and many that are not, a room in hell pulsing with pain and gurgling screams, screams that are strangled at birth, screams at a pain that obliterates all the other smaller pains, that gives to understand that there are endless variations and reserves in the pain arsenal. "Help me," I croak, "help me." The white face comes back. "The drug will help you soon," the face says, blinking worriedly. It doesn't. It rips my head apart, hammers at my brows, glues my lips together, squeezes out my last breath. "I've got an allergy, I'm allergic to the drug," I mumble through my glued lips. The white face tries a little smile, bends down through the infusion tubes, a hand feels my forehead. "I'm done for, end of the rope," I mumble, falling back on battlefield jargon, back to the war and its screams, its death rattles, pictures of ripped-open guts and bleeding entrails.

"It's the plaster that's hurting," the quiet voice says. "Your stomach's in a plaster cast, so the wounds won't burst open." She pushes the dual nozzles into my nose, oxygen fizzes through my sinuses. Happy Olive suddenly appears and says, "Now, now, what do I hear? An allergy? Pain?" He fiddles with the infusion bottle. "I've put a catheter to your heart. It's my specialty," he adds. The last I hear is my own gurgling; I see the back of his head, the finely combed black hair, then no more. Blackout.

•

"I'm Mathilde," the white face says. "Help, please help me," I croak. "I'm not allowed to give you anything, not unless he specifies it," Mathilde says. I want to cry out but the cry tumbles back into my burning belly, hurls me at the blackness billowing toward me. There's a polka-dot dress dancing the samba in the blackness, black dots on a white background are bobbing over my stomach, rapping my head, jumping on my neck. Briefly I see Kaiser P.'s face, gray-green, his eyes bedded in black streaks. "We'll have to drain the gall bladder," somebody mutters. I choke, splutter, hordes of starving rats are gnawing at my belly. My bed is standing in the middle of the room, it didn't quite make it to the wall. Happy Olive, cast-iron, ironhearted, armor-plated, shoots past. My room in hell has been lifted out of time, out of the town, country, place, it's a capsule hanging in space with dying going on inside. There are no more Swiss streets with shops that open and close punctually, no more neon signs that never have faulty letters, no more sidewalks that never have dog droppings or piles of vomit; there isn't any clean gray forecourt with bicycles, gleaming mudguards, bells, pumps, oiled chains, no more middle-class cars under spreading brown branches.

Long slender butchers' knives with hooks are churning in my stomach, the plaster is like a slab of concrete. "Fever," Mathilde whispers, "you're running a high temperature." She shakes her head and looks frightened. "Help me," I say. She bends to my ear. "I can't. He doesn't understand, doesn't want to. I'm not allowed to give you anything, not even if the pain's unbearable." "The professor . . ." I grate. The rest of what I want to say gets tangled with the tube in my mouth, sticks to the palate and the plastic. Mathilde nods and hurries away. I see red thick hair and two tired dark-velvet eyes coming nearer and nearer. "I'm a doctor," she says in a clear voice, "you've got to, you've got to . . ." She leans forward imploringly and touches my wrist lightly. "You've got to live," she pleads, "live." Her tears drop into my face. All at once men are enemies, vindictive torturers. "Help me," I gurgle. "I'll get the professor." The red hair goes away, the crocodile-green walls of hell reassert themselves. Mathilde hurries back silently, I feel a sting in the hip. "Mo," she breathes and smiles, her white face creasing and crinkling distortedly. "Mo?" "Morphine, that'll help, the professor prescribed it." Olive is standing behind her, clearing his throat, the rasping sound cuts through my belly. "If the professor prescribed it . . ." his strained voice says. His cool eye is merciless, even the right one promises terror. Once more the rasping noise, then short hard footsteps.

Mathilde is sitting quietly, humbly. Her gray-streaked blond hair is mussed under the cap. The emergency light throws a blue circle on her forehead. Her face is like a pencil drawing, lovely clear lines, gentle, unobtrusive; you wouldn't notice it on the street, men especially not. Mathilde, with her manless, childless life, Mathilde, who absolves post-narcotic confessions, confessions no priest has ever heard, desperate stammered confessions that are spewed into her unobtrusive face.

Mathilde looks at her bulky wristwatch, checks the infusion bottle and the drainage tubes, pushes a thermometer under my left armpit. "You've been here a long time, nobody's ever in intensive that long, nearly six days," she says. She holds the thermometer up to the light. "Over a hundred and five," she whispers.

It's night and there's a glimmer of light behind the window opposite my bed, I can see a doctor, and now a woman stands up. They can't hear me chanting "Help." They smile at each other guardedly. The pain forces my teeth apart and I slowly begin to choke, silently, as though it's my last breath. The light dims like a spluttering oil lamp, green smocks swirl around me rustling excitedly. Two bleepers are bleeping. "A hundred and six-point-five," a hoarse voice says. "We need an X-ray," says another. An ice-cold plate is thrust under my back, hands pull me this way and that. The chant begins again, "Help, help, help." It is drowned by the rustling and swirling and the clamor of a bell. My bed rolls over the smooth floor, over tiny ridges. It's still nighttime—or is it the next night? Which night? "Nearly midnight," the hoarse voice says. I can see the theater green in a blinding light; to the left there's an unfamiliar face hidden behind the mask and the cap and gold-rimmed spectacles, the eyes are fierce and concentrated on my body. Then I plummet down the well of anesthesia. I want to scream, want to die, want to live, the pain is an inferno of pains, millions of glittering spears.

They operate for the second time. The old one-two.

•

To digress from the present doctors' subject, which is me, in order to examine some of the past doctors and their deeds in connection with the subject: some six years ago at five o'clock on a beautiful cobalt-blue, Munich morning, the pregnant subject awoke from a deep sleep to find herself in moderate pain and bleeding copiously. Her husband, whose self-control is usually quite reliable even in moments of extreme danger, rushed to the telephone, stubbing a toe and cursing loudly as he did so. He called the gynecologist and quickly described the situation. The doctor's level soothing voice assured him that an ambulance would be there right away to take his wife to the hospital. Somewhat steadier now, her husband paced back and forth between the window and the bed his wife was lying in for exactly eighteen minutes before calling the doctor again, telling him that the ambulance had still not arrived and suggesting that he carry his wife down to the car and drive her to the clinic himself. The doctor applied the medical profession's stock-in-trade panacea, saying, "Now, now, don't let's get excited," and reassured the husband that there was no great hurry anyway since he had only just begun to call the members of his operating team, some of whom lived many miles away from the clinic and all of whom were still in bed, and furthermore, that the husband wasn't helping matters any by tying up the line. What he didn't do was tell the husband to take his wife down the road to the state hospital, where a team of surgeons, anesthetists, doctors, and nurses was on duty round the clock. It must be admitted that the thought didn't occur to the perturbed couple either, even though neither of them were all that stupid or all that young any more, just greenhorns at the business of having babies, that's all.

After a total of sixty minutes, the wife was carried on a stretcher into a small, white-tiled room with windows looking onto a garden full of May's freshness, and lay there with chattering teeth, staring troubledly into the faces peering down at her. The faces belonged to a jolly although sleepy-looking gynecologist of bull-like stature, a slender, retiring chief doctor, and two nurses. Prepared, now, to leap into the breach, they stood around their bleeding patient exchanging (it seemed to her) uneasy glances, while a third nurse proceeded to shave her. The patient was by now very weak, and although she was constantly aware of the magnetic effect her fame had on a great number of all sorts of people, she never dreamed of attributing the odd occurrences of the past one and a half hours to it and to the beneficial light a little publicity might shed on the small, struggling private clinic. Her condition had grown critical and the chances that the child would be delivered unscathed diminished by the minute. The team finally set about their belated task and performed the Caesarean section, and found that the placenta was situated in front instead of behind the child, a circumstance known as placenta previa, which is, in spite of its agreeable-sounding name, acutely dangerous both for the mother and for the child. After they had extracted the child and cut the umbilical cord, removed the placenta, sewn the wound with catgut, and dispatched the incubated baby girl to a children's clinic in an ambulance, the mother wouldn't wake up. She couldn't, because the clinic didn't have enough coagulant to stop her heavy bleeding, nor did it have blood transfusions of her particular group, although it's very normal and her blood count had sunk to 15 percent hemoglobin. She did eventually regain consciousness after some highly adventurous hit-or-miss emergency measures on the part of the doctors, only to find herself in a bed full of blood again eight days later. The wound had opened, incredibly and of its own volition. The anesthetist immediately put her out; the others went to work with needle and thread.

Over the next five years, it became more and more apparent that all was not well inside the patient's abdomen; whether the circumstances surrounding the childbirth were the cause or not will never be proven. It is possible that tiny gaps were left among the internal stitches which in time developed into pouches of pus. And time proved to be their long suit. Throughout the five years, during which ever new, ever more erroneous diagnoses were pronounced over the ailing patient, the pouches grew into acute abscesses, became infected, resisted all antibiotic attacks, and rallied themselves for the final onslaught. That May, the surgeons had dismissed the patient, relished the publicity, sent off their not-inconsiderable bills, and turned their attention to fresh deeds.

Then came Kaiser P., five years late, and found himself confronted with his colleagues' calamity. He was speechless at first, then gave vent to an un-Kaiserly outburst and tried to make amends. It was nearly midnight when the night doctor summoned him from the warmth of his double bed. He hurried to the half- or three-quarters-dead patient and decided right away on what is profanely called a second-look operation. He made the decision with grave misgivings; the risk was great, the degree of temperature extremely dangerous, but he had no choice. He cut into the discolored swollen belly and found fresh abscesses, necrosis, ileus or obstructed intestine, decomposition of the bowel lining, and acute peritonitis.

He completes the operation and orders peritoneal drainage: antibiotics in liquid form are infused by means of a tube into one side of the peritoneum and drained off by another on the other side. He also orders a vena-cava catheter, a tube inserted into the heart which ensures direct control of the blood and the level of artificial nourishment. The slim tube is inserted at the wrist and carefully pushed along the vein to the heart. Kaiser P. checks the placing of the tube by X-ray and now leaves the theater, exhausted and with little hope; he goes slowly, creeps almost, to his consulting room and lies down on the narrow sofa, listens to the sounds of the awakening hospital, asks himself how much longer he will be able to bear his profession, asks himself whether his allegiance hasn't committed him to a situation that becomes more and more a vendetta, considers his bank balance, weighs the possibility of retiring and enjoying life at the side of his wife of many years, who has the positive sunny disposition common to many gynecologists' partners. He doesn't smoke a cigarette, nor does he drink a cup of coffee; he tosses and turns, gets up, sits down at his desk, looks at the green leather surface, allows himself one small sigh, and, understandably in his exhausted state, comes to no decision.

•

The patient on the other hand wakes in the certain knowledge of having experienced something awful. For the moment she doesn't realize exactly what: she had come out of the curare narcotic for a short period of time during the operation. Her subconscious had registered the gruesome fact, but now it blocks out the memory; terrified of new iniquities and torture, it recommends her maltreated and willing consciousness to give up and die, not risk any further excesses. The memory is also suppressed by a barking noise she hears on awakening which, after the few moments she needs to orient herself, proves to be a voice saying, "What are we supposed to do with her in isolation?" "Is she still alive?" follows. Although she's hardly conscious, she quickly gathers that, wherever it is that she is, she's not welcome. Through one eyeslit she can just make out a large number of tubes hanging around her like jungle undergrowth. To the right there's a hazed oblong of blank pink which she takes to be morning sky framed by a window, above it a strip of ultramarine-blue venetian blind, and below the pert white of many chestnut blossoms. Pain and weakness force the slit shut again; before it closes she sees several white-covered hips.

"Who can we call now?" a soprano voice squeaks desperately; then an alto: "Who do you think? The doctor on duty of course, who else?" There's an uneasy pause, then, "Don't you think the professor should . . ." Yet another, furiously: "Why on earth did they bring her here?" The alto: "Because the intensive's closed, stupid. They've got to disinfect it because of her, that's why." Determined footsteps come nearer, then a cocky Hamburg accent: "What are you all standing around for? And what's that?" "That" seems to refer to me. A pitiful groan from the patient puts an end to the discussion.

The wide-open door admits the familiar hospital cacophony. First the dull thud of the wax polisher hitting the wainscot, then the furious grim screams of many vacuum cleaners, the piercing babble of women's voices, the clatter of plates and cups and glasses, which reminds her of a film-studio canteen, in between bleepers and the rattle of clogs, free-and-easy slamming of doors. She has traded the still inferno of the green room in hell called "intensive" for a fury-infested white one know as "isolation."

"Would you recognize her? I mean, the way you know her from TV?" says a seriously disappointed voice. The soprano answers, "I certainly wouldn't." The uninhibited exchange of

impressions continues and indicates that the patient is still showing little sign of life, if any at all; even so, the next casual remark
still jolts her: "Well, even if she doesn't pull through, we've
still got to change the sheets." And up she's heaved. She feels a
tearing in her body and a tube ripping from her side. She
screams and her bearers drop her instantly, as though the corpse
they'd been carrying had suddenly sat up and talked. The pain
opens her sweat-caked eyes. She sees that her inconsiderate outburst has brought a look of speechless panic to the row of faces
peering down at her. A stocky nurse gasps for breath. "Your
bed was soaked with sweat," she says indignantly in a high
soprano voice. "The tube," I rattle, and feel the liquid spurting
out of the wound like a park fountain. "Now, now," the stocky
one says in Happy Olive fashion and whips off the blanket
together with a lot of bandages and tape and tubes. They exchange looks at my admittedly self-pitying whimpering and the
exchange expresses the thought: Typical. "Can't go on like this,"
an emaciated nurse with a rough alto voice says and marches
out. "I'll get the professor," says another and follows her.

Judging from the pulsing piercing pain in my hand, the
transfusion needle has slipped. Calling their attention to it, I
hear a snarled "There you are, she should be in the intensive."
A small oval face with a red nose bends over me and whispers,
"Help's on its way." The eyes behind the horn-rimmed glasses
are anxious and the incongruous mascara is smudged. "Right
away," she whispers again, just as the stocky one bawls, "Get
out of the way!" She thrusts a towel under my back and bares
her teeth as I scream again. The sight of the bared teeth summons up a great rush of fury in me; grappling with the gall-
bladder tube in my mouth, I hiss at her, "My helplessness
doesn't make me into a vegetable!" This is followed by a tropical
burst of sweat and ice-cold waves of fever. Her chin drops like a
bull readying for the attack and her eyes signal punch in the jaw
at the very least, just as the sound of male footsteps commands
her attention and miraculously transforms her into a humble
angel. Olive comes in smiling benignly. "What do I hear?" he
begins, cribbing Cottbus's text, and bends forward with a syringe

in his hand. "No, please don't, your drugs don't agree with me,"
I say. "Well, well," Olive grates, "it's an excellent drug, pain-
killing, the professor administers morphine but I don't, mo
makes you addicted and we don't want that now, do we?" He
repeats his speech like a sanctimonious country priest conducting early-morning Mass to empty pews.

"Does my husband know I've been operated on again?" I
mumble. The sweat is still dripping into my eyes. He raises his
hand as though he's about to bless something. "Of course, of
course, we talked on the telephone, everything's fine." He plants
his legs apart firmly and twiddles the empty syringe between his
fore- and middle fingers like a cigarette holder as he says, "How
do you like the heart catheter, hm? My latest invention. Good,
what?" I don't answer, first because the catheter is an old hat
I've already had in another clinic, and second because the allergy
is on its way back, tearing at my throat and bursting my head.
"The allergy," I croak, and hear him mutter, "Imagination,"
before I pass out.

•

Once more the patient drifts through a ghostly timelessness;
on several occasions she thinks she can make out Kaiser P.'s
lined and withered face, but before she can reach out to him
she crashes back like a clipped fowl into the crackling, sloshy
undergrowth where Olive's loathsome split visage glowers at
her. Once she sees a light and a white apron and a white cap
over a wide, plump face. "I'm dying," the patient says. The
realization surprises her. She feels herself begin to cry, to sob,
feels the sobs grow into a pain that concentrates itself on her
more and more intensely. "My husband . . . he's in Austria; I've
forgotten the number," she says, "and Bertrand B. in London,
friend of mine." A telephone receiver appears through the jungle
of tubes, someone presses it to her ear. "What's up?" the distant,
sleepy voice asks. "I'm dying," she says. "I've been operated on
again." The voice and the receiver recede.

•

Outside the window blue-black and orange mingle and inter-change like pictures superimposing themselves on each other. At the bottom right-hand corner in front of the flapping vene-tian blind she recognizes the Giraffe. He's sitting hunched forward and his chin is covered with straw-colored stubble. "Hello, Captain," she whispers. His head snaps back and bangs against the window. "What?" he says confusedly, "who?" jumps up, and gropes through the tubes for the bell hanging over her head. The bell must have been a prearranged signal, rows of doctors and nurses now tramp through the room. They gather around the bed muttering, surrender their places to the next batch. A pitifully ugly, stringy woman addresses the patient. "I'm Erna, the day nurse. Professor S. is on his way."

The gold-rimmed spectacles I had seen in the operating theater bob through the crowd. "You've given us a few sleepless nights," he says in a disquietingly hoarse voice. His smile is self-ironical, the way he holds himself emphatic and vigorous, only his hands betray insecurity; they wander from his pockets to his hair, link behind his back, steal back to the pockets, and jiggle things there. His eyes are deep-set and gray-green, his nose is straight and a little sharp, the soft mouth doesn't match the rocky chin. He looks like my father, the father I never saw, who died when he was twenty-eight and I six months. He resembles the only photo I still possess. "Do you remember me?" he asks, coming closer. I try to nod but it doesn't work. "I assisted at the second operation." The Giraffe is absently stirring something in a paper cup. Gold Glasses says, "I'll take over now, you go off and get some sleep." The Giraffe looks at him as though he can't remember ever having seen him before. "Yes," he says finally, "yes, that's right," and clomps out, pulling the bleeper from his pocket as he goes. Gold Glasses picks up a chair by its back, maneuvers it nimbly past the infusion stand, and sits down, crosses his left leg over his right, then his right over his left, doesn't seem able to find the desired comfort, and says, "I've changed several of the nurses you had, I hope that's all right with you." "Thanks," I answer, desperate that I can't formulate my gratitude more explicitly. At this point Olive slides in.

"How's the pain?" he grates, brandishing a syringe. "No," I hear myself screech. Gold Glasses looks up quickly, the orange sky slashes across his spectacles. "She's to have morphine," he says, his hoarse voice sharp and impatient. It's clear to see: Gold Glasses doesn't like Olive. Struck by a thunderbolt, Olive flaps his arms. "Yes, yes, as you wish, but I feel bound to warn you . . ." he begins animatedly. "For God's sake, spare us your non-sense about addiction, that's the least of our problems at the moment." Olive slinks off reluctantly. "He scares me," I say. He shrugs his shoulders in embarrassment. "I'll be representing the chief from tomorrow on. He's earned a little rest," he says, dodging the issue, buttoning and unbuttoning his smock. "Who was it who said, 'The secret of evil is the secret of restricted good'?" I ask, proud that my memory seems to be rising from the dead, and am overcome by raging thirst and shabby exhaustion.

Dr. W., the X-ray specialist, trots in with fresh-scrubbed red cheeks and lungs full of early-morning air and thunders, "Oh, maiden, my maiden, nobody thought you'd pull through. Four days and four nights, a madhouse." He looks across at Gold Glasses for confirmation but there's none forthcoming: Gold Glasses ignores him haughtily and most uncolleague-like, crosses his legs again. Dr. W. looks disappointed. Thrown out of his conversational step, he says, "What'll you be up to next?" moves heavily to the door, and adds, "Keep it up," rather limply as he goes out.

A laboratory assistant enters in a tiny skirt and a tight sweater; she looks as though she's on her way to the ice rink. Balancing her tray like a butler, she squeaks, "I must make little blood test from finger, excuse not speaking good the language, me from Teheran, yes?" Gold Glasses likes short skirts. He twinkles with interest, thoughts from the back of his mind leapfrog up front. The Teheran beauty appreciates a good audience. She moves in wagging her hips under his nose like a belly dancer and somehow manages to smile sweetly at me at the same time. "Bad, very bad, wonder that you live," she says, ruining her performance. Gold Glasses repels his fetishist curiosity, drops it like a hot potato, and snarls, "Are you finished?" She looks a trifle hurt and stalks without the wagging to the door, where she collides with Kaiser P., who seems to have found his old frantic pace again. He flies in and settles on the windowsill, retracts into himself, looks grimly from Gold Glasses to me and back again, and whispers, "One more anesthetic, just a short one, we have to change the tubes, we can do it here." He sags and the brush sinks down to his drawn-up knees. Gold Glasses rings the bell, three nurses spill in, stand in line, Olive follows them, beaming benevolence and light. Kaiser P. whispers his instructions. I sense a tightening in the throat which tells me I'm about to vomit. My attempts to fight it back only make things worse; I gulp and swallow and end up clucking like a hen about to lay an egg. They watch with surprised interest. The stringy nurse called Erna fidgets about close to the bed and is sent scurrying into the corridor by Gold Glasses's snarled "Get a bowl." The Giraffe comes in, clearly still climbing out of a very deep sleep. He stares about him in a daze, realizes wondrously why he's here, gallops uncoordinately to the washbasin, starts to pour antiseptic into it but forgets the stopper, and watches sadly as it all runs away again. Olive goes to work, the patient takes leave of the gathering for a short period and then wakes up, to find a new battery of tubes sticking out of her in every direction. Gold Glasses is there, and my husband. He's leaning against the window with a gray face. "I actually came to get you a psychiatrist," he murmurs, staring reproachfully at Gold Glasses, who bends forward and gives me an injection. "You should sleep now," he says and goes out.

"What do you mean, psychiatrist?" I ask my husband.

"They didn't tell me about the second operation," he says. "Bertrand called me yesterday and said you'd called him in the middle of the night and told him you'd been operated on again, you'd said you were dying. I've been calling here twice a day since I left and each time the anesthetist said you were doing fine but you needed rest and shouldn't be on the phone. Last Friday, which was the morning after the operation as it turns out, he told me you'd asked for your make-up and were doing your lashes again. Not a word about your fever, the abscesses, or anything. Bertrand and I concluded that your nerves had packed up and I came right away. I've confronted the anesthetist and he says you expressly forbade anyone to inform me, you didn't want Christina and me to worry."

"It's not true." I feel weak, beaten, and doze off.

•

I awaken with a start and the feeling that I'm being watched. Yellow mastiff eyes are staring at me. "I have bad news, I'm afraid," Olive says; my heart does two somersaults. "My daughter, my husband? What's happened?" I gurgle, with visions of a car wreck, twisted metal, splintered glass. Olive grins, waits with his answer. "No," he says weightily, "I mean, we'll have to operate again." "Why?" I blubber. He inclines his head from side to side as though something's gone wrong with his neck. "The intestine is in bad condition. Only surgery can help." Erna comes in wagging a syringe and cooing, "Eight parts mo, Professor S.'s orders." Olive screws up his mouth as though he'd swallowed cod-liver oil and bolts for the door, clearing his throat noisily. "It's nothing to do with him," Erna babbles, "he's only an anesthetist. You'd think he was the professor to hear him giving orders. I'll set S. on his tail." She adjusts her cap and snaps it to her hair with the aid of a clip, then stands irresolutely at the washbasin. Her ugliness remains distressing, even though she's standing in the flattering morning sunlight; her face is apparently devoid of all bone structure and has the color of wintry lemons, the red-rimmed eyes and the pugilist's nose add to the impression of a George Grosz caricature. She suddenly casts off her lethargy, hops over to my bed, and asks, "May I smoke?" Erna's question is to prove the first of a long line of similar requests put to the patient in the course of her stay. Swarms of nicotine-addicted nurses will drop by and state their case either directly by asking or indirectly by hesitantly pulling out a pack of cigarettes (always a soft one —no telltale outlines in the pockets of their aprons) or by discreetly rattling a box of matches. Erna asks directly, albeit quietly and shivering slightly, but still directly. She lights up behind her cupped hands and hurries into the bathroom, leaves the door ajar, and sits on the toilet seat, cramped and getting more and more nervous by the puff, the cigarette in one hand and a peppermint lozenge in the other. I'm not too comfortable either; the thought of a professor blustering in and flaying us makes Erna's cigarette pauses more and more enervating. Erna is the timidest smoker in my group. Others lean nonchalantly against the wall in the small hallway, still others stand in front of the open window and puff away at the chestnut tree's proud blossoms, a third minority section stand in the middle of the room holding the lid of a jar of Nivea cream filled with water in one hand and drop the cigarette, regardless of how much there is left of it, into the water the moment the door opens; the dejection is heartbreaking when the intruder turns out to be a fellow member coming in for a drag.

Erna sits glued to the toilet seat and relates through the half-open door that the head nurse will be the end of her one day. She warms to her subject, burns her bridges, and comes into the room still holding the cigarette and the lozenge. Her hands begin to shake violently, and in a desperate shrill voice she tells me that she doesn't know how she's going to cope with every-thing, especially since her husband insists on a rigid diet and she has to bake cakes and biscuits at night and prepare his very complicated meals on a two-ringed stove in her tiny nurses'-home room and all because the man she married five years ago and loves very dearly even though he's thirty years older than she still hasn't got them an apartment. He always sleeps in his bohemian bachelor's studio (Erna's expression) and doesn't dream of moving with her into a larger flat like a normal hus-band. On top of everything, Erna is a light sleeper and seldom closes her eyes, which is partly due to the location of the nurses' home, right bang on the busy main road, and partly because they'd had to put the kitchenette he'd insisted on in her bedroom, leaving her very little space to lay her bones down in, not to mention the smell of cooking. The story unfolds and I learn that her husband is a sworn outsider by choice, which is only understandable after all, seeing as how he'd been confined (Erna's expression again), through no fault of his own, no, he'd been the victim of a mean and downright cunning plot, and of course of his own good nature in taking the blame for others who didn't deserve it, and so he'd been confined for the best years of his life, convicted of (here Erna started to stutter and became very indistinct) embezzlement—and—living on the—immoral earnings—of—prostitutes . . . Erna pulled herself together and assured me that she wished for nothing more than to be able to help him out of the dreary, resigned rut of the life he led and just once be allowed to introduce him to the many relatives so dear to her. Tears now poured from her red-rimmed eyes and rolled over downtrodden paths in her prematurely lined, wintry-yellow cheeks. She pulled out a bottle of Valium pills, swallowed three, cupped her hand under the tap, drank noisily from it, and resumed her narrative: Her family had been refugees from the Sudetenland, and even though Erna couldn't remember too much about it, as she'd still been a child when they left, her family cherished memories of their homeland. Her husband didn't understand this bond at all, of course, being Swiss and you know how haughty the Swiss are with foreigners. So Erna went on cooking religiously and undertaking time-consuming journeys by bus, train, and bicycle to far-flung markets and health-food stores, felt bound to do her bit toward preserving his fine masculine good looks, which fooled everybody about his age, sixty-five he'd be next birthday, and she always felt proud and just a little bit jealous when they went for one of their rare strolls and the other women fairly craned their necks to get a look at him. She hadn't had to think twice that day when he came to her and asked her to lend him the money for a tiny operation which would get rid of the little lines under his eyes and the teeny-weeny pouch under his chin, he only wanted it done for her sake after all, so that people wouldn't talk about the difference in their ages.

Erna now pulls out a photo from their wedding day on which very little can be seen of her husband, as he's looking away from the camera. "He doesn't like to be photographed," says

Erna. Since the operation he looks as good as new again on the outside, but on the inside nothing has changed; he still lives for nothing but his looks, his drums, the two mice he keeps in a bird cage, his transistor radio and color TV set. Depressing too is the way he insists on her calling him up and telling him exactly when she would like to visit him in his bohemian studio, she daren't just drop in, and then his morbid dread of bugs and bacteria, to say nothing of the two long trips to Paris he makes every year and won't even let her see him off at the station, saying, "A man needs his freedom and his little secrets," every time she suggests it. She has to go over straightaway when he gets back though, because he never comes home without a cold and stays in bed wrapped up in woolies and scarves, sipping the tea she makes him and taking his temperature by the hour; he won't let anyone near him but her, not a doctor, not ever. She feels nearest to him at these times, although, as she said, she sometimes doesn't know how she'll cope. She shakily lights a second cigarette and hurries back to her toilet seat.

Parts of Erna's narrative reach me as though she's talking through a filter, or wads of cotton wool; other parts are amplified and reverberate, as through an echo chamber. My apathetic, bedridden presence would appear to offer an ideal form of confessional, the drugs can be relied on to haze the outlines of memory.

Erna changes the subject and calls through the half-open door: "You haven't had the pleasure of meeting our head nurse yet. She was on vacation. I had to go to a psychiatrist on her account, she bullied me to a pulp, she did, really finished me. During the day she spreads her poison, and at night she goes to the Salvation Army. It's a fact, she's a member. Her fiancé killed himself, put a bullet in his head. I'm not surprised. What we're all wondering is, Why on earth did you come here? The doctors are all right but everything else . . ." Erna leaves a pregnant pause and I hear her turning on the tap. Over the sound of running water, she asks, "What do you think of our Turkish delight?" Only as she goes on to mention short skirts and tight sweaters do I realize that she means the Persian assistant. "Have you dug the way she walks?" Erna comes in, undulating her skinny hips in a grotesque parody. A noise from the corridor causes her to jump like a startled cat and listen intently. False alarm. After a few seconds she continues like an old turtle: "She's after a man, got a bee in her bonnet, she has, wants to be a professor's wife . . ." She snorts in disgust, then continues sunnily: "We had a nurse here once, she drank like a fish, she even drank the alcohol out of the thermometer glasses, I used to wonder why they were always empty in the morning, and our head nanny goat blamed me for it. Then the one who's on duty at midday, she's got a screw loose, she has; she pours the bedpans into the bed and we have to clean it up. Another one, she's gone now, used to take money from the patients for every shot she gave them that wasn't ordered by one of the doctors. And the rhinoceros from Cottbus—you must have seen her—she was in the cancer ward, she led the patients a merry dance, I can tell you, she never gave them anything but a bit of Librium and a bit of Valium to quiet them down, nothing for the pain they were in—that's the way things are here. Whenever a patient's in real pain, like after a big operation, the anesthetist comes along and says, 'It's all imagination, it can't possibly hurt that much.' Even when they are dying, when you put a dog out of its misery, he still goes on complaining. He should lay himself on the table and see what it's like. He gives himself airs, just because we haven't got an internal specialist, plays God the Father. Don't tell anybody I told you, but I've got another theory: Morphine's so cheap they don't even bother to put it on the bill, but the other synthetic stuff costs a fortune, enough to make the patients' eyes water. And he goes on about addiction, he's got a real thing about it, doesn't drink and doesn't smoke, all he does is complain and get het up when the patients say they're in pain."

Erna goes exhaustedly to the washbasin, looks mournfully into the mirror, squeezes her lumpy nose, and says, "We'll have to change the dressing in a minute. I'll hold your hand."

But she doesn't. She's called away and Barbara takes her place. Barbara is the one with the oval face and the red nose and smudged mascara behind the horn-rimmed glasses. Barbara holds my hand tenderly, but not for very long, because her hands are like blocks of ice; rubbing and blowing on them doesn't help, nor does warm water or a spell of hot weather. They remain like the snowballs mischievous children thrust up the sleeves of unwitting victims. I ask for a rubber glove and attempt to help in the hope of distracting myself from the discomfort but only succeed in making things worse; Gold Glasses's precise and careful manipulations are nevertheless so painful that after a short time I'm covered with sweat and gnawing on my thumb and lower lip, trying to count the number of blossoms on the chestnut tree. At last he applies the fresh dressing and I ask him, "When are you going to operate on me again?"

"Who said anything about operating again?"

"The anesthetist."

"We have no intention of doing so," he mutters and boils with considerable fury.

A fresh bottle of antibiotic fluid is attached to my tubes and it courses through my belly like a glacier stream. I gasp and Gold Glasses explodes, "Why wasn't it warmed?" His outburst knocks the swarm of nurses down like ninepins. Only Barbara remains cool and unperturbed; she smiles at me encouragingly. As soon as the instrument trolley is wheeled out and Gold Glasses has taken his leave with a "That's enough for today," Barbara pulls out her soft pack, murmurs, "*Permettez?*" and lights her cigarette with a gold Dupont lighter. Her accessories are altogether incongruent with the normal concept of an underpaid nurse. Her shoes could be from a leading Paris shop, her bracelet from Hermès, her leather bag, from which a batiste handkerchief is peeping, from Gucci; she could be the daughter of rich parents who has donned the nurse's uniform as a joke and is helping Mummy at the charity bazaar. Barbara stands absolutely straight, the perfect curve of her back indicates firm upbringing, horses, and ballet training, and her profile is of a simple beauty surrounded by thick black hair gathered loosely at the neck; one might be tempted to apply the word "madonna-like" to her. Smoking contentedly, she gazes down into the courtyard and says, "I'm a failure." She says it rhetorically, with a tinge of singsong Schweizerdeutsch coloring her slow, high-German diction. Throwing the half-smoked cigarette through the window, she turns around and chuckles, as though to relieve the gravity of her statement. She sits down, arranges the folds of her smock, places the tips of her blue fingers together. "I flipped out, you know," she says with great pleasure. "My father's a banker, I had no point of communication with him, not with my mother either. I needed a task." She sighs and lowers her hands with the palms uppermost. "I sleepwalked through the first terms of training, they'd only take me in the psychiatric clinic to begin with." She laughs dryly and a trifle theatrically, leans forward, and cries out nervously, contemptuously, "You think they help? They pump them full of sedatives till they're zombies. Their help is unfeeling, insensitive, like robots. After two years I was ripe for them myself." She raises her fingers again and positions her chin on them, looks at me thoughtfully. "You're in pain," she says suddenly, as though telepathy were a routine form of intercourse, and goes out without waiting for an answer. She comes back within seconds, feels my hip, gives the injection without my noticing it, accepts my "Bravo" with naïve delight, and says self-deprecatingly, "If you don't learn it in the psychiatric, you never will." She screws up her face to convey bitterness, pulls her chair close to the bed, and continues, "Right afterward I started taking acid." She repeats the word "acid" as though I mightn't understand or take her seriously. "I went to Madras with a friend, then on to Calcutta. At first we lived on a peninsula in a hippie commune, went on trips, expanded our consciousness." She throws her head back proudly. "It was the happiest time of my life," she says defensively. She clicks her lighter. "Then everything fell apart, they all went their separate ways. We got sick, lay in a hotel for weeks on end, nobody bothered about us, somehow we got to Calcutta. My friend died." Holding her face in both hands, she begins to laugh, not at all hysterically or uncontrolled, more the laugh of someone who has heard a good joke and finds it funnier and funnier the more she thinks about it.

A fieldmouse-gray woman sidles through the door. Even though she's wearing a crackling white uniform, she's still fieldmouse gray. She tiptoes up to the bed, gazes aghast at Barbara's shaking head, and stops. Barbara's mirth gradually subsides; she murmurs, "Crazy, crazy," reaches for her batiste handkerchief, and, in raising it, looks straight into the fieldmouse gray. "Well," the Mouse pipes, "we're very gay, I must say." No doubt about it, the Mouse doesn't hold with gaiety, no doubt she's Erna's nemesis, the restored head nurse. She turns to me and addresses a point on the pillow some six inches away from my head. "And how is our patient today?" The patient answers, "You're the head nurse, I take it." "Yes, indeed," the Mouse says and puckers her mousy mouth as though about to whistle. She stands there for the moment a little at a loss and not sure what she should do, decides to inspect the row of infusion bottles and the patient's chart, then strides to the door saying, "To tell you what's for dinner won't be necessary, as I see you'll be getting yours from the bottle." She turns to go with the Swiss farewell, "*Auf Wiederluaga,*" on her lips, and I stop her dead with a sweet "Aren't you German?" She remains absolutely still for a moment, one foot forward, and then says to the door, "Well, yes," and, a little higher-pitched, "but I've been here for some considerable time." She turns and looks about two feet away from Barbara, adds, "You should go and report to Sister Sophie," and disappears, closing the door without a sound.

"Grand Guignol," Barbara chortles, "Sophie, the sister of Dracula." She shudders, demonstrates her revulsion. "Sophie is in charge of personnel; as soon as a patient and a nurse become friendly, the nurse is moved to another department." She jumps up, flapping and fidgeting. "I can't stand it much longer. I'll work until I've got enough money, then I'll fly to Calcutta, my friend's dog's still there, I couldn't bring it with me because of quarantine laws. Then perhaps I'll go to Israel, kibbutz, the last hope for human community." She begins a pirouette, spins and grabs at the chair back for support. "Played about with drugs too long," she says. "I kicked it not long ago, I'm O.K. now, but sometimes I get . . ." She runs back and forth, lays an icy hand on my forehead, and says intensely, "People have to find a way to each other, they must," and runs out.

Gold Glasses finds the patient in a desolate state a few hours later; she's whimpering, sobbing, crying. She laments abysmally, howls like a jackal, swims in tears, would be dried out but for the replenishing tubes. "What has happened?" Gold Glasses asks, without the jovial patronizing tone doctors seem to think indispensable to their bag of tricks. He takes off his glasses and looks plucked and helpless without them. "I want to see my daughter," the patient manages.

"In a couple of days," he says and clips his glasses awkwardly back behind his ears.

The patient sniffs, tries to control herself, makes use of a strictly masculine prerogative, and asks stupidly, "What do you do with yourself in the evenings?"

From his perplexed reaction it's clear that he's well acquainted with this form of inquiry, has probably used it himself a time or two; he sniggers embarrassedly, clears his throat, and says, "When I'm not on night-duty I go home and read, or sleep; sometimes I go ice skating or swimming, skiing on weekends. I attend quite a few congresses too."

"Do you have any children?" the patient asks, knowing full well that she's knocking down keep-out signs left and right.

"Two," he says and fingers his bleeper as though hoping it might put an end to this highly irregular conversation. "One's about the same age as your daughter." He's sitting on the windowsill like Kaiser P., feeling his neck and chin thoughtfully. The patient, meanwhile, is trying to imagine him in an anorak and ski pants instead of the green smock, tries to see him in a knitted cap instead of a surgeon's, gives up, he'll always be green for her. "My little girl's been in the children's clinic for four weeks now," he continues, crossing the border between patient and doctor, dependent and independent. "She has a constant temperature, blood test's miserable, twelve thousand leukocytes, nobody can find out why." He slides down from the sill, stretches himself in an ungainly fashion, says, "You'll be getting an injection" and "See you tomorrow."

The patient calls out, "I hope your daughter will soon be well." She says it partly because it really is her wish, and partly to help him not regret the excursion into no-man's-land. She wishes to gain his favor; parallel to the confused vision of the feverish child, her own fainthearted ego, trained by brute self-preservation's merciless hands, is vying shamefully for pity.

•

The eyes grow used to the emergency-light blue, the noises deplete and diminish, the darkness swallows exaction and disquietude, suspends all temporal divisions, allows a selfless, sleepless twilight. At first light, which tinges the sky a cheesy white, the chestnut blossoms a gruel gray, the spell of stagnant rocking-chair repose is broken; it succumbs to the heave-ho of the clinic's early day, the bugle's urgent summons. The advance guard breaks in, works up a lather, rinses down, scrubs hair and hide, sees that the mouth's washed, takes the temperature, spits and polishes, changes linen, charges from task to task. Order rotates through the morning mill, beats a solid tattoo on the stupored heads, barks commands, signals the regiment, regales Kaiser P. with his crown and scepter, invites him to inspect the bedraggled captives. Pressed by the morning's plan of operations and inhibited by his matinal shyness, he swoops through the realm surrounded by his veteran lieutenants, at the fore Olive, with arched brows and a baleful eye, looking like a summerstock Iago. Regent and retinue have hardly quit the scene when the main body of troops moves in led by the X-ray drum major; bright and boisterous, early riser through and through, he posts his unit about the disabled's camp bed, scrutinizes her innards elatedly through his screen, beats a retreat, leaving the mopping up to the rearguard action headed by the Persian Mother Courrèges. Now a field priest, female; she takes her place during a lull, improvises a prayer to suit the stage of the battle, is succeeded by the Mouse, who plays Gunga Din and sounds the arrival of a delayed divisional commander whose duty it is to tend the dressings. He too is sorely tried by the Kaiser's sweeping operations and the bleeping of his bleeper; he carries out his duties dauntlessly and relies on a lone patrol to search the ground and dispose of enemy dust. After them it's quiet. Cease-fire. No, there's a reconnaissance scout called Erna. She throws herself at the bed sobbing, "That beast, that ogre." Tears streaming, she gropes for a cigarette, but is shaking too much to be able to light it, a severe case of shell shock. The patient learns that the Mouse has halted the column right in front of Erna and given her a severe and unwarranted dressing down for not having number three ready for the theater. Erna blubbers and slobbers, for not only the Mouse has done her an injustice: her husband is incensed because he's lost two pounds in weight. The cigarette, now crumpled and limp in her fingers, finally shows signs of igniting. The smoke curls to the patient and makes her retch, but she doesn't dare to mention it for fear that Erna will misunderstand and do something rash. She endures nausea together with the fact that the fluid flowing through her belly is again ice-cold and the transfusion vein in her right arm seized with cramp, and resigns herself to the inclemencies of the early-morning siege.

The muffled explosion of a mop thwacking against the door causes Erna to jump and stick the burning cigarette in her pocket. More woebegone than ever, she races to the bathroom, comes back with ugly blisters on her hand, and swallows the daily ration of sedatives. Shaken now by hiccups, she gasps, "He wants a divorce, he says I'm trying to murder him, he's leaving for Paris in the morning and won't allow me to see him off . . ."

Trude enters. Trude is pink and chubby like a baby, has grand pillars of legs and no waist, wears a petite watch on her massive wrist and back-combs her hair into a beehive that's probably too high for her to be able to affix the regulation cap to, for she never wears one. Trude stands in the doorway and pretends astonishment. She looks over to the patient's corner, widens her pale-blue eyes, rounds her ruby mouth to an O, stretches it to an Ah, and plays out a pantomime indicating that she'd reckoned with a whole lot of things but not with the likelihood of finding the same patient in the same bed for the third week running. She knows only too well that I'm not capable of taking one step alone, but it's her daily opening gambit and she never tires of playing it. Her spiel over, she says, "Well then, anything new?" in her awful accent, a mixture of Baden and Saxon. Looking across at Erna, who is jackknifed over the back of a chair sobbing her last, she says, "Your hubby been naughty again?" Soothingly she pats Erna's jerking back, catches sight of the patient's pain-contorted face, feels the tubes and the bottles, and cries out, "The ninnies took the bottles straight out of the fridge again, her bowel must be like a block of ice." She stamps out and returns a few minutes later with her beehive trembling indignantly and the Mouse in tow. "Just you take a feel," she says aggressively, ignoring the Mouse's lofty station. The Mouse's mouth disappears almost completely; silently she binds a thick towel around the bottle and retires with a don't-push-your-luck glance at Trude. The towel slips and dislodges clips, disconnects the tube, and the patient finds herself taking an antibiotic shower. Trude rings the bell, Erna sits suffering from her generation's lack of women's lib and the effects of the sedatives, the Giraffe bowls in and stops the flood; he announces apologetically that the skin and tissue where the tube enters the peritoneum have been torn and that running repairs with needle and thread are necessary. I hear Gold Glasses's crisp footsteps, he stands in the doorway with his surgery mask pushed down over his mouth, looking like John Wayne tackling a stampede. Erna gets up and knocks over the instrument trolley; she's having a bad morning all around.

Gold Glasses orders five parts mo and starts plucking and threading. Again I count the chestnut blossoms, growing more ostentatious by the day, rattle off a nursery rhyme, try to find some truth in the theory that deep breathing helps relax, and hear Gold Glasses say, "You can get up this afternoon for fifteen minutes." "And what about the bottles?" I ask incredulously. "We'll take 'em with us," he answers. He turns away abruptly and goes out, slamming the door behind him for the first time, creating a misogynous impression. Trude feels her left forearm, trying to locate her watch, and says, "I'll have to be off, time to collect my little one from the kindergarten. He does nothing but cry. And my old man does nothing but shout, you know, that comes of working on the bulldozers, they have to shout or nobody'd ever hear them, and at home he always forgets." She turns to Erna and says, "Let's take off, dearie." Erna murmurs incoherently and follows her out like a newborn calf.

Noises are the patient's most reliable chronometer. Judging by the present noises, it's lunchtime. My door is half open and suddenly Olive glides in, hovers around the bed, sniffs and clears his throat, then comes to the point: "It's time we made a little test to see whether you're addicted or not. We've got a new drug."

The patient loses her cool and hollers, "If you come near me with one of your new drugs, I'll scream the place down—" and chokes to a halt.

Olive looks surprised. "Now, now, now, our nerves are in a bad state, all the more reason to do a test."

The patient plays for time. "Even if I were addicted, which I'm not, this is hardly the time to try and break the habit."

Arguments are not up Olive's street. "All the more reason," he repeats, and his distant eye glitters.

I try to draw his fire. "Why did you lie to my husband?"

"You wanted me to," he answers, not at all put out.

"What did I want?"

"As I gave you the anesthetic, you asked me not to inform him; it would only upset him and the child, you said."

"Since when do doctors take any notice of what patients say under narcosis?"

He doesn't answer, doesn't need to, he has a better method of attack. He moves toward my arm with the syringe in his hand; as if in answer to my prayer, Kaiser P. comes in before Olive can reach me. I bubble my thanks and Kaiser P. reacts in a strangely ponderous manner; only as he sees the syringe does he regain his customary alertness. He lowers his brush and orders Olive to go down to his consulting room and wait for him there. Climbing up onto his sill, he begins to tell me an astonishingly obscene gynecologists' joke; he tells it fluently, it's as though a tape recorder were playing. I laugh dutifully, Kaiser P. whinnies rather dejectedly, then we relapse into silence. At last he whispers, "I'm flying to Moscow tomorrow, a sure sign that you're on the mend." He puts a light hand on my arm and continues, "It could have gone wrong. From a medical standpoint you hardly had a chance, the only hope was the patient's willpower." His smile is warm, open, appreciative. I lie there speechless under the spell of a smile he'd kept secret till now.

Erna, Trude, and the Giraffe stand me up. The perspective of a six-year-old I've been looking from for the past weeks alters: noses get longer, foreheads higher, eyes more open. Even the tone I'm addressed in changes from patronizing condescension to one of respect and equality. We muster each other on the new level, arrange ourselves between the stands with the bottles and tubes, carefully push them along with us, and move off across the corridor, stopping in front of a window. I look down at the street below. The activity I see seems incomprehensible, the orderly flow of traffic incredibly reckless, the carefree parade engenders envy in me, is desirable and frightening at the same time. A girl on a bicycle misses a truck by a hair's breadth, a child holding a woman's hand is hopping along the curbstone, two pipe smokers are trotting across the intersection, they've all come together to dance a somnambulant pas de deux with catastrophe, appear neither to see nor to hear nor to suspect the presence of death, are immune to his tricks and foibles.

"I'm scared," I say.

"Everyone's like that when they come out the first time," says Trude.

"No, I mean something else," I answer and feel that I'm back in Dr. Albertini's elegant office. "We haven't seen the end yet," I say, certain of it, ignoring their astonished reaction.

Gold Glasses comes by to tell me that he'll be taking Kaiser P.'s place until he gets back from Moscow, then asks casually, "Do you remember anything about the second operation?"

"Should I?" I answer in the irritating knowledge that I won't unless he helps me; "I always thought the memory fails to function under narcosis."

"Of course, of course," he says uncomfortably, in the manner he probably uses with his students, and vaguely mumbles, "It was just a thought . . ." He has stirred the embers of an inferno that has been glowing in the refractory dungeons of the subconscious; my consciousness battles with the flames, my attempts to reconstruct produce a series of black-and-white photos: In one, Gold Glasses's fierce eyes, in another, ropes of bright light pointing at my stomach; the flames rear up in revolt, the fire fighters put them down, cow them into unconcentrated flickering. Our eyes meet and lock, grapple for a second, then break apprehensively. He tries to clear the air. "How was your walk?" I follow suit. "Not so good, after fifteen minutes I was only too glad to crawl back to bed, I was almost homesick for my tubes and bottles and sore backside; I'll never wish to turn on my side or drink a pint of delicious fruit juice again, just as long as I can lie quietly." He riffles the pages of my chart concernedly and doesn't seem to like my subservience. He says, "You'll be getting a new night nurse tomorrow," and exits.

The day shift comes to an end; cheerful "so longs," slamming doors, and jolly giggles mark the absconders' exodus. The hospital takes a moment's rest, puts its feet up, listens as the last footfalls echo through the corridors like an office building settling down for the night. Night nurses grimly check the lists of what is to be given when and to whom, make coffee, read newspapers, synchronize their watches, stare at the dials on the oxygen cylinders, get up heavily when the bell rings or the red light flashes and a patient asks for water, a bedpan, a shot, or mere company.

In the isolation ward, Nana makes her rounds. Nana's from Africa. That's all one knows of her background, since Nana haughtily declines to give more, ignoring all inquiries as to which town or nation she's from. It's not clear either whether it's just the bedridden ones, or the white race in general, or human beings as a whole that she hates. She plods up to the bed with her long body and yells, "Injection!" Her German is terse and it's obvious that she's acquired it in Switzerland. I prattle away in a manner befitting a colonial overlord's descendant bent on making amends, getting meeker and meeker by the second. My reference to the sweat-soaked pillow sends her eyes to the ceiling; she appears to implore some higher being to bestow strength upon her. Two hours pass and seem like six; I press my bell hesitantly —nothing. I press it again, keep my thumb on it a little longer this time, and Nana, rudely awakened, shoots in. You've got to hand it to Nana, she's got an excellent memory. Without a second's hesitation she yanks the closet door open and rips out the reserve pillow; lots of bowls and plastic bottles come away with it and clatter to the floor. When she's changed the pillows, I'm grateful and don't like to ask her for a bedpan, I've always found this part of a nurse's job to be particularly obnoxious and with Nana I feel it would be like asking her to give me a shoeshine. Nana spares me further conjecture by glaring at me, screeching, "Will that be all?" and departing, chips of plaster dropping from the ceiling as she goes.

•

I'd made up my mind to be carefree and gay when she came, which again would have probably seemed strange to her, but when my daughter finally did enter my room for the first time, my emotions refused to obey and I broke down completely. Her defenselessness and vulnerability were my own. And my state of dependency was equal to hers. Even our level of vision had become the same. The victims of the May catastrophe looked at each other, the one at the beginning of her life, the other in the middle of what would appear to be a beleaguered one. I wanted to warn her. I wanted to say: Be on your guard against those who are bigger than you and those who are the same size; doubt everything and everybody, never allow your trust to go further than your possibilities of defending yourself, for I can no more protect you than I can myself.

Even here, in the strange surroundings, she had the natural grace which most children possess, which adults don't comprehend and try to destroy. She sat down beside me, laid her head on the back of my hand, kissed the skin between the bandages, and remained so for a long while. Then she sat up and looked at the floor, as though understanding that a direct confrontation could destroy the moment of unity, understanding intrinsically that one doesn't stare at a person who is emotionally disturbed.

The Mouse squeaked that the visiting hour was at an end, a child's green cap was left lying at the foot of the bed; it became the focal point of hope, desperation, and the will to live.

I had hardly noticed the presence of Libby and Bibba; resplendent in new hairdos and new hats, they had hovered in the background, mumbled their heartfelt sympathy, and then gleefully filled me in on every catastrophe that had happened in the world during the weeks of my confinement. Libby had pulled out her small camera saying, "So we'll be able to look back on the bad times," and made a few snapshots. After they had told in outraged tones of the infamous reporters who were waylaying doctors and nurses in the hope of getting a juicy quote, and had deplored the fact that public figures were doomed to public illnesses, they were asked to leave. Puffing and blowing, Libby popped back a short while later and hissed excitedly that she could sell the photos she'd just taken for huge sums to the newspapers, that agents had accosted her in dark passageways, and that she had to decide immediately which major power should get the material. My protests were rudely interrupted by: "You're in no condition to judge the situation. Just think, Bibba and I could buy a good-size car from the proceeds." She stamped out on her stovepipes, exhausted and heady at the same time. The first steps to interdiction, outside the clinic walls as well as inside, had been taken.

•

Nana from Africa is replaced by Leopoldine from Austria. Leopoldine resembles a great many dressers and wardrobe mistresses the patient has had the good fortune to meet during her long career in the theater and in movies. (Although she's given up acting, she sometimes sorely misses the casual community of a film unit which is formed for the months of shooting; and although she tends to make precipitate decisions in small things, it takes her ages to make up her mind about larger issues. She participated in fifty-four films before she drew the line and hung her thespian cloak on the hook. She had come to realize that the so-called film star's lot is an infantile and precarious one, since critics and public alike are apt to make him responsible for the final product; the ugly truth is that whatever a star's box-office standing and however much he may exercise his power during the making of the picture, there is a whole battalion of other participants lurking in the background just waiting to gum up the works, namely, author, producer, director, editor, and, last but by no means least, distributor. On rare occasions the finished article will turn out as good as, perhaps even better than, the star expected it to, but here again, it's through no fault of his. Whatever the outcome, the success or failure of the movie will be automatically linked with the name above the title, the star carried the day or carried the can, earned undeserved fame or deserved blame. As she says, it took her a long time to act on this realization, to decide henceforth to earn her living by singing songs and writing lyrics and books.)

But to get back to Leopoldine: like a good dresser, she is considerate, lenient, and always ready for a hearty gossip. The patient catches herself counting the hours till Leopoldine returns. In the afternoon she listens for the familiar squeak of her shoes, the rustle of her densely starched smock. Leopoldine always asks if she may sit down. The unexpected courtesy had boggled the patient's mind at their first meeting; she had said, "But of course" and "Why do you ask?" to which Leopoldine countered, "I don't like to disturb" and "Perhaps you want to sleep." Earnest entreaties were necessary to stop her beating a retreat. Leopoldine sits quite still. After a sigh, more of contentment than complaint, she places her calloused hands together and smiles with the corners of her eyes, without moving her mouth, and looks down with a friendly, conspiratorial expression. Leopoldine, born in Vöcklabruck, Upper Austria, sits and emanates warmth and grandmotherly peace and gives the impression that she's just been reading a beautiful fairy tale. Although it's no great distance and presupposes no particularly adroit wander-lust, Leopoldine's road from Vöcklabruck to the Swiss hospital had been long and arduous in that it entailed many stopovers, some of lengthy duration, before she finally arrived. Her face attains beauty at the mere mention of Vöcklabruck; it smooths her brow, flushes her cheeks, and conjures a gleam to her eyes, for to speak of Vöcklabruck is to speak of Walter; Walter, young and handsome, active and good, had been a fine carpenter, Leopoldine a seamstress. She had become pregnant, Walter had married her right away. Leopoldine's flow of narrative stumbles at this point, her brow furrows, the flush dissolves, and the gleam in her eyes is scattered as tears splash down her cheeks. Before the child was born, Walter was sent to Stalingrad and didn't return. Walter's son is the spitting image of his father. Leopoldine's face brightens a little, for a moment her brow regains composure, simultaneously her hands begin to screw up the starched white seams of her apron as she continues: "He was two years old, on his birthday he suddenly got fever, a hundred and three. Children often get high temperatures; he couldn't swallow anything; in the middle of the night I got panicky and went to the doctor. You should have heard how he shouted at me for disturbing his rest, told me he'd come in the morning. When I got home, the boy was making rattling noises and then he stopped breathing altogether." Leopoldine bows her head, her neck is slender and wrinkled. Cowering, as though expecting a blow, she says, "Everyone has his cross to bear. A child's so helpless, the poor kid suffocated. He had diphtheria, I carried him about in my arms until midday, I couldn't believe it."

The Mouse pitter-patters in, squeaks, "Is there no work to be done?" and bats her eyelids cocksuredly. "No," says Leopoldine calmly, not even turning around; "and if the bell rings I can hear it just as well from here."

"Since when are you on night duty?" I ask.

"I'm not," the Mouse answers loftily. "I forgot something, that's all." A sharp tooth glistens. She hovers capriciously, then chirrups, "By the way, you'll be getting your first meal tomorrow, a bit of porridge." "Bit of porridge" relegates me to high chair, bib and tucker, puts me under tutelage. "There's an injection due in number four, Nurse Leopoldine," the Mouse pipes fearlessly. Leopoldine's face swells, threatens to burst; raspingly she says, "In twenty minutes." The Mouse patters off. "Those bitches," Leopoldine hisses and gets a nosebleed. She dabs her nose and her brow with a wet cloth and says, "That's why I do night duty, because of them; I can't stand the bitches any longer. They squabble like a pack of hyenas." She looks up, perplexed. "Do I really have to stand for that?" she asks. "I'm nearly sixty-four."

Before number four gets her shot, I learn that Leopoldine had adopted three children, her own grandchildren, in fact. After her husband has succumbed to the Russians and her son to the doctor, Leopoldine marries a forester named Franz. He drinks heavily, beats her, and the cupboard is usually bare, but Leopoldine sticks with him, she's expecting a child. She gives birth to a daughter and, determined never to be reliant on a doctor again, studies to be a nurse. But her daughter needs neither nurse nor doctor; she never gets sick, not even a cold, but she does get pregnant, as often as nature allows, from her sixteenth birthday on, and has soon accumulated three illegitimate children. Leopoldine gets a divorce from the slugger-drunkard, is excommunicated by the Catholic Church, adopts her grandchildren, and goes west with them and their promiscuous mother. Fifteen years later, prematurely aged by work and worry, Leopoldine has her bosom operated on, has it lifted, tautened, refurbished, and enters into matrimony with a child-loving but barren Swiss widower who furnishes her and her adopted grandchildren with Swiss passports, peace, and a roomy apartment.

Leopoldine stands up at this point, takes the empty infusion bottle from the stand, warms the refill, inserts it, and is just showing me a photo of her oldest grandson standing in front of a cake in a chef's hat on the day he received his diploma when the door flies open and an agitated nurse hurries in. " 'Scuse me," she says, wiping her wet mouth with the back of her hand, "I've gotta see Leopoldine. —What shall I do?" she asks Leopoldine, "there's a girl in my ward, she's only seventeen, they took out her uterus yesterday and she's screaming with pain, but they've only got her down for Valium on the list." She has come to a halt but is still in perpetual motion. She scratches her arm, then her ankle, plucks at her cap and her crewcut hair, tugs at her belt and her collar as she babbles. "It's downright barbarous, that's what it is, no jokin'." Leopoldine rubs the girl's arm quickly, turns to me, says, "This is Marianne, she's a good girl," and, superfluously, since I know my hometown accent when I hear it, "She comes from Berlin." Marianne's motor seems to run down; chewing her thumbnail and staring absentmindedly at the tubes and bottles, she says, "They're doing it to you too." With a start she begins fidgeting again and asks, "Can I smoke here?" This excites Leopoldine. "Your nerves are bad enough already," she snaps, almost aggressively, shakes her head, and sighs, "She's got a hard life, our Marianne." Marianne leans against the washbasin and smokes, her triangular face with its short stubby nose, wide mouth, and long green-gray eyes is bright and cheeky and attractive in an amiable way. The light from the low bed lamp accentuates the lines running from the corners of her mouth to her nostrils and the deep cleft between her blond bushy eyebrows, giving her face a false harshness. "D'you know Wuhlheide?" she asks. I say that I do. "That's where I'm from," she says and, without pausing, "What am I goin' to do with the kid over there?" She asks this with the certainty that only someone who knows Wuhlheide can proffer sensible advice. As Leopoldine and I exchange helpless glances, Marianne continues, "That damned foreigner with his chatter about addiction, it's nothin' but sadism, that's what it is. Don't talk to me about doctors, they've got both my little ones on their consciences."

Leopoldine interrupts her. "Don't start talking about that, you'll only get worked up again."

"Give me one good reason why I shouldn't get worked up," Marianne cries. "Two kids I've got, one gets a fever so I take her to the hospital. 'It's a virus,' they tell me and give her the usual pills and send us home. D'you know what it was? Meningitis, and now she's stone deaf—five years old and stone deaf, you try livin' with a child that can't hear nothin'." She spits the words at us, propels them from her lips like bullets from a machine gun; her consonant-slurring Berlin accent becomes a whip, brawling, picking a fight. "And the other one—there they weren't quick enough when the time came. My doctor was playin' golf so they gave me a little injection to delay the delivery, and by the time he got around to it, the baby was suffering from oxygen deficiency. Now she can't stand and can't walk, cerebral palsy—two children and both of them wrecks, thanks to our wonderful doctors. Just you try and take them to court though, you don't stand an earthly, with a smirk and a smart lawyer they knock the legs from under you. What I wanta know is, what's a gynecologist got to do with a newborn baby? He's there for the mother. But who's there for the baby? Nobody. Talk their heads off about the abortion laws they do, but when a child's born and needs a specialist, all it gets is a gynecologist who hasn't got a clue about babies and what oxygen deficiency can do. And when it's too late, they give you the twaddle about complications during the pregnancy and the trouble started when it was still an embryo and all that. Nothing went wrong with my pregnancy, I didn't smoke and didn't drink, it happened during childbirth. Bastards."

The patient had visited a center for cerebral palsy six weeks previously, had seen the children crawl on their elbows and knees, children that had never stood or walked, children with sharp clever eyes that understood every word. They had crawled in a dark dilapidated house under the supervision of a warm-hearted woman therapist; the house and the therapist were dependent on donations; the children, delivered to the house in the mornings by their parents, had been conveniently forgotten by the gynecologists and isolated by youth-worshipping posterity. "The damage occurs almost exclusively during the childbirth phase, oxygen deficiency," the therapist had said.

Leopoldine tugs a wad of surgical gauze from her bag and wipes her face with it. It's as though the night magnifies and coarsens sorrow, presses you to the ground, and hammers the ungraspable, unbearable into your brain. One horror gives way to the next, even greater one, is overtrumped by a deeper sorrow; it seems it must be made clear that there are no limits to the depths, that they are unfathomable, and that man pushes the limits even further where he can, digs deeper, broadens the possibilities, burrows in the bowels of distress.

"One small blessing is that I don't have to work in the cancer ward any more," Marianne says. "The dear relatives all come and visit at the beginning, then they leave them alone. And we hack around with infusions and try to give them a couple of days more. In another clinic I worked in, we had a nurse who gave the dying patients distilled water and kept the morphine for herself. You can only die at home, otherwise you're up the creek." She throws her cigarette butt into the courtyard and says, "I'll come by later."

Leopoldine and I stare at the chestnut tree. The sky grows leaden-gray, the day shift becomes audible.

I begin to distinguish weekends from weekdays, register the visitors'-hour busyness in the corridor on Sundays, smell clinic-strange odors, wet raincoats, coffee.

Gold Glasses strides in to change my dressings and says, "Four weeks you've been our guest now." I don't feel in the mood for pleasantries. "Are you ambitious?" I ask. My aggressiveness seems to amuse him. He checks himself, assumes his impersonal doctor-patient expression, is clearly of two minds; a confessional yes would be equal to a breach of etiquette, like picking one's nose or putting one's feet on the table. Smiling coyly, he says, "Up to a point," presses the bell, purses his lips, and hisses, "Where's the sister?" Trude saunters in chewing, there's a line of sugar over her upper lip. Still chewing, she declares, "Almond cake." Gold Glasses measures her with an I'd-love-to-get-my-hands-around-your-neck look which makes as much impression on Trude as water on a duck's back; balancing her beehive carefully, she saunters out at the same pace as she'd entered and soon comes back with the instrument trolley, rubs her chubby infantlike hands with antiseptic, strokes on a pair of rubber gloves with great deliberation, opens a plastic bag, and extracts a second pair with the aid of tweezers, strokes them over Gold

Glasses's hands; he's at the end of his parsimonious tether and yells, "They're too big," but keeps them on anyway.

The patient says, " 'Up to a point' means you'll be head of the clinic one day."

"Ah, well now," he says and suddenly grins like a student whose treatise has earned him prophecies of a glorious career.

The patient follows through. "In your capacity as a gynecologist, would you welcome the presence of a pediatrician during childbirth?"

"It's not usual," Gold Glasses answers, not relishing the laywoman's suggestion, nor does he seem impressed by her trade vocabulary; no doubt about it, he'd like to get her foot out of the door.

Undaunted, she continues, "Isn't it high time, in view of the rate of cerebral palsy? One doesn't go to a proctologist to have one's tonsils removed either."

I must say this for Gold Glasses, the surgical tweezers remain steady and his hand gentle as he tests and changes the tubes protruding from my belly. Trude makes herself useful, passes him gauze and instruments, gives no indication of her burning interest in our discreetly contentious conversation; after a while she asks in a voice as sweet as whipped cream, "Finished?" but gets no response.

"I must say you're merry and bright considering your condition," Gold Glasses says casually. "Coli and streptococci en masse, the little beasts are probably resistant to antibiotics already." He allows himself a "God Almighty," grips his biceps, plants his feet wide apart, and stares at his toecaps. "I've no idea what we can give you now, have to try something new. We'll have cortisone ready in case of allergies."

"She's in pain," says Trude.

"How could you know that?" he asks amusedly.

Trude's phlegmatic character doesn't hold with bragging. "I just know it," she answers simply.

"Is she?" he asks the patient.

"She is."

"Women," he grunts, feigning vexation. Getting ready to leave, he says, "I'm not here tomorrow, have to go to a conference. A lady doctor will take over."

"I shall miss you," the patient says, "you'll not be able to say the same."

"Who says I won't?" he asks, a little too roughly, his voice even hoarser, uncertain whether his tricks will work at this bedside.

There's been no sign of Olive since Kaiser P. asked him to step outside, but the Mouse still patters by. "I hear you're in pain," she squeaks, pouching her mouth and wagging a cloth smeared with paste. "This is a good cream, you should apply it to the wounds."

"Did the professor prescribe it?" the patient asks, filled with mistrust.

The Mouse is in a tight corner. "Not exactly, but I think you should know that I don't always approve of the medication that's prescribed."

"Neither do I," the patient answers, "but we're not going to get very far with lotions and liniments."

"You'd do well to follow my advice," the Mouse says peevishly.

"I'd be delighted to if you were a doctor."

She comes up for air, breathless piping issues from her constricted throat, the thought seems to activate some sort of choler. Slowly she finds her way back; she stands there limply, rasps, "As you wish," turns, and runs straight into Trude's mighty breast. "No, no," the Mouse complains, bouncing out of the masses of flesh. She stands for a moment as though suffering from shock and then stalks to the door, flickering harassed glances about her. Trude's beehive has weathered the storm; so too have the syringe and the infusion refill she's carrying.

"I can live without her," Trude babbles, lifts the blanket, and darts the needle into the skin squashed between the mattress and my hipbone. "She gave Erna another drubbing, Erna got so upset she vomited all over the stairs. I had to clean it up, as though we didn't have enough vomit around here to start with. Now she's gone on sick leave." Trude lights a cigarette and asks, "When's your husband coming again?"

"He's building us a house near Salzburg," I say.

"Heavens above, I lost weight when we built ours," says Trude and anxiously fingers her packets of fat. Relieved at finding them still there, she crows, "My old man loves fat ones," her peachlike skin turning purple as she guffaws. "No, but really, you couldn't have picked a worse time to start building," she adds, stifling her chuckles.

"It picked us," the patient says ruefully.

10

.

Days drip into each other like the drops trickling down my
infusion tubes. The patient hardly knows any more exactly when
her husband had sat at her bed, how many hours pass between
his visits. He usually comes in the early morning and again
before dusk; she looks forward to his visits like a girl at the start
of a love affair who can't wait for the next meeting. Each of his
movements finds its place in her memory and repeats itself
during the innumerable sleepless nights, suggesting ever new,
important meanings. He's no stranger to hospitals, his own
teenage bout of tuberculosis and the patient's regular sojourns
have formed him into a hard-boiled professional, so to speak, but
still he sits uneasily on the hard visitor's chair, which, as in most
hospitals, is not conducive to cozy tête-à-têtes anyway, reminds
one more of visiting hour in prison; the door too, liable to be
opened at any time without a knock or other warning by some
doctor, nurse, or charwoman, is a constant impediment to easy
intimacy. Questions and answers straggle by; the patient, although eager to hear the news from "outside," remains grumpy-
sensitive-glum, frightened by contact with the active world, by
his participation in interests which do not coincide with her
sole one, that of survival. These hours are comparable to parents'
Sunday-afternoon visits to boarding school, long awaited, exu-
berant to begin with, then simmering down, finally reproachful.
Points of secondary importance become overblown; a helpless,

friendly remark seems benevolent, remiss; words of encouragement have been carefully worked out with the jailer-doctors.

Only eight months previously they'd gone looking for the "prison" he'd been in twenty years ago. They'd driven from London in a southeasterly direction, toward Dover. At the top of the hill just before Swanley, the wind had pressed their car to the side of the road; it had bounced over the rough stones, slid on the gravel. "It's down there," he'd said, "on the left between the trees." I saw potato fields, a few poplars, a lot of bushes, finally the gates. They were open, the drive was overgrown with weeds, hardly traceable, the wooden fence sagging and rotten; chestnuts and acacias, tree-high rhododendrons, laburnum, ferns, and ivy heaved and swayed in massive entanglement, as though eternally at each other's throat; a cold warring jungle hidden between emerald-green English meadows. "We should be able to see it from here," he said puzzledly, "it's three stories high. We were downstairs, the women on the second floor and the nurses up top. The ambulances used this driveway at the side."

A broken gin bottle was lying in the undergrowth; we noticed the man only when we were standing right in front of him. He was leaning against a rusted lamppost. Very slowly, as if with considerable effort, he raised his bushy, sand-colored eyebrows. "You're looking for the house," he said, without looking at us. His hair was like fur, thick and short; his trousers were pasted around his thin legs as though he'd slept in them for weeks. "It burned down," he said loudly and jerked his head back so suddenly that it startled me. "Right down to the ground it burned," he continued, and stared at the violently jostling treetops. Just as abruptly as he'd jerked his head back, he now turned and vanished into the bushes. "That was ten years ago," he shouted, then, chuckling childishly, "and you're David, aren't you?" Although the man was no longer visible, David nodded and looked disquietedly at the shaking bushes.

"The chief doctor's house was over to the left; on the right there was a smaller clinic for TB of the eyes," David murmured. We were standing on the open spot where once the sanatorium had been. The ground was covered with weeds and high grass, there was no sign of foundations, not a brick to confirm its erstwhile existence. "It was November when they brought me here the first time," David said. The sky was deep blue, the racing clouds were heavy and white, compact, keeping their shape. He parted a clump of clover with the tip of his shoe. "It was a very cold day," he said, almost embarrassedly. We stood there uncertainly, as though we'd suddenly realized we'd been lying and were wondering how to confess.

We walked back down the neglected drive. Next to the gates, on top of a pile that had once been a rock garden, the man was sitting chewing a piece of grass. "How do you know my name?" David asked him. The man grinned arrogantly; "I know a lot, I do, I live next door," he said and waved his hand casually in the direction of the wooden fence. I looked, but there was no house there, no hut. He bent forward and added another knot to his already perfectly tied shoelaces, then stood up, flicking the blade of grass over his shoulder. "You were in ward two," he said, moving away, "old fatty was in the next bed." He turned around and blew out his cheeks. "What was the name of the place? I'm afraid I've forgotten," David asked him. The man shrugged his shoulders as though he didn't care to continue the conversation, as though he didn't give a damn, and walked away. "Kettlewell, that was the name," David said as we got into the car, "and I was in ward one." Through the rear window I saw the man walk after the car, then go into a grotesque, malicious imitation of a tubercular coughing fit.

We drove back to London and in a dismal suburb called Peckham David stopped the car in front of a church. It was dark brown and hardly bigger than a village pub. "This is where my mother and I used to fetch our powdered milk and orange juice during the war," David said. We went up the four worn steps and opened the door. The church was full of Negroes. Most of them were squatting on the entirely bare stone floor, others were leaning against the whitewashed walls; they wore a hodge-podge of West Indian, African, and European clothes and were apparently listening to the loud rock music coming from a large loudspeaker hanging under two fluorescent tubes, one of which flickered on and off incessantly. A man came toward us and gestured that we should go.

We drove on and soon came to the borough of Dulwich. David stopped the car at a corner on which a prefabricated house was standing. "That's where our house used to be," he said; "this is where I lived until the doodlebug, a V–1 rocket, dropped on it."

The rest of the houses in the street are old and shabby but intact. They are tiny, like dollhouses, and divided up into pairs: two stories, four sash windows upstairs, two bay windows downstairs, two doors; two half-houses stuck together, then a tiny gap, then the next pair, all the same size, each with two yards of front garden protected by a knee-high wall. Prim poverty in prim houses under prim roofs which sport six-potted chimney stacks; they stick up ostentatiously as in the gleefully overdone finale of a surrealist farce. The sky hangs lower here than in other places, as though consciously adapting itself to the unrelenting miles of demureness down below. It's a different kind of poverty from that of the big-city apartment barracks of my childhood, with rats in the trash cans, lavatory next to the stairs, with bugs and "prohibited" signs, screams and squabbles and nocturnal black eyes; it neither intimidates nor challenges, it's a soft-shoe poverty, orderly, steady, avoiding trouble; it would never provoke a rebellion, unleash an uproar.

A red bus stopped at the corner, towering above the houses. People alighted and walked down the quiet street; they walk slower than the pedestrians in the heart of London, wandering along as though they're not sure which house is theirs. Two children jumped over a wall, but the display of energy seemed rehearsed; I felt they wouldn't have done it had we not been there to watch. They disappeared and the street became still again, so still that one might have believed a curfew had been imposed on the district. "Down at the other end there was a dentist," David said. "Poorer children got a certificate and the state paid for the treatment. I was eight when I went to him, he pulled one tooth and drilled seven others in half an hour; it was years before I went to a dentist again." As David is some six and a half feet tall, I couldn't imagine how he ever managed in these puppet houses, why the dwarf landscape had tolerated his growth. "My father was taller than I am," said David, as though I'd spoken my thoughts. "My brother too. I was the smallest."

At the corner there was a sign bearing the name of the street; it had the same noble format as the signs in Curzon Street or Pall Mall. David said, "My father didn't like the work he was doing but he always said, 'I'm a worker so you'll be workers too.' He contented himself with being tall and going down to the Magdala to drink."

We went to the Magdala. It was closed; through the windows we could see red-glass balloon lamps and bast screens. "I don't remember it that way at all," David said.

Until we met in London sixteen years ago, our lives had run in very different directions. David's, although not at all monotonous or free from catastrophe, had followed a more or less consistent line down the middle, in keeping with his temperament; mine, on the other hand, could only be compared to a paratyphoid patient's temperature chart.

David's began on the sleazier outskirts of pastoral Dulwich, in the street with the half-houses, two and a half rooms upstairs, one and a half plus kitchen downstairs, no central heating, coal fires. The front room with the bay window downstairs is the living room. As in all the other houses, it is used only for weddings, baptisms, and Christmas celebrations. David's family sets no store by baptism, and the last wedding had been that of the parents, so use of the living room is limited to the twenty-fifth of December. David lives with his brother, whose seniority of seven years makes theirs a remote relationship; his sister, who's even older and a girl to boot; his father, of whom he's afraid; his mother, whom he loves most of the time; and a lodger. The lodger works at night, his father during the day, both for Esso. He never sees the lodger, his father seldom. Seldom is Sunday morning. Father sits in the kitchen reading the Sunday newspaper; he reads it so slowly that one would think he were committing it to memory, reads until the Magdala opens at eleven-thirty. Seldom is every night when he comes home from the Magdala smelling of beer and falls into bed. At a tender age David already begins to wonder how he ever came to be conceived; as long as he can remember, his parents haven't been on speaking terms, and since he shares the same bedroom, he can vouch for it that here in particular the vow of silence is rigidly upheld and that connubial rites have been abandoned long ago.

The next-door neighbor to the right is Mabel Pritchard. She's the only person on the street who possesses more than one coat. To be precise, she owns three: one for winter, one for summer, and a raincoat for all seasons. Mabel Pritchard is also the only person in the street of half-houses one might just have expected a whole one of, but no, she lives semidetached like the rest, although she owns three coats, keeps six cats, doesn't go to work, and always looks as though she's just been to the hairdresser. Mabel Pritchard, fifty years old and a spinster, has her funny ways. She uses the living room in summer. The children stand on the street in front of her window and watch her do it. She sits there with her long narrow feet carefully placed side by side and knits or sews or reads, holding the book straight in front of her with outstretched arms. She gives a little nod when she first enters the room, but that's as far as she'll go in acknowledging her audience; it swells by the hour, when school breaks the pavement is blocked, only when night falls does the crowd gradually diminish. Then she nods once again, stands up, and goes into the kitchen with her cats. With this, her last hardy admirers disperse, for now she's on familiar ground; the aromas that exude from her kitchen are the same as in the rest of the street, cabbage, fish, or bubble and squeak, roast lamb or beef on Sundays. The smells of cabbage, fish, and lamb drift from door to door, waft up and down the street, mingle at the corner with the other streets' smells of cabbage, fish, and lamb.

The time is the late thirties and the street is suddenly surprised by the addition of two exotic families. Over the tiny gap to the left, Herr and Frau Kirsch and their daughter, Elsie, move into the next half-house. They drink coffee instead of tea and, hanging in their kitchen, next to the zinc bathtub, on the wall, there's a view of the river Spree in Berlin. Herr Kirsch is employed at the gasworks in Peckham. He's a bag of bones and wears nickel granny glasses that always slide down his nose and tug the wire from behind one enormous ear or the other. At six in the morning he rides off to the gasworks on an ancient bicycle; whether he's riding his bicycle or not, the turnups of his trousers are always held by metal clips. The bicycle itself, even though it's old and rather rusty, has a fixed wheel and drop handlebars and invests him with a certain status, for it's one of the very few of its kind in the neighborhood. Confused by the attention he and his bicycle attract, Herr Kirsch looks more and more frightened and helpless; even the most harmless questions seem to upset him, he fumbles with his glasses and refers one to his wife. But at six in the morning, when he's alone and fairly sure no one's watching him, he's a different man: erect and with his chin held high (possibly on account of the slipping glasses), he whisks away with a flourish as though he were holding the wheel of a dreadfully expensive limousine. These limited moments of self-assurance crumble entirely whenever Frau Kirsch is around, against her prodigal girth he appears more frail than ever. Frau Kirsch seems to have been as little predestined for the narrow half-house staircase as she was for the zinc bathtub she crams herself into every Saturday night. The tub, stairs, and floors in the whole house groan under the massive load; majestically she thrusts her huge solid bosom through the narrow doors and passageways, majestically she enjoys the false impression her mammae make. Frau Kirsch's inherent good nature and *Gemütlichkeit* are camouflaged by the aggressive character of her imposing warhead. Their daughter, Elsie, resembles her father and arouses sympathy, one feels that her mother's strength is more of a hindrance than a help to her, and the general surprise is great when, at the age of eighteen, pigeon-breasted Elsie up and marries.

Across the road live the Jackmanns. Although they've changed their name and adapted their habits to those of the street, they are nevertheless interned at the outbreak of war.

To begin with, the war means little other than an interesting topic of conversation. The rent collector still comes every week to collect the fifteen shillings which are religiously deposited in a pot on the kitchen shelf each Friday night when Father hands over the housekeeping money but which have invariably been reduced to much less by the time the collector calls. Monday is still washday for the whole neighborhood; wooden duckboards are laid across the kitchen floor, the zinc bathtub is filled with linen and heaved onto the stove. The week begins with clouds of steam and bubble and squeak—the remains from Sunday lunch, meat, potatoes, and green vegetables fried in the pan. Father still commutes between Esso and the Magdala. The neighbors show temporary concern when the nocturnal lodger is the first on the street to be enlisted into the air force and gets shot down over Holland on his maiden flight.

David flees to the uninterned Kirsch family whenever the silence between his parents explosively changes into the opposite, and this happens on the rare Saturday nights in the year when they go to the Magdala together. David has witnessed a few of these outings, and the result could be listed under "depressing experience with a traumatic effect"; they teach him once and for all time that silence is indeed golden when the only alternative is a stand-up fight. The Saturday nights go something like this: Father, who is six foot six and a half and holds a lot of beer, leans against the tinny upright piano and tosses off twenty to thirty songs in a sturdy baritone voice which is nothing if not loud. The songs deal mainly with England's illustrious seafaring heritage; he opens with "I Will Go Down to the Sea Again," moves on to "Hearts of Oak," a ditty in which both the ships and the hearts of its mariners are described as being of the same noble timber; in between, and particularly toward the end, he cleverly mixes in sing-along songs such as "Nelly Dean" to encourage the others and, on especially good nights, winds up with "Rule, Britannia," no less. Mother, in the meantime, has been intent on downing gin-and-tonic, which she never touches except on these occasions, and takes her cue from his finale. She now raises her clear, ear-splitting, untrained soprano voice and moves resolutely through her lengthy repertoire of romantic ballads. Father quenches his thirst with several pints and makes a second appearance; in this manner the "handsomest man" and the "belle" of the street wage an "anything you can do" battle. (Mother's small regular features, her grace, green eyes and auburn hair had attracted a film producer's attention and earned her a small role in a silent film in the early twenties; Father had been against it.) Their mutual hatred swells with each song and each glass, reverberates through the fumes and smoke of the dingy local pub with the turgid name Magdala.

David, cowering behind the bar and praying ardently that the ground might open and swallow him, nevertheless survives these initial shocks unscathed to all outward appearances, physically takes after his father, shoots up to dizzy heights, grows accustomed to seeing first people's scalps and parts, then their humble upturned faces, and begins an altogether extraordinary existence as regards outlook and point of view.

David's memories of his father, apart from the singing duels, are limited almost exclusively to Christmas festivities. Among the fonder ones, one might mention a works' celebration at which Father, dressed in an old-fashioned uniform with a peaked cap bearing the word "Esso," had driven an open veteran automobile and then hoisted the four-year-old David onto his shoulders for the photographers; among the more traumatic memories, another Christmas, some years later: Father has reluctantly agreed that his Boy Scout son needs a sheath knife and presents him with it. David, overjoyed, can't wait for the next scout meeting and tests its weight and balance then and there in the kitchen. The knife slips from his hand, sails across the room, and buries itself in the newspaper that Father's memorizing until it's time for the Magdala. The knife slices through the thin pages and hangs quivering between the sports news and Father's nose; David and the other members of the assembled family freeze in their tracks. Very very slowly, Father lowers the newspaper to the floor, raises himself to his full alarming height, picks his way through the pages at his feet as though selecting a path through a soggy bog, goes trembling to the kitchen stove, and picks up the ax lying next to the pile of firewood. Obeying primeval instincts, David comes out of his hypnotized state and hares out onto the icy windy street, races down the full length of it, hears labored breathing gaining on him, races back up again, shoots through the Kirsches' ever-open back door, up the stairs, and under their brass double bed, sees his father's immense shoes approach stealthily. They are joined by lace-up boots and bicycle clips, granny specs peer under the counterpane, a wooden spoon comes into view; the boots and shoes shuffle about, change direction, and disappear.

David starts school, not at all unwillingly, which one may well understand, but his first day begins with a debacle and ends in the general hospital. His very opulent lady teacher stumbles as she welcomes him, knocks him down, and sits on his spindly legs, breaking them both. An ambulance is called and David is brought to the hospital, where he spends several weeks in plaster casts and surrounded by dozens of whimpering children who have one and all had their tonsils removed. David rather enjoys the novel interlude, misses only the morning searches for shrapnel and other relics of the nightly air raids that London is now subject to.

When his legs have mended, he returns to the half-house and finds it in a state of turmoil. His parents, holding their tongues as grimly as ever, are frantically packing everything in sight; David manages to drag out of them that Esso has ordered evacuation and that the whole firm is moving to a nest near Didcot, west of London; that Father's position as gauge checker is unimpugned; that his brother and sister, both having reached school-leaving age, will henceforth likewise be in Esso's employ; and that Esso emergency quarters have been arranged for the Esso-dedicated family. Relieved of the responsibility of making a decision of their own and without so much as a grumble, they leave the street, the Magdala, the neighborhood, the shrapnel, and set out for Didcot. Father, thrown out of the rhythm of habit, avails himself of the opportunity the enforced evacuation offers to change the course of his aborted life; he strikes up a warm friendship with the owner of a Didcot lingerie shop, accepts the consequences of her ensuing pregnancy, and decides on divorce and remarriage. Due no doubt to the English habit of ignoring illness, he fails to notice that the expectant mother, who is otherwise hale, hearty, plump, and jolly, is the victim of cancer of the palate; only David, with the clear perception of youth, realizes vaguely that the clicking and clucking, together with a speech impediment, augur no good.

His brother is called up and joins the Airborne Parachute Corps, his sister follows the call of an apparently hereditary thespian trait and shocks the small-town community to the roots of its moral sensitivity by appearing in the Esso amateur dramatics production with her lips painted a lascivious scarlet and wearing a risqué nightie. She cocks her pretty nose at the outraged petite bourgeoisie, marries a gentleman from an upper-crust family, and says goodbye to Didcot and Esso forever. David is left alone with his mother, whose beauty declines visibly from day to day; unable to cope with the divorce and the lawyers, she cries almost continuously and withdraws herself into a reticence that is no longer dogged or aggressive but submissive now, defeated, done for, finally capitulates under the pressure Esso exercised to evict her from its quarters now that its employee has moved to the lingerie shop, and returns with her youngest son to the empty half-house, which, in the meantime, has suffered minor bomb damage and is more rickety than ever. In order to fill the pot on the kitchen shelf, she takes in work and a new lodger.

His name is Adrian. Adrian is big, with black hair, thick glasses, and a jaundice-yellow complexion, is an undertaker by profession and a homosexual by inclination, a circumstance he celebrates with almost wanton openness. Adrian is extremely excitable and precipitous and would seem at first glance to be the very last person one could imagine in the somber world of undertaking; one sees him mixing up the corpses and not being able to tell one set of bereaved from the next. Adrian derives great benefit in his profession and his general attitude from the fact that England at this time is overrun by American servicemen and that the English are being confronted with a different way of life for the first time in centuries. The American influence is everywhere in evidence, and just as Adrian moves into the half-house, an undertakers' conference takes place in London at which it is unanimously decided that the whole system of undertaking must be revamped, the positive relaxed approach adopted here too; the word "undertaker" is thrown on the scrap heap and replaced with the down-to-earth, businesslike term "funeral director." Adrian needs no second bidding and soon appears wearing startling wide-shouldered jackets and ties with hand-painted palm trees, brilliant suns, and luminous exhortations to "Be happy." He greets his lachrymose clients with bubbling vivacity and is not at all put out when they fail to share his revolutionary enthusiasm for the job in hand. Each evening he comes home and jubilantly relates the events of the day, underlining the funny bits with expansive gestures that often spell the end for one of the few pieces of crockery left the depleted family, but Mother and David take it all in good part and experience a hitherto unknown exhilaration through Adrian's infectious delight in a good chin-wag. Alice, Mother's robust older sister and Father's archenemy for many a year, now resumes her visits and adds greatly to the air of conviviality.

Alice is a widow and lives in a whole house four streets away. She's an expert businesswoman and, with the aid of Jules, her head salesman, runs a shop that sells practically everything in the way of food and has no competition anywhere in the neighborhood, for Jules, known as Julie to his many friends, is, like Adrian, rampantly homosexual and proud of it and takes each customer, regardless of sex, under his warm wing and elevates the mundane action of buying a can of peas to a sublime erotic experience. The dour Dulwich housewives, used to dour service and blissfully ignorant of the very existence of homosexuality, fall over each other for the opportunity of crossing Julie's blatantly outstretched palm with the last of their hard-earned silver and fill the shop from morning till night. Julie is portly but rosy and appetizing, with rosy, wavy hair; he resembles an exorbitant baby. One of Alice and Julie's strongest bonds is their common delight in throwing parties. They plunder the cellars of their shop and roll out the port, gin, and beer, even brandy, pile the table high with hams and smoked salmon and other delicacies the street has never even heard of. They invite relatives, neighbors, and favored customers and so create a thankful public for Alice's one great passion: piano playing. Alice's dexterity, one must admit, has been sorely impaired since she got her left hand caught in the electric slicer at the beginning of her delicatessen career and maimed it for all time, but she didn't lose heart, she practiced with obstinate dedication until she'd strengthened the virtuosity of her right hand to such an extent that she could satisfy the most demanding requests from her respective audiences, using the left more as a drumstick, rapping groups of keys in the lower register to stress the rhythm when need be. In the wee small hours Adrian and Julie team up and sing love duets, Julie's vibrant tenor voice soaring over Adrian's nicotine-racked baritone.

David's sister now reappears on the idyllic scene, together with a very young infant and her gentleman husband, Roger, who has been discharged from the army with a mild case of tuberculosis and whose family has cut him off without a penny. They move into the half-house with six vast trunks, creating earnest problems as regards space. They camp down in the untenanted living room, the narrow collapsible sofa, which bears a certain similarity to a camel's back, serving them as a nuptial couch. Roger's thirty custom-made suits and one hundred shirts are the talk of the town, his Oxford accent and impeccable manners strike awe into the neighbors' hearts to begin with. They've hardly installed themselves, however, when fate deals Roger a sharp and considerable blow: a letter slips from the pocket of his hand-stitched jacket and reveals that the short rest cure he had undergone on leaving the army had not been entirely devoted to mending his groggy lung; the letter is from a woman who declares her undying love for Roger in no uncertain terms. Although he swears by everything holy to him that the liaison is over and done with, David's sister shows him the door, musters all her energy, and shoves the six trunks after him onto the street. She takes her place at her baby's side and retreats into silence.

Now silence, which had been so gloriously exorcised by Alice, Adrian, and Julie, makes a triumphant comeback. David finds himself looking after his infant nephew and secretly grieves over the departure of Roger, whom he'd become attached to. Doodle-bugs have begun to plow through Dulwich's low-hanging sky and offer a dubious diversion. They chug along like old lawn-mowers and resemble fat Havanas with a stovepipe stuck on the end, seem to have been invented to amuse the children until the engine suddenly stops and they point their noses at the ground and become violent. And that's exactly what one of them does as David is babysitting in the garden one relatively bright June morning; the doodlebug stops chugging, aims its snout at the half-house, and swoops. David scoops up his nephew, dives into the kitchen and under the steel table issued by the Ministry of Defense for this very purpose. The half-house collapses with a whiff and a pouf like soot falling down a chimney; under the table it's pitch-black and hard to breathe, but the dust settles and David sits quietly, almost peacefully, with the sleeping baby in his arms and imagines himself in a beleaguered wigwam waiting for Chief Sitting Bull to return and beat off the attack-ing cavalry.

A rescue squad digs them out and ascertains that neither of them has suffered so much as a scratch. The whole corner of the street has been flattened and many of the neighbors killed. Mother, who had been out shopping, sets off to search for a new residence for the family. They are assigned a garret in a requisi-tioned house which has an exotic monkey tree in the front garden, but Mother, David's sister, and the baby undertake the business of moving alone, for David's whole school is abruptly evacuated to Devon. He is taken in by a pleasant, warmhearted laborer and his unpleasant, witchlike wife, who has fearful talons and beady eyes. Fred, the laborer, goes off to work at sunrise and returns at dusk, falling into bed exhaustedly after his meager supper; the witch never sets foot outside the door. Although the state pays for David's keep, she feeds him nothing but bread and water; at the end of three months he is emaciated, with skin eruptions all over his face and body, together with ugly bruises caused by the witch's knobbly stick. David is forced to write comforting letters home and only an unexpected visit by his mother saves him from total starvation. They board the next train and return to the garret and David's taciturn sister, who is to remain silent for the next five years. The time has come for David to take an examination; he is awarded a scholarship and sent off to a boarding school, Rossall College, tuition and lodging being provided for by the state. The full meaning of this step will not become clear to him until later, for it is only now, in wartime England, that such a leap over the class and financial barriers can be achieved with such facility.

Rossall, near Blackpool, is large, austere, sport-oriented, and overlooks the sea. Its customs may well be called spartan, the morning runs along the seafront in shorts and singlet, regardless of weather and the towering waves that break across the course —barbaric. The prevailing chill in the classrooms prompts the unhardened London contingent, along with a French student-teacher who is even less adaptable to the raw climate, to smash chairs and burn them in the stately but empty fireplaces when no one's around. Otherwise, the pupils spend their free time sticking little flags into a map of Europe, marking the advance of the Allied troops; they greet the fall of Berlin with the same mild satisfaction they demonstrate on the soccer field when their team wins. With the end of the war, the London boys are sent back home to continue their quest for knowledge at a noble edifice by the name of Alleyn's College of God's Gift.

David's admission to Alleyn's at the age of twelve marks the beginning of a positive phase. The school had been founded by one Edward Alleyn, who had been a prominent actor in Shakespeare's day, possibly the first Hamlet, Othello, or Macbeth, and besides maintaining its high academic standards, the school is intent on furthering the arts and upholding the theatrical tradition. Here, behind the russet façade and amid spacious playing fields, David spends six happy, crucial years. It would be thoughtless and unfeeling to leave unmentioned the fact that David, during these years at Alleyn's, is of spectacular beauty and begins to employ the many gifts that have been bestowed, one might even say showered, upon him. He is soon playing the leading parts in the Shakespeare productions, singing with a captivating soprano voice (as long as it lasts) in Gluck's *Orpheus*, Gounod's *Faust*, Gilbert and Sullivan, Verdi's *Requiem*, oratorios, and whatever else comes along; on the playing fields he bowls faster, jumps higher, shoots straighter, is made captain of several teams, in short, becomes one of the pillars of Alleynian society. In the classroom his principal teacher is a solid Welshman named Thomas. Mr. Thomas is in his forties, married, with four sons, a heavy smoker, and writes glowing reports on David's prowess to his mother. "God, in his bounty, has blessed your son . . ." one letter begins. The highly sophisticated music master with the preciously common name of Clark endorses Thomas's eulogies.

Clark is round and sleek, wears expensive sport jackets and large flowering ties that bear abundant evidence of Clark's Falstaffian approach to the dining table, and is an ardent Germanophile; he even flaunts his partiality on London's postwar streets by driving a prewar Opel, which, due to the lack of spare parts, is more often to be seen being pushed by a crowd of the boys than running under its own steam. In the first summer holidays after the war, he patently ignores the current weight of opinion and palpable proof of Nazi atrocities and drives off in a cloud of smoke to the land of Brahms and Beethoven. Spurred on by Clark's and Thomas's praise, David rolls up his sleeves and surpasses even their expectations, is first in this and first in that; nothing stands in the way of an Oxford scholarship and a brilliant academic career, it seems. A small cloud appears on the clear blue sky of David's destiny, however: Thomas gets an offer of a better job and moves away from London. David's interest wanes and he relapses into the familial apathy, relying on his physical attributes and a photographic memory to keep him above water. Mother's possessiveness sees to it that his sexual awakening takes place within very tightly drawn boundaries.

The family has now moved into a whole house; it's drab and has no bathroom, but does boast a small garden with a cherry tree. Although Mother is very nearsighted, she proudly declines to wear spectacles; between them, she and Adrian steadily demolish everything breakable in the house, and Mother's cooking suffers from the fact that she frequently places the ingredients next to instead of into the frying pan. David's sister has got a job with a market-research company in the West End of London but is still very subdued and remains silent even in the midst of the total destruction going on around her.

David's blossoming libido teaches him the use of guile, and he devises ways and means to visit a passionate Cypriot girl he has met. She sweetens his existence for several weeks, but the attachment is soured by the heavy Greek food her mother prepares in lavish quantities and insists that David eat. Also, her habit of leaving her daughter alone on the living-room couch with the wretchedly belching David, locking the door behind her as she goes, gradually cools David's ardor and fills him with a feeling of claustrophobia. Disturbed by the uproar in his digestive tract and by the sad realization that his first attempts at coupling with the Cypriot fireball are proving rather awkward and jolly painful to boot, David turns in his hand.

His youthful potency lies idle; the grumblings in his belly subside with time but are followed by a period of listlessness and languor, also by rapid loss of weight. His pubescent spate of industry dries up and would seem to have been wholly dependent on the immediate reaction of an audience, on the Welshman Thomas's incentive. He is no longer first in anything, his performances on the sports field deteriorate dismally. He spends the nights next to his ever-adoring mother (they still share a bedroom) coughing violently. She plies him with tea, engenders in him the feeling that his very presence is equal to deed and achievement, and in this way nurtures his sense of self-satisfaction, a sense he is going to need to be able to cope with the ordeal awaiting him.

His cough gets worse and he wakes up one morning to find his pillow full of blood. Accompanied by his mother, he goes to the nearby general practitioner; they wait six hours to then be scoffed at by Dr. MacPherson; first he laughs, his waxed mustaches bristling; then he booms, with the unrestrained bass-drum voice of a pukka brigadier, "You're wasting my time, who ever heard of a star athlete like you getting sick? A little blood vessel's probably ruptured, that's all, be off with you." Mother summons up her courage and says, "Don't you think he should be X-rayed?" but the disciplinarian sweeps her under the thread-bare carpet with a glance and thunders, "Don't you think the radiologists have got enough to do as it is? And what about the money it costs the state?" They go home, comforted on the one hand, still troubled on the other. The bleeding doesn't stop, David loses some twenty pounds in weight, repeated efforts to engage Dr. MacPherson's interest fail abysmally. Finally a series of alarming hemorrhages persuade the stiff-upper-lip advocate that all may not be quite well after all and David is sent to the radiologists. X-rays are taken and David is told to go home, get into bed immediately, and stay there. A district nurse comes the next day and injects streptomycin, repeats the procedure every day for the next few weeks. David swallows dozens of big PAS pills daily, stays in bed, and awaits further developments. What exactly it is that he's got remains the doctors' secret and they never come near the house. The hemorrhages stop abruptly, color and fullness come back to his cheeks.

Mother enjoys the months of undisturbed togetherness and the radical elimination of her chief worry, girls; some of David's more erudite school friends, one teacher and several old boys of the school, pay him a visit and Mother encourages them to come more often, quite unaware of the fact that they're all homosexually inclined and enchanted by the idea of lovely David wanly doing lonely combat with consumption. They turn up in droves, and the soirees that take place at David's bedside are such as to turn the most radically chic circle of aesthetes green with envy. The suddenly imposed state of invalidism doesn't disturb him in the slightest; on the contrary, his mother's love and the new form of popularity boost and strengthen him, he seems free of any form of emotional engagement at this time. Indifference and a latent death wish, later to prove a godsend, prevent unchanneled feelings from bursting their banks.

From his bed David paints pictures of the florist's shop on the corner and sells them to the owner, thereby making a small contribution to the pot on the kitchen shelf. Three and a half months pass, during which time he regularly sees his friends, his mother, his sister, Adrian, Julie, and Alice, but never a doctor. Then he's picked up by an ambulance and taken to the hospital for further X-rays. He goes with a light heart, for he has regained his old weight and looks the picture of health; indeed, some friends speculate that there's been some mix-up with the first X-ray plates. The same doctor examines the new exposures and promptly dispatches David with very un-British haste to Kettlewell sanatorium in Kent.

It is November and the day is cold; they drive in a southeasterly direction, slow down on the hill just before Swanley, turn off to the left, pass the iron gates, and approach the turreted, chateau-like building. David is signed in and told to change the gaudy suit he's borrowed from his funeral director friend, Adrian, for a pair of pajamas. He then meets the lord of the consumptive manor, Dr. Wyss.

Dr. Wyss is Swiss. With an icy, immobile smile he rattles off his unembellished, bloodcurdling diagnoses in awkward, unctuously intoned English, and in no way corresponds to the conventional concept of sanatorium life. He shows no sign of affinity with the lulling timelessness, the soft gracious resignation and gentle elegance coupled with erotic longings that accompany the withering, painless disease. It's possibly the first and only time that David experiences a feeling of simple animal fear as he faces his Swiss overlord; his antennae signal danger, a dependable knee suddenly buckles, he's defenseless, there's nothing to fall back on. He had entered the room easily, in full control, but now he finds himself dodging the close-set eyes that gaze at him relentlessly. Dr. Wyss leads him to the screening room, rattles away impatiently, "We must be patient, we will make an artificial pneumothorax, if this is not good we will make a thoracoplasty in Brompton." Dr. Wyss has shot his big guns too soon, for David still has no idea what the word "Brompton" implies; later, among the veterans in ward one, it will find its mark, will cause hearts to miss a beat, bring cold sweat to the brow of the patient it's directed at. Brompton is the hospital in London where all major thoracic surgery is performed, is the great black scrawny bird that hovers above them, waiting to plummet like a thunderbolt. Thoracoplasty is the biggest operation they have to offer; it takes twelve hours and is divided up into three sessions to enable the patient to recuperate from one and muster his strength for the next; the surgeon first snips away large sections of the ribs and shoulder blade, then strips the lung, rather like peeling an onion. The patient emerges temporarily cured of TB, at least, but disfigured for life.

Ward one awaits the newcomer. He immediately disappears behind a screen. A very tall spindly lady doctor and two male nurses built like nightclub bouncers come to his bed, the doctor holding a long thick needle. He feels a blow like a kick from a donkey; although he's never been kicked by a donkey, he's sure that that's what it's like. The kick is the prelude to the artificial pneumothorax, known simply as AP. Air is pumped through the needle into the intercostal cavity, surrounds the sick lung, and squeezes the life out of it, puts it out of action. Apart from a feeling of constriction, David suffers no great ill effects. The doctor and the bouncers depart, taking the screen with them.

Eight faces are staring at him. To the left: a small, drawn one, peering over the top of *The Times*. He's a draftsman, hasn't been married long; from a medical point of view, his is a mild case. He's an obedient patient, but tends to be overcareful, worries about himself. He'll waste away in the coming weeks and the bouncers will say, "'E's off to anuvver department." Next to him there's a mountain of a man, flabby, with a tiny head, his bloated body protruding over the edges of the bed. He's unpredictable, illiterate, has a vile temper, spends his time staring at comic books and biting his nails. His wardmates tease him to pass the time away, throw his comics from one bed to the next; he chases after them, coughing and wheezing with fury, then collapses on his bed muttering darkly for hours on end. He'll be taken on a stretcher to the tiled room next door in four weeks' time, will die there, with his comics pressed tightly to his breast. To the right: an architect who owns a record player and the complete works of Moussorgsky. He reads Marx, Arnold Toynbee, and Mallarmé. Medically he's considered a hopeless case. In eight months he'll walk down the drive in perfect health. Opposite him: an abrasive cockney automobile mechanic with an endless repertoire of jokes. Things go wrong with his AP, the needle goes in a little too far and pierces his lung. The screens topple over as he whoops frantically and the doctor loses her head. It's touch and go for a few minutes, but then he pulls through. Next to him there's an eighteen-year-old with chubby rosy cheeks who looks like an advertisement for baby food. He's been in ward one for a year and knows every trick in the book, knows who stands a chance and who doesn't. "It never lets you go," he says warmly, and the fact that at least half of the inhabitants are relapse cases seems to bear him out. In the corner bed there's a professional soldier who neither speaks nor reads, just plays with a Moroccan dagger the whole day long. This is his third visit to Kettlewell in the past five years.

Once a week Dr. Wyss sprints in, checks the temperature charts and X-rays. If he sprints on, everything's fine, but if he stops and moves nearer, trouble's in store. On the second day he moves in on David and says, "AP has not taken, too many adhesions. We will try pneumoperitoneum." The screens are wheeled in again and this time the donkey kicks David in the stomach. Air flows into his belly, pushing his lungs up under his collarbone and swelling his abdomen monstrously. When the screens are wheeled away, David looks as though he's in an advanced state of pregnancy and can't sit up. A short while later he's given a local anesthetic in the neck and taken to the operating room for a phrenic crush. This proves to be quite a bizarre undertaking, the object being to paralyze the diaphragm temporarily by crushing the phrenic nerve which controls it. The problem is that once the incision in the neck has been made and all the nerves are nicely exposed, the surgeon doesn't know which one is which and is bound to proceed by trial and error, tweaking each one in turn until the patient has the right reaction. The operating team stands around David and the surgeon starts tweaking. A leg shoots up, now an arm, then the other leg; it's as though they're trying to get the hang of a very large puppet. David suddenly feels as though a whole army of donkeys have kicked him in the solar plexus; he roars, they sigh: got it.

Even the most dramatic events of these months leave him relatively unimpressed; he is protected by an enviable immunity to pain in general, due in part, no doubt, to his unburdened nervous system and to a naturally impervious disposition when confronted with adversity. Apart from Dr. Wyss's repeated allusions to Brompton and thoracoplasty and the smile on his lips as he does so, one sole instrument of torture in the sanatorium's arsenal disturbs him. He has happily stopped coughing altogether and is therefore unable to deliver the sputum imperative to ascertaining the disease's progress and has to swallow long rubber tubes by way of which gastric juices are drawn off. He has begun to appreciate the unique round-the-clock community of ward one. The motley assembly which has one common bond and is kept in total communion for months on end becomes a conspiracy, a plot; fears which would bear heavily on one individual's shoulders are alleviated by common participation. Even the knowledge that no one, least of all themselves, can apprehend the outcome of their separate cases proves a further link; irrespective of intellect, position, or approach to the capricious and indomitable illness, they are all totally at its mercy.

Removed from the driving competitive atmosphere of the school and his mother's overpowering love, he makes his pact with TB and death, faces the prospect assuredly, and attunes himself to the soporific rhythm of the sanatorium days and nights, instinctively robbing the disease of its chance by offering only passive resistance. Death, in this painless muted form, becomes a partner and ward one the clan in which a dog-eared copy of Thomas Mann's *Magic Mountain* goes from hand to hand. The uniformity of the days shortens the weeks and months, Dr. Wyss's weekly visits and the refilling of the AP's and PP's (pneumoperitoneums) being the only variations. They smoke, they read, they talk, they swindle a little when the thermometer creeps up to dangerous highs. Their arrogant distaste for anything that has to do with "outside" gives way to thoughtful sorrow when a suitcase is packed and hands are clasped to the accompaniment of well-wishing phrases, when one of them gets well and deserts. Then they remember the outside they've discarded like an insufferable burden, the outside that exists only as normal and incalculable, laughable and futilely active, and which becomes more and more irreconcilable with their soothingly sauntering dreams and the sabbatical dalliance with death.

After three months Dr. Wyss stops at David's bed, examines his latest X-ray pictures, and announces that his condition has reached stagnation point and that the sanatorium can do nothing more to help him at the moment. He recommends that David go home and allows him to get up for two or three hours a day, providing he spends them quietly in an easy chair. David struggles to get Adrian's trousers buttoned over his PP and trundles back to Dulwich in the ambulance. Neither his mother, his sister, Adrian, nor the hordes of friends that come hurrying over are a substitute for the community of ward one. Among the healthy, he comes to learn the meaning of loneliness and loses his detachment toward the illness and its possible consequences. At the slightest sign of sweat or abnormal temperature, visions of Brompton romp and frolic through his mind, threaten to unbalance him. In an enlightened moment he realizes that this condition of teetering humility is not for him and decides to live a normal, if careful, life; he goes to the theater, to the cinema, smokes suicidally, cultivates anew the friendships that had been interrupted by the months in the sanatorium. Among others there's Lewis. Lewis is a gifted poet who ekes out a living by gardening and whose remarkable good looks are therefore always tanned the color of a pickled walnut, giving him the appearance of a nonchalant film star, rather than an earnest, impecunious artist. Lewis is aware of this and uses his façade to good purpose in warding off boorish allusions to his suspect profession. He develops David's taste for literature and presents him with a very old and shaky but beautifully kept Citroën car. Then there are teachers who try to draw David's attention back to the business at hand, his set books and other, less romantic studies which he must keep up with should he be able to return to school and sit for his exams. Above all, there's Stephen, who had come to the school straight from Oxford just as David was taken ill. He visits almost daily and talks for hours on end, insisting on a university career, encouraging David's interest in the arts, in theater, and in books particularly. He becomes his best friend and soon moves into the house, which by now is full to bursting point.

On top of all this, there's Nancy. Nancy, daughter of a local restaurant owner, is a black-haired, warmhearted beauty and is devoted to David, who smuggles her through the back door under Mother's watchful but failing eye. Nancy brings more than just her physical attributes to the scene, namely, cigarettes and other amenities from the restaurant, but the teeming inhabitants have hardly had time to grow accustomed to the Lucullan delicacies when the supply is suddenly cut off. Nancy's father has had a businessman's hunch and decided to dedicate himself to the manufacture of nougat, undeterred by the fact that he has little knowledge of the tricky technique involved in making it. His grandiose visions of a worldwide export coup (he often relates that the Japanese are insatiable when it comes to nougat) soon wither on the wobbly kitchen table; disregarding the loudly protesting neglected diners, the whole staff buckles down and produces great slabs of nougat, which are then hacked up into mailable portions while still warm but which, on cooling, turn into leaden, granite-like nuggets and prove less than profitable from the outset, since the postage rates are higher than the wholesale price Nancy's father has agreed on with the dealers. His faith in his hunch is unshakable, however; he urges his team on to even greater efforts, many hands stir and knead the brown-gray mixture—in vain, all attempts to refine the faulty recipe won't alter the rock-hard consistency of the end product. The first order comes from the rapacious Japanese, is sent off at great expense, and comes back at even greater by return mail, as there's no one in Japan either with the millstone teeth it takes to tackle the Dulwich nougat. The restaurant is now completely deserted except for the depressed mother-in-law sitting behind the redundant cashier's desk, bankruptcy seems inevitable. The nougat appears to have had a strange effect on Nancy's father: he kneads on obstinately over the forfeited cooker, mumbling dementedly about his world-shattering nuggets.

Nancy is passionate to become a dramatic actress and spends her time working as a photographer's model until the big chance comes along, returning each night to Dulwich, the smell of nougat, and David. He now goes back for a long-overdue check-up to Dr. Wyss, who surprisingly tells him that he's made enormous progress, unsuspectingly praises his doubtless self-castigating conduct, and releases him from all further treatment except the filling of the PP, which must be continued for a year at least. David is free and from now on becomes a confirmed fatalist, allowing the course of his destiny to unfold with as little interference as possible. Above all, a conviction forms in him that fortune's arrows are not meant for him, that he has been selected for some special position which will reveal itself to him in its own good time.

The comfort of this newly formed enviable disposition is to be shaken once more. Almost immediately, as if she'd only waited for him to get over his illness before attending to her own, his mother gets into the same bed, in the same room. She is pitifully thin, weak, and suddenly senile. Dr. MacPherson bristles in, quite uncowed by the confrontation with the subject of his spectacularly inaccurate diagnosis, David, and promptly roars again that his time is being wasted, that Mother has a touch of gastritis and will be as right as rain after a week's diet.

Mother's decline is swift and terrible. Her vanity increases with each sign of decay, what had once been endearing coquetry now becomes pathetic; holding an old scratched magnifying glass and a piece of broken mirror, she furtively tears out the rapidly multiplying gray hairs in clumps, accepting yellow wrinkled bald patches rather than the telltale streaks of gray. The pains in her swollen belly grow worse and a French doctor, who has mysteriously taken up practice in Dulwich, advises surgery. She's taken to hospital but it's too late; the surgeons close the wound over the completely metastasized body and send her home to die. She has no idea of the hopelessness of her condition and adheres blindly to the story she's been told—a small cyst on the uterus had to be removed, pain and the continued swelling are only to be expected following abdominal surgery. She believes it until her last minute, and believes also that the frequent injections and the white medicine David gives her are vitamins and not morphine. She asks David to buy her some henna; sitting up in bed with an enamel bowl balanced on her knees, she smears the paste on her thin wisps of hair, washes it off again, sinks back exhaustedly, and peers blindly but contentedly at the flaming red halo around her gray sunken face reflected in the piece of mirror. Henna-red is youth, is a flat belly, is once in a film studio, belle of the street.

Father, who has been informed of his former wife's condition, sends her an old TV set and David a card on which he clumsily informs his youngest son that he now expects him to forget the advanced-schooling nonsense and settle down in a respectable job and earn some money.

One night, as Nancy lies in the next room and the rest of the house is sleeping, Mother asks her son to hold her gnarled, arthritic hand. Her hennaed hair shines brightly, a sickly sweet aroma exudes from her shrunken, pot-bellied body, above her flaring sightless eyes the lids are painted vivid blue and brown. Smiling, and with no word of complaint, no show of resistance, exactly as she'd lived out her sorry life dependent on a man whose temper, reticence, and bigotry had toppled her pride, she dies; destroyed by a lifelong futility, she gives herself up simply, asks just once, "Will I soon be well again?" and smiles peacefully, invincibly, still full of hope.

David sits beside her and remembers the only holiday they'd ever had together; they'd gone on a day-trip steamer in the English Channel when he was five years old; at the end of the day there'd been a raffle for the children and Mother had bought two tickets, both of them duds. Mother had stood there and couldn't bear his disappointment, had suddenly dipped her hand into the barrel, had stolen a small rubber ball and been caught. She had never cheated at anything in her whole life and was desperate. Her shame had been heartrending to see.

David gets up and goes into the next room to Nancy. They go to bed and make love ardently, lustfully, violently, throwing all precautions to the wind, as though they must negate the presence of death with an act of procreation.

Adrian volubly proves his worth as an undertaker, organizes a priest and a crematorium; Mother's ashes are scattered over the cemetery as is the family custom. After the ceremony they all go to the Magdala and manage to get paralytic before the English licensing laws send them on their way. Arriving home, they find that a window has been smashed and the house entered; while they were at the cemetery Father had come and collected his TV set.

It soon becomes clear that Nancy is pregnant; gin and hot baths, pills and bone-breaking car rides over plowed fields eventually rid her of the unwelcome embryo that was conceived under death's nose. David goes back to school, passes one exam, and must take another in six months' time if he wishes to go to a university. He decides against it, has terrible rows with his friend and mentor, Stephen, resolves to become a professional actor. He is nineteen years old, is disgusted with poverty, zinc bathtubs, soggy towels, freezing rooms, and the eternally empty pot on the kitchen shelf. He plumps for financial independence. Stephen and his other academically ambitious friends turn their back on him; he leaves for the provinces and learns the trade the hard way, going from one tottering repertory company to the next, living in the murky industrial catacombs of northern England, having his PP refilled from time to time, still breaking into a cold sweat at the thought of Brompton; he applies himself with dedication to the profession his friends have so reviled, even shows signs of becoming ambitious when in the company of like-thinking colleagues, but these are few and far between. Realizing that too much fervor will only cause disappointment at this stage of the game, he relapses into an easygoing indifference which not only enables him to walk on to any stage without the slightest sign of nerves but also to view the whole business of living with amusement and to deal with unavoidable unpleasantness with as little strain as possible. Some years later he will return to London and begin the march from agent to agent which is an actor's routine, will make his way and have his share of success, and, out of the blue one day, will suddenly be confronted with the author; from then on he will often need every last vestige of his innate repose to prevent himself being thrown by the violently bucking character of her life and temperament. Sometimes she succeeds in dragging him along to her heights and her depths, but most of the time he declines to change levels, remains on his own home ground, and watches her hurtle around her private helter-skelter, exchanging troubled glances with her whenever her daemon-driven carriage charges across his path.

11

•

"I've got a lump here," the patient says, nodding her chin downward. The Giraffe, who's been dozing fitfully in his capacity as allergy night watchman, stretches his legs and crinkles his brow, gets up. With a delicious display of Swiss delicacy he murmurs, "May I?" and "With your permission," lifts up the loose hospital gown, feels the spot indicated, and grunts, "That's all we needed. Does the professor know about it?"

"Yes," the patient answers, "they X-rayed it weeks ago, did mammography, thermography, the works."

"And?"

"The radiologist said it's a cyst, said I should hold my horses and drink a cup of tea."

"Why tea?" Trude asks with a giggle.

The Giraffe wastes his time shooting her a reproving glance and says brusquely, "We'll check it again on Monday."

"It's grown bigger," the patient says in a small voice.

"Since when?"

"Since I've been here."

"It's nothing," Trude says. "I feel it in my wee-wee. The breast's always a secondary carcinoma anyway."

"God give me strength," the Giraffe moans and clomps over to his chair, shrugging his shoulders and rubbing his forehead as he stifles a yawn.

"Why do you all wear clogs?" the patient asks.

"Because the amniotic fluid splashes over our legs when the babies are born." From the manner in which he says this, it's clear that he's supplied the same answer to the same question a hundred times already. Again he stretches his mouth open as wide as it'll go, showing splendid teeth and a tongue with no vestige of fur on it, his prominent Adam's apple jutting out sharply.

"Why aren't gynecologists all gay?" the patient asks, breaking the drowsy silence.

Once more the Giraffe jerks his head back and cracks it sharply against the wall; he stares in astonishment, as though someone had shouted "Fire!" then starts chewing his tongue, which doesn't improve his already bovine expression. "How do you mean?" he stutters feebly.

"Well, you can't possibly rummage around in vaginas the whole day long and then go home and do the same for fun."

Trude's breathing heavily, her bosom quakes and shakes, strangled squeaks struggle from her mouth and blossom into helpless sniggers. "I've never met one who's the other way around," she gargles delightedly.

The Giraffe, on the other hand, is showing renewed evidence of the delicacy of his upbringing in that everything about him that had once been salmon pink is now geranium red; even his hair starts to glow. "I know of no homosexual gynecologists," he says in a state of shock.

"What did I tell you?" Trude blubbers.

The Giraffe folds himself up and murmurs, "Well, have we got an allergy or haven't we?"

Trude propels herself to the door. Still sniggering, she says, "I'm through for today, and tomorrow's my day off. See you Monday then."

"We're understaffed to the tune of eighty doctors," the Giraffe sighs. "Eighty doctors too few. The state won't pay for more. Can't pay for more. The younger ones are on half salary. Madness."

"I wouldn't like to know what goes on in the third class after what I've been through here in the first," the patient says.

The Giraffe's thoughts are apparently still centered on the half salary; nevertheless, he says, "Sometimes the third's better. I knew a professor who always wore a tab around his neck which said, 'In case of accidents or emergency: *Third class.*' Then his appendix burst and he was taken to the hospital. They recognized him at reception and put him straight into the first class; by the time a top professor had been found to operate on him he was dead. Wouldn't have happened in the third, the duty surgeon would have taken him right away, no problem." He taps a cigarette on a worn leather case, opens the window, and puffs away furiously. "I've just bought an apartment. Paying for it over fifteen years. On this salary I can hang myself. And I don't think I'll ever leave the hospital again anyway, won't ever sleep again. I'd like to know who makes these decisions." He makes no attempt to disguise his anger any longer, veins swell on his forehead, forgotten ire bursts from the back of his memory. "In the last clinic I worked in, I was called one day to an emergency operation, fallopian pregnancy. I raced off and couldn't find a place to park my car, so I just left it in front of the hospital and dashed into the theater. We operated for hours and saved the woman, then I was told to report to the head of the clinic. He ranted at me, 'We too have to respect the parking rules,' and fined me two hundred francs. Would he rather have had the woman die?" He throws the cigarette into the courtyard and slams the window shut, his bleeper bleeps, absentmindedly he grins and inclines his head to one side, saying, "It's unlikely that you'll get an allergy now. I've given instructions to the night nurse, she'll give you cortisone should it still turn up." He stalks to the door pulling his bleeper clumsily from his pocket. "A sick person in our society is as exposed as a nonconformist in a dictatorship," the patient says. "A few doctors too," the Giraffe answers, and turns off the bleeper.

•

The patient is dreading Sunday. The hours slither and squirm like slugs, noisome, loathsome, smearing their slimy progress through the day. She tries to read but doesn't know how to hold the book without resting it on her sensitive belly; she props it to one side, grabs at a few sentences; they all seem to have been written exclusively for her, doom leers from very word. She lets the book fall to the floor. Streams of visitors flood the corridors: she hears the rustle of paper as they unwrap their flowers, they tap first on the outer door, then on the inner, subdued voices bubble up in delight, now and then there's a sob. The venetian blind flaps, the chestnut tree too, the sky's a brilliant pompous blue, too cocky by half.

The Mouse patters in noiselessly with porridge, bats her eyelids at every spoonful, stands there stiff as a ramrod, watches the struggle with every swallow, squeaks, "Just one more wee mouthful." The patient feels blown up; "I can't any more," she grumbles childishly. A little later her innards start jumping about, she begins to count the stabs and jabs that still sting so murderously. The door cracks open: a blonde superstar in a green smock is standing there eyeing her purposefully. She's as crisp as a rusk, crackling with power, incentive, and energy. High white boots she's wearing and looks as though she's ridden swiftly through a menacing forest. There's just a touch of rouge on the wide-pored skin of her cheeks, the eyes are brown and challenging; she reminds the patient of many of the physiotherapists she's had to engage to teach her daughter how to walk. The body-conscious swagger, the determination to enjoy it all, to take it as it comes, the *dernier cri* boutique clobber stretched over their muscular frames, the steely glance when any potent male appears on the scene, the spontaneously expressed opinions offered on every subject under the sun, the total collapse during the menstrual cycles, pills galore, ice packs to the forehead, frail femininity. There she stands, the frisky Frau Doktor, physiotherapist, equestrian; she speaks surely and unwaveringly, the voice is clear and loud, she might be addressing a hall full of the hard of hearing. "I shall change the dressings today," she announces and pulls back the bedclothes. The Mouse trundles the instrument wagon into the room. "Are you a gynecologist?" slips from the patient's lips; she knows immediately that the question has been booked as "impertinent" and that a lesson will be forthcoming. The white boots slap together, the green body stretches upward a few inches, the narrowed eyes zoom down as she says, "Would I be here if I weren't?" The Mouse chirrups contentedly. "Our professors have all flown off for the day," she squeaks, and red blotches appear between her scraggly eyebrows. The patient's heart grows less stout by the second, she sees the rubber-gloved hands coming nearer, she watches them as though they were a pair of rattlesnakes moving in for the kill; she feels the rip as the first tape comes off the troubled area and tenses to meet the variety of pains it unleashes in protest. "Professor S. told me you'd be coming today," she gasps, and losing a sharp skirmish with her pride, she adds, "I didn't mean to insult you." The horsewoman ignores her; she's screwing tubes and snapping clips, snipping tugging ripping, warming to the job. The patient starts to sweat, it courses down from her hair and makes a puddle at the base of her neck. "Tsk tsk," Frau Doktor clucks, "you're that sensitive?"

"Yes," the patient answers, "after a couple of weeks one grows soft."

"It can't possibly have been as bad as you make out," the liberated lady says and raises an eyebrow.

"Some patients are more sensitive than others, isn't that so?" the Mouse titters.

"Professor S. always administers morphine before changing the tubes," the patient says, getting more and more breathless.

"Quite unnecessary," Frau Doktor calls out poisonously. "One should be able to take a few little twinges without getting squeamish." She gives the dressing a final pluck and the patient howls like a hyena. "Keep still," the lady roars.

Bitch, the patient thinks to herself, goddamn bitch, and knows she's emanating for all she's worth. The gauntlet has been thrown down, battle can begin. She'd been to another lady gynecologist some years previously, the woman had examined her with the delicacy of a butcher. "Why are you so brutal?" the patient had asked. "As a woman you should know that hurts." "What hurts?" the woman had barked.

The patient's positive attitude to emancipation topples like a sand castle when she's confronted with the grim pacemakers, the give-'em-hell foragers, the incorruptible indomitable Amazons. She feels as uncomfortable in their presence as in that of "feminine" women, a term she always associates with petty intrigue at the court; softly purring diamond and mink devourers with a bone-hard plan for their leisured future comfort. She forgives them every degradation they ever brought and bring to the name woman when she sees the new pretenders to the throne, the rabid insurgents intent only on reversing the dictatorship instead of outlawing it altogether.

Christ's idea of charity doesn't seem to have gotten promulgated, the patient thinks to herself in a vacuous attempt at being cynical, and promptly starts to retch, watches delightedly as Mouse's porridge spatters all over the lovely green smock beside her. "Good gracious," the besmirched equestrian yelps and stares at the heap in her lap. "Do something," she hisses over her shoulder at the Mouse, who's standing gummed to the spot, fluttering her eyelids. "Hold a bowl to her mouth or something." The voice is like an electric saw. God help her children, if she has any; she'll talk of herself as the "reference figure," give them the smallest, easiest-to-manage room in the house; there they'll be made to play with sober contemporary games that develop their powers of logic and incentive, they'll grow up as guinea pigs trained according to the latest giant breakthroughs in making us all alike and colorless. Without so much as raising a hand, she'll drill them into becoming gregarious earth inheritors, she'll thrust them into the nearest kindergarten and scoff at the idea of children possibly not wanting to be surrounded by other bawling dwarfs the whole time, wanting instead to be allowed to choose, to be allowed to dream in a solitary atmosphere and escape the sterility and insanity of sensible planning. She will be convinced of the correctness of her revolutionary function but will still keep her son away from handwork, washing up, and vacuum cleaning, will uphold all the age-old masculine prerogatives on which she, despite all protestations to the contrary, is astoundingly dependent.

The patient feels as though she's sliding down greasy

smudged-brown walls. She feels as though she's been dumped in a caldron that's shrunk to the size of a rain barrel, the walls are wooden and covered with wet moss. Noises echo around the barrel, thin and metallic, like the sounds that used to come out of the wartime radios; they gather together and make martial music, tinny trumpeting raspberries threaded with static squeals; then the noise collapses, notes fall over each other and die away. "Pulse," Frau Doktor's voice peals into the barrel. A sourly stinking arm waves around in front of the patient's nose; she feels a prick in her hip and notes that her own left arm is waking up; it prickles as though someone has got the longest thinnest nerve on a hook and is pulling it ashore, firmly and obstinately giving a tug and then a jerk, unrhythmically, short then long, reeling it in, now her heart feels the stab of the hook, it's being hauled through her ribs— "Left arm," she crows and has a glimpse of the Giraffe before it grows dark, before the venetian blind, chestnut tree, and courtyard fade away and the pompous Sunday-blue sky narrows down to the glimmer of an emergency light.

•

"You certainly keep us on our toes," the Giraffe says as he injects something into the heart catheter.

"Is it my ticker?" the patient asks.

"Your what?"

"Ticker, heart."

"That too," he says.

"Where's the jockey?"

He laughs.

"How did you know who I meant?" she asks.

"She really does ride horses." The Giraffe chuckles.

"I messed up her smock and her Sunday."

"And it was to be my day off," the Giraffe says resignedly. "I'd planned to sleep." He puts everything he has into the word "sleep"—one can see him stretching, grunting, nuzzling the pillow, drifting away.

"Sorry," the patient says.

"Didn't mean it that way," he whispers, really concerned. "You been here long?"

"Since midday. The jockey called me in."

"If she handles her horses the way she did me, she'll be riding a bicycle before long," the patient says. He likes this; he waggles his neck, scratches his back with his long fingers, then a yawn puts a stop to the hilarity. "I'm glad you're back," the patient says simply; a couple of tears trickle down her cheeks, then she dozes off, glad he's back.

Olive turns up in the morning. He's taken extra-special trouble with his hair today. Keeps his distance. Trude's on duty. He turns his attention to the catheter, carefully peels back the tape, Trude rubs the clinging skin with alcohol, scrubs away as though it were the kitchen floor. One last tug and the tube slips out of the vein and coils up like a bloody snake, twitches down into the bowl, gives a shiver, and is still. One transfusion bottle less. The patient can move her arm again; she feels her body, feels the lump. Olive is very reserved, his mouth a thin cramped line. He strokes off the gloves and rubs his shapeless earlobe, pinches it, turns his uneven gaze to the courtyard, and unexpectedly barks, "Tape, nurse!" "It's already on," Trude purrs and grins maliciously. He picks up my chart with great deliberation, turns a page, looks up, and pauses, staring at some distant point, looks as though he's about to quote a poem by Goethe at least, clears his throat twice, and says, "Are you really still getting morphine?" The patient forgets all the niceties her finishing school might have taught her and says, "D'you make all this fuss because it's so cheap or because it really helps?" Olive slaps the chart down on the table and leaves with an enormous bang of the door. "I think we've seen the last of him," Trude chortles.

The patient discovers that the bed she's been lying in for so long is electric and that she can change her position by pressing a button. She tries it and rears up, leaving her tubes behind as though she were emerging through the beaded curtain of an Italian hairdresser's salon.

•

Gold Glasses breezes in that evening. "How was it?" she asks.

"Same as always," he answers.

"I don't know how it is any time."

"Everybody makes a speech which nobody listens to, then we all go to dinner, then we get drunk, then we go to bed."

"I've got a lump here."

"Shall we call a nurse or can I examine you alone?"

The patient probably resembles an owl in the way she looks at him.

"Please don't look at me as though I were in need of a psychiatrist. I have to ask you that."

"I may take it, I presume, that you have no intention of raping me through all these tubes?"

Yes, of course, she carries her one-armed freedom much too far, revels in the fact that her tongue no longer has to cope with catheters or drugs, and kicks the all-enveloping dread in its tenderest parts with everything she's got. Gold Glasses grins pardoningly and complacently but starts to fidget again, ease his throat—could it be that Gold Glasses has some hang-up here? some entanglement that needs attention? The patient carefully closes the blabbering cubbyholes of her mind and raises her shirt with her liberated left hand. Gold Glasses bends forward with closed eyes, feels the spot, and shouts suddenly, "These women!"

"What do you mean, 'these women'? I've been to mammography and thermography over and over again."

"That's not possible."

"It certainly is."

He stares at her indignantly, enraged, shouts at her again, "You're to go to mammography tomorrow morning, then a biopsy." He's a little late in noticing that his reaction is causing panic. Beside himself with anger, he beats the windowsill with the flat of his hand, clicks his teeth together, tries to control himself, and says with a frog in his throat, "The chief will be back tomorrow. We wanted to send you home the day after."

The patient is trying to check the shaking, which seems to start behind the knees and travels the length of her thin body before taking hold of her shoulders and head. " 'One has to have a fairly healthy body to be able to stand one's nerves,' a doctor friend of mine always says," she rattles.

Gold Glasses pats her hand, looks around bitterly, and hammers out his next words: "I'd arranged for a colleague in Salzburg to look after you. It's time you got out of here. Your husband has ordered a helicopter, a doctor will fly with you. Tomorrow morning we'll pull the tubes, the wounds will heal pretty rapidly. But you're not leaving till that's been checked out." He points with his index finger, then massages his wrists. Suddenly weary and disgusted with his own failure to behave in the proper implacable manner, he mutters, "Why didn't you tell me about it before?"

For a moment she doesn't know what to answer. "The others knew," she says finally.

"Ah well, it'll all work out for the worst," he grunts, and bends his head back, trying to get rid of a cramp. He goes stiffly, uncoordinatedly to the door, saying, "Forget it. I'll send you down a shot so you can sleep."

"D'you know that silly joke: 'If you don't think of a bear, I'll give you a thousand dollars'?"

Nonplused, he pushes his glasses up onto his forehead and stares down at her with four eyes. "Forgive me, I'm a little slow on the uptake today," he whispers sadly.

The injection doesn't put me to sleep; on the contrary, it does the opposite. I lie there wide awake and as taut as a bowstring, torn between exhilaration at the prospect of leaving tomorrow, of seeing my child, taking her in my arms, stroking her hair, feeling her hands around my neck, and the slimy, scalding, sickmaking dread of "You're not leaving till that's been checked out."

"Right here and now it's nothing," I say defiantly and loudly, then wait for a chuckle to come from a dark corner. Testing time, I think to myself, testing time for my nerves. Who's doing the testing? The patient begins to tick off a list of banner headlines: She's had everything, a full life, a rich one, success, failure; she's been kicked when she was down, picked up and dusted off, raised on high, pitched into the gutter. Love, fury, hate, love. "Happiness" she leaves out, the phantom that became a centaur. There's no denying it, they were after her skin from the word go—there was nothing personal about it, it just happened to that decimated German generation. I see the tank once more, see it careering over the prisoners, see my feet in Stepfather's boots squelching through the bloody clumps. My films of memory are silent, Berlin houses collapse without a sound, the Russian guns drum silently, showers of bombs puff up the dust as quiet as mice—the perforation rips. A new film: Mother's face as she stood at the airport the first time I flew to America; frozen, hungry, postwar shrinkage. She never saw her grandchild. Cancer metastases—the surgeon took one look and sewed her up again. "I can't breathe," she screamed and the nurse came rustling up, gave her morphine at last, at last, as if it were important whether she became addicted or not, whether it shortened her life or not. Fellow human beings? Anti-human beings. It's twelve years ago; in the meantime, a shot to the moon, space programs, Vietnam, laser, napalm, money—money they don't have for cancer—they're still back there where they started. "Research means finance." "The world's overpopulated anyway." And the venerable Swiss man of letters chats about euthanasia. Blah, blah for the healthy, the fitness brothers' club. They check out their lists of statistics and let cancer do the dirty work. "He/she died of cancer," they murmur, keeping the last word down to a whisper, an unkind stroke of fate it was; the calendar winds back to the Middle Ages, cholera, pestilence. How about introducing anti-cancer witch dances with incense and sacrifices to keep the plebs happy? Till then: Let them bawl themselves to death with their metastases, let them crawl off into a dark corner with that bellyful of lead called cancer, there are too many people anyway. That's what they say who still haven't got it, they put the fear of God into their grandchildren too, fill their heads with demented terror of longevity, issue pistols at the grand old age of twenty-five: Do away with yourself before you get it and become a burden. —"Not yet," the patient shouts, "my daughter's only five." "Who the hell cares, we're overpopulated," the darkness chuckles.

Twenty years ago, in New York, George S. Kaufman had sat in the empty auditorium with his legs intertwined as always and said, "My dear Hilde, there's one thing you must never forget in our business: The people in the audience are sitting on uncomfortable seats next to people they can't stand. It's drafty and they're not allowed to smoke, eat, or drink. They've paid a lot of money at the box office for all this discomfort and it's our job to make them feel privileged." The euthanasia propagators would have us believe that cancer is a privilege, that it's necessary, indeed imperative, and that it's up to us to see the positive, beneficial aspect. What was it that the emancipated journalist with the ape-look wig asked me as she scanned her list of prepared questions over the top of her tinted glasses, then tilted her head at me quizzically? It's a few years back—ah yes: "If you were to contract an incurable disease like cancer, would you feel that fate had been unkind to you?" Not that I was at all irritated, oh no, meekly I trotted out my opinion, civilly I tendered my points of view on this and other subjects, but it took a deal of control, for the bland lady tiptoed into the realms of metaphysics with the same felicity she'd displayed in discussing cosmetics at the outset of our meeting; fate, karma, reincarnation, cancer were neatly ticked off her list as she kept a cool eye on the control dials of her tape recorder and visibly showed her approval of my answers in degrees like a primary-school teacher: good—average—could be better—more industry needed!—does her best. I slip in and take my place in these strident choirs very easily, raise yet another dissonant voice which pretends to do its own thing and abhors the all-together-now limits of the standard melody, but which knows full well that you can't sing scat unless you know your way around the basic laws of harmony. Isn't that why I sometimes get bogged down in the spider's web of the small-bore cynicism I used to raise my nose at? Hasn't one corner of my mouth permanently drooped, and doesn't it stubbornly refuse to crinkle up again, even when the laughter's good and too silly for words?

"Does it disturb you to know that you're being marketed?" a sporty type with a beard blathered; he played tennis at a leftist club in his leisure hours. You need farm-fresh cowlike dumbcluck optimism in order to be able to communicate, hate and latent anger too. —Here's another: A conservative fella this time, tie and white collar; it was at a press conference and he'd seen it all, his service whipped over the heads of the fumbling novices: "Why do you write?" I unleash my retorts like greyhounds when I feel they've gabbled on long enough, but it's usually wrong, no, they prefer pauses; pauses lend weight to the shallow procedure, allow them to believe they've provided food for thought. (Example: The journalist asks, "How do you like F.?" Straight answer: "Very much." —Very wrong. Won't bring a thing. Try again. Journalist: "How do you like F.?" Knit your brows, breathe deeply two or three times, look him in the eye, and then: "Very much." Perfect.) Now then: "Why do you write?" Leave the pause, and then explain, truthfully, tell of the times of cramped deadlock at the typewriter, of the Cyclopean glare of the well-rested white paper, of how it can tell when the paralysis sets in. I've been pounding out these confessions for quite some time now, first about films and theater, then the record business, concert tours; now it's books and literature; I'm always ready to let myself be plundered for reasons and motivations, my moral and ethical standpoints, political too, of course. The princely freedom of writing turns into a corset and splits open at the seams, busts the suspenders. Once more the apewigged lady: "How can one bring children into the world today?" Who's bringing? Just because the abortion-law reforms have caused such a ruckus, we're not to have any any more? Not even one? —Now that we're against the pill and for abortion. Let them conceive, let them starve, let them have cancer and wars, God will look after them, last unctions and yet another slogan. The one demands uninhibited conception, the other the uninhibited pill, both demand that humanity inhibit itself.

Now wait a minute, I feel like hollering; but no, she doesn't holler, the ever-ready sponge, she needs their benevolent balsam, the comforting sparkle of admiration in their dumb dull eyes. "You've gained a lot of experience," says a puffy-faced gentleman in too-tight jeans who's almost certainly gained his initially at one of the elite Nazi schools, now a white unexplored terrain on the atlas of his life, brashly covered with pop shirts and chunky sideburns. "Experience," collected like rain in a barrel and scooped out in the last third of one's life, the cannibal finally eats himself. "What are your views on youth?" he continues, and means the babies that were inadvertently "brought" into the world not so long ago and who become a shrine of worship the moment they shed the vulnerability of childhood, stagger along under the burden of their irreplaceable puberty with its pimples, or the peaches-and-cream complexion the industry loves so well, and wake up to find that life, none too long to begin with, has been slashed up and stashed away into a dark chest of drawers, youth: top row, middle drawer.

Prosperity's disciples build careful bastions against age and change; they watch their weight as they stifle the burp, live in fear of the self-induced, avoidable heart attack, and, in this age of enlightenment, much prefer the shrouds of mystery surrounding the social necessity cancer, need the shivers it sends tingling up and down their spines, just as genteel ladies used to crave their little upsets in order to be able to reach for the smelling salts. They loll back in their protective aspic and gaze at the label clearly marked INCURABLE, let those affected believe in the callousness of the way nature's dice roll until their heads start to swim and their screams mingle with all the screams ever screamed by fate's hostages through the ages. They'll learn what goodness looks like with its mask off, and should they happen to be in a profession that has earned them fame and envy, then the mystery will become a precedent, a comforting confirmation that nobody's safe from the fickleness of fate. Thanks to the slipshod fashion in which research has been conducted up till now, our century has succeeded in reinstating a form of that ever-popular pastime: burning at the stake, coast-to-coast, worldwide.

•

Back in his youth somebody must have told the drum-major radiologist that he was "keen." Reeking of fresh morning air, piping hot coffee, and heady after-shave, he keenly plants himself in front of my bed and booms, "Now we shall see what's behind the hero's breastplate. Nothing can stop the Teutons. They died on their feet, riddled with arrows. You had to knock them over before you could bury them, the Teutons." The information misses its mark, his attempt to cheer the patient up ricochets off her wall of fear, causes her left eyelid to start fluttering. Trude comes in without her cap, her beehive higher than ever, doesn't dream of skipping her entrance spiel with the astonishment at finding the same patient still there. "Well, I never, what are my old ears hearing at my time of life? Don't tell me they want to take a sample?" she chimes. Now Kaiser P. saunters in, which is very odd for him; he's followed by Gold Glasses and then the Giraffe. "How was Moscow?" the patient asks. Kaiser P. musses his brush and whispers, "Oh, well," and "How are you?" His eyes flip back and forth, get caught by the Mouse, who's just come in, show no sign of delight, and flip away again. There's a hiatus. The Giraffe suffers nobly, squints at his bleeper, which doesn't respond. Gold Glasses fidgets, the Drum Major sniffs violently and irregularly, and the patient ransacks her mind for a suitable release. "Since you're all here, who's watching the shop?" is the best she can find. Gold Glasses exhales happily and mumbles, "Due to the celebrations of our proprietor's return, our workshops can only accept minor repairs today." Kaiser P. grins distantly but retains his worried aimless stance. They all stand there keeping as much distance between each other as possible and appear to sink into a quagmire of murky thoughts.

"Can I go home tomorrow?" the patient whispers with a promise of tears in her voice. Kaiser P. bolts to the radiator and sits down on it; it takes him several false starts before he finally says, "Professor S. has informed me that the lump—well, of course, yes, we'll do another mammography test and thermography, you are already acquainted with the procedure. At all events we can remove the catheters today and seal the wounds, it won't hurt . . ." His monologue peters out, he looks down into the courtyard distraughtly, compares his wristwatch with the big clock below, and takes several seconds to remember that the big one hasn't been working for some time now. He knits his brow, turns, and shoots for the door, whispering, "It's bound to be all right," dodges the Mouse, smiling frostily as she scuttles out of his way. His retinue follows him out.

The jungle drums have spelled it out; Olive sidles into the camp and says, "I will freeze the spot, desensitize it with ice, you understand? Then we will extract a few cells with the needle to see if they are malignant."

"I thought there was just going to be mammography?"

"Well yes, but afterward we will make the little test." He spreads his feet and folds his arms and is just about to go into detail when Trude comes in pushing a wheelchair. "Mind your backs," she whoops and runs a wheel over the tips of his Italian shoes.

There's a narrow bicycle track running between the meager bushes on the hill in front of the X-ray basement. A candy wrapper is drifting over the grass, a rubber ball rolls down out of the bushes followed by half a doughnut. Shrill children's voices and the insistent ringing of a bicycle bell penetrate the thick soundproofed glass, even drown the sharp monotonous commands to "Breathe in, hold it, breathe out." The Drum Major has adopted his introspective pose; the moment he sets foot in his domain he seems to lose all feeling for the connection between the solid patient he knows from upstairs and her transparent contents revealed on his screen; if you speak to him while he's peering at it, he looks up frostily, indignant at having been wrenched from a clairvoyant, translucent paradise into thick-skinned, dense reality.

Kaiser P. is sitting behind me. He's been offered a heavy rubberized apron against radiation, but declined tersely. I turn around and look at him. His nose is quite white and seems longer and bonier than usual; he nods at me and wheezes, "The Russian hospitals are very Prussian." He laughs mirthlessly and immediately pats his pockets, rubs his brush, checks that his smock is properly buttoned, as though laughing were a sign of disorderliness that must be set right on the spot. The Giraffe is leaning against the door, wagging his head from side to side. "Be careful that you don't touch yourself any more before the test," the Drum Major bellows. I sit there half naked, keeping my back as straight as possible in spite of the pain in my stomach. I concentrate on opening the sluice gates of my emanations and directing them at Kaiser P. I inform him that I shall leave the clinic, that I must leave, that what we are doing here is all a terrible mistake due to our frayed nerves after the trials of the past weeks, that we have programmed ourselves to catastrophe and are making mountains out of molehills. I wind up my message with "I'm going home tomorrow," and add a postscript that I'm reckoning with his help, fade out with a series of SOS signals. This is the first time that I've consciously emanated outside of my profession and the effort exhausts me. Sweat pours down my face and chest as I tap out a last "It's nothing."

The Drum Major stands up abruptly and wrests me from the depths of my telepathic drama. I give a jolt as though I'd been struck with a whip. "Our nerves are not what they were," he says and slaps my shoulder. Trude wraps me up and wheels me to the door. Once more I hear the thin children's voices and see two red ice-cream cups sail down the hill.

Trude is markedly silent on the way to the elevator; she carefully pushes the wheelchair over the ridge and then murmurs, "If they allow you to fly, we'll have to strap up the incisions good and proper; you'll need something for the pain as well." She searches her arm for her watch and says, "It's really too bad that I'm always hungry." Two women stare at me in the passageway and grab Trude's elbow. "Isn't that . . .?" they giggle. Trude blocks the attack and snaps, "Let go of me, for God's sake, you can see she's not up to the mark," and quickly heaves me into my room.

The Mouse creeps in right away. "Is there any news?" she pipes. "No," Trude rasps and drags her out, coming back alone with a full syringe. Then she sits down, lays her chubby hand on my arm, looks gloomily at the graying chestnut blossoms, and says, "They'll be over the hill soon too . . ." She gives only a slight start as she realizes what she's said, probably relying on the muddling effects of the injection. "Only neurotics refuse to accept the fact that something's irrevocably over," I say. Trude looks at me blankly. "Try to sleep a bit," she says.

We hear the outer door click open, hear footsteps and voices; the inner door flies back and Kaiser P. chases in, followed by Gold Glasses and the Giraffe. Kaiser P. grips the foot of my bed and hisses, "A cyst. Quite big. Clearly outlined. Nothing to worry about. We'll advise our colleagues in Salzburg to have a look at it again when you go in for your first checkup. They might puncture it and examine the cells. Until then, have a good rest. You can go home tomorrow."

I forget my belly and everything else as I let my body fall forward over the bedclothes, my stringy clotted hair dangling around my face and covering my eyes. I feel myself being engulfed by a surge of emotion which I coolly and contemptuously despise but am powerless to stop; the more I try to control the deplorable gulps, the bigger and worse they get. "Forgive me," I try to say, but only succeed in making animal-like guttural noises.

The three of them stand there and present a perfect picture of male helplessness. They've become mere men instead of doctors, the professional shell has shattered and they've not a clue how to deal with the geyser of emotion gushing from the bed. Kaiser P. is the first to try his hand. He moves gingerly up to the bed, taps the patient on the head with his index finger, says, "We're going to take the tubes out and patch up your stomach now," and stares down at her apprehensively. This suffices to break the grip of her cramp-like sobbing. She pulls back the bedclothes, only whimpering a little now, and looks up to find three heads shaking at her. The Giraffe points his finger at the door, stalks over to her, takes her arm, and leads her across the corridor into a room opposite, peering about all the while as though he were leading a bleeding buddy through no-man's-land. He helps her clamber up onto a table and says, "The professor does it wonderfully, it won't hurt a bit." A stick about the size of those big matches one uses to light an open fire approaches her. The fear that "patching" means burning and searing turns out to be groundless. She feels nothing other than Kaiser P.'s light delicate hands, under which the tubes and stitches seem to evaporate. The right instruments are handed to him at the right time without him having to say a word; very soon he says, "Finished," and smiles at her with such utter exhaustion that one would think he had just completed a major operation. The patient sits up and says, "You saved my life. If you hadn't decided to operate a second time that night, I would have died. What does one say to one's savior? Thank you? Just that? Thank you?" Kaiser P. is perplexed, bright red seeps into his forehead, spreads down to his cheeks. A little light of joy starts to flicker in his eyes but his embarrassment doesn't allow it. It appears to be none too easy to accept sincerely felt thanks, especially when you're Kaiser P.

•

Trude's beaming as she packs my things. She pulls out my fur coat and boots and says, "My God, that shows how long you've been here. What on earth are you going to wear tomorrow?" The Giraffe brings in packets and bottles of pills and test tubes, tells me what to take when, and then adds, "By the way, I'm flying with you." Trude fetches a plastic bag with an anti-airsickness injection for the flight, a box of morphine ampules, and fresh dressings. The room looks like a druggist's during inventory.

"My nerves gave way, didn't they?" the patient says. "Once before too, while I was in the intensive."

"Yes," the Giraffe says in surprise. "I didn't think you'd realized it."

"I'm afraid, it frightens me. I'm afraid of the split—one knows all about it but can't do a thing to change it. The same as with . . ." She was going to say "cancer."

"Have you ever flown in a helicopter before?" the Giraffe asks, obviously excited by the idea.

· 185 ·

"No," she says, "I've been in everything from one-engined grasshoppers to jumbos, but never a helicopter."

"Me neither," he says and seems relieved. "We've ordered a cot. You can't sit up the whole way."

"When do we leave?"

"At nine o'clock," he replies and grins shyly.

"I'm beginning to believe it," the patient says and falls asleep immediately.

•

Once more the ensemble goes marching by as at a curtain call in the theater. The Drum Major strides in rubbing his beefy red hands, raises his stentorian voice in mock menace: "If I catch you back here again . . ." and reminds me of those robust comedians whose faces are always easy to recall but their names never. He's followed by the minor but recurrent character of the Persian belly dancer, resplendent this day in a see-through chiffon blouse. For the last time she pricks my finger, squeezes my punctured hand to wish me luck, and waggles to the door under the malignant eyes of several sisters. Now Erna—thinner, yellower, more of a mess than ever. A wreck, her husband has just completed a trip to Paris and taken to his bed, demanding Erna's undivided attention. She bursts into tears the moment she enters the room, gulps a handful of Valium tablets, and lights up a cigarette with a violently shaking hand. One doesn't need a crystal ball to predict that Erna's heading for a sticky end. The next, more than surprisingly, is Olive. He oils his way in, words drip from his mealy mouth, he's more the ham Iago than ever. Our little chat might well have fooled an outsider—Olive avows his relief and delight in the results of the mammography tests to such an extent that one would think two bosom friends were taking painful leave of each other, not the inquisitor and his prisoner.

Barbara doesn't show up. The patient inquires after her and hears that she's left, is on her way to India and the waiting dog. The Mouse keeps her distance too; she probably never runs the risk of a thin final-curtain accolade, prefers to squeak her malice at those who can't yet run away. A nurse comes in and declares that she'd been present during the first operation, which the patient can hardly remember at all, even so they shake hands as though they've been linked in perfect harmony for many a year. Now Leopoldine; she's stayed on after her night shift in order to say goodbye and give grandmotherly words of encouragement. "Should you ever come back to Austria . . ." the patient says. "Ah yes, I'm bound to one day," Leopoldine replies, and goes off to bed to gather strength for the next endless night. A stream of uniformly clad bit-part players are directed in and smartly out again by Trude, who stands in the middle of the bedlam like a traffic cop at rush hour. Outside, the morning battle is raging, the patient is truly grateful to be able to slip from her foxhole. Trude shuts the door firmly on the last of the well-wishers, leaving us alone to finish our preparations.

Now she starts to wrap me up. She fastens bales of cotton to my stomach and begins to circle around me unrolling yards of bandages, so that my middle section gradually resembles the trunk of a tree. "If you bump into anything it's all over. Better be careful than sorry," she mumbles as she goes on winding. She gives me one more injection, then takes a list from her pocket and listens intently as I recite what I should take at what time of day. Finally she gives me a letter for the professor in Salzburg and takes her leave simply and sincerely. I sit down on the edge of the bed and feel more and more like a child being sent off to rich relations for the summer.

Two nurses the patient feels sure she's never seen in her life before now appear and maintain they were present at both operations and that these were "no joke for anyone, that's for certain." The patient lowers her head in shame and assures them that she's dreadfully sorry. One of them goes on to relate the torments she'd suffered with the patient on her first night in the intensive; if she were to sit down and write the things patients say when they come out of the anesthetic, it'd make pretty interesting reading, she adds meaningfully.

The room fills to bursting point again, they all stand around as though they're wanting to say goodbye but don't know how;

they stammer and stutter, and the situation begins to resemble a railway station with people waving handkerchiefs at the receding train. The bold clear lines that have guided the finale till now waver and then break up altogether as the actors shed their discipline and start improvising wildly. Just as the injection begins to make itself felt, Gold Glasses comes in, says adieu curtly, and withdraws like a psychiatrist who's determined not to get emotionally involved with an increasingly dependent patient. He shakes hands with her and they look at each other briefly, neither of them too sure as how to end the shake or the look, so finally they just turn away from each other at precisely the same moment, he already busying himself with the new patients and the new operations awaiting him, she trying to contain her rising excitement at the prospect of freedom.

•

The helicopter was in the farthest corner of the airport. Sitting in the middle of Boeings, Douglases, and Ilyushins, it looked no bigger than a bumblebee. Due to the persistent wave of terrorism and hijacking, the airport was full of armored cars and jeeps loaded with soldiers in camouflage outfits. Even though the reason for the display of military alertness was clear, it was hard to believe that one was at a commercial airport in a neutral mid-European state. The sight of all this had a strange and sudden effect on the Giraffe. His whole body stiffened, his shoulders went back, and his profile became sharp and daring; in short, he turned into a captain before my eyes. I could see that he was dying to salute and was inwardly cursing the casual civilian clothes he was wearing.

We were checked and double-checked at the gates, then allowed to proceed onto the tarmac. Our taxi driver, who had been most uncommunicative all the way from the hospital, suddenly woke up at the sight of the soldiers and planes, leaned out of his window ecstatically as he followed the takeoff of a giant jet, and forgot the steering wheel altogether until the Giraffe clapped him on the shoulder, causing him to wrench the wheel so violently that we drove straight into a wire fence. There was a lot of shouting, several soldiers heaved the taxi out of the entanglement, and we set off again, only to be stopped by an armored car, its driver insisting that we were trespassing and banishing us from the field. Back at the gates we were issued new writs and directions for finding the bumblebee without coming into conflict with the army, set out again, and, with the help of the Giraffe, who now barked his commands like a field marshal, finally found the insect sitting behind a large fuel truck.

A young man in jeans was leaning against its slender body yawning desperately. The Giraffe got out and went up to him resolutely, fairly bobbing on the balls of his feet, and began a shouting match with the screams of the jets. After a good deal of gesticulating, he came back shaking his head, helped me out, led me over to the sleepy young man, still shaking his head constantly, and introduced him as the pilot. The young man raised his arm in a form of salute and pointed to the inside of the insect, where a bench the size of an ironing board was situated. "You'll have to sit, I'm afraid," the Giraffe yelled unhappily and rolled his eyes up to the sky. "There's no room for anything wider," the pilot yelled back. "When I pick up people who've had skiing accidents, I strap them to the runners outside." I said I didn't think I'd like to spend two and a half hours strapped to the runners outside and would sit on one of the tiny bucket seats behind the pilot. He reached in to pull out the bench and slipped on a patch of oil, banged his head sharply against the edge of the door, and staggered back, grabbing my hand and pulling me with him as he sank to the ground. I would have gone down too had the Giraffe not reacted like lightning and pulled my hand away. The pilot was now lying in a pool of blood with an ugly deep gash in his forehead. The Giraffe raced to the taxi and got the first-aid kit he'd brought along for me, hurried back to the pilot, and set about examining the wound. While I hung on to the side of the bumblebee, desperately trying to cope with the effects of the morphine I'd received before leaving the hospital and an increasing desire to throw up, the Giraffe supported me with one hand, cleaned the pilot's wound with the other, decided that it didn't need stitches, patched him up with tape and bandages, and washed the clotted blood from his hair with alcohol. The pilot sat up, crossed his legs, and stared vacantly at our feet for quite some time, looking like a meditating guru in his turbanlike headdress. Then he got to his feet and stood there swaying giddily, lurched away as though someone had given him a push, staggered around the bumblebee like a drunk who's trying to show that he isn't, swung himself up into the pilot's seat, and signaled for us to get in. The Giraffe shouted, "You're in no condition to fly, you've lost too much blood!" The pilot shrugged his shoulders, adjusted his earphones over his headdress, and yelled, "Fasten your seat belts but good. We've got a storm warning, I'll have to hedgehop."

"She can't wear a seat belt," the Giraffe hollered and pointed at my tree-trunk belly.

"Then she'll have to hang on to you," he yelled back and switched on the ignition. The bumblebee seemed to explode; it heaved and shook so that I thought it would fall apart; the tiny seat I was sitting on bucked like a berserk dromedary. "Good Lord above," the Giraffe cried and tried to press me down onto the seat.

I looked out of the window and saw Olive. At first I thought that my eyes had been shaken out of focus and were playing tricks, but then I noticed that the Giraffe had caught sight of him too and was staring out of the window as though transfixed. Olive was standing behind the wire fence and staring at the helicopter with both hands raised to his eyes to shield them from the bright early-morning sun. Without the hospital green, seeing him for the first time in normal clothes, beige jacket, brown tie, baggy trousers, with his immaculately combed hair flying around his forehead, he seemed smaller, humble even, almost pitiful, like the little people who flock to the airports on Sundays and gape from the terraces.

The bumblebee suddenly shoots straight up like a rocket, hovers for a second, and then whips away sideways; Olive shrinks to a point the size of a pinhead between the armored cars and camouflaged soldiers.

With the lift-off I am filled with a sense of defiant, vengeful, exhilarating, delirious joy—I've made it! I've escaped! I'm over the wall and on my way, it's just like 1945, when I escaped from the Russian prison camp; a little wearier now, warier, a little more worn, but the appetite's still there, the same lust for life, the present you don't look in the mouth, the new chance, reincarnation.

We chop along over the town, over a lake, over boats; the bumblebee rears with the storm, describes semicircles, bobs over hills and treetops; for the first time I experience fear in the air, see my unique chance ending in a heap of burning metal. The Giraffe moans dreadfully and goes green; tears stream from his eyes as he grabs a paper bag and stares fixedly at the back of the pilot, who's staring desperately at the map lying on the seat beside him. With a snort he picks it up and passes it over his shoulder to Giraffe, yelling, "Have a look and see if you can make out which river that is down there." The Giraffe knows his way around maps, immediately forgets his air sickness, and starts barking commands in a highly imposing manner. This doesn't change the bumblebee's highly erratic flight, however; it bucks and careens; we're so low that I can see faces turned up to us laughing. They seem to think we're putting on a show for their benefit.

Six years ago, I was in a Trident jet which was struck by a silver-red ball of fire as big as a pumpkin; it ran down the fuselage and hit the tail, knocking out vital components of the steering mechanism. The plane dived toward the telegraph poles and pulled out just in time, while I raised my knees and crossed my arms over the three-month-old embryo that was to become my daughter and whispered, "Not yet—not yet, please." The landing gear refused to function and we landed on a carpet of foam, dislodging things in my spine but, mercifully, not in my womb. "Not yet." —Years before this I'd been in a rattly old Constellation that had coursed through a fearful storm for hours on end; it had been flung upward, then dropped like a stone; that had been like being trapped in the gullet of a snoring belching giant. —Once, over the wastes of Canada, three of the four engines had failed and the plane had limped on ruefully; everyone but me had thrown up, and if looks could kill I'd have found an early grave, but it didn't trouble me in the slightest at that time. I weathered the storm and the looks in the certain knowledge that my contract said nothing about crashing or dying young. —Two years ago, my reaction was different as the Caravelle thundered on and on down the runway at 7 a.m. in Helsinki and should have lifted up long ago but still didn't. The pilot brought it to a halt within touching distance of the birch forest and said casually over the intercom, "One of our fuel pumps hasn't woken up yet." We eventually took off for Turku, in the southwest of Finland, which, when we got over it, was blotted out by the thickest fog I've ever seen, but nobody gave a damn, least of all the pilot; we went straight down into it as though it were a fine summer's day in Nice. Then once over the Irish Sea, with raindrops like grains of rice slashing down the windows, the captain's very British voice informed us that "various parts of the airplane aren't working." —Oh, and the test of valor in the Swiss mountains. The pilot flew up to the tip of the Piz Palü in the tiny two-seater, single-engined plane, landed on the glacier, told me to get out and wait for him but not to move— "There are lots of eagles, and wide crevices under the snow"— then flew back down to the valley to pick up the photographer. I sat there shivering and clutching a thermos flask for three quarters of an hour; then he came curving in, gave me a sign that I should still not move, and landed within an inch of my nose. "Not yet." I remember quoting Strindberg while I was waiting: "If it weren't for the fear of death, we would never have had a spark of life in us at all."

"We'll have to refuel," our turbaned pilot bellows, "we'll never make it to Salzburg." The mention of Salzburg doesn't stir any feeling of belonging as yet. But it'll come, when the house is finished, when we can move in, when there's water, light, a bed . . . It's on the same degree of longitude as Berlin, exactly the same, due south.

We swoop down toward a corner of Lake Constance. The bumblebee hops up, settles down, stands on its wobbly knees, appears to breathe out. I feel my belly, the pilot feels his head.

"How are my patients doing?" the Giraffe asks and laughs a hollow solitary laugh. The bumblebee hops up again as though somebody'd kicked her in the backside and comes to rest exactly in front of the fuel pump. We get out creakingly, feel our way into the brilliant sunshine, and run into the arms of a substantial customs officer who sets about taking us apart.

Then we sit in the shade of a tree, light cigarettes, and the Giraffe says, "What on earth was Olive doing there? Looked like a gnome . . ."

"No idea," I answer and, without knowing why, ask, "Is mammography reliable?"

"Yes, of course," he answers, and looks down at me in astonishment.

We stroke our bumblebee, talk to her like a good, overworked horse. The rocketlike start doesn't surprise us any more, we shoot up into the cobalt-blue sky, dip to the east, peer down in disdain at the crowded freeways and chockablock lakes, rock gently on the waves of a summer storm toward Salzburg's empty airport.

Exhaustion and pain don't have a chance against my buoyant joy as I step down onto the promised land where a man and a child are waiting for me. Not the terrifying house David's rented on the Wolfgangsee, not the dragons, Libby and Bibba, not even the necessity of crawling right away into one of the damp beds can spoil the perfection of this day.

"In three months we'll be in our own house," David says. The end of vagrancy, the beginning of stability, a new life, a new chance. There's a sharp cry from outside; the Giraffe has trodden on a good-size snake. He flails away at it with a rusty spade, draws and quarters it, vivisects it with a surgeon's steady hand; its jaw still snaps open although the head is severed, long pieces of its black and yellow body slither around in the pool of blood.

"Nice house," Giraffe says as he shakily takes the glass of whiskey David offers him. David sweeps away the remains of the still-twitching snake and says, "We regard it as a displaced persons' camp, we'll be out in a couple of months." Queasy rumblings are going on in my stomach, dark thoughts of bad omens hammering in my brain: Olive at the beginning of this bright-blue day and a snake at the end. I straighten up and shake off the superstitious associations that have started milling around my head and now see my surroundings clearly for the first time. The hideous antlers, hunting trophies, windows and corners are fairly clogged with cobwebs. "Doesn't anybody do the cleaning?" I ask. David shrugs his shoulders and waves his hand disgustedly, picks up the bottle of whiskey. The dragons come in with a girl called Rosa they've engaged to help in the house. Rosa is young and brazen with long slender legs. She immediately throws herself at my feet and begins to sob wildly, "I can't go on any longer, I have to do everything alone, it's too much . . ." A sharp kick in the backside from one of Libby's convex shoes puts an end to her histrionics. "That's enough of that nonsense," Libby barks. Bibba darts her avian profile from side to side. "Get rid of the slut," she screeches, marches over to one of the dark windows, reaches through the curtain of cobwebs, and brings out a bag of nuts. "Gurr gurr," she croaks, moving to the French window. She opens it and a gang of squirrels spring into the room, jump on the tables and chairs as Bibba starts throwing nuts around. The Giraffe picks up our daughter and watches the performance with an expression of horror; David slumps down into a lumpy leather chair and narrows his eyes dangerously. Feeding time at an end, the dragons suddenly turn on me and yell, "We're not Aunt Klara." "Who's Aunt Klara?" I ask stupidly, missing the point. "We're not cooks and we're not charwomen," they chant simultaneously. "We're used to giving interviews now." They exchange triumphant glances; Libby pulls at one of her loose ears and snarls, "First of all, we need a car." At this moment a van drives up to the door and a woman gets out carrying a hair drier. "Ah, there's my hairdresser," Libby barks contentedly.

"Am I going crazy?" I shout, forgetting my raw scars.

"Libby has to look good for the press," Bibba cackles.

"And who pays for it?"

"You, of course," she giggles and marches over to the door, the antlers and cobwebs swaying as she goes. Libby turns to follow her on her stovepipes and is brought to a sudden stop as David, very softly, says, "Out."

"What?" she calls out loftily, without turning around.

"Out," David repeats, just as softly as before.

She spins around wildly. "Just you try it," she says. "We're here for good and you'll have to lump it. Or do you want to read all about your private life in print? I'll set the lawyers on you if you turn us out; we're in a social welfare state, don't you know that? Bibba and me, we're being exploited, workers are protected nowadays, just you wait and see what the courts have to say about it, just you wait." The house creaks, the stuffed swans shed a few feathers. "That's what you get for doing your best and helping people," she bellows dementedly. Andreas peers around the door, Rosa cowers behind him, chewing her nails. Bibba comes marching back to the rescue. David gets up suddenly to his full height and shoos them all from the room, bolting the door behind them.

"How long has this been going on?" I ask him.

"I really can't tell you," he answers grimly. "Christina and I are hardly ever here. We go to the building site at seven in the morning and often sleep in a hotel."

Bibba's hammering at the door. "She could have been a millionaire, you're forgetting that!" she shrieks. "Just you wait!" roars Libby.

Doors slam, suitcases are hauled through the dark passageways, a taxi comes and goes.

"Who were they anyway?" the Giraffe asks, refilling his glass.

"Friends, helpers, fellow human beings, paid enemies," I say listlessly.

"While we are about it," says David after a heavy silence, "the man we bought our house from is in trouble with the tax people. Some fraud or other. When I went to sign the papers and look at the land register, I discovered that they've attached all his property to the tune of three and a half million schillings. I decided to start building anyway, I've found a good lawyer and we'll work it out somehow."

"You seem to be especially lucky with people," the Giraffe says.

A fuse blows; David and the Giraffe blunder about in the dark knocking over elephant tusks and tables as they search for matches and candles, Christina lies beside me asleep, breathing steadily, occasionally snorting softly.

The Giraffe takes his leave in the morning. "Back to the treadmill," he says shyly and raises his arm. "The professor from Salzburg takes over today."

My daughter leads me to the antediluvian toilet, each of my steps senilely uncertain, each of hers a reminder of the circumstances of her birth. "Tell me about the time you had polio," she says. "I had polio as a child," I tell her, "and when it was over, my left leg was shorter than my right one. All the other children laughed because I had such a funny walk, but they didn't laugh long. 'Think quickly, but don't walk quickly,' I always told myself. And a friend of mine called Henry Miller told me a story about a famous geisha girl one day. The girl was attacked by a madman who cut off one of her arms and slashed her face with a sword. A year later she was even more popular than before." Christina listens reverently, her magical face shining up at me.

A big shiny Mercedes comes crunching up the gravel driveway that afternoon. A tall man gets out, fumbles with his keys, leans back into the car, shuts one door, opens another, finally approaches the house. He stands there puffing and blowing as though he'd run a mile. "Hello, hello," he says loudly, "I'm the rearguard action." The patient and the professor—ex-submarine commander—shake hands. "Good Lord," he says, as we walk down the dark stag gallery, "how on earth did you come by this? It's not what I'd call ideal for a convalescent patient."

"It was the best we could find at short notice," the patient replies. "We'll be moving into our own house in a few weeks."

"Well, well, let's have a look what my Swiss colleagues have sent me." He removes the dressings and blinks. "Jesus Christ," he says, "that must have been quite a carve-up." He bends forward to examine the scene more closely. "And the incisions are acutely inflamed," he booms. "You'll have to stay in bed a few days, no walking about, complete rest." He stands up, mutters, "Gracious me," waddles over to a chair that collapses the moment he touches it, mistrusts a second, and carefully lowers himself into a third, sits there sipping a whiskey and surveying the wreckage, then says, "It's a pretty kettle of fish, my word."

"I've got a lump too," the patient says; "it's been tested though, mammography and all that." He screws up his face as though he'd swallowed a foul oyster. Undaunted, the patient continues, "They said it's a cyst, nothing to worry about, but that you should keep an eye on it in case it gets bigger."

He clears his throat and gets up again. He feels it, squeezes it, taps it. "No, no, no, mammography is not enough, we'll do a proper examination of the tissue," he mutters and shrugs it off with a chortle. "Let's get rid of the inflammation first, then we'll see about the rest. We'll give you a good anesthetic and make a tiny incision, only takes a few minutes, but then we'll know where we stand. Mammography . . ." he blubbers deprecatingly and blows into his whiskey, spilling some.

"I could live without another narcosis," the patient says numbly, "I've had fifty-four already."

"Your very good health, madam," my U-boat commander says, raising his glass.

•

Three weeks later our friend Martin helps me into his VW jalopy and we drive to Salzburg and the hospital. David is at the house, directing the construction crew; clad in high army boots, old velvet jeans, and a beaten-up hat, his daughter in his arms, he's in his element. There had come a point when we'd tacitly agreed that a marriage can stand just so much of clinics, the visitor's chair beside the high narrow bed, the well-tended sheets, glittering washbasins, kidney-shaped bowls, and the habit of looking past each other as we say, "It'll soon be over" and "It'll all work out for the worst."

We'd called Martin and he'd shouted, "I'm on my way!" Martin always shouts on the telephone, for the first few minutes at least, then he gradually gets off his happy high horse and settles down to normal volume. (With us anyway, perhaps he stays up there with others.) His normal volume is quiet, understanding, the ends of his sentences are either turned up in a question mark or dropped altogether; in between he lobs the tenor of the conversation up on high, pulls all the stops of his profession. Martin is a priest, descended from a long line of Bavarian priests. "We're a pretty good couple," he once said as we caught sight of our reflections in a shop window: I, the insurgent evangelist, and he, the faithful but obstinate, hairy, refractory, and critical Catholic.

Martin steers his VW as though he were sitting behind an old and incalculable nag; he leans back with his arms stretched straight out in front of him and his head stuck forward, ready for the worst. As always when I look at him, I see him as he must have been when very young, an infant almost—his unobtrusive straight nose with the rounded point and the dark-brown eyes that dominate his face give the impression of a being that has never been taken to task, and is endangered for this reason; the fact that his hair is thin and his cheeks and forehead are deeply lined can't change this impression. The other people in my life, with the exception of my daughter and my husband, appear older than they really are. Their skin, however smooth, seems to suffer from the way they neglect their fantasy, and grows slack and stale, their faces drawn or swollen—the exceptions here are few and far between but have undoubtedly set the standard: the enjoyment of experience, of whatever type, reflected in the bony skull of Henry Miller, or the sumptuously upholstered face of one great German, Carlo Schmid. All other faces seem to tarnish in front of my eyes, lose their shape, and go into a huddle.

Martin wipes the sweat from his face, the sun blinds like a brute spotlight trained exactly at us, we stutter along behind a tractor pulling hay. "I don't believe it," he says. I don't feel like talking. I've talked myself out of fears and tensions all my life. ("You never said a word as a child," my mother had once said. "Whenever somebody asked you something, you clammed up." Am I coming back to that? End of the line? Circle?)

"What don't you believe?" I ask, wanting to know nothing of ends.

"That it's what they think it is," he says.

I sit up and hunch my shoulders. "Why do you avoid the name?"

"You're right," says Martin, with no sign of balsam, "but I still don't believe it's c—cancer."

"I read somewhere that Catholics have fewer heart attacks than ordinary people," I say. "They even proved it. Or is it a campaign slogan?"

Martin grins and dodges around the tractor. Coming toward us and not too far away there's a yellow bus. He looks suitably surprised, brakes, changes gear, almost kills the engine, smiles apologetically at the purple bus driver, and says, "It's a good idea."

"Do you have less cancer too?"

"I'm afraid not," Martin answers and starts to sneeze dreadfully, our course of progress matching the convulsive explosions.

"The Mormons have a head start on you, also according to the books." Martin makes a search of his pockets, no doubt looking for a handkerchief. I hold on to the wheel. "I need a fight," I say.

"Let off steam," he splutters, "that's what friends are all about, or am I wrong?"

"You could be right," I say limply; he's taken the wind out of my sails. "If it'd only rain, it might be easier," I say and laugh.

"What's the matter?" he cries and stares at me, forgetting all about steering wheels.

I hold on to it again and excuse myself. "As if cancer would be easier in the rain."

"You haven't got it, for God's sake," he cries, wielding the whip. "After they've done the operation, you'll come up to my house with Christina and stay there until David's finished yours."

"People will talk if I come without my husband."

Martin laughs uproariously and turns the wrong way into a one-way street and nothing happens.

It's Wednesday, August 8, 1973. As always I'll be operated on on a Thursday. I've always tried to dodge Thursdays but it's a losing game. They've had it in for me, the Thursdays, even in my childhood they took on a laughable but unshiftable importance. At school the teacher I feared most took the last period on Thursdays; she invariably ignored the bell, made us sit out extra time. The first big air raid was on a Thursday, the one that shook me out of all my childish anxieties. The very first operation I had, at the age of thirteen, was on a Thursday. Later, for many years, they settled down and became solid ordinary weekdays. I never noticed them in the film studios and they had no special importance in the theater—except in New York, there the Thursdays labored under the strain of Wednesday's two performances, and yet held a promise of respite, one could count the hours till Sunday, our day off. But with operations there was never any doubt: Thursdays. Christina's day in May, a week later when the stitches came apart, the last one and the one before last, with an interval of seven days, from Thursday to Thursday. Was I put in the prison camp on a Thursday? I don't know, we'd lost all sense of time, didn't know one day from another. And the day I escaped? I'll never know. But I do know that they'll operate on me again tomorrow, Thursday.

"Are you in pain?" Martin asks.

"There where they cut me already, yes, but not where they're going to."

"There's nothing to beat good health," he says and tries to light a cigarette.

"You can't drive in here like that," the gatekeeper bawls at us in front of the hospital. "Please keep your trap shut," Martin says sweetly and treads on the gas. The old man waves his arms and runs after us; a nurse appears, intercepts the gatekeeper, bends down to my window as far as her bosom allows, and says excitedly, "I've been expecting you, I'm Sister Erasta." Puffing and blowing, she runs ahead, waving her short arms like clipped wings, showing us the way to a parking place. There is only one and it's extremely narrow; Erasta tries to guide us in with gusto but it soon becomes evident that she's no great shakes at it; she throws up her hands and looks desperate as Martin shunts backward and forward, jumps up and down ecstatically when it looks like we're on the right track, claps a hand to her mouth as we graze a fender. Finally Martin succeeds in wedging us in, but the doors won't open. Erasta squeals and sobs, we start again from the beginning. It's getting very hot, and by the time we reach the cool entrance to the gynecological department, Martin and I are bathed in perspiration. Not so Erasta. She throws the door open with a grand gesture and then steps aside as though she were ushering us into the Presidential suite at the Ritz. She crinkles up her eyes and whispers, "You've no idea how thrilled I am to look after you. Tickled pink, I am. Now, you take your time, I'll be back in a while." She manages to make the dreadful act of moving into a hospital room cheerful and gay, even the high metal bed looks inviting, holds no threat of operations and pain.

She's hardly closed the door behind her when a laming sadness befalls us. I sit on the edge of the bed, Martin leans against the wall mopping his dripping forehead. The venetian blind has been let down and creaks as it sways back and forth, knocking against the open window. Through its slats we can see a terracotta church, the sky is a violet blue, colors that belong to a hot summer's day in northern Italy. "Shouldn't you get into bed?" Martin asks and is suddenly at a loss. A mighty sneeze sends him reeling against the table; "Good heavens," he sniffs as he tries to ward off the next.

"A French physicist has just announced after a lifetime of study that everything's coincidence," I say.

"Did he define coincidence?" asks Martin and releases the next salvo, his eyes now as red as a rabbit's.

"What do you think?"

Martin shakes his head, crosses to the washbasin, and holds his face under the tap.

"I envy you your ritual," I say, feeling belligerent again, bloody-minded.

"The ritual's of secondary importance only, perhaps even pagan," he says underwater, "and not necessarily in keeping with Christ's intents. Many see him as a rebel, the truth is a little more complicated. At all events, he represents a challenge to authority. In the Church and in government."

"Would you say something like that at one of your company's board meetings?"

"Why not?" he says and pulls his head away from the tap.

"Then I envy you all the firmness of your faith."

He waves his handkerchief at me. "You're confusing faith with dogma."

"What I hate is your power."

"We seem to be doing everything we can to lose it," Martin says and lays the wet cloth across the back of his neck.

"Your tariff's too high and your greed insatiable. You've been caught out."

"Perhaps now we'll become Christians again."

"You don't become a virgin when you stop copulating."

Martin laughs and sneezes at one and the same time.

"And not one of you had to pay for your past crimes."

He slumps down exhaustedly onto a chair and says, "Every great thought has its inquisition. It might be better if the thought were to be restricted to a small community, then it might remain intact." He chuckles absentmindedly and adds, "Virginally intact." He suddenly jumps up and calls out, "When you leave here you're coming to stay with me at the presbytery, and if you're willing I'll give you Holy Communion at an evening service."

"You'll be excommunicated," I say, very impressed.

"Not on your life, you underestimate them. And I hold you to be a Christian." He moves to the door and murmurs, "I'll be back tomorrow. Don't be too brave."

Memories crowd around my bed, the gray oblong and fading chestnut blossoms blot out the violet-blue sky and the terra-cotta corner. The window's to the right here too, the washbasin and the door to the left. It seems to be the hottest day of the year. Erasta gallops in and fizzes, "How are you feeling? Can I do anything to help?" She hangs my linen pants lovingly over a hanger, beams at them, and says, "I'd give anything to be slim again, anything."

"Why don't you have air conditioning here?"

"The professor won't have it," she says and rolls her eyes. "It brings in the bugs. We haven't got it in the theater either, especially not there, we haven't. They all sweat like—" She chortles and corrects herself, "You've no idea how they perspire."

•

Ten days later Red Fluff, the U-boat commander, and Erasta lean over me, peel off the dressings, and pull the tube from my armpit. "Don't look," they all cry out together.

I look very determinedly.

"What are you doing?" Red Fluff cries excitedly.

"I'll have to get used to it, I hope."

"What does that mean?" he babbles, bending over my armpit.

"It means that I hope to live."

All three start growling like a pack of frustrated hounds. "We found it in time," the U-boat commander booms in his dark-brown voice.

"A couple of cells always escape," I bleat obstinately. "The only question is whether my ill-treated body can cope with them."

"We found it," Red Fluff echoes.

"You have to forget it. It's going to be all right," Erasta says softly.

The blood-red streak, held together by black threads, runs diagonally across the ribs and disappears in a Y shape under the shoulder. Erasta raises my arm and for a moment the pain quells the shock. Strange, I feel no regret, no tears drop for the loss of beauty; I feel physical pain, but it's manageable, and fear. I'm scared stiff of the disease and its inscrutability, its enigma, I'm very much afraid of death.

The beauty is no more, of course; the body which had always

been sick and intractable but passionately, head over heels, in love with life is beautiful no longer. A stream of high-sounding pompous words break into her thoughts, words like "branded," "disfigured," "marked"—strange, they're no longer important. Her bosom had been small, widely spaced, no brassiere had ever fitted, had ever been needed; it had been firm, supported by reliable strong muscles. The muscle's gone too, and what about the arm? She can't move it. The reflections on her lost beauty are laughable compared to the dread, nothing but memories; her "beautiful" bosom hadn't even served its purpose when Christina was born, the milk had been contaminated by the transfusion and medications, they had shot her full of hormones until the bosom contracted to even less than its normal size. "Too many hormones at once can be a decisive factor in activating a carcinoma," Red Fluff had hazarded, but he wasn't sure. The word "mercy" is now blinking at the back of her thoughts. She spells it to herself, trying to find the meaning in the vowels and consonants. She looks down at her body, the uproar subsides, the alarm it has caused ebbs away. Calmly, to all outward appearances, she looks down at the scars on her flat, sunken stomach, then at the diagonal slash with the black stitches. It was beautiful, she thinks, the long back and wide shoulders, splendid bosom, narrow hips, long thighs, the neck a little too short, the legs from the knees down too. People had hardly noticed the shortening that polio had caused. It was this body that had launched the first big scandal after the war; she'd been the first to appear naked on the righteous postwar screen. She smiles.

"That's more like it," the U-boat commander murmurs and heaves a sigh of relief as he picks at the stitches.

"One might almost think you were looking for fleas," she says.

"These Berliners," he says, trying an awful Berlin accent. Red Fluff chimes in: "I had some in my regiment, don't talk to me about them."

Her body seems truncated; absurdly, she feels that it doesn't belong to her at all. It's a hell-raising component that's always been a menace. She can't identify with it—sometimes it had carried the burden, at others it'd been she; sometimes it had fallen down on the job, at others she'd been the failure. They have an odd relationship. As far back as she can remember, they had been bound in insidious fellowship, just how odd and insidious only now becomes clear as she stares at the livid scar, which is hideous, she must admit. Perhaps the schizoid alliance began with the calamities in her childhood, with the polio, rheumatic fever, ruptured appendix, and broken bones, perhaps they decided it was the best way of dealing with the increasingly perfidious attacks. We have a bond that may be broken at any time, by either party, she thinks to herself. She sees her body as a stern and sadistic private tutor who is unwaveringly bent on self-destruction, but who is capable of springing a delightful surprise, of protecting her against the disciplinary punishment inflicted on her by their common overlords, the professors.

"You've got a nice case of hepatitis," the U-boat commander had said last night, "and masses of coli too, a pretty kettle of fish. And my Swiss colleagues still haven't sent me their report on you. How much did they remove when you had the ileus?"

"I neither saw it nor measured it, nor did they tell me any-thing. In case it interests you, I've got gallstones too."

"Why didn't they take them out while they were at it?"

"They had enough on their hands with the other."

"True enough," he says and splits his face from ear to ear in a smile.

"One would think that everything else would leave one in peace when one gets cancer. It only seems fair."

"One would think, you're right," he says and quickly clears his throat. "Now listen, you don't have it any more, we re-moved it. O.K.?"

Red Fluff patches me up again. "It's a relief to get rid of that reptile under your arm, isn't it? The tube, I mean." He looks up and smiles at me. "Everything's fine, no abscess, nothing."

Erasta dodges out in what she hopes is an unobtrusive man-ner, skips back in again holding a carton behind her back. When she thinks I'm not looking, she passes it to Red Fluff. He stands there rocking on the balls of his feet, strokes his imaginary hair, hems and haws, looks unconcernedly out of the window, then at the commander and at Erasta. The bakers' aprons rustle. Taking a deep breath and nodding his head, like an actor running through his opening lines just before his entrance, he swings the carton from behind his back, holds it out like a present, beams haphazardly, and says in an unnecessarily loud voice, "You'll be able to wear the most risqué dresses with this. No one will notice a thing if you wear . . ." He struggles to get it open, lays it on the bed. The words TRUE LIFE are printed on the lid. I reach for it and a tiny squashy cushion filled with air, or water, embroidered with pink lace, falls out of the box. The bakers' aprons rustle again, their bearers shift their weight from one leg to the other, Erasta is scrubbing the washbasin, drying her hands thoroughly, retying the belt of her smock, testing the tidiness of her bun. At last she seems satisfied and folds her arms over her mightily protruding bust. Erasta's breasts reach out into the room despite the sharp starched white creases encasing them. They seem to gain size and importance as the patient looks at them.

"Thank you for thinking of it," she says with convincing ease. They all start talking at once. Red Fluff runs up and down, the U-boat commander sits up as straight as a pole and beats on her hand mechanically. Their enthusiasm grows in leaps and bounds. "No one will have the slightest idea . . ." "We've had women before, you'd never believe it . . ." "And you'll get used to it much quicker than you think . . ." The cascades of words come tumbling down.

I look at them, one after the other, intact people with intact bodies. A foretaste of not belonging any more, of being on the other side of the fence, slinks in. Erasta is standing as though she's been soldered to the floor; she stares squarely out of the window, what seem to be hiccups grow louder and more frequent. She turns around resolutely and says, "I've still to get the operating room ready for the morning," and runs out. Red Fluff waves a hand, blinks his eyes, plods after her, and says, "Be back in a minute." My commander tugs at some loose skin around his throat, scratches beneath his jaw, sniffs, "We must look pretty dandy, sweaty, unshaven, a sight for sore eyes." Then, quite simply, he says, "It wasn't easy for us either. Nobody likes these operations." He gets up and wheezes, rubs his buttocks as though he were having an attack of sciatica, groans and grunts and wades to the door, turns his head toward me, fumbles for the knob, and suddenly bellows, "I'll look in again in about an hour." The patient says, "I'm sitting on a time bomb and I know it. Most of the others don't know it."

"Eyewash," he says, disgruntled, "that's no sort of talk for a convalescent. If we didn't have hepatitis, I'd say we ought to get drunk tonight."

"I slowly start to wonder what else I've got left that could possibly give up the ghost."

"We've got lots of adhesive tape and gauze." He grins and goes out, his creased smock swishing through the slit as he quickly closes the door.

•

"There's somebody on the phone who says he's the Cherokee from Ireland." The head nurse is standing in the doorway with the telephone under her arm. She plugs it in, looking very confused, then stands up and stares questioningly, amusedly, at the patient. She says, "Who?" and "Oh no" and "Oooh yeees!" takes the receiver, and says, "How the hell did you know I'm here?"

And there it is, the deep voice spluttering wonderful things erratically, relapsing into sleepy wide Maryland English, plowing through every language it has at its disposal to pep up a thought or an exchange which might otherwise grow boring. In answer to my question, he laughs his gurgling laugh; it's proud and means well. "That's my job, for Christ's sake!" It's Jim, the Irishman from Washington, D.C.; Jim, who wouldn't harm a fly, with his streaked flaxen hair that always looks as though he's just pulled a wet comb through it, but which soon bunches up into a tight mass of curls at the back; Jim, whose bright-blue eyes twinkle through a permanent blaze of hangover-red;

Jim, the sentimental cynic, old pro of the best American journalism, religiously stalking that phantom prey, objectivity, drinking too much and managing it well, waxing poetic in the bars at night, as is the custom of his forefathers and of people who are too often alone, writing at night, sleeping little and badly in the mornings; Jim the rover, systematic and pedantic in his work, infatuated with the inconsistency of the German character, in love with Berlin, above all its elevated railway, always riding it, never in a car. Jim, Berlin correspondent for the worthiest American journals, has been working on an interview with me for the past eleven years. We meet at irregular intervals and he's written down the outcome of our conversations in a number of neat pads that are piled on a shelf in his apartment: on the rare occasions his subject visits her hometown she's usually rushing around like an egg beater. Jim, whose honor and integrity must have cost him a lot of scoops, always and only calls when he hears that the going is bad. "I'm an old irascible Irish Catholic and I've just been down to light a couple of candles for you. The question is, how bad is it?" he asks in a mixture of Berlinese and Maryland. I wonder for a moment: Shall I tell him? I don't owe the truth to anybody. But who would I tell it to, if anybody? To Jim. I tell him. He grunts and groans, coughs heavily, asks sillily, "You still there?" and then, after another pause, says, "Christ Almighty." More grunting and groaning.

"Can you put an end to these animal noises?" I ask him.

"How long d'you have to stay in the hospital?"

"Two or three weeks."

"I'll write you every day."

"What's new in my fatherland?"

This wakes him up. "You wouldn't believe it. I bumped into one of your quaint newspaper publishers yesterday, you know, one of those left radicals with houses in Hamburg, St. Tropez, and the North Sea islands, well, we got to chatting and d'you know what he said? After I'd ventured to question the German habit of sticking a knife in the back of anyone who gets his foot on the first rung of the ladder to success, he turned around and said, 'We conform with the German mentality when we criticize and negate. You fair-play Americans will never understand us. We're against, not for. Whatever it may be.'" Jim laughs, splutters, and coughs, gets over it, and chuckles on: "So the sadomasochism's still intact. Your fatherland's got more laws than order; if you write with humor it can't be literature, if you bore the shit out of people you must be a great thinker; the nouveau-riche explosion has doubled and tripled, to each inhabitant there's at least one manager, every pickpocket has an image, still no sign of a capital city, and Bonn is deader than the proverbial doornail. The vocabulary gets more Anglicized by the day, the United States is as misunderstood as ever, there's a marked trend to the right, and I'm writing a book on Adolf's last days in the bunker with the title 'Germany's Underground Leader,' but nobody wants to read that sort of thing anyway, and I don't give a damn if I'm right, as our Bavarian friend Ludwig Thoma once said."

"When did we see each other last?" I ask him.

"Berlin, at the Philharmonic," we say, overlapping each other and then, perfectly synchronized, "It can't be true." Jim guffaws and adds, "Our memory and the oil sheik's money . . ."

"Time's running out and we botch up what we have more and more. It's like doing a concert tour or going to the dentist— let's get it over with, the next one's waiting . . ."

"Prussian, very Prussian," Jim says half praisingly, not at all unfond of the Prussians. "Did you know your last TV show's on tonight?"

"I'd forgotten. I've forgotten the profession. In the meantime, I've made a new career. I'm now a patient, doctors' property."

"Get back on your feet and go to work," says Jim. "It doesn't have to be a tour, but get back to work."

•

Jim's done it. He's shaken up the patient's professions like the sediment in a bottle of wine.

One of them started off so harmlessly, like for fun. The carefully concealed, lethal mantrap: singing. Not one tone that came out of her throat could be called brilliant, nothing, if one disregarded the words she sang, to stagger the ear at all; there was a small hoarse voice of limited range, musically fair-to-middling, sense of rhythm not too bad. What she had to offer was again the emanation of her thoughts and emotions dressed up in a cascade of words, coupled with a soupçon of self-irony and a telling dash of sentimentality, served with the experience she'd gained as an actress. After hitting the jackpot with her first records, she sat down and began writing the lyrics herself, made a hugely successful concert tour with a friendly five-man combo, then asked herself, Why not? and set out again, this time with a big band, seventeen men with trombones trumpets saxophones clarinets drums bass guitars and other noise-making instruments. They gathered together and went on the circuit, five years ago. David produced and directed. Their child was just six months old. The seed that was to shoot up into a tour of hospitals and into a verdict slumbered peacefully, hidden behind ragged scars.

12
.

The rehearsals began just as all rehearsals begin. Not at all. The participants stood around sniffing each other. The first steps toward a musical performance of any kind seem to be born under a sad and sloppy, droopy star; only the singer, she who'll be thrown out alone in the circles of light at the still far-off premiere, has any feeling for the twinges and tweaks, a premonition of the murderous things to come. The others will scratch themselves, yawn, horse around, lay spread across chairs like zombies, bored stiff, talk about their tax returns, or just sweetly and simply succumb to the enmity that daylight hours represent for purveyors of jazz. That's when they take place, rehearsals, during the day, usually mornings, nobody ever bothers to ask why. Since they're all jazz musicians, they'll react to the presence of the actress-turned-singer in a manner which is either hale and hearty or dire and morose. The songs she sings are called chansons in Europe, little stories where the lyric is more important than the music, melody and rhythm serving the word; so why the hell does she need jazz musicians? they'll ask. It's David's and her idea to try a new fusion, but they can't know that. This she accepts. For the moment jazz and the word are in separate camps.

If one sits down and concentrates on imagining the worst possible surroundings for rehearsing a musical show, it's never as bad as the rehearsal rooms one actually lands in. They stink of cold cigar and cigarette ashes, beer, schnapps, and greasy sausages. Opening the window never helps; the atmosphere they exude seems deliberately created to deaden the chances of men and women coming together to trip the light fantastic by means of instruments, voices, and words. Acoustically too, they're constructed in a fashion which is the exact opposite of what's needed; either they suck up the sound like sponges and give nothing back, or they are like caverns, swallowing the notes and digesting them with great ramblings, which fizzle off like the dying buzz of a fly that's tarried too long.

One after the other, the musicians slouch into the evil-smelling hole. One naked dusty light bulb hangs over the rickety dais; spread around the floor are flaccid balloons, paper streamers, and dragons that roll and slither about obscenely with each draft from the door, thick cups with opaque remains of coffee, cardboard hats, and funny noses, with and without the specs attached, piles of spindly chairs stacked on top of each other. Although the singer has seen a lot in the way of dirty dressing rooms and backstages, she's not quite sure where to begin with this one, starts by lighting a cigarette in an effort to banish the smell. With a jump she remembers her touchy, cricketlike voice, kills the cigarette, considers the possibility of sitting on one of those chairs, decides against it, and settles down to a standing wait.

The European musicians come up and shake her hand, the Americans say "Hi" and keep their distance. A young trombonist grins mischievously and rips off a chorus of "Getting Sentimental over You" at full blast, shaking the dust from the light bulb. The drummer raises one finger and starts building his battery of drums and cymbals; he goes about it with an air of bitter determination, as though faced with the prospect of putting a totally wrecked automobile back on the road. What one can see of his skin between the masses of black hair and beard is light green, the color of young cucumbers. He doesn't seem sociable at all, neither greeting the musicians as they pass by his construction site or answering their polite inquiries as to how he's doing, just goes on bitterly turning screws and joining rods. Now he swings onto his stool, adjusts the height, picks up his sticks, and batters a furious tattoo, stops abruptly, leans back, and opens a book of crossword puzzles.

A lofty saxophone player comes up to the singer, mumbles "Hello," waves a long arm in her direction, allowing their hands to touch briefly, attaches his saxophone to the strap hanging from his neck, and blows a superb run, ending with a rasp like a shot from a cannon. He lowers his instrument; nobody else has taken any notice at all, only the singer chuckles softly. Egon, the tall orchestra assistant, comes in. Egon has the function of sheepdog, chief secretary, bouncer, waiter, is needed everywhere by everybody at the same time. Egon, no stranger to rehearsal rooms either, stands in the door, takes one look, and roars, "Who the hell rented this?" Nobody answers as Egon sweeps in muttering to himself; he opens a cupboard on the wall, throws a switch, and three fluorescent lights flicker to life, leaving no detail of the ghastly room unilluminated. Egon is wearing a suit of the finest matinal gray, in sharp gentlemanly contrast to the general jumble of T-shirts, sweaters, baggy jeans, and corduroys. Egon unfolds a spotless white handkerchief, rubs his face and hands as he watches the pianist make his entrance. His eyes become very alert, as though he were preparing himself for the worst. The pianist is a tiny man with crinkly dark-red hair. He stops in his tracks at the sight of the piano and stares at it as though it were a rotting corpse, advances cautiously, and lifts the lid as if expecting serpents and vampires to come hurtling out at him. For a long moment he stands motionless, then carefully raises a hand and strokes one of the yellow-brown keys, then a black one, then pulls up the stool and sits down charily, like a man with a carbuncle on a sensitive spot. He kneads his hands, lowers his head over the discolored keys, plays an arpeggio, and rears back, looking about him uncertainly. He catches sight of Egon, whose breast is proudly swollen. "I ordered a tuner this morning, I did, now you've got nothing to complain about," Egon calls out to him. The pianist still looks uncertain, but raises his right hand with the thumb and forefinger forming a circle. Egon nods in satisfaction and swaggers to the door like a sailor, muttering that it's time to see about the morning beer.

A young man who is shaped like a cooked asparagus struggles up onto the podium, carrying a slender bass guitar which seems to weigh a ton. Just as he's about to collapse, he finds a chair and sinks down onto it, holding the guitar like an umbrella. He looks around blindly, leans forward, and launches himself to the edge of the podium, grabs an enormous amplifier which is standing there, and drags it back to his place on all fours. He lies there puffing for a few minutes, then picks up two extension cables and starts searching for an outlet. After inspecting all the walls within reach of his cables, he gives up, slumps back to his chair, and pulls several bags of health food from the pockets of his caftan; he picks at the grains and seeds like a ravenous canary, letting his pale-gray eyes travel around the room. He catches sight of the singer and blinks, stops picking for a moment, looks away and then back again; the memories of the many recording sessions they've done together seem to be coming up like a slowly rising tide. With a small gleam he says "Hi," and raises the hand with the bags in it a little way, lets it sink back again weakly. The singer approaches him as one should approach a debilitated patient: carefully, quietly, feel-ingly, making no sudden gestures that might frighten him. When she gets close enough she hears him breathe, "Oh, man, I've been off speed for a month now, no pills, not even a joint. I feel terrific, wheat germ, nuts, and sunflower seeds, really great."

The woodwinds file in. They're all old hands, well-kept, with rosy complexions, steady reliable pros. Behind them: Hansi Hammerschmid from Vienna. Hansi is blinking furiously, which means that he's extremely nervous and tired too. Hansi's car-riage is the standard one common to jazz musicians all over the world: the body bent forward from the waist with the arms and shoulders swinging loosely, as though the bones had been removed. Looking at his chubby child's hands, it's hard to believe that he once was a first-rate pianist, touring the world with the best American jazzmen. For some years now, Hansi has turned his attention to composing and arranging with great success, has built a fine house near Munich, and settled down. Hansi tends to obesity and wages a constant battle with his expansive waistline, going on regular diets, which he abandons after forty-eight hours. He now lollops bonelessly across the room, drops a great heap of sheet music onto a greasy table, spreads his arms as he turns to the singer, blinks, and says, "What d'you think of that? I've lost five pounds." She congratulates him enthusiastically, even though he looks just as fat as ever. She and Hansi are a team, they write her songs together, and like most teams, their relationship is subject to violent fluctuations, short bursts of sheer hatred interrupting long periods of serene rapport. He runs a hand through his thin blond hair, screws up his forget-me-not-blue eyes, and beams, his broad face looking ridiculously young as he does so. "Where's the maestro?" he asks softly, with an undertone of sarcasm. The bandleader, he means. "Let's hope he's not stoned already," he adds, loosening his alligator belt. He hoists himself up onto the table with a great sigh. "We work too much. My old woman . . ." he says, rolling his fluttering eyes, referring to his young and attractive wife, "my old woman never stops nagging, her mother dropped by and stayed six weeks, the kids drive me crazy, my taxes are overdue, and the record company doesn't do a damn thing for our discs." Except for the blinking, his expression as he says this is positively radiant; he continues his tale of woe and the singer ascertains that Hansi is still as mad about his family and life in general as ever a Viennese can be.

The maestro now enters through a side door nobody has used till now; he's wearing a long flowing gown of an overcoat which billows out behind him as he lurches with short uncertain steps across the room and climbs onto the creaking podium. He seems to be sucking something, with his lips protruding, like a baby sucking its pacifier. A kind of spasm sweeps through the band. The drummer's skin turns a deeper shade of green, the second sax player bends forward and fiddles incessantly with his shoelaces, the pianist takes a dirty cloth from his pocket, unwraps it, and extracts two blue porcelain eyes, lays them next to the keyboard, and starts talking to them; everyone is fidgeting and fumbling except the bass guitarist. He stops picking at his seeds and stares at the maestro with parted lips and a puzzled frown, as though trying to remember where on earth he's seen him before. Within seconds it becomes all too clear that the band does not love its boss; some of the musicians make no attempt to hide their contempt, others react obsequiously to his commands, which is astonishing, for each and every one of them is first-rate and would be difficult to replace. The whole band is permanently employed by one of West Germany's biggest radio stations, and the musicians, after insecure years of freelancing, have sold their independence for a long-term contract plus pension, provided the boss keeps them on.

He raises his dainty hands with their overlong polished nails and strokes his hair, which is white and has been silver-rinsed and conventionally cut and looks very out of place among all the wild beards, Jesus- and Afro-looks. He has stopped suckling now and his mouth is set in what one might call a "smug" smile. His nose is short and unimposing, his chin weak and receding; the eyes alone, large and droopy like a basset hound's, begging sympathy and understanding, relieve the overall impression of affectation. To get things straight from the outset, even this seemingly endearing feature proves misleading on closer acquaintance; the only really positive thing one can say for the maestro is that he has the courage to leave his hair white in a profession which, in Europe, is totally devoted to youth.

He lurches over to the singer, suckles again a little, and delivers an astonishing opening gambit. Peering up at the light, he says, "Do you know if it's correct to say 'adaption,' or should it be 'adaptation'?" Without waiting for an answer, he continues, "You'd be surprised how many people say 'adaption,' but . . ." He stops and raises his first two fingers, looking for all the world like St. Francis of Assisi; "strictly speaking, 'adaptation' is the proper word," he concludes confidentially and enjoys the stupefied look on the singer's face. "And another thing: do you know whether it's correct to say 'promiscuousness' or 'promiscuity,' and if so, how do you spell it?" With that he turns away and gives Hansi's pile of scores his undivided attention. A massive Negro with a flute comes in and ambles over to the dais; "Hi, boss," he drawls as he passes the maestro's table. The maestro turns a page of the score and shows no reaction, then leans over and whispers into the singer's ear, "Have you read Durrell? Or Genet?" "Both," she answers; "now that you mention it, that's not such a bad idea, I could go on and give a series of readings instead of the concert tour. Much better. Only where does that leave you?" Archie—the maestro's nickname since playing for the British troops in servicemen's clubs after the war—is not amused. His carefully planned opening round, demoralizing, no doubt, for jazz-oriented band singers, has not had the desired effect. The fight will go the distance, every point will count.

While they've been sparring, the band has been getting increasingly bored. They unwrap sandwiches, reach down for the beer bottle at their sides, smoke, sticking the cigarette in the holes of their flutes or saxophones while they eat or drink. Egon moves from desk to desk distributing the sheets of music; he moves on tiptoe, avoiding all unnecessary sound. The bass player gazes at his part and cries, "Man, oh, man," nodding his head in Hansi's direction. The drummer suddenly crashes out a roll and smashes the cymbals, finishing off with a comical, exaggerated effect with his brushes, as though announcing a striptease act. Archie whips around and glares at him like a furious schoolmaster, but the drummer has already stuck his green face into his crossword puzzle. Egon looks up, stares at Archie, and hurries to the door. As he passes Hansi he mutters, "High time. When he starts chewing like that, he needs the bottle." He's hardly out of the door before he's back again, a bottle of Vat 69 in one hand and a tumbler filled to the brim in the other. Archie looks at the glass with apparent loathing, turns away as though he were about to vomit, then shoots out a hand, quickly brings the glass to his mouth, and pours the contents down his gullet in one draught. Hansi shouts, "Any chance of starting today?" which means that he's ready to lose his cool. Archie considers for a second, then lurches over to the metal washbasin and starts to wash his hands; he rubs and scrubs and washes for what seems like a sheer eternity, one would think he'd been down in a coal mine.

Archie's tactics succeed in bringing even David to his feet. Until now, our producer has been sitting, or lying, with his long legs spread over three chairs, in the background, smoking peacefully and unconcernedly, his attention riveted to the sheaf of lyrics he always carries in his hand. He moves up to the podium, gazes over the seventeen heads, and raises the hand with the cigarette to his ear, clearing his throat as he does so. Only Hansi and the singer know that this means he's profoundly irritated. "Shall we try the opener?" Hansi yells, putting it as a question, since the opener, a purely instrumental number, is the bandleader's business. Archie staggers back, drying his hands, stares intensely at the score, and whispers, "Opener." He sheds the towel and starts to tap the palm of his left hand with the index finger of his right; one shoulder goes up, his feet turn inward, not one musician looks at all interested as he now starts to count: "Ah—one two three four, one two three four," and goes on in this vein repeatedly until suddenly all seventeen men start playing at precisely the same moment. "Jesus," the singer says, not in love with the rhythm at all. Hansi listens for a few bars, then murmurs, "He must have learned his timing on the parade ground." Both are startled by a withering look from their producer. The singer is used to Hansi conducting the band in the record studios, used to his hunched back and easy countdown: "One and one and two and three and three and four and go." Once they're off, Hansi leans away and leaves them to it, beating the rhythm with his fist and turning back only to stress an accent or lead in a new section, whereas Archie stands right in front of them, hopping up and down on his toes and staring at them intensely. After watching him for a few more bars, both Hansi and David begin to look very nervous. Archie waves his arms in wild sweeps as though beating off an attack of hornets; the palms of his hands are a brilliant red, raw, unpleasant to the touch, which, the singer-patient thinks to herself, would indicate a long-term liver disorder.

"There's something wrong there," Hansi calls out loudly, "let's check the brass parts." Archie starts to suckle again, he's looking more piqued by the minute. He and Hansi examine the score for wrong notes, find them; Hansi comes down from the podium again. "The musicians are great," he says, "but Archie—wow."

"I might as well hang myself," the singer says.

"Give it a little time," Hansi answers.

They get through the opener and come to the first song. "Go up and sing it in his ear so that he gets an idea of the tempo," David says, towering over the singer. "From the top," Hansi cries.

For the moment we have no sound equipment; it and its engineers will come when we've run through the whole program. Missing too are the lighting technicians and the singer's dresser, Moritz. Her real name is Angelika but somebody called her Moritz at sometime or other and the name has stuck ever since. Moritz is young and plump and pretty, has a husband she can't stand and three children she adores; on account of the husband she likes to go on tour; on account of the children she cries at least once every day and spends most of her salary telling them long bedtime stories over the phone. Moritz does the singer's hair, makes her up, and sees to it that her stage dresses are always immaculate. More important, Moritz is a Florence Nightingale of the road, helping everyone through the torment of the tour. She'd been on the first stint the singer had done with the combo and is now an old hand in the music business; she's even learned the language from the American musicians, says "Cool" and "Crazy, man," which sounds quaint with her Salzburg accent.

The singer climbs up beside Archie and sings as loud as she can. Hansi joins them and leans toward her, listening. "You're way off, lady," he says and grins. Archie starts waving his arms again and the drummer suddenly comes to life, which delights

Hansi but not Archie. He taps on his stand and brings the herd to a halt, leans forward and starts to shout at the hirsute and green American in unintelligible school English, divesting himself of his liverish wrath. "They all get on each other's nerves," says Hansi and shrugs his shoulders. "Life in a big band is hell."

David reserves his opinion. "The English are playing it cool as usual," says Hansi. From the way he keeps rubbing his ear and chain-smoking, the singer knows that David's anything but cool. That he moves to the door whenever spoken to is added evidence; he places his hand on the doorknob, turns as if to go, listens to whoever's complaining, nods or shakes his head, and disappears. He's moved into his evasive phase, is intent only on keeping his objectivity, avoiding the danger of making precipitate decisions. For the moment his job is limited to determining the order in which the songs are played; the detailed work with the singer, the orchestra, the electricians, trying out entrances and exits, stage effects, etc., will follow when the band has mastered the scores. He'll be infuriatingly gay and optimistic when the singer enters into her black period, seeing nothing but catastrophe winging toward her; his icy self-control and endless patience will drive her either up the wall or sobbing into Moritz's comforting arms. But Moritz is nowhere around and panic still in the embryo stage. The singer busies herself with counting the milestones between now and the premiere: first of all, they must record the whole program for a double album. The studio's booked in two weeks' time, her record company wants to be on the market before the tour begins. Then, after the final series of lighting and dress rehearsals: the premiere, the deluge, end of the world, failing vocal cords, defective mikes, wax-polished stages, control loudspeakers with faulty wiring, the gaping, curtainless monster which is the concert arena.

They're taking five. The pianist practices a run, rests his elbows on the keys, lets his head sink down, and takes a nap. "Helluva cat," says Hansi, meaning that he's satisfied with the piano player, and trots over to the vacant drums. "Gimme an A," he says, not shy to ply one of the hoariest chestnuts in the business. The pianist raises his head wearily, stares at his blue-eyed marbles, absentmindedly hammers out an A, and then sinks down again. Hansi dispiritedly rattles off a roll on the drums, then slides down from the stool again.

"O.K. now, let's get with it," Egon cries and claps his hands. Seventeen men trample across the podium yawning and scratching their backs; the brass players blow short blasts on their horns, Archie quickly downs a second glass and says "Three," he wants to rehearse song number three in the pile of thirty. There's a pause. The drummer's not there. Archie stands completely still, looking at his shoes. The door opens and the drummer wanders in with all the time in the world and settles down on his stool without a word. Archie regards his shoes for a further long moment, then jerks back his head and begins his enervating countdown. Little blue-and-white blisters are puffing up on Hansi's cheeks, a sure sign that Hansi's not quite himself any more; the effort to suppress his discontent is playing havoc and causing water retention. "The trombones are not in time," he mutters, waving his arms. Archie stops and says, "Check your parts at four bars before B, B for Bessie." "Bessie, Bessie," Hansi snarls, "they weren't playing wrong notes, they were dragging, for Christ's sake." The singer feels more and more redundant in this cockfight. She sings along, more to get acquainted with the arrangements than to make any earnest attempt at phrasing; the band can't hear her, nor can she hear herself, except when she raises a hand to her ear like a deaf woman.

David wanders in again and says, "There you are!" as though we'd moved since he'd last seen us and he has spent hours tracking us down. The opposite is true, of course; he's the only one who's been anywhere, but it's his station identification, his method of signing back in, no one will change it any more, even the band musters no more than a nod.

The singer jots down notes on key changes, orchestra choruses. She's still at that stage where the marvelous arrangements give her the feeling that nothing can go wrong, they're good enough on their own. She purrs along with the slow numbers, cuddles into the romance, the up-tempo rhythms lift her out of her seat, scatter control to the winds, make her a slave of the big-band magic. One thing is alarmingly clear and she's used to it: The songs she didn't write are difficult enough to memorize, but her own are almost impossible. It's as though her brain refuses to be reminded of the excruciating hours it spent hatching them; only later, on the road, will they come to mind as readily as the others, but by then she'll have other problems. Above all, she'll have begun to hate music. Bass notes, drum breaks, whole phrases by the trumpets will have settled in her brain and will repeat themselves at full volume whenever she lays her head on a pillow, will pick up the rhythm of car and plane engines while she's trying to doze, will even drown out the nervously fluttering booms of her own heartbeat.

David and Hansi are looking more optimistic. A trumpeter suddenly blows a wrong note. It slices through the chord and jolts the harmony, like a burp at the royal table. David laughs. Very loudly. He's not given to bursts of loud laughter and the team wheels around in amazement; even Archie drops his arms and looks stupefied. The laughter seems exaggerated, like that of a ham actor moving into the demented scene in the last act; only the team knows that it's perfectly genuine. The musicians boggle as they listen to the strange whooping and cackling, then decide that David has chosen a weird but friendly method of breaking the tension, telling them to relax and enjoy it. The whole room starts to shake with laughter, the trumpeter blows the wrong note again, others join in, it's as though they've been waiting for this cue to throw off the stiff sterile rehearsal atmosphere and turn the session into a ball. It also serves them as an escape valve for their various degrees of antagonism toward Archie; every last man down to the pianist, the guitarist, even the green drummer, adds his voice to the atonal uproar. Archie's scalp seems to stiffen and his ears stretch back like a hunting dog taking the scent; Egon puts two fingers to his mouth and ends the jamboree with a shrill whistle. Hansi's enjoyed every second of it; he laughs and murmurs, "I'd rather have a good fat wrong note any day than a weak right one, it shows they're trying to get moving, not just reading the notes."

•

After three days we've completed the first run-through of the thirty numbers. The singer still hasn't done any serious work; she's been singing to herself, muttering over wrong tempi and difficult pickups, getting more convinced by the minute that she's heading for destruction. On the fourth day, the sound engineer and his assistant arrive. They run back and forth joining up miles of cables, the loudspeakers crackle and whistle the moment they're turned on; the soundman cuts them off, adjusts something, moves them downstage a little, turns them back on, they scream even louder. The band and its leader sit around with the expressions of people suffering from acute neuralgia. The singer flirts outrageously with the sound engineer, flaps around him like a starlet around a producer; the success of the evening depends largely on the way he will color her voice and keep it in front of the solid body of sound from the band. The screaming stops as the assistant adjusts her microphones and begins testing. David strides over the chairs that have now been set out in rows; he moves from one corner of the room to the other, advances to the front rubbing his ear, letting the engineer know by nods of his head or frantic waving whether the sound's right or not as the assistant repeats, "Testing, testing, one, two, three . . ."

Archie's leaning in a corner fussing with his beautifully manicured half-moons, the pianist shifts and makes room on his bench for the singer. "I'm scared," she whispers. "What of?" he asks, opening his huge auburn eyes wide. "Of the first dates," she answers. He chuckles like an old woman, knowing all too well, delighted to hear it on the one hand, anxious to help on the other. "I know what you mean," he says. "I couldn't play in front of an audience for a long time, they drove me crazy, you understand? I went to a psychiatrist and he found out that I had a guilt complex, about the war, although I was only just so high"—he indicates the size by holding his hand over the floor at about the height of a dachshund—"that's what it was." Suddenly embarrassed, he starts to tinkle on the keys. "Quiet!" the sound engineer roars. The pianist looks hurt, then continues, "Now I don't give a damn, the hall can be as big as it likes, the people don't worry me any more." His name is Ivan and he's from Poland. He's been in Germany for many years but still has a heavy accent and can't get the hang of the jazz language at all.

The electricians turn up in the afternoon. Rudi, Bubi, and Ken. Rudi and Bubi are Berliners, Ken's from London. Rudi's the boss, he works the dimmers, does the fade-ins and blackouts. He's tall and thin, and suffers from stomach ulcers and constant doubts about his wife's fidelity. The show can't go on without Rudi. To look at him, one would think that Bubi was playing truant from school, but he's thirty, drinks lots of Slivovitz, wears jeans that are no wider than an umbrella sheath, and ties up his long golden hair with rubber bands during the day, letting it out at night, after the show, when he goes "marauding," as he calls it. Bubi's not good at flying. Even the sight of an airplane turns him purple; he advances toward it over the tarmac with a paper bag held up to his chin in readiness. During the day he lives on gruel, at night on Slivovitz, endures the daily spasms of sickness willingly, for Bubi is mad about touring. He works one of the big spotlights that we take with us. The flight has been short today, and Bubi is only moderately weakened; he's bubbling with enthusiasm, which doesn't suit Rudi's ulcers by any means. "How's the young mother?" Bubi asks, and looks up at the podium. "Now, that's a sight for airsick eyes, big bands really send me, sister." Rudi is seething. "Our equipment's still at customs, the stupid idiots're making trouble again." "Then I'll just go down and shake them up a little," says Bubi with the twinkle in his eyes he gets when he's going marauding, and disappears for the rest of the day.

Ken, the delicate English flower child, smiles happily, doesn't understand a word. Ken is very young and has jumped at the chance to go along on the tour as an electrician in order to learn German. David and the singer have known him since he was sixteen years old and fetched the tea and coffee in the offices of their English record company. His jet-black hair and dark-blue eyes with long sumptuous lashes remind one of Snow White. We ask Egon to keep an eye on him. Egon walks around him in a full circle, inspecting the goods, nods, and says, "Will do."

That Ken doesn't have the slightest idea about spots or electricity we don't mention, they'll find out the next day anyway.

We work until midnight. Archie, who's "full to the brim," as Rudi murmurs, is also in fine fettle; he tells meandering, sophisticated stories and reveals a completely new and not at all unpleasant side of his character, so that one begins to wish he might remain full to the brim for the rest of the tour. There's one snag though, the songs are hardly recognizable at the tempi he now takes them. Hansi's blue and white cheeks are mightily swollen.

●

The work between David the director and Hildegard the singer began on the ninth day. For the others, the only changes in circumstances to be noticed were that the singer now stood at the two functioning microphones and that her voice was audible to all, and that David had placed a chair directly in front of her, some ten feet away; with his legs crossed and a cigarette in his hand, he sat there in an attitude of complete relaxation. Now and again he looked up at her and, as always, the turned-up corners of his mouth gave the impression that he was smiling. To any outsider looking in, it must have seemed that here was a friendly, indeed loving couple come together to set about surmounting a lengthy but not too formidable task. The way they exchanged just a couple of words at the completion of each song was a model of respect and harmony and no one (except Hansi, who, through long years of working with the couple, had certain inklings, if not thorough knowledge of their methods) would have dreamed that this was the beginning of a deadly new phase in the rehearsals, a phase which would grow progressively more brutal as time wore on, a phase of incredible toughness, in which there would be no compromise or concession, no quarter asked or given between the two. When things went right and her talent made itself felt, flashes of brilliance maybe even flickering through, delighting humbler bystanders, he would react as though perfection was the very least he had a right to expect; when things went wrong and the effect she'd reached for went sailing past the mark, he would raise an eyebrow and look away, pretending not to hear it. Profound disgust lay in this looking away, and it would often drive her to the ends of her sorely limited self-control, but he'd learned how to deal with her brawling too, he simply ignored it.

They were mobilizing the forces of their very contrary but complementary characters and talents, and preparing themselves for a further clash; it would certainly be productive, of that they were sure, at what expense to their personal relationship remained to be seen. First of all they dispensed with all forms of ceremony and conversed in the blunt, elliptical language they had developed for this purpose. By looking away, he would needle her to ever greater efforts; with ambiguous acerbity she would demand his absolute attention and goad his inventiveness. His capacity for complete concentration, plus an ability to analyze the structure of any written work, to see its weaknesses and potholes and correct them, coupled with her talent to grasp and transpose his thoughts before he'd finished expressing them, had bound them together in an attachment that had fetters of steel. He understood her demoniacal obsession with her work, knew too that she must expend herself totally in order to experience regeneration. These were her terms. They had not yet found a rational way of dealing with the demands they made on each other, knew only that they would never again find professional partners capable of satisfying the constantly escalating standards they set themselves. David's quick smile, the rare peck on the cheek he accorded her, the finger he would place on her brow, tracing a line there, were accolades five thousand clapping hands couldn't compete with; she too was well aware that her whispered "You were right" was the only reward he sought. These were their ways of praising each other's tenacity and closing the door on the weeks of castigation they'd inflicted on one another.

To come upon her in a weak moment, to see her succumbing to some frailty or other, filled him with an almost physical loathing, and the help he offered her in these moments was the help one extends to the strong, not the billing and cooing men resort to when tending a member of the gentle sex awash with self-pity.

Their work was a duel in which they were perfectly capable of cold-bloodedly directing their weapons at any confederate unwilling to share their ideals and intemperance. They were born gamblers and loved nothing more than to set off on new adventures, to hack their way through the virgin jungles of untried professions without regard for loss or gain, and this always in front of a broad public and under the malicious eyes of the Federal German press. They had no time for those who say, "You have to know your limits," since they were unaware that such limits exist. They had worked together for fifteen years with a remorselessness which, had they ever thought about it, they probably wouldn't have wished on their worst enemies, and had anyone ever bothered to ask them why, they would possibly not have known what to answer.

As always, his easy manner and his considerateness gain him the affection and sympathy of all those working for him—to begin with. After a while they realize with a shock that the hail-fellow-well-met has nothing at all to do with the professional David, and their attempts to distract him from the exacting goals he has set them founder on the sharpness of his perception, on the patience with which he insists on having his wishes fulfilled. They find out also that his retiring attitude is not quite as noble as it would seem, but rather a means to an end, employed wittingly, designed to awaken a feeling of insufficiency in them, of not coming up to his expectations.

The very first independent production they had undertaken had ended in a type of nervous breakdown for her. David had announced one day that he'd found a new play he wished her to appear in and that they'd tour it for seven months through German-speaking Europe. She agreed, they formed their first company. During the rehearsals they were surprised to find that their own stamina and disregard for tiresome bodily needs such as food and sleep were not qualities common to all dedicated artists; the other actors started to mutiny. Director and star had stood their ground and demanded that the rehearsal plan—not at all in harmony with the dictates of the unions—be adhered to. Actors who came out of a rehearsal looking fresher than when they went into it didn't stand a chance with them.

The part she was to play was of a New York taxi driver's wife who was gregarious and loquacious and very slowly going out of her mind; her only child had lost its life due to negligence on her husband's part; her surroundings, her isolation, and her incapacity to accept reality finally take her sanity. For all the experience the singer-actress has had in her long professional life, she has never been able to understand what is meant by the term "routine," or detaching oneself from the part. She was never able to; she began to identify with the taxi driver's wife more and more with every performance, and the combination of her own repugnance for routine and her husband-director's exactions gradually took its toll.

After a few weeks she had reached a point of total immersion in the part which would have satisfied even Stanislavsky, forgetting herself to such an extent that she traveled and went on stage with a temperature of over 100 degrees for days on end without ever giving it a thought. And just at this time he had upbraided her in front of the complete, astonished company for skipping a line in the text, a line which was completely unimportant to the development of the plot. And although she'd tried to hit him with a kitchen chair, she'd secretly admitted that he'd been right and felt deeply ashamed. Later, when she suffered a series of violent gall bladder attacks, which doubled her over like a jackknife, it was clear to both of them that this was a most regrettable circumstance, certainly, but not one to prevent her playing the evening performance. During the final weeks she broke a bone in her hand and developed an abscess in the hollow of her knee but still never missed a show, although an overcautious doctor did warn her that her leg might have to be amputated if she didn't stop. Before she met David she had played in a long run on Broadway and had learned to her cost the meaning of the phrase "The show must go on," but she couldn't know then that Broadway was child's play compared to the times she was to experience with an Englishman who professed to be without ambition.

At the end of the seven-month tour she was frazzled, hoarse, and morose, an exact replica of the woman she'd played, and was, if not quite ripe for the madhouse, at all events in dire need of a psychiatrist. As usual her director-husband reacted to the foibles of his actress-spouse with the aplomb of a field marshal on learning that his foot soldiers have fled the field. But the despots didn't give up; the longer they worked together, the more unbending they became. Their behavior was of a neurotically determined character, as if they must pay dearly for the fusion of complementary talents, and the complement was vividly clear: the moment she switched from acting to singing, he took over the production, proved to be perfectly at home in the world of music, and told her composers and arrangers how to enhance her thing. When she sat down one day and tried her hand at writing, he encouraged her, sat down himself, and translated her text, winning a major prize at first try. Even when she thought she might steal off and dabble in a little painting in her spare time, he breezed in and corrected her efforts, showing a quite diabolical knowledge of technique and the art of mixing colors, also of the lives and works of countless painters hitherto unknown to her.

•

There's a row on the eleventh day. Archie is still at loggerheads with the tempi and the band's much too loud; Hansi and David take turns working on him. The room is cleared of hangers-on for the umpteenth time, two photographers who claim to have been invited by Archie are escorted unceremoniously to the door, Archie suckles and washes his hands. His girl friend, Didi, has been present for the past two days, talking loudly and disturbing the rehearsals. She traipses after him wherever he goes, nattering into his ear. "Throw her out, for God's sake," Hansi mutters. "She should get back to her beat, on the street corner where she belongs." David reaches for his walkie-talkie, whispers directions to Rudi, Bubi, and Ken. The spots seem to have caught Bubi's air sickness; they wobble and sweep around the hall, illuminating everybody but the singer. She, on the other hand, sings away into a black hole and always hears the tour manager hissing, "The band's too loud, for Christ's sake, can't we do anything?" between songs. Hansi is getting fatter every day, his cheeks are puffier and bluer than ever. He slouches over to the pianist and says, "Keep the arpeggios for your spare time, you're doing much too much, this doesn't need the Chopin touch." The Pole is not happy and hardly touches the keyboard at all from now on.

The singer can't stand it any longer. She grabs her mike and barks, "Would those people not taking part in the show kindly scram?" Didi pushes up her platinum-blond hair, blinks in outrage, and heads for the door with her hips undulating. "Everything's out of whack today," says Hansi. Egon rushes in waving a magazine and howls, "Take a look at this—they've got a review of the show already!" The singer takes the magazine and reads an extremely negative account of her show which, as they all know, is still some way from its premiere; chunks of "her" lyrics are quoted out of context, but they're not from her pen, the critic spares no effort to deride the way she delivers them, finally the band comes in for its share of vitriol. The singer's reaction is unladylike; she vituperates and hurls the Germans' idea of what *Time* should be like against the wall. Even Archie forgets his tricks and joins in the protest. "Goddamn rag," Hansi grunts. They stand there united in justified indignation, only David appears to be wildly amused by the whole thing. He pulls up a chair, sits down, and regards the three of them with undisguised delight. He lights a cigarette and says in Hansi's Viennese accent, "What did you expect?"

Just as the singer is feverishly searching for a blunt instrument with which to murder her director-husband, Moritz appears—that is to say, she falls through the door and lands in a heap, squealing like a stuck pig. This doesn't surprise or excite anyone at all as this is Moritz's normal method of entering a room, happening four or five times daily. Moritz has a stormy temperament and it requires no alcohol to send her sprawling. She falls headlong into airports, restaurants, buses, and cars; studios are particularly insidious on account of all the cables lying around and, more important, because of the music that's always being played there; Moritz, although unmusical to a pitiful degree, is immediately seized by an irresistible urge to dance the moment she hears the first bars of any rhythm whatsoever, even jingles send her shaking and jerking like a voodoo lady in heat. Blubbering with excitement, she picks herself up, scrapes her ash-blond hair from her face, revealing an ugly black eye. "My old man gave me that as a going-away present," she says and opens her good eye wide, throwing her head back to let the tears run away over her cheeks. Her husband has a habit of giving her these presents, especially before she goes on tour; perhaps he feels that in so doing he is helping her resist the temptation to go astray. Moritz, monogamous and devoted to her pugilistically inclined husband in spite of everything, had always firmly rejected all suggestions that she get her own back until a short while ago. "A new affair for every uppercut," the singer had advised her in a fit of rage. Moritz had cried and sobbed and sworn that she couldn't and daren't because of the children and the Church, but had quickly altered her opinion on finding out that her banger was banging elsewhere as well.

Seventeen pairs of riveted eyes brighten visibly as Moritz stumbles across the room in her white boots and clinging Pucci blouse; most of the musicians are married with nice homes and regular meals and holidays at opportune prices, living solidly with their rubber plants and expensive stereo sets and an assortment of Oriental and Mexican bric-a-brac they've bought at duty-free shops around the world. Once off the leash, however, they revert to the habits of yesteryear and bloom at the sight of the first appetizing female. The only eyes that soon wrench themselves away from Moritz's bobbing bosom belong to Tom, the bass guitarist. Tom married a breathtakingly beautiful Eurasian girl only eight weeks ago and carries her photo next to his heart and the bags of health food.

Moritz says, "Don't come too near me, I've got a terrible

cold." She kneels down and delves into a huge bag, pulls out black and red French underwear, stockings, scarves, a hairbrush plus comb, false eyelashes, cosmetics and curlers, and eventually comes up with the white package she's apparently been looking for. She opens it, takes out a white surgeon's mask, and ties it around her face, setting off her black eye beautifully. Only Ken looks surprised. He pops out from behind his spot and giggles hysterically, "What the hell is this?" Bubi takes a deep breath and explains to Ken in indescribable English that we can cancel the tour if the singer gets a cold.

"Have the dresses arrived?" Moritz mumbles behind the mask and waves an iron. "No, of course not, they never do until the day of the premiere," the singer answers. "Oh, all right then," Moritz says happily, which means that she'll now pull up a chair and start listening and jerking.

"What d'you think?" David asks as they take a cigarette break. Neither Hansi nor the singer react; "What d'you think?" belongs in the same category as "There you are!" and is another of David's signature tunes. At every salvo of worries, gripes, and hysterics we fire at him, he lets down his bulletproof visor and goes into a huddle with himself, looking for the watertight solution. And we do have problems: the band is not getting quieter, the tempi still tend to run away like racehorses in sight of the finish line, the pickups are harder to find than a cab in the rain, and the running order of the songs is not right. Hansi has taken to sucking handfuls of peppermint candies. He mumbles, "I've got the musicians together, the studio's O.K., sound engineer's O.K., we'll start at ten the day after tomorrow." He's talking about the recording date. We won't be using Archie or his band for the studio takes, the routine is quite different and studio musicians specialize in playing for microphones and not for audiences. Only Tom, the bass guitarist, is ideal for both worlds. He'll be along. We leave in the morning for Berlin.

•

At the beginning, things are quiet. The singer takes her throat pastilles from her bag and looks for a comfortable chair, since she knows that she's in for a five- or six-hour wait until she can start singing; the musicians will record the playback tracks alone first. The big studio doors are open, three taxis drive up between the tall pines, stop, their drivers complain loudly about the state of the driveway. Across the courtyard there's a derelict water-works with a tall red-brick tower, next to it an open-air, mussel-shaped bandstand with a sloping roof. Standing on its stage are two lopsided cane chairs and piles of rotting cardboard boxes. The studio is a long converted dance hall, built at the turn of the century, and has four double doors; two give onto the court-yard, one leads into a dim corridor where there's a dusty billiard table and several broken one-armed bandits, the fourth is situated at the other end of the hall at the top of six steps and is sound-proofed; right beside it there's the large square window of the control room.

It's shortly after ten. The team is ready to go, but tired, not too bright this morning. Hansi yawns exhaustedly as he goes from desk to desk, distributing the band parts; they're the same ones we've been rehearsing with Archie for the past weeks. An old man in a gray work coat is laying cables and setting up mikes; "I retired years ago," he says toothlessly, "but what am I supposed to do at home all day? Can you tell me? My old lady died, and although I love my canary very dearly, it's not quite the same. Tell me if you need anything, I'll go down to the bar, O.K.?" "O.K.," the team answers.

Kalle's bright-red face is peering through the control room window. Kalle is the sound engineer. He raises a big rheumatic hand and waves. Kalle served in the navy during the war and his ship was torpedoed on his eighteenth birthday; he spent thirty November hours in the waters of the North Sea and has been plagued by rheumatism and kidney trouble ever since.

Hansi and the singer clump up the six high steps, push the heavy door open. "Where's the offspring?" Kalle shouts. "At the hotel, Bertha's looking after her." "That you have to start hatching on top of everything else . . ." he says and grins broadly, waving a cardboard plate. His large mixing board is covered with cardboard plates—there are four different types of sound engineers: the first eats the whole time, the second drinks the whole time, the third smokes the whole time, and the fourth eats, drinks, and smokes the whole time. Kalle belongs to the fourth group. At the moment he's eating cake, two meringues are ready to hand, around midday he'll start drinking, beer and schnapps. In order to hear imperfections, sound engineers listen to the takes at maximum volume and many of them land in a sanatorium before they're forty; one and all are victims of a grueling apprenticeship and bad pay.

David comes in, lowering his head as he does so, but bangs it against the frame just the same. "What the English didn't bomb they hit with their heads," Kalle whinnies. "Why don't you buy him a crash helmet?" He pushes the second meringue into his mouth and mumbles, "What's on the program?"

"Twenty-four numbers," Hansi says guiltily and blinks like a silent-film star.

"Twenty-four?" Kalle splutters. "Twenty-four in four days?" He stares at them with eyes like fried eggs, swallows the meringue, pushes the cardboard plate across the mixer, and adds, "Which asylum have you booked me into afterward?"

"Hilde's rehearsed the numbers already, no problem," says Hansi.

Kalle jumps up and goes into a tango routine, gaily singing, "Well, I think I'm going out of my head," and falls back onto his swivel chair with a deep sigh.

Fritz, the drummer, is busy setting up his equipment in the hall. Kalle gazes at him through the window, presses the knob of the intercom system, and calls out, "Morning." Fritz nods and answers with an old-fashioned Gene Krupa–style break. "Oh, he's been going to night classes," says David. "Have you gotten over the attack?" Kalle asks over the intercom. He sighs again and gets up, picks up two slabs of plum tart, goes into the hall, and starts pushing microphones about; Hansi and the singer follow him. David remains in the control room and won't emerge again for four days and nights; his job here is to listen with the sound engineer and let Hansi and the singer know if a take's good or not, suggesting corrections when necessary. The studio is equipped with a 16-track recording system, the engineer records each instrument or section on a separate track; in this way he can juggle the balance between the instruments and the vocalist, can control their timbre, adding echo, bass, or treble as need be during the final mix.

Hansi calls into a mike, "Can Ude make some coffee?" Ude is the editor whose job it is to watch over the tapes on which the music is recorded, and keep a constant flow of coffee coming at the production team. He has a little cabin beside the mixing room; it has a tiny window that looks onto the flaking trunk of a pine tree, and on the wall, beside man-high stacks of tapes, there are three color photos. The biggest of the three shows a fat, leering bandleader who was a local giant during the fifties; he's wearing a strawlike toupee and the face has been retouched to make him look about twelve at the most. Beside him are two pop starlets who, judging by their hairdos and heart-shaped necklines, must have been wowing audiences at around the same time. Above the photos there's a sign: NO SMOKING. Ude is short and thickset, could be a boxer in fact, with a round head and curly hair, and although he's the best editor in the business, he's never without a drink at his side. Five days ago he ran into some cops late at night and they confiscated his driver's license. Understandably, he's not very convivial today. Chomping on his cigarillo, he listens to Hansi's request for coffee, says "Shit," and tramps off to put the water on.

Hansi calls out, "Which number shall we start with?" David gets up, comes to the window of the mixing room, and raises his arms, as though to say, Whatever you like. Sitting in a semi-circle at the front there's Fritz, at his drums; next to him Tom; next to him a gentle nearsighted guitarist who wears sandals without socks at all times of the year—he slumps over his guitar with his head held to one side, smiling at nothing in particular. Then there's a rhythm-guitar player from England with long black hair and a leather jacket, and a slim young pianist from Iceland who has a splendid, classic nose and green, close-set eyes. Sitting diagonally across from the rhythm section are the trumpets: on the outside left there's Benny, "the jazz giant," an enormous

American Negro; next to him a young and incredibly healthy-looking Yugoslavian; a fat German; and a red-nosed, pot-bellied Irishman with a Stalin mustache.

Kalle has finished positioning the mikes and trots back to the control room, starts pulling knobs and levers there while Hansi claps his pudgy hands and says, "O.K., let's take a look at the masterpiece, fellers, warm it up slowly." None of us are strangers to each other, we've either done records together before or been on some date or other, TV or concerts; we meet at irregular intervals, greet each other as though it were only yesterday. The freelance musicians are a breed different from Archie's big band members; they work here and there, go on tour, play for records, TV, and radio, sometimes for their own pleasure in one of the few jazz clubs in Germany. They're their own boss and don't have the problem of living constantly together.

Kalle's voice comes over the intercom: "The bass oven's sizzling." Tom leans back and twiddles the knobs on his amplifier, replugs a connection, looks up to the window. Kalle nods. Hansi counts four and they're off, but after only eight bars there're two sour notes. He raises his arms, says, "That hurts, it really does . . ." and the usual banter about how they'll murder the copyist when they see him starts. Kalle's voice again: "I need to hear the bass once more, alone please." Tom plucks a few chords, Kalle says, "O.K., now rhythm guitar . . . O.K., drums . . ." We see him twiddling and hopping around, then he says, "It's my pleasure to inform you that we're ready." Not that this causes any ripple of excitement among the musicians; in fact, they look even sleepier. Hansi claps his hands again: "A one and one and two and three and three and four and go," turns away from the orchestra, and blinks at the singer, who's mouthing the lyrics to see if the tempo is right for her.

They get to the end of the first number. Hansi looks up to the window, David and Kalle are in a huddle. "They're playing at goldfish again," says Hansi. "Let the water in," Fritz guffaws. "Come up and listen," David says finally. They all get up, tramp up the six steps, and squeeze themselves around the mixing board. Ude spools the tape back, squeals and screeches come from the loudspeakers. The take begins; after thirty seconds Hansi starts to pull his hair and rub his neck, then pouts. "It's heavy as lead, man, don't get its ass off the floor," he says. They stand there forlornly, hating the whole thing, especially the morning sunshine streaming in. Hansi suddenly grins in appreciation and nods to the lead guitar. "I like the E chord," he says; then to Fritz, "Take sticks, not brushes, it needs more pep." To the flutist he says, "Less wind and more notes would suit me better." All in a friendly tone, without admonishment. The take gets very loud toward the end and the needle on the control dial shoots up into the red zone. "I wonder if it'll ever come back," Fritz says between his teeth. "If it does it'll be bent," says David. Hansi turns to him and says, "The strings'll give us a lot, especially in the second chorus. I've ordered them for three o'clock." The strings will be synchronized this afternoon; thirteen orderly looking gentlemen who look like bank clerks in comparison to the rest of the group. "How about a choir?" Hansi asks. "Maybe the 'Swindle Singers' would give us a lift?" "Oh no, they tear your ears off," Kalle groans, "but there's an Inkspot down in one of the clubs, he's great on bongos, we could synchronize him." "For God's sake, no," says David. "We don't need anything else, it's just got to move, that's all." Hansi says, "He's right, if we pack in any more, we'll drown Mama altogether." David puts his arm around Hansi's shoulder as they move to the door and says quietly and worriedly, "The main trouble is the piano, it's not his cup of tea. Can't you do it? Give it a Garner touch?" Hansi nods and answers, "I'll synchronize it tonight."

They pour back into the studio. "From the top." Fritz feels his head carefully and says, "Man, I crashed last night, landed in a barrel, I think my head's died." Hansi claps his hands loudly, means business now. "All right, let's see that we get a good feeling. A one and one . . ." Twice more they stop in the middle; then David whispers over the intercom, "It's dead and buried," which means he's satisfied, on to the next.

Six hours later he sends in a round of drinks. The old man in the gray coat comes in with schnapps, beer, and whiskey, they all blow their horns, Fritz hammers a deafening break, Hansi yells, "I'll pay for a whole piano!" which means the next round's on him. They place their glasses on the floor beside them, Hansi whistles like a locomotive and mumbles, "Sit back, man, relax, O.K. now, a one and one . . ." and turns away.

At four in the afternoon they pack up their instruments, drain their glasses, and drive off to the next job. The strings are waiting. At seven they take their first break, at eight they're finished too. The singer arranges her sheets of lyrics at the desk in front of her and puts on the headphones. The old man has turned off all but one fluorescent light. He's sitting in the corner munching a bread roll and drinking from a bottle of beer, otherwise the studio is empty. When the red light goes on, the old man lays his roll on his knee and lowers the bottle. She's standing a few inches away from the microphone; she tells them she's ready, the playback drones in her ears, she nods her head in time with the rhythm and starts to sing. "D'you have it a size smaller?" a voice rasps over the intercom. She tries again, this time the voice says, "You're about three yards behind the field, it won't swing unless you catch up." This is serious remonstrance. After the fifth try, David's voice is frosty: "You're doing too much," which means too emotional, trying too hard. Finally he says, "Good," in a Bavarian accent but without any tinge of praise or admiration. Hansi mutters, "Mama, you're in a class by yourself," but after six more songs he's almost dead on his feet and says, "Let's let it lie overnight, maybe it'll improve by the time we listen to it again tomorrow." Kalle, coughing violently, says, "Wrap it up." The mixing room is full of smoke and smells awful, Kalle's board is littered with cardboard plates, glasses, bottles, ashtrays full of butts.

We stand shivering and silent in the courtyard at four in the morning waiting for a cab, tumble into the hotel bed, get up and crawl back to the dance hall–studio with the feeling that we've only just left. After four days we all look gray and green. As we take our leave, Kalle goes into his tango routine again, this time to the tune of "Goodbye, Sweetheart." He turns his swollen wrists this way and that, yawns so that his jaws crack, and says, "Show 'em how it's done on the tour, little girl." Ude grips her shoulder with his heavy boxer's hand and says, "It was great, really groovy, keep your chin up."

Hansi, Tom, David, and the singer drive to the airport in a sad mood; the best part of the production is over, the monster tour still to come.

•

They drive through Schöneberg, along the Hauptstrasse and Kolonnenstrasse, pull up in front of Tempelhof airport. As always, a rush of sentiment overcomes her at the sight of the round building with its roof sticking out over the grid; in spite of its monumental ugliness, it always succeeds in activating corners of her memory which otherwise slumber over decades; the air loses the heavy smell of oil and jet fuel, and whiffs of smoked sprats, bloaters, and wild strawberries fill her nose, the warm scent of hot white sand permeates the great hall mixed with the sweet sickly odor of the brewery she passed every day from her tenth till her fifteenth year on the way to church; the bittersweet scent had clung to the psalms and Protestant hymns and colored them ale yellow forever. Still, they had seemed more reliable, dependable, than the Catholic ones, more suited to her forthright nature; the others smacked of prohibition, paganism, of incense and murky deeds. The way the church-goers hid themselves behind headscarves was suspicious enough, and then the way they furtively dipped their hands into the water and hastily made the sign of the cross confirmed what everybody said: There's something fishy somewhere. "The Catholics aren't genuine" was the general opinion in our street; their churches were always stuck in between houses, never stood free in the middle of a square like ours. They've got something to hide, we thought to ourselves as we sang our beery songs in the severe unadorned Protestant church, which was kept firmly locked between services: our stringent God had office hours, the way it should be. Ours was just and incorruptible and not stuck in a pompous house laden with gold and silver like the other one, always available for any old Tom, Dick, or Harry who felt like bothering him with his silly complicated sins.

Looking out from under the jutting roof onto the airfield, she sees sharply defined pictures: Grandfather's shack in Zossen, where they spent the summers, the asparagus beds, the curve of his back as he bent over them, his deep-brown neck, the string undershirt he always wore, his broad face with the high cheekbones, wide mouth, and big healthy teeth; she even feels the warmth his love filled her with, tangible, unforgotten love, the unconditional trust she would never know again. When she was five years old, he had taken her to Tempelhof airport one afternoon, and somehow the building had become a storehouse for all the memories of this short period of implicit trust. Landscapes now blend themselves into the pictures of Zossen, Grandfather and asparagus beds: the Baltic Sea, that corner between Usedom and Wollin, up to the right from Rügenwaldermünde on the school map; summer holidays, the whole day in a threadbare one-piece red bathing suit, freckles on her nose, blisters on her back, and Mother always furious in the evenings. "How often must I tell you to put some oil on?" No bathing the next day, no speckled ice cream, nothing for it but to lie still on her belly in the shade and hear Mother say, "Serves you right."

The thought of the Sunday after next explodes like a hand grenade among the halcyon memories: in nine days she'll be back on the stage of the Berlin Philharmonic, back in the arena. For an hour before the band begins to play she'll pace the corridors backstage like a tiger close to insanity. With the first bars of the opener she'll take her place at the door beside the stage and stare into the triangular emergency light as her cue advances on her like a naked bayonet. Here in Berlin her hands will shake as they never do elsewhere, for here is where her roots are, this is where she belongs, if she belongs anywhere; she must confirm it and have it confirmed, as though the impunity of her memories of the only time in her life when she had not had to constantly prove herself and stand judgment, when she had been protected by the unequivocal love of her grandfather, depends on the grace and favor of those people now sitting there waiting for her to appear, as though she could bring back the *temps perdu* by winning here in the arena.

At the end of the Tempelhof runway there's a cemetery which contains urns with the ashes of her mother, her father, her stepfather, and her grandmother; only Grandfather was buried in a cheap postwar coffin after he committed suicide shortly before his eighty-second birthday. He had been sitting next to the paneless window when she came back from the prison camp; he had looked up calmly and said, "I was only waiting for you."

The plane flies over the cemetery. "Sleep a little," says Hansi, in the next seat; "the pictures they have in hotel rooms drive me crazy," he adds.

"I suppose there are hotel-room painters just as there are ice-rink composers," she answers.

"Probably."

"I'm going to miss you on the tour," she says.

"Call whenever you need me. And if Archie gets too loaded, I'll come and take over. Don't let 'em get you down, O.K.?"

•

The "one-man" show has destroyed quite a few of us. Garland, Piaf—they were murdered by their three-minute plays, warmly known as popular songs. How can one determine the degree of stress? Where's the yardstick, who's to do the measuring? No one is so alone as the one-man going out to do his show. There's no partner to chatter your teeth with, no rails of plot guide you slowly into the role and carry you through the stickiest evenings. Who's going to blame the second trumpeter for that wrong note he blew which threw you just at the crucial moment? Who will notice that the pianist went into the wrong key at the change? Twenty-seven to thirty songs a night and God help you if you haven't got them by the third, they'll cough you from the stage. How do I know that there's a man sitting on the edge of the third or the sixth or ninth row who can't stand my guts? I can't see him but I know he's there. Why is he there? Why didn't he stay home? Is he there to see me fall on my fanny? He's not a critic, they get better seats, gratis. "You're the thorn in his side," your antenna whispers just as your brain is starting to reverberate between the loudspeakers and your heart misses two beats because you fumbled for a word and couldn't get it, so you improvised and the one that came to mind had more syllables and threw you off balance, but you had to go on, if you stop they're not going to wait for you. Why does one man's silent malice in the third or ninth row come through more strongly than the good will of the other two thousand? Why can't I block him from my wavelength? At that moment a delicious morsel springs up out of the crowd, something like an understanding, a warmth, now they're all joining in as if to say, "Welcome home," I can hear the first creaks as the ice breaks. "Welcome home, come on now, show us what you can do, you haven't any voice to speak of, but show us, let's see if it's worth the money." And what swine causes the stage to be waxed? Backstage looks like the morning after the night before: the dressing rooms are littered with cups and glasses, everywhere you touch there's chewing gum that was stashed away and then forgotten, the taps drip, what comes out of them looks like Worcestershire sauce, and when you finally find the only toilet, you think you've been lured to the casbah—but the stage they polish! The rush you like to come out with turns into a skid and already you hear the first buzz from the front row: "Whoops, she's had one too many again—" This is the unkindest cut of all, one sip and she'd blow the first of the thirty soliloquies, Hamlet's a bit part in comparison.

She comes out of the skid and holds on to the mike stand for dear life, stands there in the blinding pillars of light, and tells herself that everything's going to be fine, she's prepared herself well. For weeks on end. But for what? For the telling of a lot of stories written in telegram style which are over almost before they begin and which demand the utmost concentration from the singer and the audience; they must listen and live every word with her, otherwise the connection will break down. She must warm up and move to a frequency on which thought and emotion will impart themselves without being sieved through the filters of the intellect, there where the reservoirs of instinct and awareness respond. How she does this is as much a mystery to her as the mechanism of her emanations, she only knows that she must use the one to attain the other, to "get" and "hold" the audience. So what does a chanson singer backed by a big band prepare herself for? For the audience? It's different every night. Does she train her voice? The way hers is, it doesn't help. She learns her lyrics certainly, and has planned the ways of delivering them. She knows that the first song must be light, come-hithery, give them time to take it all in, make it easy, no demands; with the second she can beckon them a little closer, lend me your ears; with the third she can raise the level, take them by the hand and lead them through the sly play on words, by the end of it she must have them firmly on the leash. With the fourth she can throw them a tidbit, camp it up to get them ready for the naïve lament of the fifth and the lovelorn grief of the sixth. The seventh she can throw up high, right to the ceiling, give them a glimpse of stocking, and then take her first pause, skid off the stage.

These tools of the trade she has whetted and honed, to be sure, but what does she really prepare for before she goes out to meet the six thousand or four thousand, perhaps only two? For the monster whose tentacles will reach out and take possession of her muscles and her nerves, for the tension that will grope its way along every vertebra before it finds the spot it likes and sucks the marrow from her spine with relish, slobbering with delight while she plants the thoughts and scatters the emotions with the hoarse, harsh allusions rasping from her throat, persuades the audience that she's having a ball, which it too can enjoy, if it'll only take the plunge. How can applause be warm or cold? How can the same hands making the same motions send up a yes or a no? If by the third number the clapping straggles, then they're still brooding on their own problems, are still busy with the gas-stove heating taxes household budget, and where do we take next year's vacation, for God's sake? Then they're still not prepared to shake off their ordinary identities and let down their hair; then you must take a step back, make them realize they could lose it all, go into your private mystery, and hope they'll follow.

With the next song, tread on the applause, don't wait for it to ebb, kick the pickled bandleader in the seat of the pants and leap into the next number, take them by the ears and rape them. As the flashbulbs flare from down below, between songs bow very low, get the blood back up into your head—they'll write that you made a mannered humble obeisance, but what the hell, the blood's more important, not even the Queen's guard can stand for two hours at a stretch without keeling over. The moles will bleat from their hillocks whatever you do. But there, in some hall or other, on some spit-and-polished stage, there's the second of time where it suddenly ignites, the seduction is complete, lechery can begin; the wavelengths interlock, signals fill the air like a flock of gulls, a cry, a chortle, a shriek, a tidal wave sweeps the polished floor, heaving the jaded jazzmen off their stolid butts, sending them on highs they don't find in the weed; all at once the loneliness of the arena never existed, they were always on your side, never the bull's. For this one second in time she can allow herself to fall headlong into the delirium, if she stays too long she's lost. At precisely the right moment her personal intercom must tell her, "Hear this: it's gone far enough, there is no place at this banquet table for you, you are the cook and the fodder too, but you are not the partaker. Now then, next number. Take a deep breath before the bridge, otherwise you won't get through."

There's no time for ceremony, and there's no net to catch you if you fall; the musicians can't even hear the man next to them, let alone you, and if the bandleader isn't on his toes the coordination will come apart at the seams and the euphoria will come tumbling down around your ears like a ton of bricks.

Two and a half hours later she'll hold the bouquets to her sweat-drenched breast and bow for the last time, even deeper than before, arise in the exaltation of exhaustive self-realization and totter back to the airless hole called the star dressing room. She'll sit there for a long moment in front of the smeared mirror trying to recognize the face she sees there, letting herself fall completely as she feels the sap of success flowing, glowing.

It's a masculine victory, and all those ladies who dabble with the abstruse pleasure of raping a thousand or more unknown entities will use up their masculine reserves far too quickly, must soon admit that the aggression needed to carry it off isn't coming the way it did. They'll grow weary and footsore, and will seek to restore their strength through love and affection, will crave gentleness and become more feminine than the daintiest house-wife, devoted, fragile, doting. They'll bring their success home like a dog its bone, proudly show off their acclaim like an order of merit, all the more reason why they should be loved; in doing so, they'll completely misjudge the nature of a man's needs, realizing too late, perhaps, that a staple diet of champagne and oysters must bring about a surfeit.

The vicious circle will close; the friends and admirers they have gained with their strength will want no part of their weak-ness. They will turn from one cold shoulder to the next in their search for gentleness, and finally break, for all they ever wanted was to be loved, perhaps more immoderately than other people, but less selfishly too.

•

It was only to be expected that Dimitri, ridiculously "Dimi" to his friends, would come to the dress rehearsal. Dimi always comes to the singer's dress rehearsals, although from a profes-sional standpoint it's much too late for anyone to help any more; the dresses can't be changed, or the songs, or anything at all for that matter, twenty-four hours before the premiere, but Dimi insists on being the first to offer his expert opinion in spite of the fact that he can't abide music in any shape or form. He takes trying journeys, expenses, and all sorts of discomfort in his stride just to be there when the mania reaches its height. He quite blatantly admits that he adores to see people going off the rails, it sets him up for weeks, but the real reason for his fervor in our case is that he loves to annoy David. Dimi, by his own admission "easily hurt, overbred, homosexual, and grossly cultured," takes particular delight in rocking David's proud and lofty pedestal; indeed, he's the only person under the sun capable of upsetting him at all, forcing him to give vent to furious speeches of astonishing length. Even David's proficiency in the art of dodging trouble falls afoul of Dimi's terrierlike pursuit, for although Dimi is about half David's size, and has his work cut out to keep up when David takes flight, there's no getting rid of him.

Dimi, who is employed as an editor in a small but important leftist publishing house, is an enigmatic figure. His doubtless meager salary bears no relation to the princely fashion in which he lives; to begin with, no one has ever seen Dimi in the same suit twice, not that they're cheap, or off just any old rack, oh no, each has its individual, modish touch, with accessories to match. Then there's the apparently inexhaustible succession of plump young men in thin Cardin getups that are always in attendance, not to mention Dimi's passion for giving presents of an opulence that leaves their recipients speechless, even those, like the singer, who have no feeling for money.

Dimi is standing in the center aisle with a packet of Gauloises, matches, and a lighted cigarette in his right hand, as always. As always, he's looking irritated, staring about him aggressively, as if one had dropped in on him at an inopportune moment. His thick curly hair is clipped short and shot with very becoming white streaks. The moment he started working on an essay about Lenin he grew a beard; it doesn't suit his delicate, finely boned face at all; it seems to stifle it and reduces his long anthracite-colored eyes to sinister slits. Followed by a plump young man who's dragging a number of chic leather shoulder bags behind him, Dimi sprints up on his tiny legs to David, who's sitting in front of the stage glowering at the singer. She's parading up and down in the white Balmain dress that has just arrived, desperately trying to avoid coming into contact with the grimy walls and chairs. Moritz squints into the blinding spotlights and asks, "Is the make-up O.K.?" As David grudgingly answers, "It'll do for now," Dimi puts his left hand over David's eyes and tickles his neck with his overloaded right. David rears up and turns fiercely on Dimi. "Don't make a face as though my caresses were an insult," Dimi says mockingly, "there are worse things in life than being loved by me," and stares at David with a well-practiced Gloria Swanson look. The plump young man jiggles the roll of fat around his waist as he laughs, and Dimi kills any chance of repartee David might have had by turning to the stage and calling, "And how's the Sappho of rock 'n' roll?" She yells, "Be as bloody-minded as only you know how, maybe it'll take my mind off doomsday." Dimi springs up onto the podium, disregards the suspicious looks of the musicians and Moritz's outrage, kisses the singer full and lingeringly on the lips, and whispers, in a voice that carries far, "I'm your slave, your songs alone will rescue me from premature impotence." In a trice he stands on tiptoe and places a long silver necklace around the singer's neck. It reaches to her navel. "It will bring you luck, my angel," he cries satanically. "You are an angel and you never deserved this unresponsive Englishman, whatever atrocities you committed in your previous lives." He chuckles and strokes the necklace. "My Russian great-grandmother always wore it when she went to the opera."

She knows he's lying. He always lies. Each time he refers to his background and upbringing, a totally different version emerges. The first thing that had struck her was that all the geographical locations his far-flung family was supposed to have lived in sounded wrong; if one confronted him and said, "But listen, Dimi, there are no wind-swept deserts in Macedonia," he would simply say, "Oh, really? I've never felt a burning interest in landscapes, they all look like wind-swept deserts to me," and the subject would be closed. But she had been determined to get to the roots of his family tree, and once, when he had been extemporizing for rather a long time on the Russian tinge in his multicolored blood, she'd dug out an old Russian friend and brought them together; it turned out that Dimi had not the faintest clue about the language or the national customs, and this after having spent hours telling her about the strength his grandmothers had implanted in him as he sat on the footrest next to the samovar while they told him one fairy tale after another. A little while later he himself admitted that he'd gone too far with the Japanese episode, the story of his father riding bareback on an elephant hunting down a man-eating tiger at the foot of the Sayonara Mountains was too much, even for her. He retaliated, though. One afternoon he turned up with an appropriately yellow photo of an Indian-Thai and announced proudly that this had been his father. He'd shed a tear or two as he stared at the bearded snippet and sobbed that he owed this man everything that he'd become in life, and that his end had been a tragic one—he'd been squashed in bed by Dimi's monumental mother (still Russian!). None of Mama's mates had ever learned to deal with her properly, he added apologetically.

That I appeared to disbelieve him hurt him deeply. He took off his shoes and showed me his verily tiny feet, removed his shirt and displayed a tea-colored back; just as I was beginning to feel uncomfortable, his current plump friend sniggered and dug me in the ribs with his elbow, told me that he was a Pan-Am steward and that he'd got the photo along with a phony Buddha from a con man in Bombay's duty-free shop. The plump friend scuttled off, the friendship seemingly come to an untimely end.

I didn't see him for a year after this. Then he suddenly turned up again at some dress rehearsal or other and topped it all with the confession that he was in reality a Jew, that he'd been taken to a concentration camp at the age of three, and for this reason had been schooled in the art of lying; his life was still in danger: underground and other movements were still keeping a close watch. Of course, he was only a quarter Jewish, but he nevertheless felt strongly attached to the Jews—he was often on the verge of St. Vitus's dance, so he told me, because he didn't know which quarter was affected, whether it was the top or the bottom, the left or the right, it didn't matter, he was doomed to persecution for the rest of his life.

This took the cake. Even his best friends said as much. Now real researchers went to work. They found out that Dimi had been born the only son of humble carpenter-folk in Silesia, and had been given the names Oskar Dimitri. His parents had dropped his second Christian name when Father became a member of the Nazi party, reinstating it again quickly with the arrival of the Russian troops. At the end of the war the whole family had moved to Berlin, where the parents took a job as janitor and housekeeper of a large apartment block near the Savigny Platz. His father had died of a weak heart four years after the currency reform, and his mother had been running a flourishing florist's shop for the past seven years.

Dimi still insisted on opening conversations with "We Jews . . ." and one day the singer could contain herself no longer and told him what she knew. Dimi withdrew, sulking. He popped up again a short while later and promised by everything holy to him that he would henceforth restrict his fantasy to the present and, apart from occasional sly slips, kept his word. There was no doubting the fact that he'd been a brilliant scholar, winning scholarships left and right, as he said, and had enjoyed the advantages of a first-class education; nor was there any reason to doubt the story of his prolonged battle with tuberculosis. It was possibly this last that persuaded David to put up with him at all, the bonds of sanatorium experience, pneumothorax, and their common disregard for the value of life being perhaps stronger than their totally contrary personalities.

"Where've you come from?" David asks him roughly.

Dimi describes a wide arc with his right arm as though illustrating a trip to the moon. "There where Sweden is called Norway," he says.

"In other words, from your Munich office," the singer says.

"Oh no, you're wrong. I've been on a fascinating business trip that offered all manner of side benefits." He flings an arm in the direction of the new plump youth and says, "This is Detlef."

"My name's Karl," Detlef barks.

Dimi sucks in his cheeks and answers decisively, "Detlef sounds better," turning to Hansi with outstretched arms as he does so.

Hansi ducks and says, "Enough baloney, let's get back to work."

Dimi gives a little wave up to the stage, numerous bracelets tinkling at his delicate wrist, and takes a seat beside David.

As usual the dress rehearsal is a catastrophe of the first order. During one of the many pauses necessary for the technical crew, the singer sits down and sucks on a cigarette, Moritz tries to comfort her with well-meaning phrases, and Dimi suddenly jumps onto the stage, trots up to Archie, taps him on the shoulder, and asks, "Do you do this professionally?" Hansi stuffs a handful of peppermint creams into his mouth in an effort to prevent himself from exploding. Archie stops suckling, looks at Dimi with a disconcerted expression, and mumbles, "I'm actually more interested in literature." "How lovely," Dimi coos delightedly and seizes Archie's hands; he lets them drop again immediately and stares horrified at Archie's unsavory palms. It's a bad moment for Archie, and the singer almost feels sorry for him as he stutters, "It's an allergy, awful, especially as I'm an aesthetic . . ." Seventeen musicians lean forward in their chairs.

"No matter," Dimi says sweetly, then in deadly, infernal earnest, "Since you're devoted to literature, our meeting may well have been arranged in heaven. I'm an editor, and if you'll allow me, I'd be delighted to enrich your doubtless irreproachable taste and experience. How d'you get on with Trakl? And what about Claudel? He can be delicious, although not quite up my company's street, of course—I know, Rainer Maria Schickelgruber! The poor darling's been terribly misunderstood, God help him, but those of us in the know are just waiting for the day when his 'Songs My Mother-in-Law Taught Me' will take its place beside the all-time greats. Which brings me to the question of the Westphalian Romanticists—you must let me send them to you, they capture quite perfectly the naïve rotundity of yesteryear, which, alas, is sadly lacking in the world today."

Archie's looking as if he's just been told he's been elected this year's Queen of the May. The singer pushes herself between them, shoves Dimi from the stage saying, "That'll do, he's in a bad enough state as it is, if he doesn't get the tempi by tomorrow they'll think I'm singing Korean opera."

At the end of the rehearsal we avoid each other's eyes and whisper, "Till tomorrow." Tomorrow means Hamburg, premiere. Egon bawls like a sergeant-major, "Takeoff at thirteen hours fifty. Warm up in the hall at eighteen hours fifty. The truck with equipment and technical crew leaves here tonight at twenty-two hours promptly." He goes on to read out a list of hotels and telephone numbers, then relaxes out of the official tone and says from the corner of his mouth, "I'll be standing beside you the whole time tomorrow night, nothing to worry about, use my shoulder when you need it." The singer nods appreciatively.

"If I'm not fed soon I'll bite somebody," Dimi says, quite uninterested in our little problems. Herding us all to the door, he takes David's arm, gazes up at him, says, "No measure of reason can fathom the depth of our affinity. Even I, with the breadth of my vocabulary, must admit failure," and places a gold, horseshoe-shaped key ring in David's hand. David stops in his tracks, holds it up in his fingertips with a look of utmost distaste, and groans, "Oh my God." It's exactly what Dimi had expected. Excitedly, as though he were the one who'd received a present, he looks at the company and cries, "Our David can't accept a gift. What d'you think of that? My psychiatrist would say, 'That's a grave sign, my friend,' neurotics view presents as worthless rubbish and only see themselves obligated by them." David does him the favor. "What the hell do I need that for?" he says. "You see!" Dimi says jubilantly, and gazes up earnestly at David. "Try to model yourself on your drearily normal lady love. She accepted the great-grandmotherly costliness with the same grandezza with which it was given."

We are standing on the street in a deserted neighborhood; it's very foggy and there's no sign of a taxi. Dimi is turning his head from side to side as though trying to dodge a wasp; his fingers are clamped around the pack of Gauloises and the matches, his mouth opens and a dull sound escapes between his bared teeth, develops into a violent fit of coughing. David pulls him into a doorway and binds his woolen scarf around Dimi's face. The coughing doubles him over, sends him staggering from one side of the doorway to the other, large childlike tears drop down onto the scarf and his beard. He pulls a delicate handkerchief from his breast pocket, mops his streaming face, leans his head on David's chest, and says, in a tiny grating voice, "It's not what you think, just a cold, that's all."

Hansi and Detlef have moved on into the fog and soon come back with a taxi. We drive to a restaurant that Dimi knows and enter its candlelit, red-plush atmosphere with the suspicion that only he will feel at home here. After endless wranglings over who should sit next to whom, we take our seats. The singer couldn't care one way or the other, all she's interested in is a decent meal; from tomorrow on she'll live on frugal hotel breakfasts and those gay little boxes they give you on today's airlines which contain an apple, two rubbery rolls, and a bottle of healthy black-currant juice. She can't eat before the show, and she'll never leave the hall before midnight; the chances of getting a warm meal then are remote.

Dimi bends his head over the large handwritten menu and sinks his teeth noisily into a stick of celery. One and all react with varying degrees of feigned outrage; Dimi surveys our pursed lips, bites off another chunk, and says, "I abhor people who chew radishes and crackers, but celery is a different thing again, especially when I chew it with my splendid molars that cost ten thousand marks."

"We'll remember to bring ear plugs the next time," says Hansi.

"I'd no idea you were so sensitive," Dimi murmurs, leaning back in his chair and looking up at the mirrored ceiling. He turns to David abruptly and raises a hand to his forehead. "Don't tell me you're losing your glorious mane?" he cries aghast. David squirms a little, for this is a play on his avid interest in the way people carry their years; within minutes of meeting anyone, regardless of sex, he will blatantly ask for their birthdate, insisting on the year, month, and day if the case interests him, which leads people to suppose that he's another astrology buff, which he isn't at all; he just wants to judge how they've weathered the storm. He decides to ignore Dimi's provocation and turns his attention to the wine list. "Silence is not unfailingly a sign of inner noblesse, just as not all loud people are absolute boors, as one is inclined to want to believe," Dimi announces. He resumes his inspection of David's hairline and says, "I do feel obliged to warn you though, my dear, that there are glimpses of scalp glistening through which weren't there last year, the first teeny-weeny step toward decay, one might say, of resigning oneself to the ultimate dissolution which must overtake us all."

"You're not getting any younger either," Detlef says meanly.

"Ah yes," Dimi answers, reaching for a second stick of celery and munching happily. "Yes," he repeats, "there's an element of truth in that too. But, you see, I possess charm and culture to an alarming degree, and I've only to go to the seaside for two or three weeks and I become so beautiful that I can't take my eyes off myself."

Only the singer laughs. She doesn't really like him at all. She's known him for ten years now, during which time he has proved himself as a friend, though she's never called on him in time of need; when they part company it's always with the feeling on her side that he's a black, negative person who has survived war and illness for the sole purpose of leading tentative candidates into the realms of suicide, a kingdom in which he himself is very much at home. But when he pops up again, she quells these discomforting thoughts, feels guilty, and wants to take him under a motherly wing; in short, she's constantly of two minds as to how to deal with his dual personality.

Dimi's voice penetrates her thoughts: ". . . you all had that benevolent sanatorium look. Whenever I cough, there's invariably somebody at hand who will stare at me with a look that says, 'Such a pity, and still so young.' I can't stand that look any more than I can stand the thought of phrenic crushes, X-rays, weigh yourself once a week, and don't forget your refill." He stuffs his food into his mouth as though afraid someone might take it away from him, and swallows two or three glasses of wine.

Hansi is slowly and lovingly chewing the last of his lamb chops. He turns to Detlef and, in an effort to change the subject, asks him, "What do you do professionally?" "I want to be famous," Detlef answers, and straightens his head, as though prepared to face a battery of cameras. Everyone stops eating and stares at him, everyone except Dimi, that is. "Jump off the Eiffel Tower, you'll be famous overnight," says David.

Dimi stretches himself, wheezes noisily, and lights a cigarette with a haste that indicates he's only eaten the better to be able to smoke. Detlef is wriggling about on his little gilt chair looking pleadingly at Dimi. Dimi ignores him and tells David, "Hilde's dresses for the show are indescribable. The orchestra is strident, to put it mildly, and the conductor would really be in more suitable surroundings collecting tickets on a bus. Regrettable as it all is, I do see on the other hand that since your good lady insisted on retiring for so long in order to reproduce herself, it's high time that one shows her to her adoring public again."

"On the contrary," the singer retorts, "it would have been far better had I been allowed to stay at home for a good while longer but, as your perceptive eye will no doubt have noted, I am not the youngest of mothers, on top of which I'm equipped with an excellent memory, which constantly reminds me of my own childhood and its impecunious circumstances. We must gather the rosebuds while we may, while there are still a few people around who'll pay for the dubious privilege of seeing and hearing me. With one good tour we'll be out of the red for the first time in nine years."

"I do adore people with the gift of articulation," Dimi sighs.

"And I adore people who go easy on demented entertainers twenty-four hours before the premiere."

Immediately Dimi lays his head on her hands and kisses them. "I adore you and love you, my love, but you never believe somebody loves you unless he shoots himself in front of your bedroom window, and even then you surmise that he had tax problems. Nevertheless, I admit that I'm a philistine, self-centered, tasteless, deplorable."

The singer repents. When Dimi says, "It was only a scream of loneliness," it sounds like the beginning of a soppy song from a drag show. And say it he does, with a bittersweet melancholy and glistening anthracite eyes; Hansi, David, and the singer hoot uncontrollably.

Suddenly, as though several buses had pulled up at the door at the same time, the restaurant is filled with men of all age groups. They sidle through the door, mostly in pairs, and stand there waiting for the agitated waiter to show them to their tables. Their deportment, as they wait, appears to fall easily into one of two categories: it's either exhilarated, as though a tingling adventure were awaiting them, or studiedly bored, letting one and all know that they're used to nothing but the best. Well-preserved, tanned, mature gentlemen stand next to pale slender youths who take in the whole clientele with a few flickering glances as they light cigarettes with quick, nervous movements, then fumble with their frilled shirts and carefully dressed hair. Every single one of them takes a long look at the painting on the wall, which depicts a well-endowed naked young man of Southern origin, and is quite nauseating in its overblown fleshiness.

Detlef gives a little wave to a man who has sat down at the next table; the man lowers his admirable eyelashes and blows Detlef a tiny kiss. Dimi has noted the exchange carefully. He strokes his beard and considers for a moment, then says in an unnecessarily loud voice, "I had my first homosexual experience while still a lad in Russia—" My glance calls him to order. "All right then, Silesia. Our school was situated next to a railway station which boasted a public lavatory. The gents was large and stank quite dreadfully, and I remember that it always swayed as the freight trains rattled by. There were toilet cubicles at the back which had faulty locks and large holes in the wooden partitions." He pauses and then continues, almost sadly, "That was the beginning. But to further your education, you should know that homosexuals invariably do have complexes about their practices, and when they couple, there are nearly always disputes as to which one will assume the coveted 'active' role, the theory being that it's not really that perverse if one's on top.

And now to serve you the *pièce de résistance*. When a so-called normal man succumbs to seduction by a homosexual, he will quite willingly adopt the passive role, accept the volte-face, as it were, without a murmur. Fascinating, what? During my years in the Orient—" He has folded his hands and looks as though nothing can stop him any more, but he suddenly remembers his promise and says, "Yes, well, perhaps the Orient is going a little too far for the first lesson. You see, homosexuals are looking for themselves. My psychiatrist maintains that a determination to belong to only one sex must end in insanity. Women who suppress their masculine traits, and men their feminine ones, must go round the bend."

Just at this spellbinding juncture in Dimi's monologue, a platinum-blonde film agent known to them bursts through the door and stands there trembling, as though plugged into some invisible generator. She dashes up to our table and squeals, "I just love handsome men." Her face has been lifted so often that she has trouble closing her mouth. "You don't mind, do you?" she says as she sits down next to David. "I went to a séance," she whispers, craning her neck over the table. "Two lives ago David and I were brother and sister." She looks at us as though expecting applause, then leans up to David's ear. "I knew we'd meet today," she says.

"Does this mean we're in for some incest?" Dimi says very loudly. "Not that I've anything against it, but I do feel you might wait until we've finished the cheese."

"Are you a friend?" she breathes and tries to take Dimi's hand.

"No scenes please, madam," he says, rapping her over the knuckles with a stick of celery.

David engrosses himself with a piece of Gorgonzola, whereas Hansi does something not at all typical of him. Blinking wildly, he straightens up and says to the woman, "We were having a nice cozy chat until you came. Would you mind getting lost?"

The agent gets up with a look of fury, but it bounces off Hansi's blond locks as he attends to a large portion of chocolate mousse.

"No wonder there are so many gay types," says Dimi, "with ladies like that. And since the time for leave-taking has apparently come, I'd like you too, dear Detlef, to follow suit." Detlef looks at him like a cow and turns ever-deepening shades of red. "Off you go," says Dimi, as though he were sending his favorite son to bed, "and leave the handbags here, if you don't mind."

As Detlef staggers blindly to the door, Dimi tells them, "Revenge is best partaken of when it's cold. And the little whore was up to all sorts of tricks to swindle me, so no false sympathy, please."

Hansi shoves back his dainty chair and says, "I think I've had enough gaiety for one evening."

"Spare me ten more minutes of your precious time, I beg of you," Dimi implores like a small child, and places his fingertips together. "I only wish that you'd got to know the really one great love of my life, he was a scrumptious, conniving, silent specimen of masculine glory. He had an exceptional talent for making me unhappy, and yet I've never loved like that before, or since. He never said a word. I used to squat next to his enormous feet—he took the biggest size in shoes there is—I would squat there and beg him to say something, anything. He would stare in front of him with eyes as empty as a carp's, you could actually hear his atrophied gray cells grinding in an effort to produce something, but they never could. His sexual organ was his weapon, and his brain to boot. He used it like primeval man used his club, not as an implement of love or joy at all, but as a weapon with which to fight his way out of the railway station pissoirs and into the mink-covered king-size beds. He looked down at his battering ram one day and actually spoke: 'When I'm thirty I'll give it to a millionairess,' he said in dire earnestness. And I loved this cretin. I swear to you, it was not only sexual—why do I say 'only'? Anyway, it wasn't just that. One night he sat there in the kitchen in my dressing gown, and after about an hour he said, 'It's over.' He stood up and cleaned his gigantic ears with a Q-tip, then he took down my most expensive Gucci suitcase and packed everything that belonged to him and a few knickknacks that didn't. He paused at the top of the stairs, turned to me, and said, 'I've found a better deal. He's got a Mercedes and a yacht and he's putting me in his will, I'll get the lot.' I remember saying, 'You'll make a fine heir,' and then I made four suicide attempts, one after the other, and didn't set foot outside the apartment for a year. I lost my job, of course, and then one evening I was walking along the Maximilianstrasse in Munich and I looked up and saw a man standing beside a Rolls-Royce grinning at me. I had never seen such a vulgar face in my life, and I didn't recognize it, although I'd thought of nothing else for months on end. When I finally realized that this monstrosity standing there in a fur-lined leather overcoat was the love of my life, I ran into a doorway and vomited for what seemed an hour. After that I was cured."

"Let's go sleep," says Hansi, unimpressed. David stretches himself and says, "I hate hotels," without any animosity, more the stating of a simple and immutable fact; he might just as well have said, "I love hotels." Dimi murmurs, "Now don't start treating us to wild emotions this late in the day. One particularly obnoxious teacher of mine always used to say, 'There's no denying one's roots.' The longer you stay away from your island, my dear David, the more insular you become. You squat on your roots like a nest egg. My envy knows no bounds."

"And your self-pity even less," David answers, suddenly angry. They both turn on me as though demanding intervention.

"I'm not prepared to be your bone of contention," I say.

They stare at me critically, two teachers without a pupil. Dimi rises and picks up his cigarettes. "There are times when I hate you both, but it was a lovely evening, nonetheless." Again he turns his head this way and that, collapses in a burst of coughing. David whispers, "There's a decent doctor here, go to him tomorrow and have a checkup." Dimi splutters, "Why are you whispering? I don't need an abortion."

On the way back to the hotel, David says gloomily, "By the way, I got the news today that the first ten concerts are all sold out." Hansi and I gape at him. Dimi says, "It might be nice if you were to inform us one day why you always tell good news as though it were bad, and bad news as though it were good—or is that part and parcel of being British?"

At this moment I feel the pain for the first time; it shoots up from the back of my knee to my stomach and nestles in with an ease and singularity of purpose that stops me dead in my tracks. It travels on and seems to explore the whole region of my abdomen, gleefully giving a tweak here and a tickle there, then slamming me in the guts with everything it's got.

"What's the matter?" Dimi asks, and sounds more irritated than concerned.

"I don't know," I answer breathlessly and hold my hands to my stomach as though they can rescue me from the pain. David and Hansi come up and say, "Probably a cramp . . . nerves, no wonder . . . premiere." Hansi trots off to his room with bleary eyes, saying, "Sleep's the best medicine."

Dimi sits down on the edge of David's bed and says, "My reaction to couples can only be compared to the excruciating tortures a drug addict suffers when deprived of his poison." The pain is depriving me of my hearing, his voice seems to be coming from another room. Dimi takes no notice of my discomfort. He strokes his beard and continues, "I shall never travel to Italy for this reason. The Italians always parade about in couples, as though they were born that way."

David is standing in the bathroom doorway, brushing his teeth slowly and methodically. He stops and yawns loudly, has clearly had enough of Dimi for one day. Dimi ignores the hint and says, "Enough of the small talk, let's get to the point, first things first, as they say, although I much prefer second things first since the first things seem to do nothing but accelerate the misery. I need your help, or more precisely, some of your money. My illness is making a comeback, and I might even like to stay alive."

"How far on is it?" David asks professionally.

"It's still negative and the paraffin-pneu is still effective, but there are other signs."

David hesitates for a second, then begins to search for his checkbook; he rummages in a suitcase, sifts through a mass of papers, finds it eventually, and now looks for his pen. Dimi rolls over and pulls the sheet from my face. "It's important to know that a human being has five lobes to his lungs, two on the left and three on the right. He can make do on only one, however, just as he can get by with only a third of his stomach and a twentieth of his intestines. So, you see, a lot is superfluity, whereas other parts are in dreadfully short supply." He takes the proferred check without even looking at it and sticks it into his breast pocket behind the gray and red silk handkerchief. "Koestler says that tolerance is an acquired virtue and apathy a hereditary vice. And Freud said something quite delightful: 'When I have forgiven you everything, there will be nothing left between us.' "

"I can only hope and pray that he's right," I wail.

Dimi looks at me in surprise. "Why aren't you looking more seductive in bed?" he asks.

"Because I've got a terrible pain."

He gets up with a look of distaste. "I'm not fond of illness, excepting of course the manic-depressive variety, enchanting confusion. I'm not really up to survival any more, ambition bores me, work is a potent potion that only makes one drunk, and you, my enviably beautiful David, you live on the periphery of despair and passion and couldn't be better equipped for the battleground of life," he says, but David is already asleep. Dimi moves to the door, still talking. "We are the speechless society, firmly committed to not communicating, and I am only waiting for the day when I shall be empty and inviolable. But it must never become the story of my life that I say, I suffer no more because I feel no more."

"Be quiet and go to bed, for the love of heaven," I say, almost in tears. He goes at last.

The singer doesn't dare to take a sleeping pill, which will make her hoarse voice even hoarser, and she doesn't care to call the hotel doctor. She hopes that sleep will overtake her and dull the pain which is still circling her belly like a coil of wire. As yet she doesn't know, of course, that this is just the beginning, a scratching at the door, so to speak.

•

Moritz is waiting in the narrow dressing room. There's a smell of fresh paint and the windows are wide open. She's looking very distraught as she searches for an iron in her bags. She slams the windows shut and cries, "That's all we need, that you get a cold too. Today of all days they have to go and paint the dressing room . . ." Tears run down into her gauze mask. "Where on earth has the iron got to? I had it in my hand not a minute ago." I'm sitting under the hair drier, my hands are cold and my efforts to apply a line to my right upper eyelid are not meeting with success. Moritz starts to beat my face with a powder puff; she pushes the drier away into a corner, it falls over and the plastic hood smashes into a thousand pieces. She howls into her mask. "We've still got ten minutes," she says. "I'll wait outside."

I lie down on the floor and fall asleep immediately. I have learned to murmur the magic formula: Empty your mind, there'll be time for these thoughts later, you can hear nothing but your own breathing, sleep sleep, tired tired . . . David shakes me awake. He's in his dinner jacket and white frilled shirt, smiling, no sign of nerves. I can hear the unmistakable humming of an audience outside. David helps me up and the vicious pain shoots up from behind the knee again. Archie comes staggering in and slobbers, "I'll be with you, no need to worry, I'll watch the whole time. I love you, you must know, I love you." He's waving his hands about. I take hold of "I love you" as though it were a life belt.

Moritz has found the iron; she's pressing the hem of my white dress for all she's worth, and burns her fingertips as she tests the heat. She pulls the dress over my head carefully, zips it up, then looks at me encouragingly but very uncertainly. I stumble along the long corridor between David and Egon as though I were being escorted to the scaffold. The linoleum on the floor is light brown and smells of disinfectant. Egon hands me his snow-white handkerchief, I rub my wet palms, Moritz is lolloping along behind us trying to pray but can't get her hands together for all the make-up and sprays she's carrying; she mumbles away anyway, and the mask, which is now soaked with a mixture of perspiration and tears, slips down lower and lower over her nose until it finally lands on her chin like a bedraggled Santa Claus beard.

Dimi suddenly comes racing up to us, beaming crazily and dragging Detlef along behind him. "Sweetheart," he pants hysterically. "Leave her alone, otherwise you'll get one on the jaw," Egon barks. They skip off toward the auditorium, gazing deeply into each other's eyes. Again the pain startles me, rippling up insistently. "What'll I do when I have to breathe deeply? The pain'll knock me over," I say. "Take it easy," David answers, "come now, settle down, everything's going to be fine, you'll be wonderful. The house is packed, we've had to put extra chairs in the aisle. Quiet now, settle down."

"You didn't shave!" Moritz screams, and grabs Egon's lapels. "Hilde hasn't shaved her armpits, have you got an electric razor? Quick, quick!" Egon shoots off and hurries back with the razor but we can't find an outlet; Egon finally discovers one behind the door. The musicians file past us onto the stage, there's a polite round of applause, Archie lurches up and asks, "Shall we start? It's ten past already." "No, not yet," says Egon. The cord on the razor's too short and I have to squat down in order to get at my armpits. Moritz inspects first one, then the other, and nods. Archie bobs up and down, takes a running start, and sails onto the stage like an aging chorus boy. He picks up his baton, taps on his stand like a woodpecker, the opener begins. Egon whispers, "Take care, right behind the door there are two steps with ridges, and they've polished the stage again." He gives me my hand mike and arranges the yards of cable behind me. Somebody tugs at my sleeve, I turn, and there's an evil-smelling fat man with a tape recorder hanging from his shoulder and a microphone in his hand; he almost shoves it down my throat as he pants, "I'm from the *Presse* and my question is, Do you feel your songs have a basic message, or are you just offering another form of escapism?" "Could you come back in about a year?" I say, beginning to feel very nervous indeed. Egon takes him by the collar and kicks him in the shins. The man staggers back against the wall snarling, "You'll pay for that," looking at me with unlovely bared teeth. "I'm good at karate, too," Egon says, "and I'll turn your head around the other way if you ever bother Miss Knef again."

Egon takes me by the arm, he knows my cue exactly. He opens the door and holds on to my wrist as I clamber down the steps and into the spot; it blinds me completely as I start my skid across the Olympic-size stage, the beam of light following me like the barrel of a rifle. Applause wells up and flowers fly past my head. One lands on my control loudspeaker, another gets wedged in the border of my dress and refuses to budge—a few well-meaning chuckles from below. Thank you, I want to say as my subconscious somehow gets me to my mike stand as planned. The rhythm's good, what's my first line? Ah yes.— Don't think ahead, just let it come. The nail of my middle finger is ripping into the skin of my palm, steady now, for Christ's sake, O.K., I'm O.K. now, breathe steadily, good. No frog in the throat, off we go. The timing's fine—there's the first twinge in my stomach, as I hit the high note something seems to tear, it's like a seam ripping inside me, so loud they must hear it in the last row. Now the left loudspeaker's splutter-ing like somebody coming up for the third time—we're through the first song, applause, take the bow. Archie's beaming happily. — "Start in on the next!" I yell. —What wouldn't I give for the actor's fourth wall, the invisible screen one can lose oneself behind when playing a part, shutting off all awareness of the audience. Here the medium demands the exact opposite: direct contact, the singer standing head-on, facing the firing squad, spots instead of blindfold. Everyone in the audience should have stood up there just once, not as a form of punishment, or to show that it's not as easy as it looks, making them grateful for any old thing when they get back to the safety of their seats, no, they should stand there once to test the reliability of their arms and legs, and to discover how docilely their loyal egos will leave them in the lurch.

Standing at a noble lectern is entirely different; it discreetly obscures the lower half, shields the cramped hindquarters sticking out behind, or the obscenely jutting pelvis, blocks flapping hands from view as they grope through pockets scratching this and that. Half concealed is doubly secured. The speechmaker can use his desk as a crash helmet, or an armored vest, and can't be compared with the soft-underbellied one-man as he stands alone in the thick of the fray; nor, really, can those fainthearted troubadors who duck behind the piano at the drop of a hat on the pretext of showing you that they can accompany themselves—as though another couldn't do it just as well! And quite despicable is that modern breed of minstrels that takes no chances from the word go, protecting its solar plexus—stomach —liver—gall bladder—spleen—colon with its guitar–machine guns. Absolutely excluded from any form of sympathy should be the type of so-called performer that sits at a table with his arms folded or stretched out in front of him reading—true, the head is free and could be knocked off, but just think, a table! Half the battle's won already, just as it is for a doctor or a judge when the prisoners are brought in. He sits there and subtly recaptures wavering attention with a slight variation in posture and pace, leaves pauses, and ups the tempo at will as his well-oiled eye glides over the passive page with a facility calculated to turn the one-man, trapped as he is in the corsets of time signatures and dependent on the wiles of his own fickle memory, green with envy.

There's an intermission after the sixteenth song. Moritz catches me at the end of the skid and together we stumble back to our freshly painted cell. She peels off the damp white dress, puts it on a hanger, climbs up on a chair, and hooks the hanger over the catch of the upper window. She rubs me down with a towel, dries my hair with a hand drier, rolls my hair up in heated curlers, burning my ear only once. She holds a glass of lukewarm tea under my nose, her hand shaking so much that drops of tea spit up into my eye; at last she finds my mouth and pops a throat pastille in after the tea for good measure. Behind her fresh white mask, she says, "It went just great, you were terrific, great, I really mean it." She takes out the curlers and fetches the black gown for the second half from the "coffin," a six-foot leather case made especially for the dresses.

The musicians are standing in the corridor smoking and drinking. Only now does the singer notice that they're wearing black velvet tuxedos with big Mickey Mouse bow ties, and look very smart, even the pear-shaped ones. "Going well," says Tom, his fingers deep in a packet of health food. "We can't hear a word you're singing, but you sure send 'em," says a saxophone player. "Crazy man, what'd I tell you?" Ivan chuckles. Hansi leans around the stage door in a dark-blue dinner jacket. "Tops," he says, "coming through strong." David sprints around the corner and says, "Marvelous, and the sound's superb, you can be as soft as you like."

"On your marks!" Egon bellows and claps his hands. They file back onto the stage with their heads held high, a remarkable transformation has come over the sloppy jazzmen; only Archie is still fussing and barking at the green drummer. The drummer looks at him with a friendly expression and says, "Motherfuck-ingsonofacocksuckingbitch," knowing full well that Archie's English isn't up to that yet, and drifts back to his post. Egon beams down at me, sacrifices his last white handkerchief, and says, "Take 'em apart now."

After twenty-four songs and six encores, a delirious flower-laden heap of happiness sags back along the corridor and drains a glass of sickly German champagne, pours a beaker of clammy warm Scotch-and-soda down after it. Moritz locks the door and stuffs the gowns into the coffin; the truck with all our equipment will leave for the next town in an hour. The singer collapses onto the lumpy sofa and right away the pains, which she'd forgotten all about after the third or fourth song, worm their way back, knocking her off her ego trip with sly insistence. She sits up and stares at the stained carpet. Outside they're hammering at the door already. "You'd better get dressed," says Moritz and pours a glass of neat whiskey down her throat.

Smiling, and wearing a little black something, the singer welcomes her guests. Fifteen to twenty journalists and photographers pour in. Egon maneuvers them like a riot cop, ignoring their protests; five microphones appear under her nose and two movie cameras seem to want to inspect her tonsils. "What does it feel like to have so many cameras kneeling before one?" a young man asks her in a tone that assures her he'll remain standing.

"Good," she answers after two beats, the picture of guileless simplicity.

"We haven't heard too much of you recently. Would you describe this as a comeback?" the next one asks.

"The way I understand the term is that you come back from being down and out, which I wasn't at all. I just didn't think it would make a good impression if I were to go on and sing 'Love for Sale' in the sixth month of pregnancy, that's all."

Moritz shoots a warning glance.

Now a man with a dome-like forehead and a nose like a saddle: "Do you feel that your songs have any message for the youth of today?"

Before she can answer, a lady as tall and thin as a bean pole elbows her way into the assembly and begins to stutter abysmally, which causes her colleagues to snicker. It takes some time before her question emerges in a clear form. Jabbing her ball-point pen at Moritz, she says, "Can you tell me if this mask your companion is wearing is a publicity gag?"

Moritz doesn't react kindly. She tears off the mask and snarls, "If you think we'd stoop to such methods, you're very much mistaken, I've got a cold and—" and sneezes right into the bean pole's face, "so have you now." Moritz lets loose a salvo of sneezes and they all take cover.

A man in a cloth cap asks, "Do you think that your work contributes anything to the working classes?"

Rudi has pushed his way in through the door. "I sure do," he says loudly. "I'm an electrician, and when Hilde goes on tour I earn a lot of money."

"I was not thinking of individual cases so much," the man says, frowning irritatedly.

"What else is there to think about?" Rudi answers. "Workers aren't born in bundles."

One of them decides to come to the point. "Why don't you sing protest songs? Antiwar songs? I notice these themes are sadly lacking in your program, together with sociological statements." The meeting promises to deteriorate into a display of swollen vanity, a Kafka cross-examination in a singer's dressing room. A woman with large round eyes in a worn face says, "I enjoyed the evening very much, congratulations. I shall write a glowing review." The others look at her with open disapproval, she's broken some sort of rule, it seems. Now a young man with long blond hair that's black at the roots gets up. Perhaps his bathroom mirror's too low, or broken? He whispers, "I used to go to all your movies when I was a kid . . ." The others laugh heartily. "Oh, I didn't mean it as an allusion to your age, but . . . are you afraid of age?"

"No," the singer answers.

"What are you afraid of, if anything?"

"Mostly of people, least of all of age."

"Why not?"

"Because, provided we're not sick or infirm in some way, or dependent, old age could be the best time of our lives; we'd have time to read the things we'd always wanted to, and learn the things we'd always wanted to, and above all to love, selflessly, which we probably couldn't do before, to love with less emphasis on sex and therefore without being influenced by jealousy and egoism and hate. Lust for life doesn't bow out when a few lines and wrinkles appear. If you think that, then you're overestimating the beauty you see around you and underestimating your own. Old age is a time to look and not to be looked at." Admittedly, she feels like some Bible-thumping crusader the moment she's said all this and would dearly love to add that she didn't mean it that way at all; her audience stares at her silently in a manner that suggests that it too could have done with less. Again the sting in the stomach, the poisoned arrow; the pain seeps up like a watercolor, tingeing here and there, gathering in a pulsing clot.

"Could you please define the word 'chanson'?"—"Would you take part in a protest march?"—"What do you regret?

What are you proud of?"—"Don't you agree that our government—"

"Please don't put words into my mouth." He gapes and combs his brain cells for another formulation. They stare at their tape recorders and seem to be conducting their interviews more with the cassettes than with the singer: they never look at her.

"Has success changed you?" one of them asks his microphone. "How do you bring up your child?"—"You look very exhausted."

"Wouldn't you be too, after a two and a half hour show?"

Burping and grunting in the background. "Most of it's technique, isn't it? Second nature for a circus horse like you," the one with the saddle nose trumpets.

"If only I knew what my first nature is," the horse answers.

Moritz snarls, "Throw the idiot out."

"What do you live for? Have you ever thought about it?" a brightly painted child in Carmen raiment twitters, but is shouted down by an elephant of a man who roars, "Tell us a couple of anecdotes, you Berliners are supposed to be famous for your humor and I need something funny for my readers." He snaps his fingers as he says this, life and soul of the party. "I can't concentrate with all this unrest going on," a mature lady says breathlessly, "I need peace and quiet for my work."

"You should have been a war correspondent," the singer says and laughs, but no one follows her example. Moritz suddenly squeals like a cat getting raped, "You get away from me, you vile pig," she screams, her bosom quivering heatedly. "This beast put five hundred marks in my hand and said I should tell him what goes on in here before the show—whether you drink or take pills or shout at me and the like . . ." The thin elderly gentleman behind her looks around for an escape route. Egon moves to the door. The man says, "There seems to have been a misunderstanding, madam. I assure you that I'm one of your greatest admirers, any of my colleagues here will confirm it." He smiles ingratiatingly and fingers an eyebrow pensively, strokes his silver watch chain and inclines his head to one side in a fine display of Old World charm. More confidently now, he repeats, "A regrettable misunderstanding, my dear lady, I assure you." "Misunderstanding, my eye," Moritz bleats. "What d'you take me for, stupid?" "Now, now, now," he says, placating her nobly, forgiving her rude outburst. Egon opens the door and murmurs, "Don't let me catch you here again, sonny."

The fans are kicking up a row outside. Dimi, still clutching Detlef's hand, pushes his way in with a whoop as though he were coming late to a riotous party. Giggling and gurgling, they pick their way among the journalists and cameras, throw their arms around the singer, and exclaim, "Divine," in unison. Sure of his audience, Dimi loosens his high shirt collar and gets down to brass tacks: "The third song must go. The microphone stand obscures your heavenly mouth from the orchestra seats and must be changed. You bow much too deeply, and the houselights must never be turned on during the encores. The buildup to your entrance is not quite right and—well, yes, there's a great deal more but I hardly think this is the right moment . . ." He looks up triumphantly and, indeed, several of the journalists seem impressed, nodding reverently.

"Save it till later," the singer says, "unless of course you need an audience to inspire you."

The media members slowly start to pack their cameras and recorders, mumbling, "*Auf Wiedersehen*," and, superciliously, "My review will appear in due course," quite forgetting that we'll be gone by the time it appears and that it can only influence the local public in retrospect, since the one-night stand is over and done with. The flagellation seems at an end for another night, but one of them turns back and says with the unshakable self-confidence peculiar to the very dumb, "It's said that you write the lyrics yourself." He measures me with a look that says, "Tell it to the Marines," and adds, "Is that true?"

Her fur is rising all the way down her back; Grandfather's warning flashes through her brain—"Never let them needle you. Just because others behave badly, it's no reason to follow suit"— but the warning's no match for the titanic fury bursting up inside her. "Let's get one thing straight, now and for all time: I never let other people act for me under my name, nor do I let them sing for me under my name, and I certainly don't let them write for me under my name. Do you put this question to every author you meet? Or do you reserve it for those who have the impertinence to change their profession?" To her amazement he throws himself down in the chair and lolls there with his massive thighs cocked over the arm, as happy as a clam. "I'll overlook that little outburst and put it down to exhaustion," he says nasally. "Take off," the singer yells, wondering if he'll hit back if she socks him. At this moment Archie careens in with a bottle of whiskey in each hand; he raises one to his suckling mouth and guzzles as though it were Coca-Cola, says, "I love you all," between two lengthy slugs, and throws his arms around Dimi, then Detlef, and is about to do the same to the stolid newspaperman, who's still draped across the chair, when Egon bundles him to the door. As the door opens, the fans pour in and hurl themselves at the limp singer, tearing out locks of her hair to remember her by and dodging Egon's fists. Hansi is borne in on the second wave. "You're the greatest," he says as he goes sailing past.

After another one and a half hours, Moritz and I are left alone in the dressing room; the smell of fresh paint has now been joined by that of sweet perfume, sweat, and cigarettes. We circle around, checking that nothing's been left behind, smile wearily at each other. There's nothing to indicate that four hours ago this same room had been charged with panic. We wrap ourselves up in warm coats and scarves, and shuffle to the stage door. Waiting outside is a small knot of the most ardent fans, those who don't like to disturb in the dressing room. They are blue with the cold, and the flowers they present me are frozen stiff. We shake hands like old chums, and a clicking tells me that David is near. His knees click when he walks, nobody's ever bothered to find out why. He clicks up the corridor, has finished his chores of counting the receipts, seeing that the trucks are properly loaded, paying the hall rental, checking the details for tomorrow. "O.K.," he says, "where do we eat?"

•

From now on, the towns, hotels, and concert halls seem to flow past us. The madness that comes with touring creeps up on us. From the cab I gaze enviously at mailmen, policemen, women with shopping bags, old men on street corners reading their newspapers, people whose days are not focused solely on two and a half hours in the evening. The pains spit and fume; when they subside, I tell myself that they're probably part of the professional hazard, no more, no less, but then come the nights when I sit at the hotel window with tears streaming down my face and a hot-water bottle pressed to my stomach, watching the first gray light come up over the roofs and TV aerials. Whenever I finally do fall asleep, the hotel comes to life; they're building new elevators or a splendid swimming pool, my neighbors start to gargle, telephone, cackle, and shout, bathe like dolphins for hours on end, shave their whole bodies. At the airports we fall down on sofas and sleep propped up against each other. At some time of the day I run through the lyrics with Moritz, reel them off like a litany. The pains grow worse, I call the gynecologist who'd performed the Caesarean. "Nothing to worry about, I'm sure, nerves and a little soreness still around the scars . . ." he says, warming to his telephone diagnosis, and ends with, "No problem for old troupers like us, what?"

Our faces begin to take on the color of domestic mice, we hide as much as we can behind large sunglasses, our clothes cry out for a dry cleaner louder each day—who cleans between two and nine in the morning?—the troupe schlepps itself from concert hall to hotel to airport, in between the half-crazed cry "Where the hell are we today?" Our appearance is beginning to excite public disapproval. "A disgrace!" we hear outraged voices saying wherever we go; "in the good old days they'd've been packed off to a work camp!" Bubi's tresses with the rubber bands and Tom's Jean Harlow look don't send solid burghers.

One night, while we're on stage, a thief goes through the dressing rooms. The green drummer's suitcase and Tom's bag with his health food and salary are missing. The police arrive and one of them says, "Oh, I see, you're mu-si-cians," spinning out the syllables to show what he thinks of them; he seems to prefer thieves. "Jesus," says Tom, "how'll I pay the rent, man?"

I'll never grow weary of musicians' easy optimism, the murmured retorts when Egon goes into his sergeant-major routine; they yawn and stick a four-letter pin in every fat balloon. Archie is still leaping out onto the stage like Nijinsky's drunken brother —he's drinking more than ever, and the band's slowly going to pieces; sometimes they play like amateur night at the village hall. Flying every day is wearing them down, all of them chew sedatives, Bubi even vomits at the airport now. After three weeks the singer has lost twenty pounds and her haute-couture robes hang like a forsaken tent. Sometimes an audience stimulates her and picks her up, but rarely; she'd never really belonged to that group of actors who nurture themselves solely from applause, always having preferred the camera. At the end of the thirtieth concert, her voice gives up the ghost, the last tones of her limited range refuse to deliver the goods.

A professor, no less! comes to the dressing room and is clearly not expecting the hellhole he sees; he beckons to his devoted nurse, she gives him a piece of gauze, he adjusts the mirror on his head with an admirable flourish, hissing through his teeth all the while, and demands an "Ah" in no uncertain terms. He grabs the patient's tongue, uses throat spray on the troubled areas, grunting volubly to express his displeasure at what he's seeing there. This done, he writes a prescription for antibiotics and cortisone tablets, then his bill, which he allows his nurse to present with what one might almost call festive ceremony, lets her help him into his custom-made overcoat, and goes his solemn way. Moritz opens the noble envelope and screeches, "Six hundred marks!" sinking down into a bamboo chair that gives way under her weight. She takes no notice, sits there giving little sobs. Then, strongly, she says, "The price of fame. God, you'd think we'd inherited it, or had a money machine rattling away at home. I bet he'll take the floozy out tonight, two dozen oysters apiece."

"They lifted thirty thousand from me for Christina's birth."

"Let's drop the subject, otherwise I'll sock the next one I see."

The next one is not a doctor but an unfortunate female fan who makes the mistake of insisting on an autograph just as the singer is about to go on. Moritz gives her a left and a right with a wet sponge as the singer goes into her skid.

Later, after the customary press inquisition, after signing her name on programs, tickets, passports, and driver's licenses, after greeting the hall owner's wife (who's managed to stuff herself into her favorite brocade dress yet again and is delighted to see the singer looking a wreck), after the swarm of groupies have made the transition from rockers to jazzmen, and much later, after the nightly search for a restaurant has ended with a sandwich in the hotel bedroom, Egon knocks on the door and tells David that Archie's missing again. David gets dressed without a word, and together they leave the hotel and head for the sleaziest part of town. As usual, they find him in the darkest snake pit the red-light district has to offer, where he's trying to persuade a dozen drunken thugs and pimps that life without Rimbaud is just not worth living. His jacket's gone, his watch and wallet too, but Archie is happiest during these hours as he sits on an upturned barrel spitting broken teeth and nursing a foot that looks as though it's been under a bulldozer, telling his circle of friends of the wondrous man that was Rimbaud. David and Egon get him to the local emergency room, the night doctor patches him up, and we move on to the next city, the next wax-polished stage.

The following night, the third saxophone player runs amok. We're in a smallish German town, the show's gone well, and the hotel has agreed to keep the restaurant open for us. The place is packed with members of the local handball team, who are celebrating an anniversary, and a great number of the concert audience, who now raise their glasses every two minutes in a toast to the singer. She's sitting at a large table with Moritz and David and several musicians. In the midst of the celebrations, the third saxophone player appears in striped pajamas and felt slippers and demands two bottles of cold beer. As he's shuffling to a table, he catches sight of an old black upright piano at the back of the room between two rubber plants. He moves toward it like a sleepwalker, smiling privately and singing a little song, feels the piano lid, raises it; it opens with a loud screech. He looks around delightedly at the riveted assembly, and it becomes clear that Charley is about to fulfill a cherished dream; Charley, forty-five and third sax player with little chance of bettering his position any more, will play the piano, alone and in front of an audience. He drinks a little beer and smacks his lips in anticipation, adjusts the height of the piano stool, and sits down facing his audience with that knowing, sloe-eyed smile the organ players used to have in the days when movie houses offered live entertainment in the intermission to help the ice-cream sales. He holds this pose for quite a while, then spins around to the keyboard, and does something that sends his colleagues' hearts to their mouths: he tries to copy Oscar Peterson's version of "Chicago." For about twelve bars he manages well, but then things start to go wrong; a run dribbles off, a glissando doesn't work; he stamps the pedal with his felt slipper in an effort to drown the mistakes, stops suddenly, and roars, "Don't shoot the piano player, he's only doing his best!" slams the lid shut, and stands stiffly at attention, announcing loudly that this here's a dump and a spy-ring headquarters on top of it. He, a solid tax-paying citizen, has found a microphone under his bed and every word one says, every breath one takes in this house, is being passed on to enemy agents, one isn't safe anywhere any more, not even in the heart of the beloved fatherland, but he'll know how to deal with them when the time comes.

Our efforts to calm him down prove ineffectual. He insists on speaking to the head of the ring, but right now, and on having two iced vodkas sent over immediately. Egon comes shooting out of the elevator just in time, for Charley has already flipped off his slippers and removed his pajama top, the knotted cord of the pants fortunately has given him some trouble. He spends a few weeks at a quiet place on the outskirts of the town and rejoins us two days before the end of the tour with only vague memories of that night when the barkeeper had refused to serve him two vodkas and there'd been a funny humming noise under his bed, voices kept waking him too.

Even Egon blows a fuse a week later. He and his ward, Ken,

the English flower child, move off innocently after the show one night and turn up at the airport the next morning in a condition that makes Archie look like Beau Brummell in comparison. Their faces are bloated out of recognition and their clothes look as if they've come out from under a bus. The spick-and-span airline officials at the check-in counter unanimously declare them unfit to travel on their plane, and it takes a lot of wrangling and promises on our part before we finally get them into the Boeing. They sag down in the last row, and Ken starts singing and making tropical bird noises, tells the stewardess that he's Carmen Miranda and that she should bring him a hat with bananas on it. After a while he quiets down, but then undoes his safety belt, springs up into the aisle, and starts goose-stepping, with his right hand raised in a passable takeoff of Adolf as he sings the Horst Wessel Lied, the rousing Nazi marching song. His performance meets with no more enthusiasm than Charley's had: some of the early-morning businessmen lower their newspapers in what could be purple indignation, but might also be shades of guilt, summon the stewardess, and demand that a stop be put to "this disgraceful behavior, and from a foreigner on top of it!" Others look as though they might just join in if he keeps it up a little longer. Ken is happily ignorant of the tumult he's causing in many a German breast; he marches back to Egon and grabs his arm, raising it high and pointing to his armpit, yelling, "SS, Heil!" as he does so. As every German knows that the SS were branded under the arm to ensure their lifelong devotion to the cause, Egon understandably looks as though he were wishing he had a parachute as every eye in the plane turns on him. His puffed face is a study in agony as he pitifully explains that he'd been fifteen when they'd called him up to serve the Führer, and he hadn't known any better, and so on. He and Ken had bumped into an old comrade on their binge last night, they'd got to singing the ditty more for old time's sake than anything else, and somehow it had taken Ken's fancy, he'd insisted they teach him the words, although he didn't understand a single one. Egon gets worked up as he tells his story. He stands up and shouts at the indignant businessmen, "Anyway, it doesn't hurt at all if young kids like him find out what was going on here not so long ago, he didn't have any idea . . ." He makes a disgusted gesture and sits down again.

Tom says, "Crazy, man," and offers the dark-suited businessman sitting next to him a selection of nuts and sunflower seeds. The giant Negro says, "That must have been some trip there," and even the green drummer shows the beginnings of a grin, but that might be just to annoy Archie, who hasn't risked a smile since his Rimbaud evening. Egon murmurs, "Every movement you make saps your strength," and snores off into a deep sleep.

•

The last day of the tour begins as usual with a dab of marmalade, tea bags, and an egg that tastes of fish. At the airport everyone turns up on time, to Egon's surprise. One of the musicians has food poisoning, two of them have hangovers, Bibi starts retching in the taxi, another three have the flu. One of the three is the singer. Her temperature's over the hundred mark and she sounds like Donald Duck; no throat spray, no cortisone, antibiotics, or 600-mark professors can do anything to help. As yet she still has no idea how she'll get through this last evening in northern Germany's biggest concert hall.

A flushed bundle of misery, she sits huddled in the airport lounge as Moritz comes running up excitedly with a newspaper in her hand: "Just look at that!" A fat headline informs her that she's been voted "best singer of the year" by a team of experts. She wants to laugh riotously but nothing comes out of her parchmentlike throat except a thin, tortured croak.

At the other end of the uneventful flight, a customs officer takes an avid interest in our coffin. Rudi edges up to him and says out of the corner of his mouth, "I wouldn't ask too many questions about that one if I were you, it'll only cause unpleasantness. It's a dear friend of Miss Knef's who used to polish stages, she's waiting until the tour's over to give him a decent funeral." This causes quite a delay, of course, and it's very late by the time we climb into the local organizer's car and head for the autobahn. On it, we move along at high speed, and after a short while we realize that a BMW is set on overtaking us at even higher speed. Our man slows down, the car shoots past us triumphantly, and its driver·sees too late that there's a construction site just ahead of us. He slams on the brakes at 120 mph and the car literally takes off—it ducks to the right and goes into a series of somersaults right across our hood, disappearing into a fir forest, on the edge of which a black and white cow is standing. Moritz screams, the rest of us sit there as though paralyzed.

As I'm standing in the wings during the opener three hours later, the images crowd in on me. At first they're just a shadow play, then bursts of sepia flood the picture, then a landscape by Caspar David Friedrich—hills, treetops, bushes, suddenly the whole scene appears in a zoom shot, in vivid colors, no detail is missing: the car seems to somersault across the stage, taking the pale oval faces in the front row with it; I see the wheels still turning as it slowly curls and rolls toward the trees and the cow. Egon's voice roars in my ear: "What's up? You've missed your cue!" I'm about four bars too late, still I can't move my feet; as the second verse begins, I smuggle my way into it and begin to move out into the spot, feel my legs sliding from under me, follow the spot like a lasso that's caught me, dragging me out to the center.

In the intermission Moritz cries, and great crocodile tears bob on her false eyelashes, sticking the hairs together; she looks at me as though through the teeth of a black comb and sobs, "Hardly anyone noticed you were late, honest." I can't speak at all any more. My throat seems to be bound up with barbed wire, inside and out. Moritz pops tablets and pastilles into my mouth as though she were feeding a slot machine, pours tea in to wash it all down.

In the second half they clap and shout, come running up to the stage roaring "Hilde!" I'd like to say "Forgive me," but don't. I bow over and over again and am filled with a bad sinking certainty that this was the last time, never again. Once more we receive in the dressing room: the quiet ones, the rabble-rousers, the shy ones, and the idiots. Once more they sit staring at their tape recorders in the airless hellhole as they pitch their challenge, demand comprehensive solutions to the world's problems for tomorrow's back page, turn at the door, and say, "Apropos, do you believe in God?"

One rowdy in the crowd wants to sing me a song, another earnest gentleman needs ten thousand marks right away to repair his electric train, and a girl with red hair to her waist has been leaning with her forehead pressed against the wall for the past half hour, making Egon very suspicious. She suddenly turns around and surprisingly has a walrus mustache. "These folks just admire you, but Jesus loves you," he says, and springs through the door like a kangaroo.

Once more Egon, as he takes me in his arms and gives me a karate hug, whispering, "Take care." Once more we pack the hair drier, the iron, and the coffin; for the last time the excited fans stream in, among them a few older ones in catalogue dresses; for some reason they all seem to be caught up in the menopause, they grow red and blotchy, fan themselves frenetically, tear the windows open as they babble, "It was lovely, unforgettable—just think, we're the same age." Once more the fourteen- and fifteen-year-olds, with their pale, tired, confused faces. Dimi's there too, with a troupe of women who all have names like Gil Zita Titi Puta Nini Rikki; one of them's dressed like a gypsy and never stops saying, "*Bella, bella,*" as she tramps around the dressing room staring at herself in a hand mirror. They help themselves to the whiskey and the sandwiches, but not one of them says hello to the involuntary hostess, it's apparently beneath their dignity.

As always, Dimi has no thought for exhaustion, weakness, illness even. Between puffs at his Gauloise, he rattles off his aphorisms: "One can bear the daily drudge only with a modicum of love." And then: "The possibilities of expressing happiness are sadly limited compared to those of expressing sorrow." He borrows from Oscar Wilde and says, "I shall die above my means," which raises a laugh from his new plump young friend, who looks like a Renoir damsel. Dimi's suit is an unseasonal beige, and a red and black silk handkerchief is spilling from his breast pocket. "By the way, I'm flying to China next week," he cries, becoming more and more unbearable by the minute. He bends down to the make-up table mirror and strokes his face and hair, plucks at his beard, says, "I wonder if our Red brothers will appreciate my hirsuteness?" and laughs uproariously. "How's your lung?" I ask him, not too discreetly. "Perfect, absolutely splendid, it was all a mistake, just a cold, that's all, *rien du tout*." He doesn't mention the check David gave him to pay for the cure; it's probably gone for the new suit, or the new Hermès bracelet he's wearing, or on new-Detlef's podgy paunch.

There's a farewell dinner at the best restaurant in town, and in the morning we meet at the airport for the last time. Rudi, Bubi, Ken, Moritz, Tom, and the green drummer are standing by the bus that's brought them, Archie is missing again, is probably reading Genet to the local whores, but no one will look for him today. Tom is leaning against a luggage cart picking at his seeds, and we don't see the small yellow car until it's too late. It comes shooting around the corner, mounts the sidewalk, and hits Tom head-on, sending him flying through the air; casually, like a rag doll, he flies higher and higher, then floats down to the ground and lies on his back smiling, as though it were nothing, his hands still gripping the bag of seeds. A thin trickle of blood runs from his ear and his nose, his soft gray eyes are half open. Tom is dead.

Two days later Moritz comes to the house to visit us and to see Christina. She's got a black eye again. She starts to cry, over Tom, and because of her husband. "I can't go on," she chokes, "he's got another woman. And I can't stand him hitting me any more."

"Get a divorce."

"I can't, we're Catholic. And what about the children?" she sobs. "Do you still have the pains?" she asks at the door.

"Only sometimes," I answer. I don't tell her that they're almost constant.

One evening the telephone rings. A woman's voice says, "Moritz often spoke of you, she liked you very much. She's dead. She was run over by a drunken driver in the middle of the day. The children are with me. I'm her mother."

13

•

Two weeks after the final concert we decided to follow the
gynecologist's advice—"A change of air will work wonders,
get some sun, relax with your family and friends"—and boarded
a Boeing 707 bound for Los Angeles and Christina's godfather,
who had invited us to stay with him.

Almost a year had passed since the patient had lain behind
windows framed by May's freshness, since her child had been
rudely severed from the maternal pulse and exiled to the still
isolation of an incubator.

The plane circled over Los Angeles, the rain streaming down
its windows and along its wings, and landed safely in a sheet of
water like a rudderless boat, shortly after a Tokyo-bound jet
had taken off and crashed into the nearby ocean. "Nobody was
saved," one of a group of panicky sunburned tourists in straw
hats with bandannas whispers in the big hall. "All they found
was sharks, nothin' else." A mixture of horror and delight crosses
their faces; they move off to get a drink, thanking their lucky
stars: "Thank God, it wasn't us, it never is us, it's always the
others."

After the passport and customs rigmarole, we see our friend
standing with outstretched arms. We embrace and hear ourselves saying, "Dreadful, how on earth did it happen?" notice
at once that he's not looking well, the dark-brown contact lenses
are new and alter his appearance considerably. "You've gained

weight and it suits you wonderfully," we say. "If you hadn't written and told us about the eye operation we'd never have noticed a thing." Twenty years we've known each other, Carroll and I. He'd started his professional life as a lawyer, then dedicated himself to astrology. A year ago he decided to undergo a major eye operation. It was performed on the same day in May that his newborn godchild and her forty-two-year-old mother sustained injuries in a clinic near Munich.

The dirty sticky-warm rain almost knocks us off our feet as we run across the parking lot. We jump into Carroll's convertible and the roof leaks like a sieve as we skid through churning rivers of rain and then hit a curb. It's impossible to make out anything through the curtain of fog and water, no streets or signs or houses are visible at all. Hollywood, which I've known for over two decades and never loved, has submerged, submitted itself to the deluge. The skidding grows even more alarming; as we start turning in circles I suddenly hear my own voice crying, "The pain, the pain in my stomach."

A woman with a bright welcoming face is standing in the lighted doorway of Carroll's house. Her expression turns to one of consternation as she sees me cowering forward on the front seat, but soon brightens up again as she helps me into the house and onto a sofa. I learn that she's an old friend of Carroll's and that she belongs to a religious sect that is responsible for her constantly sunny temperament and her nickname, Happy Adelaide. As she beds me down, Happy Adelaide says, "Isn't it wonderful that it should happen here, where we've got such marvelous doctors." A little later she comes tripping into my bedroom saying, "Isn't it wonderful, the doctor's here."

The doctor is as thin as a pencil and has a college boy's haircut and a lizard's eyes. He gazes dispassionately at my bare stomach, then presses it with his ice-cold bony fingers, extracting a short sharp gasp from his patient which he chooses to ignore. He goes on pressing and squeezing as though he were trying to find the hole in a punctured inner tube; he goes over every single inch, digging and knocking even the outer extremities, there where I'd always thought there was nothing but bones. He straightens up, flicking lizardy glances around the room, washes his hands, and picks up the telephone. "You must go to the hospital," he says, careful to smile with his lips only. "See you there."

I'm loaded into an ambulance on a king-size stretcher by two uniformed men, one of whom turns out to be from Regensburg, in Bavaria, and of course he wants to know how it is there now. I say, "Delightful," although I've never set foot there in my life, and he answers, "Isn't that so? Delightful, I knew you'd say that. It's high time I went back on a trip." He looks at my face intently as though he's certain to catch sight of a little bit of Regensburg reflected there.

The rain sounds as if eggs were dropping on the roof of the ambulance, the driver curses a traffic light, turns on the siren, and shoots across.

"What's wrong with you?" the Regensburger asks.

"I don't know, it could be peritonitis."

"Oiyoiyoi," he says, tucking up his upper lip and revealing a gap where a tooth is missing, a sight you hardly ever will see in America, especially not in Hollywood. "You'll be O.K.," he cries as they lift me out again, but I have the feeling that he says this fifty times a day and doesn't believe a word of it.

•

Lizard Eyes is sitting in my room looking at his feet.

"I'm in terrible pain," I say, "can you give me something?"

"Later," he answers, and picks up a folder from the table. "First I need your case history."

"Oh, God," I say, "do we have to? I mean, all of it?"

"All of it."

I begin the recitation, remembering some, forgetting a lot.

"Appendix?" he asks, with an expectant look.

"That went long ago."

"Sure?"

"Sure. Fifteen years back."

I'm not making his day, it's plain to see. I ask him if it could be peritonitis, but it only makes matters worse. Worried now, I remind him of the Caesarean and the belly splitting open a week later, and his silence only deepens. His jaws are cracking as though he were chewing a lump of leather, and he's turned his lips inward, leaving only a thin white line on the outside. Remembering that none of them are fond of patients meddling with their diagnoses, I change the subject and inform him of my allergies. "Please don't give me penicillin," I beg him, "or sulfa or Terramycin. Even some anti-allergics and antihistamines affect my respiration, bring on raging meningitic headaches and cramps in the neck."

He goes out looking pale and sullen; no wonder, it's three in the morning.

An inhibitingly fresh nurse comes in followed by a limp-looking doctor who's obviously been taking forty winks. Blinking wildly, he settles down to search for a suitable vein into which he can insert the infusion needle. He's more used to drilling for oil, it would seem, and after twelve fruitless attempts, willing to compromise, he goes back to the one he started with and gets a little blood. I'd like to congratulate him but the nurse pops a thermometer under my tongue, bares my right buttock, and throws a hypodermic at it like a javelin. "What are you giving me?" I mumble around the thermometer. He shrugs his shoulders and sleepily murmurs "Demerol," as though he couldn't think of something better. "You're not to eat or drink anything at all," he manages to say between yawns, and pads out. The nurse bids me a "Good night, or what there is left of it," and follows him.

The infusion trickles regularly, and after twenty minutes I know that an allergic reaction is on its way. My neck tautens and my head seems to be dancing around the blue emergency light; at the same time my lungs refuse to expand and I start gasping like a fish out of water. I wave my right arm around in hope of finding the bell—it's on the mattress next to my pillow. I press it carefully and precisely, but nothing happens for a long time. I press it again, keeping my thumb on the button much longer now. Nothing. I try a series of Morse-like signals, short-long-short, then I remember the way to do an SOS. Nothing. Now I squeeze it mercilessly, but it gets me nothing other than a distant buzzing. I begin to look my sudden *exitus* squarely in the eye. —There, there's a voice, the voice of mercy, of charity, I could take it in my arms and hug it—but where the hell's it coming from? I gradually realize that there must be a loud-speaker in the room somewhere and that the beloved voice is issuing from it. "Whaddaya want?" it says. "Please" is the most I can manage at first try. "Whaddaya want?" it repeats. "Help, help me, please." A click tells me that I've lost my Samaritan. I grab the bell and squeeze it convulsively, the voice comes back immediately and tells me I shouldn't be a goddamn nuisance. I beg it to try and understand, but it cuts me short with, "Speak into the microphone!" I start to say, "Where is it?" but realize that she can't hear me. A heavy sigh echoes through the room, a sigh that means that she's looked at the list and seen that she's got yet another novice on her hands. "Look on your right-hand side, on the bedside table." She's right, it's there, but I can't get at it—my left arm is bound to the infusion and it'll topple over if I stretch. "I can't reach it!" I cry wildly. "You've gotta learn to work the microphone," she says wearily. I work my way toward it carefully but right away the tube slips from the needle in my arm. "You daren't lose her," my alarm station tells me, and I keep wriggling toward the microphone, but as I lunge for it I hear a click as she gives me up, and the bell clatters to the floor, cutting off all hope of reaching her again.

I concentrate on my arm. I tear off the tape and try to pull the needle from the swollen vein, but fall into a black cavern.

•

I awaken to find the room full of blinding sunlight. Standing over me there's a mighty Medea and she's quacking like a wild duck; I begin to get the gist of her sermon and it seems that I've behaved outrageously, nothing like it has ever happened in the whole history of the hospital and why didn't I ring the bell? I open my mouth to answer and she thrusts a thermometer between my teeth; I lie there sucking the thermometer like a baby's pacifier but this doesn't please her; she pulls it out again and orders me to place it under my tongue. I start to tell her

· 284 ·

that it's so long since I've been in the States and that we always do it under the arm or rectally in Europe, but I don't get far as she shoves it back into my mouth and digs it in under the tongue.

An alarm bell's ringing outside. A white-clad doctor who is new to me, but familiar in the tired-testy way he holds himself, approaches my bloody bed followed by a nurse who's surely gotten the wrong address. She should be down the road in one of the studios making a hospital movie. She has long legs and her hips grind bewitchingly as she glides in, forms an O with her perfectly made-up lips, and looks at the ceiling. "Only the day before yesterday I saw you in a movie on TV," she says, and lets her eyes float down from the ceiling and then rest on my face. "You looked so pretty," she says incredulously. No doubt my face is puffed and swollen from the allergy. Lost in thought, she removes the thermometer from my mouth. Medea, who hasn't moved an inch since she came in, rips it out of her delicate hand and announces that my temperature is 102 degrees. "I'm thirsty," I say, in the hope that her announcement will make this an understandable condition, but it falls on deaf ears. The doctor takes up the business of drilling in my arm where his colleague left off last night, revisits all twelve scenes of yesterday's battle, and then decides to have a go on the other side. He trundles the infusion stand around the bed and braces himself for the attack on the right arm.

"I'm so thirsty," I say again, and with it come heavenly visions of orange juice splashing out of a pitcher.

"You're not to eat or drink anything," he mumbles, without raising his head.

"What is it that I've got?" I ask, first because it really interests me, and second to beg pause in the drilling operations.

"We suspect peritonitis," he says, digging anew.

Although I've had the suspicion myself, the impact of hearing it confirmed is still considerable, and my hospital-trained mind grimly begins to work out my chances of survival; its conclusions are not happy ones. I try to catch his eye in the hope of gleaning more information there, but he's fully occupied with my veins and shows me only his black curly locks and the tops of his clean pink ears.

"How's the pain?" he asks, not explaining whether he means in the arm or in the belly.

"Will you operate?"

"I don't think so, you've just got to stay on the bottle," he answers, and looks up with a grin.

It's a young, open grin, one that invites confidence and confessions. It prompts me to let him in on the secret of my perverse veins. "That one's a roller, I mean it always rolls away, and that one's no use any more and this one here is an artery. Why don't you take the wrist, or the back of the hand?"

"Too painful," he says, but then decides there's nothing for it, and jabs into the back of my hand, nodding at me. He's hardly connected the tube to the needle when the vein bursts and a dark patch spreads under the skin. His nodding turns into a resigned shake of the head.

"Breakfast comin' up!" a child with a face full of freckles bawls as she comes through the door with a tray loaded with orange juice, milk, coffee, corn flakes, bread, eggs, and marmalade. The doctor clears his throat, winds himself up, and explodes, "It's been made quite clear that room 1109 is to get nothing to eat or drink till further notice!" I start to memorize the number right away. The freckled child shouts, "How the hell should I know that?" and backs out with the tray, kicking the door shut behind her. Medea follows her, the film star studies a palm tree, and the doctor starts to whistle "It's Too Darned Hot." Rhythmically, he's not bad at all, but the melody gets into rough country at around the fourteenth bar and he abruptly switches to the national anthem.

We tacitly agree to dispense with nodding or any other form of mutual encouragement as he returns his attention to my veins. He jabs, connects, adjusts, and we sit back and wait. Nothing bursts, no dark patches appear, the drops trickle down. He tidies things up with adhesive tape, goes over to the windowsill, and sits down. He takes an elderly looking cigarette from his pocket and sticks it in his mouth, takes it out again, and looks at it, rolling it lovingly between his thumb and forefinger.

"Have you stopped already, or are you just about to?" I ask.

"I'm working at it," he says doubtfully.

"1109 you said?"

"What?"

"I'm in 1109?"

"Yeah, why?"

"I was in a clinic once where another patient was to have all her teeth taken out. When she came out of the anesthetic she found that they'd taken out her uterus, and the other lady, who was there to have her uterus taken out, she was minus her teeth. I'm willing to bet they didn't know their own room numbers." He smiles mildly and distantly, as though my outburst, which has cost me a lot of strength, was something one just has to accept with 102 degrees fever. "It really happened," I insist.

"Well, yeah," he says sadly. The nurse tears herself away from the palm tree and adds, "But not here." She too gives a little hearty smile, as one does to show a child waking from a nightmare that everything's just fine.

The doctor has a small name tag on his left breast with O'BRIEN printed on it. "Are you Irish?" I ask him, not really that curious, but I'd like them to stay a little longer.

"My father was," he answers, massaging his cigarette.

"I've never been to Europe," the nurse says and looks at the doctor invitingly, but he's looking at the door, which has opened to admit a black girl who yells, "Yoohoo," and prances up to my bed bringing a big cardboard cup out from behind her back and holding it under my nose. "Vanilla and chocolate ice cream!" she coos and beams at me. The stunned silence fires her to even greater efforts. "Our patients just love—" she says, with heavy emphasis on "love," but gets no further as the doctor has finished winding himself up again. "1109 is not allowed to eat or drink," he says, but not so forcibly: this time, it sounds more like a prerecorded telephone announcement.

"But it's so good, everyone's just wild about our ice cream," she says and holds the cup up to his face, trying to tempt him.

"1109 is not allowed to eat or drink, 1109 is not allowed . . ." He gives up.

The black girl drops her hand, gives me a playful prod in the stomach, and is rewarded with a shrill scream. "Easy now, baby," she says discouragedly and slinks out.

He pushes himself away from the windowsill like a swimmer setting out on the second length, circles around the bed, says, "Try and get some sleep now," and hurries out. The nurse whispers, "Bye bye," and treats me to the sight of her beautiful teeth. 1109, I think to myself and fall asleep immediately.

The clock on the wall informs me that I've been asleep for exactly ten minutes when a noise like a violent explosion puts an end to it all. I see two bent backs, then a purple face which is pouring out a torrent of Spanish, then the other back straightens and a second face comes up over the bed end pouring back. Another explosion shakes my bed. "Please" and "*Por favor*," I whimper, but don't stand a chance. They crack their mops from the wall to the bed and back again, and now a third fury with a vacuum joins the fun and games and heaves the bed out of her way as she goes at the deadly dust with a vengeance. The inferno is just reaching its zenith when a majestic nurse picks her way through the cords and pails, reaches the bed un-scathed, and puts a tray laden with bottles and tubes down on the night table. Without a word she picks up my hand, inspects it meticulously, and appears to be satisfied with her findings. For a moment I think I'm about to get a manicure, but then she takes a small envelope from her tray, extracts a tiny file, jabs it into my fingertip, squeezes out the blood and rubs it across a thin slab of glass, applies a bandage to my finger, takes her tray, and picks her way back to the door again, but the gods are not with her this time, and the one with the vacuum manages to get a loop of her cord hooked around the nurse's ankle and brings her down with a resounding clatter. The majestic lady gets up, looks down at the mess, shrugs her shoulders, and goes out. The trio is tickled pink, but now two purposeful-looking nurses shoot in and drive them from the room.

The nurses take hold of my bed and the infusion stand and wheel me out into the corridor, stop at the elevator, push me in, and we descend three floors. We glide out again and the journey comes to an end at a junction of two corridors. It's a very drafty spot and my teeth begin to chatter. There's a clock with a green face on the wall and the time is 7:45. At 8:50 I still haven't seen a soul and I'm beginning to wonder just how much longer I'll be able to hold my water. At nine it's not just the draft that's making my teeth chatter. At 9:15 the whole corridor is full of beds with wan women in them, but not one of their deliverers has answered my repeated pleas for a bedpan.

The women lie there quietly and resignedly at the mercy of a charity which can quite suddenly turn into the opposite. Equipped only with charts attached to their beds, they have entered a suppressive world where their helplessness becomes equal to infantilism; with their signature at the reception desk they have put themselves under tutelage just as surely as the prisoner when he surrenders his belongings at the portal of his jail.

We lie there with our heads pressed into the pillows, with interchangeable profiles; bathed in the loveless blue fluorescent light we all look alike, are shorn of identity. I, possibly the most experienced, begin to weigh the possibilities: Operation? Hardly, they gave me no sedatives last night, no preparatory atropine today, and anyway, I'm not shaved. I move on through the list, disturbed by the pressure in my bladder and my chattering teeth; my neighbor's starting to groan too.

I get no further in my conjecture. At the end of the corridor a shining, faultlessly turned-out blonde appears and moves along the line ticking off her list. My bed starts to move, I look up and see nothing but a bosom jutting over the iron bedstead. The bosom takes me to a tiled room and leaves me there. I look around, hoping to find a clue as to what to expect. The wash-basin, mirror, and fluorescent light tell me nothing. The tap's dripping, not helping my bladder problem a bit. The infusion bottle's been empty for some time now and I can't reach the clip on the tube. The door opens and the bosom reappears. I tell it about the infusion and my bladder, but it remains firm and unapproachable.

I begin to think that there's some code I don't know, or some form of etiquette which I've failed to observe. Suddenly two giggling nurses come in, one a redhead, the other a platinum blonde. They seem to be discussing men in general, and, at the moment, Walter in particular. Walter is a dentist and not at all happily married, it appears; his leisure hours are spent either at the tennis court or in bed with the redhead. She turns to the mirror and adjusts her cap, fluffing up the locks that peep out from under it. The blonde joins her and does much the same; together they gaze at themselves and continue the story of Walter. Walter always wants to do very odd things in bed, but then Ron's just the same, even odder—since I've never had the pleasure of making Ron's acquaintance, I fail to find his antics in bed as fascinating as they do, and anyway, I can't hold out any longer. I raise my voice and tell them about my problems, they turn and look at me like two saleswomen in a toy shop where a teddy bear has started to talk. The redhead is the first to break the spell; she fetches a bedpan and shoves it under me while the blonde moves over slowly and fastens the clip to the tube as in a trance. They move back to the mirror and resume their discussion, tentatively at first, growing more boisterous as they forget my presence. I learn that Walter can't extract wisdom teeth, his fingers are too thick, he has to send wisdom-teeth patients on to somebody else, no wonder the practice isn't flourishing as it should. His wife drinks and takes sleeping pills, wears wigs and has gotten terribly fat, and she's frigid; at the tennis-club party last Christmas she opened the chairman's fly and they don't get invited any more. Their daughter's hooked on LSD and she's only just turned sixteen. "He needs a stabilizing influence," the redhead says, and seems prepared to give it to him. "Ha!" the blonde scoffs; the redhead turns away in a huff and bangs against my bed, spilling the contents of the bedpan. She screeches and throws up her hands, the blonde advances on me with narrowed eyes. "Haven't I seen you in the movies?" she asks. "Could be," I reply. This delights them; they start to flutter around my bed like pigeons coming home from a long flight. I'm wheeled into another room, they change my sheets and then push a metal plate under my back. "What's that for?" I ask. "You gotta be X-rayed," they twitter in unison. "But I've got peritonitis, not bronchitis," I argue. They giggle, as though I'd coined a pearl of a pun. "And I need antibiotics, the infusion must be renewed." This is going too far. Their eyebrows shoot up and their expressions reflect their thoughts all too clearly: Film stars, all alike, give 'em an inch and they'll take a mile. The redhead says, from a distance, "Breathe in—hold it— breathe out," then I'm dismissed without ceremony. A thin black girl pushes me to the elevator and hands me over to a fat white girl. A doctor's standing in the elevator. "Which floor?" he asks. "Room 1109," I say. He looks amazed. "What the hell's 1109 doing down here?" he says. "How should I know?" the fat white girl answers coldly.

1109 is an oasis of peace, the palm tree a symbol of gentleness and benevolence.

"Drink that," a harsh voice commands me.

My hand stretches out to the glasses of red and yellow juice. "I'm not to eat or drink anything," I remember just in time.

"Why not?" She sounds offended.

"Peritonitis."

The tray with the glasses recedes, she looks perplexed. Her eyes search my face as though looking for signs of eczema. She remains silent for a minute, then asks, "You a foreigner?"

"Yes."

This seems to explain everything. "Aha," she says happily and goes out.

I try to sleep but can't because of the pain. The palm tree and I stare at each other.

It must be around midday when Lizard Eyes comes in and sits down on the window ledge. He seems to deflate, as though his bones had suddenly melted. He takes a deep breath and lets his hands dangle from his kneecaps, hanging them out to dry. "The things people do for one another," he murmurs, shaking his head from side to side in utter astonishment. He catches sight of the empty infusion bottle, looks away again. "We just did a transplant," he says, "kidneys. A man sacrificed one of his kidneys for his brother." Each word appears to cost him a great effort. He sinks his head and rubs a spot between his eyes, and for a moment I think he's going to burst into tears. Could it be that the studios down the road have some strange effect on them here? That they're all waiting to be discovered? "One is often faced with a complete mystery," he says haltingly. "Simple people come along and sacrifice themselves without a word of complaint. We see a great many remarkable things in my profession; I never stop wondering at people's courage and strength."

"How big is the team you operate with?"

He looks up and I see that he's suddenly embarrassed; at the same time we realize that his remarks have led me to believe that he has performed the operation, carried the responsibility, whereas in fact he's only assisted. "It's a big team," he says uncomfortably, unsure as to how to set things right.

"I'd be grateful if I could have something for the pain, and my infusion bottle's been empty for some time," I say quietly.

He gets up heavily and goes to the door. "I'll send somebody down right away," he says in profile, and closes the door behind him with unusual care.

Sometime later two nurses I've never seen before come in; they look around the room confusedly, and as always in this hospital, I have the impression that they're not really nurses at all, that they've just dropped in and donned the uniform, then wandered through the building until they came to a door or a room number that took their fancy. They drift over to the infusion bottle, regard it intently for several minutes, then go out again. There's a pause, and then two others, yet again complete strangers, enter and repeat the procedure. They disappear too, and now all four reappear together and seem to have united their strength and made a resolution. They change the bottle, one of them gives me an injection, and they go out again, leaving the field open to a girl with a tray who stabs another of my fingers, squeezes blood onto a slide, and departs. Then it's quiet. No door slams, no explosions, no shouting, nothing. The air conditioning purrs like the oxygen-supply system in an airplane.

During a conversation I'd once had with one of the few excellent surgeons it had been my pleasure to meet in a European hospital, I had made a remark and he'd looked at me like a psychiatrist who had just been about to release a patient from custody but now thought better of it. "You believe in civilization?" he said. "I'd never have thought it of you."

The quietness is uncanny, it's beginning to worry me, something dreadful must be in the making. The door opens and a man who looks like an unmade bed is standing there. He shuffles in inch by inch and on closer inspection he resembles rather a fully loaded clothes tree; his corpulent body is covered with layers of protective clothing: a shirt, a sweater, a vest, a cardigan, a jacket, and an overcoat that swirls around his ankles; the lower half of his face is hidden behind several turns of a hand-knitted scarf. He stops at the side of my bed, hooks a foot around the leg of a chair, drags it toward him, and sags down exhaustedly. His descent reveals a worried-looking Carroll, who's apparently been standing behind him all the while. "This is Dr. Abrahams," Carroll begins to say, but is immediately interrupted by Happy Adelaide, who also comes to light. "Isn't it wonderful," she titters. "Dr. Abrahams is from New York, fate has brought him into our midst today." She plucks at her petite hat and moves in closer. "Everything's going to turn out just fine now, even our California weather is back. All you need is faith." This last and her encouraging smile shame me in my speculation that she'd probably get up and sing at her own funeral. "Politicians, movie stars, writers, and singers, they all love our great Dr. Abrahams," she continues and beams at the back of his head, blushing as she does so. The head, which sports a few cleverly distributed glistening black hairs, doesn't respond. "Our dear Carroll has been working on your charts the whole night and an operation will not be necessary. Isn't that so, Carroll? You don't mind me telling her, do you?" Happy Adelaide whispers worriedly.

The clothes tree moves. It raises an arm like a motorcyclist signaling that he's about to make a turn; high enough to be noticed, but not too far from the handlebars, in case of emergencies. It commands silence, enough of the twaddle. Dr. Abrahams gives a grunt and a wheeze, which develops into a harrowing burst of coughing and tails off in mighty sniffs. "Peritonitis," he says in a rich, plummy, ham actor's voice. I'm not sure whether this is a question or a statement, and decide to wait. His long slanted eyes, which have been closed up till now, open into slits. "Well, what?" he booms.

Happy Adelaide is off again. "Our dear doctor's from Germany, he speaks German, isn't it wonderful?"

The motorcyclist's hand comes up again, Happy Adelaide simmers down.

"They think it's peritonitis," I tell him.

"Think!" he roars from the depths of all the wool and worsteds. "I'll wager they wanted to operate!"

"They thought about it."

"There you are." The corners of his mouth relax and disappear into the scarf. "It's a wonder that they didn't." The eyes close again and he seems to relapse into another snooze, but no. "Then I wouldn't have needed to come, you'd be dead by now," he rumbles and gets to his feet, shuffles himself over to the infusion stand with a series of grunts and wheezes, peers at the label on the bottle, and says "Ugh," as though manure were flowing into my veins. "Get out of here as fast as you can, I will see you in New York," he growls, and touches my arm. His hands, long and slender with nicotine-stained fingertips, creep frailly out of the collection of sleeves and don't fit the rest of the picture at all—for a moment I think perhaps there's another man hiding in there. He turns at the door and thunders, "Do you have a private night nurse?"

"No."

"How come you've survived till now?"

"I barely did."

"I'll send you one. Whether she's any good, I'm in no position to judge; main thing, she's there."

Carroll says, "The aspects'll be better in a week's time, I'll fly to New York with you."

And Happy Adelaide: "We'll pray for you, good thoughts never fail, isn't it wonderful?" She follows the clothes tree out.

Carroll bends down over the bed and whispers hastily, "I'm seeing him today for the first time too, everybody raves about him and I thought he might help. When you get out we'll go to Rose, my doctor, first of all."

Flowers arrive in the afternoon, splendid great arrangements in cellophane, accompanied by a posse of nurses. The flowers appear to do wonders for my standing, more and more nurses come in and congratulate me, offer me candy, coffee, and cookies. My firm refusal is not received kindly: they take it personally and leave me to stew in my own juice.

At five in the afternoon a man dressed like a plumber comes in with a TV set and installs it. I tell him that I haven't ordered it but he doesn't answer. "You must have the wrong room," I say, and he answers, "It's for Mrs. Brewster." "I don't know any Mrs. Brewster," I counter, but he goes on fiddling with the knobs, decides on a Western, and remains kneeling in front of the set until a good round number of Injuns have bit the dust, then straightens up, scratches himself thoroughly, turns it off, and goes. He pops his head back through the door and says, "The movie I saw you in day before last was pretty lousy."

I try to sleep but it's not to be. "Hi, I'm Dotty!" Dotty Brewster, the night nurse, bellows. A face with a great many lines, wrinkles, and all the colors of the rainbow painted there is hovering over me. Powder has been applied liberally to the worn surface, where it has settled in a pattern that resembles the grain on a piece of wood; the hair is straw-yellow; the nose, which peeks away to the left, is long and hangs over the upper lip. Balancing on the nose is a pair of moon-shaped glasses studded with flashing stones, above these the eyebrows are heavily emphasized in black, à la Joan Crawford. The eyes themselves are tired-looking and represent the only feature in the vivid landscape that is entirely devoid of color.

Her head darting back and forth like a chicken's, Dotty Brewster says, "So the TV's arrived already, I didn't believe it when I heard you didn't have TV . . ." Her voice is deep and manly.

She begins to dig around in a bag as big as a sailor's kit bag, brings out a pack of cigarettes and a Zippo lighter, saying, "You don't mind me smoking, do you." It's a statement. Then she picks up the visitor's chair, raises it on high, examines it as though it were for sale, and says, "That'll have to be changed." She goes out and comes back with a kind of chaise longue and a furious nurse behind her. "I can't do my work on that thing there," Dotty roars. She pushes the protesting nurse backward out the door, and slams it in her face. She bends down and adjusts the back rest of her newly acquired chair, throws herself into it, and gets her hips wedged between the armrests. Unable to get out again, she stands up with the whole thing wagging behind her, gives it a fearful kick, and it collapses in a heap. "Where's the telephone—don't tell me you haven't got a telephone either?" she cries unbelievingly, her massive black eyebrows pushing up into the straw-yellow hair. "We'll soon see about that." From the way she looks at me it seems she's made up her mind that I'm from a remote part of upper Asia. She grabs the bell and squeezes it viciously. "Whaddaya want?" the voice I know so well says.

Dotty gives as good as she gets and rasps, "A telephone! But quick!"

"Why?"

"Why? You have the nerve to ask me why? This is Mrs. Brewster!"

"Hi, Dotty," the voice tinkles, "how ya doin'?"

"Not so good without a telephone. How's the slaughterhouse? Same as always?"

"We gotta new one, on internal. Cute."

"A new what?"

"Doctor, stupid."

"Oh, God. Get goin' with the telephone," Dotty growls and signs off.

A man in blue overalls soon appears; he sticks the plug in the socket, checks with the switchboard, hovers around, and then goes out complaining bitterly.

"Ha! He thought he'd get a tip. Well, he can think again,"

Dotty guffaws. She turns on the TV set and switches through every station there is. "My program's at seven," she says and turns it off. She lights her second cigarette and sets about repairing her chaise. She manages well, then sits down sideways. "Abrahams said something about peritonitis. That true?"

"Yes," I say. It's the first word I've uttered since she arrived.

"Jesus, hope to God you have more luck than the last two I had with peritonitis," she says, "they're pushin' up the daisies. Pain." By the time I realize that this was meant as a question she barks, "How's the pain, I wanna know."

"Bad."

The lines around her dark-red lips deepen and her forehead furrows. "So let's do somethin' about it," she says and frees herself gingerly from the armrests, stamps out, stamps back in again with a hypodermic in her hand. "I told 'em we wanted a good sock of Demerol," she chuckles and thwacks the syringe into my buttock at the spot where the sciatic nerve lurks. As my eyes pop out of my head, I hear her soothing bass voice chortle, "How was that, eh? Bet ya didn't feel a thing. Old Dotty's famous for her shots, nobody gives 'em better than Dotty." She's leaned down and bawled the last line in my ear like a circus ringmaster. She hesitates for a moment, then straightens up, and says, "Haven't I seen you some place before? Yeah, sure I have, in that godawful movie the other night. Your hair was pretty, though. When did ya make it?"

"What was it called?"

"No idea. Burt Lancaster was in it."

"I've never made a picture with Burt Lancaster."

"Ha! You can't pull that on me, I saw it with my own eyes."

"I promise you, I've never even met Burt Lancaster."

"Now listen to me: the movie was with you and Lancaster. I'd swear to it in court, and don't you go tellin' me any different."

"Good, good."

She moves away contentedly, clacks her tongue, and all of a sudden her glasses slip from her nose and fall to the ground, one of the lenses splintering. "How the hell am I supposed to see my program now?" she roars as she peers through the good glass at her watch, moves to the TV, and turns it on. She goes on muttering as she sits down, folds her hands, and concentrates on a drama concerning country folk. I notice that my infusion bottle's empty again and try to catch her attention, unavailingly. During a commercial I yell, "Infusion," and she yells back, "When the next commercial's on I'll get ya a new one." She sits through to the happy end, sighs enchantedly, gets up, and turns it off. "Seeing as how you're from Europe, I wanna ask ya somethin.' Should I send my grandchild to Sicily or not?" she asks.

The Demerol is apparently making me woozy; I can't quite get the sense of her question. "Why Sicily?" I ask.

She looks at me testingly through her one-eyed glasses, places a hand on her hip, and says, "My daughter, the bitch, she married a lying sonofabitch Italian. After the wedding, he kicked me out into the street. Don't talk to me about men, mine was no different—take a look at my nose." She pulls off the glasses and leans down. Seen from close quarters, it looks like a tree that's been struck by lightning. "That was to remember him by. Where was I?"

"Out on the street."

"Oh yeah. Well, they get a divorce, what else? and he goes back to Sicily, never sends her a dime, nothin,' and now, after nine years—nine years!—he remembers he loves his kid and wants to have it." She's now crouching over me with bunched fists. "My daughter, the bitch, she works in a café as a waitress and don't have no time for the kid, see, right from the beginnin' I knew who'd have to take care of it, seein' as how I only work nights. And all these years not a penny in alimony. So there we are. Do I send the kid to Sicily, or don't I?"

She polishes the remaining lens on the hem of her smock and sinks down onto my bed, making it sag so that I roll toward her; I feel shooting pains of protest in my stomach and cry, "Please don't." She takes this to be my answer to her question, slaps her thigh in agreement, and springs up. The mattress heaves back up too, lifting me a few inches into the air, making me whine with agony. "What's up?" Dotty asks. "My stomach," I whimper. "Oh sure," she says, and dives into her bag again, bringing out a flowered handkerchief and blowing her nose in it noisily. She settles down in her chair and says, "One thing about my profession, you get to realize that other folks don't have such a helluva good life either." She lights a cigarette peacefully and the flame of the Zippo illuminates her lines and wrinkles, her wobbling chin. "You wouldn't believe it now," she growls, her cigarette hanging from the corner of her mouth, "but I was pretty once, real pretty." The lines around her mouth deepen as she bares her teeth in a proud grin and chuckles.

Her hips get wedged again and she pulls the chair along with her as she goes to the TV and turns it on; Grace Kelly and William Holden are mouthing sweet nothings. Dotty switches to a song-and-dance show, watches it to the end, then there's a movie about prisons. Dotty follows the action for a few minutes, then says, "I seen this before," but doesn't switch programs; during a hectic scene in which the prisoners break jail and the guards open fire, the needle dislodges from my vein. "That's no problem," Dotty exclaims and attends to it without taking her eyes from the wild car chase now underway; darting a glance at my arm, she says, "Just a little sting now, that's all," and turns back just in time to see the leading car hit a wall and spill its dead occupants all over the sidewalk. "Shit, this ain't gonna work," she says disgustedly, "I'll have to get help," and marches to the door, watching carefully as the ringleader dies excruciatingly in close-up.

She returns with an unknown but oddly wide-awake doctor. "What's the problem?" he says easily, sees the mess, and adds gloomily, "Something new every minute." He taps and nudges and tapes things until the escaped prisoners have all been rounded up, and completes his repairs to the accompaniment of a mixed choir praising floor polish. Dotty leans against the bottom of the bed and snarls "Men" as he closes the door behind him. She watches and enjoys a moving drama with Loretta Young, then switches off, and falls asleep, snoring blissfully.

The roof of the garage and the palm tree have just become

visible as Dotty packs her bag, says, "See ya tonight," and stamps off.

I get only one offer of breakfast today, and am then visited by a man who introduces himself as the chief doctor. There's a salty taste in my mouth and panic creeps up on me again, like a snarling crocodile with an unhealthy colorless pallor, albino-like, transparent, voracious.

They were prepared to release me on the seventh day. After I had signed a piece of paper exempting the hospital from all responsibility, two energetic female attendants came and told me to climb aboard a leather wheelchair and not to dismount under any circumstances whatsoever until they told me to. They whisked me from the room, I looked back and saw the shimmering outlines of the palm tree for the last time; then we zoomed along the corridor, deftly avoiding beds, vacuums, breakfast trolleys, and nurses diving for safety, and came to the entrance lobby. I was handed several cartons full of antibiotics, Demerol and Dilaudid, plus the bill, then was wheeled exactly to the end of the hospital territory and told to get up. Carroll saved me from crumpling down again and helped me into his car. I looked back as I crawled in on all fours, but there was no sign of the attendants.

•

We interrupted the drive to the airport and stopped outside a small timbered house. "This is where Rose, my doctor, lives," Carroll said. The door was open and a parrot screeched, "There's someone here," as we went in. The room was dark and full of large plants. We sat down on two bamboo-cane chairs. Sitting among the leaves was a young boy who seemed to be sleeping; after a few minutes he started, shouted, "I was first," and dozed off again. A plump woman of middle age came in and conducted us to a plump woman of advanced age. She was sitting in front of a table full of open paper bags, like the owner of a quaint candy shop. "Put that under your tongue," she said and offered me what looked like a white piece of paper. I did as I was told and stood waiting. She started sticking tabs with red writing on them onto the bags. "You can take it out now," she said, and opened a drawer, taking out a piece of cord with a weight attached to the end. She placed the piece of paper in front of her, leaned forward on her elbows, and let the weight hang over the paper. The cord shivered slightly. The woman, Carroll, and I stared at it, and it began to describe a circle, then an imperfect triangle, gradually settling down to swinging backward and forward in a straight line; then it stopped and shivered once more, like an irritated cat's tail. The woman dropped it, exclaimed, "Oh, my God!" and looked at Carroll in agony.

After a depressed pause, she struggled up from her bags, opened a narrow door behind her, and said, "Come along now." I entered a long windowless room equipped with a variety of contraptions and instruments that made it look like a torture chamber. "Lie down here," she said, pointing to a high narrow bench with leather straps. I climbed up onto it. She fastened the straps and the bench immediately sprang to life, unwillingly at first, making groaning noises and stuttering in its movements, then reaching a regular rhythm; my knees were thrust up and down, something battered the small of my back, and my head was whirled around like a carrousel. "You must have had polio as a child," she called out above the noise. I tried to say yes, but only a shaky chatter came from my lips. "You poor thing," she cried, just loud enough to be understood. I caught hold of her sympathy, howled, "My stomach, please, my stomach," and tried to point at it. She nodded, hauled a lever toward her, and the bronco gave one last buck and came to a halt. I still twitched convulsively as I told her that my stomach couldn't stand it, whereupon she answered, "Wouldn't be so bad if it was only that." Gently she led me to an upholstered couch and told me to lie down on my stomach. "Oh no, not on my stomach," I pleaded, but obeyed. She tapped my back and said, "My daughter'll help you." The plump middle-aged woman came back and I felt cool soothing hands stroking my neck and the back of my head, then a blinding flash of yellow light seared through my brain. In this moment of absolute terror, I suddenly remembered the ship I'd been on once, on my way from

Canada to France, and the gorilla-like masseur who had recommended a chiropractic treatment (which only he knew how to administer) for my war-crippled spine. I'd reached Le Havre with my head bent permanently over my left shoulder and only after a series of Novocain injections in Paris had I been able to bring it around to a near-normal position. These memories succumbed to a black fog, which enveloped me. Before I could formulate a protest, the plump daughter advised me to relax. Then a grinding crunch told me that she'd succeeded in breaking my backbone. "Stand up," I heard. I didn't dare to, but she persuaded me that things weren't as bad as they seemed and I clambered up from the couch, astounded to find that my neck and back were free of cramps for the first time in years. I thanked them profusely and we all shook hands, the mother handing me two of her candy bags, together with a large white envelope. "And stick to the times to take the various pills," she said. They waved to us from their tiny front garden with tight little smiles, as though sending us off to war.

The two bags were filled with other bags, each filled with different-colored capsules and each marked with the times of day at which they were to be taken. The letter in the white envelope repeated the instructions, and also told me when to drink water and when not to. There were capsules to be taken eight times a day at intervals of one and a half hours, others to be taken six times with two and a half hour pauses in between, and then those to be swallowed exclusively with meals, others before and after, little ones to be chewed the moment one opened one's eyes in the morning, and finally those that were only to be consumed in connection with snacks entirely free of carbohydrates, and then before, during, and after. I asked Carroll how on earth they thought that one could live, work, and sleep with such a regime, but he reassured me that it was all a matter of routine.

•

The next morning saw me sitting in the back seat of a New York taxicab, separated from the driver by a thick, bullet-proof slab of glass like a wild animal in the zoo; the absence of any kind of handle or ashtray on the doors indicated that the vehicle had been rendered serviceable for transporting psychotic patients. The driver's "Where to?" snarled out of five inches of open window, bore out this impression. I asked him, "Why the barricades?" but got nothing but furious grunting for my pains.

As I alighted in front of Dr. Abrahams's house on Eighty-eighth Street and walked toward the door, the driver leaned out of his window and shouted, "You must be new around here!" went into a U-turn, and hurtled off like a bat out of hell. I was later to find out that this part of Manhattan, which in the days when I'd played on Broadway had belonged to the impenetrably exclusive East Side, was now a happy hunting ground for muggers of all colors and creeds.

I was shown the way to Dr. Abrahams's office by the uniformed doorman's gloved thumb. I opened the French door on the ground floor and was swept into an antechamber by the wind, went through a second door, and entered a smallish square room. In the middle of the room was a desk on a rostrum; behind it a very slim lady was perched on a stool with her legs stretched out to one side. She was telephoning. She wore a great many rings on her fingers, which played constantly with the long chains hanging from her neck or with the tinkling earrings that brushed her shoulders. Her face was bony and without make-up, her hair was swept back and held at the neck by two tomato-red spheres. She gave the impression of a severe pottery-class instructress determined to go along with the times. Smiling enigmatically, she listened intently with the receiver tucked between her chin and shoulder, her hips rotating as though she had a hula hoop around them. This appeared to be part of her method of telephoning, for the hips stopped rotating the moment she hung up. She felt her hair and her rings, stroked her patent-leather boots, her belt, and her slim orange sweater. She hadn't given me so much as a glance as yet, and I stood before her desk like a miscreant schoolgirl awaiting pronouncement of punishment.

Several pleasantly chatting people were sitting on the suède sofas which had been placed around the room without any apparent regard to form or convenience. The people were all dressed to the teeth, not in keeping with the early-morning hour at all. There were feathered hats, lace mantillas, chinchilla jackets, velvet lined with mink, even an ermine cape, and several Persian-lamb coats, jackets, and hats among the ladies. The gentlemen were all attired in dark blue or dark gray, of best British cloth and cut, with the exception of one narrow denim suit over a violet shirt. The ambience and the fluency of their conversation made it clear that they were old acquaintances, and not one of them betrayed the slightest clue in their appearance as to what could possibly be ailing them; on the contrary, each and every one of them looked the picture of blooming health, odd in wintry New York, and after close scrutiny I began to ask myself whether the doorman's gloved thumb had shown me the right way after all.

The pottery-class instructress raised her eyelids slightly, looked at me with the disinterest of a camel, and pushed three printed questionnaires across the desk at me, saying, "Fill these out." I sat down next to a delicately limbed lady and knocked against her silver-headed cane; I picked it up and begged her pardon. "How charming to have a new face among us," she said. "Would it be terribly inquisitive of me if I were to ask who introduced you to the circle?"—Maybe I've walked into a séance? Or a baccarat party? Not an orgy, surely? "I met Dr. Abrahams in California last week," I said hesitantly.

They all looked at me as though, with a burst of beginner's luck, I'd broken the bank. "I don't believe it," the lady in chinchilla cried breathlessly, clutching her heart. "Last week . . ." Even the boy in denims interrupted his enthusiastic account of a ballet evening and stared at me. "Last week!" they all cried, overlapping each other, as though about to sing a round. The undisguised homage gradually simmered down and a new thought clearly crept through their minds: Perhaps she's really ill? some ghastly contagious disease? The lady with the silver-capped cane moved a few inches away, discreetly.

"You don't live in California, do you?" a lady in dark blue

asked suspiciously, and I could see her running through the possible tropical diseases: leprosy? yellow fever? bilharzia?

"Europe," I said, and watched them heave sighs of relief.

They nodded at each other, but now a new source of discontent seemed to make the rounds. "You realize, of course," my neighbor said haughtily, "that we all had to wait months for a consultation?" Then she laughed headily, as though remembering those medieval times when she'd had to get along without Dr. Abrahams.

"I have to go home today," I said humbly.

"My dear woman, what do you think Baba (a nod in chinchilla's direction) and I have to do? We fly up once a week from Mexico City!"

The pottery-class instructress made her presence felt. "The doctor won't see you at all unless you fill out the forms."

"We all had to," they say, and laugh a little.

The forms were similar to those one completes upon immigration and began with the same harmless-seeming questions: name, age, place of residence. But then, from the fourth paragraph on, they showed astounding originality. They wanted to know which illnesses one had had, reckoned from the day of birth, which medicines, inoculations, operations, anesthetics, pills—including vitamins—forms of nourishment, how long one slept, deep or light, sex life and how often, whether one was a nicotine or a drug addict, alcoholic, tea in the morning or coffee? Maybe both? And how about depressions? I started to fill them out in good faith, but soon saw that an accurate report in my case would take hours and require several supplementary sheets of paper and gave up. "You must complete it," my neighbor said, as though she were conducting night classes, and rested her head on the top of her cane. "Our dear doctor won't be able to help without your information." The pottery-class lady telephoned and whirled her hoop, hung up, and exclaimed, "Can anybody tell me how I'm to fit them all in? The poor doctor doesn't know whether he's coming or going." Nobody took any notice and she looked at her be-ringed fingers glumly, picked up a file, and began to whittle her long nails.

A gust of wind and the slamming of the outer door made her and all the others look up. Dr. Abrahams came in; that is to say, the collection of garments I had seen in Hollywood, augmented today by an Austrian hunting cape, most unusual for New York, moved into the room without a word of greeting and headed for a small wallpapered door. The untidy state of his few black hairs and the black stubble on his chin made it apparent that he'd left wherever it was he was coming from in a hurry. The chorus of hellos seemed to startle him: he looked around bewilderedly, as though trying to fathom the reason for this copious assembly. He darted through the door and one heard a dreadful fit of coughing, then the sound of gargling, then the hum of an electric razor. "The poor thing," Baba, the chinchilla lady, murmured, and everybody nodded in agreement.

Their interest now shifted to a large fat girl with cropped dyed-red hair who came through the door pushing a wheelchair, saying, "There we are, good morning, everybody." A very old lady with a head no bigger than an infant's was huddled up in furs in the wheelchair. Her head appeared to be attached to her body by a spring. It bobbed back and forth with each movement of the chair like a buoy in a swell, her thin speckled hands stroking the furs and the armrests continuously. The girl let herself fall onto one of the low coffee tables, displaying white boots, thick mottled thighs, and pink underwear under her supermini skirt. She lay there spreadeagled as though waiting for some kind gentleman to oblige her. The old lady stammered, "Give me the book, please." The girl went around the wheelchair, took a black album from a bag, and laid it on the fur rug. It fell to the floor. "Can't you watch out?" she snarled at the old lady. "Forgive me," the old lady said, and cowered down. "Now hold on to it this time," the girl said, as though she were talking to a naughty child and showing how patient she could be. The lady began to turn the pages aimlessly, stopping now and again to stroke a yellowed photo, letting her head incline. "When is the doctor coming?" she asked suddenly, looking up in alarm. "Soon, soon," the pottery-class lady called out, winking at the girl. The boy in denims looked at the old lady as though the sight of her was a personal insult.

The girl leaned against the desk, chewing on a thumbnail, and the pottery-class instructress sprang up and disappeared through the small door as a light went on over her head. "Hello, hello," a sonorous voice boomed from the antechamber. An elderly gentleman sprang into the room, fondled my neighbor's cheek with two fingers, and cried, "Where's the genius?" looking around as though he might be hiding behind one of the settees. Catching sight of me, he said, "New?" "New," I answered. He clapped his hands, sang, "Does she know how fortunate she is? He saved us all, every one of us," and looked at the others eagerly. "Sure, sure," Baba answered, and snapped the lid of her powder compact shut. He'd expected more and sat down sadly on the edge of a sofa, stretching his legs out in front of him like a cowboy. He tried again. "Look at me," he called out. "Two years ago I was a physical wreck and now . . . now I'm a boy again." He jumped up to prove it. "Just look at me, I'm fifty-nine. Would you believe that now?" "Yes," the boy in denims said and giggled unashamedly. The fifty-nine-year-old waved his remark away with a grand gesture and turned back to me. "You'll see, my dear. You'll have faith in no one but him."

The very old lady said, "I'd like some water." The girl shrugged her shoulders and retorted, "No water before treatment." The pottery-class woman came back and waved her hand in my direction. "The doctor would like to see you first," she called. My neighbor stood up and rapped the floor with her cane. "That's going too far," she said indignantly. I crossed the room in icy silence and went through the door.

I found myself in a white cubicle that was about as large as a roomy broom closet. The walls were full of shelves; lying on them were books, magazines, and two Velázquez prints. Under the shelves and along the wall was a divan, in front of it stood a horseshoe-shaped table laden with bottles and plastic throwaway syringes, beyond this there stood a swivel chair under an open window. The chair contained the sleeping form of Dr. Abrahams. He had stripped down to his wrinkled shirt, fat-stained vest, and like trousers, and looked washed-up, run-down, and in need of help. My entrance caused a draft and the window sailed open and hit Dr. Abrahams squarely on the side of the head; it was possibly the only window in New York that was constructed according to European preferences, the frame opening inwardly on hinges at the side. I closed the door but the draft remained, and the window continued to flap to and fro, hitting Dr. Abrahams at the same spot on his head each time. With each blow his knees came up and hit the table, knocking over the bottles and syringes, but Dr. Abrahams didn't stir. After a few moments a hand reached out and started scrabbling around the table, knocking off the rest of the bottles, and found what it was looking for, a pack of cigarettes. "Do you smoke?" he asked, still not having moved anything but his hand, and went into a fit of coughing. "Yes," I answered. "You shouldn't," he said, and opened one eye about a millimeter. He lit his cigarette and let the still-flaming match fall into the red and yellow pools that had spilled onto the table; the window flew open again and missed him by half an inch. His chin sank down onto his dirty shirt and the cigarette in his mouth began to singe his vest. He casually flicked at the smoldering cloth, said, "I haven't slept for four days and nights, I don't sleep at all any more," and dozed off again.

After some five minutes he stretched himself and pressed a knob on the wall. He was now within range of the window again and it promptly hit him on the brow. A nurse rushed in, took some of my blood, and rushed out again. Dr. Abrahams now woke up. He awoke as I imagine an old locomotive would, after many years of disuse; creaking and groaning and whistling, letting out clouds of coal-black cigarette smoke, he shunted back and forth on the chair until he had achieved a position from which he was able to avoid the haymakers the window had been dealing him. Kicking the bottles and syringes away from his feet, he looked at the closed door and said, "Silly bitch." By way of explanation, he continued disgustedly, "They're all idiots, they mix up the blood tests." He stood up and looked for something on one of the shelves, the proximity of his large stomach forcing me back against the wall. He fell down into his chair with one of the Velázquez prints in his hand, the window catching him a glancing blow behind the ear as he settled back. Not once did he make an attempt to close the window, or even push it away, the blows and his sporadic success in dodging them seemed part of the Abrahams routine; my suggestion that a heavy object placed on the ledge would still admit fresh air but prevent the window from opening so far that it would disturb him brought a grim expression to his face but no reply.

"My invention will revolutionize the art world," he said and began to shake an apothecary bottle filled with a copper-colored liquid like a barman mixing a dry martini. He rummaged around in the mess on the table and came up with a thick brush and a filthy rag. Alternately using the brush and the rag, he dipped them into the liquid and set about rubbing the Velázquez print with them. "Now look," he said as he rubbed, "see how the gold there comes to life? What if I went to work on Rembrandts, eh? The world of art would go crazy." And it was true, the colors had deepened and come to life, were fresh and glowing, as though the painting had come straight from the artist's easel. "What do you say?" he cried, and smacked his thick lips, already tasting his worldwide triumph. At the same time the corner of the window dealt him a wicked clout on the ear and a trickle of blood ran down his cheek; apart from hunching a shoulder and wiping the blood off on his shirt, he didn't react at all.

He now looked at me for the first time since I'd entered the room. "Why are you wearing that coat?" he asked aggressively. "Because it's cold," I said. Turning furiously in his chair, he ripped the door open and bellowed "Coat!" That was all, just "coat." The pottery-class woman sped in, tore the coat from my back, and sped out. "Stupid cow," he growled angrily, throwing up his arms and spilling the liquid from the apothecary bottle. "Bitches. Hair, fur hair in particular, is poison for my medicines. It must never, and I repeat never, come into this room." With this he slumped back into his chair.

We sat there silently among the broken bottles and the plastic syringes swimming about in the multicolored fluids. Dr.

Abrahams had closed his eyes and I watched fascinatedly as the puddles seeped into each other, forming ever new rivers and lakes. "They are my invention," he growled. "I worked for years to perfect them. They don't like fur." The window gave him another rap and he raised his hand and stroked his head as though warding off a fly.

"I didn't fill in all the forms," I said guiltily. He raised a hand and answered, "They're only to keep the idiots busy." A hand came around the door and placed a slip of paper on the edge of the table, then jerked out again, as though afraid it might get hacked off. He held the piece of paper at arm's length, coughed miserably, wheezed, "Good God Almighty," and lit another cigarette. "I smoke because I'm seventy-two and not all too keen to while on this earth much longer, but I also suffer from Jewish indecision, and this has me going down to the Atlantic and swimming at five every morning, regardless of season or weather."

"If you'll permit me to say 'goyim naches' without having me thrown out by one of your furies, I'd like to say 'goyim naches' right here and now." His reaction was in keeping with much else about him. First of all, he cupped his slender nicotine-stained fingers around his ears as though wanting to make sure that his hearing was intact, then he slowly closed his eyes, as though fighting a losing battle with a fainting fit, then doubled up, so far as his belly would allow, and slid down from his chair, without making the slightest attempt to prevent it, landing with a mighty crash on the floor. He sat there among the broken bottles and puddles of elixir and began to rock back and forth like a mourning woman of his creed, hooting and roaring anguished noises, which, I slowly realized, was his version of laughing. A torrent of tears poured from his right eye, whereas the left one yielded only tiny drops. Between noises, he asked, "Are you a Berliner?"

"Yes."

"From Charlottenburg, Schöneberg, or Wilmersdorf?" he asked, sober now.

"Wilmersdorf."

Carefully, almost timorously, as though his face were only

provisionally sewn up and might suffer permanent damage if he were to stretch it too far, he started to smile. His face fairly melted. "Wilmersdorf," he said slowly, tasting every syllable. I imagined I could see a rather fat young boy with large eyes that appeared sleepy on first glance but alert on second, protruding lips, and black sleek hair standing before me; squeezed into a tight but expensive and clean suit with short trousers ending at the knee, below them dark stockings with garters and brightly shining shoes. I saw him swinging his satchel boastfully as he and his schoolmates sprang teasingly but possessively around a row of blond, dark, and red-haired girls who'd linked their arms in a show of mock defense; I saw him run through the silver-birch wood between Rheinstrasse and Varzinerstrasse, saw him licking blueberry and vanilla ice-cream cones in the shop on Innsbrucker Platz, riding his bike over the gravel paths in the public park with the keeper shaking his fist after him, saw him throw his banana skin in the sandpit on the playground in front of the Kaiser Platz cinema. I didn't like to ask him which school he'd been to, but my emanations apparently did it for me, and he said, "I went to the Treitschke Gymnasium. And you?" "The Rückert School." We grinned at each other like members of a small gang that has brought off a big coup. "It was the best time of my life," he mumbled as he got up heavily, accepting my outstretched hand. Looking more disheveled than ever, he collapsed in his chair. "I've never been back," he said, "not since '36. One shouldn't visit one's past." The window hadn't moved the whole time he'd been down on the floor, but now it swooped in and whacked him on the back of the head, putting an end to his reveries.

After searching through several bags, cases, and drawers, he found his half-moon-shaped spectacles and put them on, took two rubber-topped bottles of medicine from a shelf, ripped open the plastic covers of four or five syringes with professional speed, stabbed the needles through the sterile rubber tops, and peered up over his glasses as he asked concernedly, "Are you afraid of injections?"

I stared at him in sheer astonishment and asked with a faint voice, "What did you say?"

"I asked you whether you're afraid of injections."

"No one ever asked me that before."

Holding the bottle up to the light, he said, "That I'll believe willingly. Unfortunately. It was always a little rough in Europe's clinics, and it's not exactly dainty here either. Did they give you enough pain killers in the hospital when you left?"

"Whole valises full of Dilaudid, Demerol, and morphine derivatives of all shapes and sizes. I could start a respectable drug trade."

He sniffed disapprovingly and said, "At least they weren't completely stupid."

"In Europe they let you go with a handshake and lots of advice, but no drugs. When you get out of the hospital there, you can call a nice little general practitioner and tell him what happened, being careful, of course, not to tell him the more gruesome bits in case he gets worked up, but explaining about allergies and so on while you bite on your finger to keep yourself from screaming with pain. Then he'll look at you sideways, as if to say, 'I've heard that one before,' and promptly give you the latest thing in synthetics that does nothing at all for the pain but knocks you sideways with a new allergy. He'll then stand at your bed and say the standard phrase in these cases, 'This has never happened in the whole of my career . . .' and give you gallons of cortisone but still nothing for the pain. Then he'll grin mischievously and say, 'We have to be careful, you know, at first I thought you might be addicted, knowing how people are in your profession . . .' "

"I sometimes wonder if it's wise that people think at all," Dr. Abrahams said, lost in thought, and relapsed into a fit of coughing. Coming back from his fit, he inspected my lower regions in search of a suitable spot to administer his injections. "You haven't got enough fat on you to keep a cat alive for two days," he said grumpily, jabbing expertly into my thigh.

"What is that you're giving me?"

"Something very delicious," he said, his eyes glinting wickedly, "but for me to be able to help you properly, you'd have to stay for a couple of months." Before I could answer, he held up his hand and said, "I know, don't tell me, you haven't got time. Nobody's got time when it's a matter of life and death. Did it hurt?"

"Not at all, I didn't notice even," I answered, almost stuttering in view of his gentleness and kindness.

He grinned with satisfaction and went grinning back to his chair; the window leaped forward and slugged him on the jaw but couldn't stop the grinning. " 'What doesn't kill you will serve to make you stronger,' our friend Nietzsche said. It was quoted to me the first time by one of my brilliant professors, who thereupon became an ardent Nazi." Once more the arm shot through the door and hastily threw a computer card onto the table. He gave it a cursory glance, fumbled with his glasses, coughed violently, and said, "These are the first results of your tests, they're worse than even I would have thought possible. Do you still have pain?"

"Well, yes," I said, "but I can bear it."

Apparently I'd said the wrong thing. He threw up his arms and attacked the window fiercely. He slammed it shut and hammered on the catch, turned it furiously as small splinters of glass tinkled down from the upper corner. Like an aggravated bear he shuffled around the tiny room, then let himself fall into his chair with a hefty "Ach. 'I can bear it'—bear it!" he said, aping my tone of voice. "What do you want, a medal for bravery, for putting up with suicidal pain for so long?" He stuffed a bedraggled cigarette between his moist lips, struck a series of matches before he found one that didn't break, lit his cigarette, and said excitedly, "What am I getting excited about?" Since his attack on the window he'd spoken German; what he'd said, together with the immense fury with which he'd said it, reminded me of my grandfather, and I smiled.

"My German's better than I thought," he said, returning my smile. He leaned forward and whispered in my ear, "Do I have an accent?"

"Only when you speak English," I said truthfully.

He thrust himself back and whinnied, and I thought that he'd forgotten his anger, but then he leaned forward again, his nose almost touching mine, and snarled, "Who gave you all this stiff-upper-lip crap? Your doctors? Or your parents and teachers? How can I prove that pain is more harmful than the worst habit-forming drugs even? How can one prove that a heart attack or a circulatory collapse wasn't caused by too much pain? Especially if you're dead already? And how are you going to judge how much pain you can stand? By the way, the bigger the idiot, the less sensitive to pain he is. It's no coincidence that torture has kept its popularity over the centuries, and not in the least surprising that more money is spent on finding new subtle ways to induce pain than to kill it. It's always been that way, from religious sacrifices to acts of vengeance, from the Gestapo's prisons and concentration camps to Korea, Vietnam, Greece, South America, and our sacred cow, the hospital."

Although he'd spoken intensely, hardly pausing for breath, he resembled a refugee who realizes that the last train to freedom has already left. With a look of complete hopelessness, he murmured, "And then along come the academic specialists—like me—and recite *their* standard phrase: 'Above all, we mustn't endanger life.' First, we harm much more than we help, and where we could help, we're mostly afraid of endangering the position we fought for so hard—once we get the position, nobody will ever question our capabilities again, as long as we stay out of trouble. A cemetery doesn't talk, and we tell the children to pull themselves together because we take a much smaller risk if we can work without anesthetics."

He sniffed noisily and put his slender hands together. The cigarette between his thick lips was down to its last fraction but he made no effort to remove it. "Illness and interdiction seem to be developing into a perfect analogue. Here we don't put our patients under tutelage with the same perfection our European colleagues have reached; on the other hand, we don't have a proper national health system either, so you can take your pick." He chose to ignore the quiet ringing of his telephone; instead he flung the window open again saying, "We'll suffocate before we're very much older," and lit another cigarette. "If we wanted to do the job of interdiction properly," he said, "we'd have to start by reverting to prohibition methods and closing all the bars. Any blockhead can drink himself to death with a few fifths of gin, but the gorgeously publicized adolescent drug problem is a much better bet for the pharmacological industry to get richer than they already are; a shot of morphine, on the official market, is cheaper than a bottle of Coca-Cola."

The pottery-class lady swept in after knocking some five or six times and whispered excitedly into Dr. Abrahams's ear. He listened to her with closed eyes, then snapped, "Put him under the lamp." She stepped over his outstretched legs and went out, whirling her hula hoop.

"Your patients seem to be devoted to you," I said.

He yawned and said, "They're all as healthy as young lions. They just need somebody to treat them badly and take them seriously at the same time."

"Even the very old lady in the wheelchair?"

He swiveled around and looked out at the gray street. "Not even Allah can help her," he answered. He stood up suddenly and said, "I'd like to look at your stomach." I lay down on the divan; he removed his spectacles and stared at my stomach for what seemed an eternity. "Where was this operation performed?" he asked finally.

"In Germany."

"I would have guessed in a wigwam."

"When I came round from the anesthetic, I had 15 percent hemoglobin, and eight days later the wound split open."

"Is your child healthy?" he asked, almost excitedly.

"Yes."

"How old?"

"Nearly a year."

"Boy or girl?"

"Girl."

"Can she sit up, stand?"

"She can sit, but not stand yet."

"And you call that healthy?" he yelled.

"We've been to several German pediatricians and they all say she's a late developer, maybe a little lazy."

"Lazy, lazy . . ." he complained and turned back to the window. "There are times when I can't help feeling that most doctors are trained in tree nurseries." He took me by the arm and said, "When you get home, go straight to Bern. There's an excellent children's doctor there. Understand? By the way, your peritonitis might still have to do with the Caesarean, and your liver test is a catastrophe. Apart from all the other small delights in your life, you must have had a bad case of hepatitis at some time."

"Twice. And after my daughter's birth they gave me a lot of blood transfusions. The gynecologist looked at my liver test and asked me if I was an alcoholic."

"They all do that, to make you feel guilty. It puts them in a stronger position."

"Later he recommended that I go to his clinic for glucose injections; I went in, once for three days and once for four, and he sent me a bill for fourteen thousand marks."

He gave a long low chuckle, not letting himself be distracted by a renewed beating by the window, and said wistfully, "Perhaps I should go back to Europe after all."

"The rest of the story's quite interesting too. My husband talked of having the bill framed, but then thought better of it and added it to the pile he likes to think about for a few months. Your revered colleague's reminder duly arrived and we were delighted to note that the new bill had been reduced by twenty-five hundred marks without any comment. We waited again and the next reminder came by registered mail, and had shrunk a further four thousand. This touched my husband's sense of fair play, and he offered a total of five thousand all told, which the man accepted with thanks."

"I went on a trip to Kuwait once, I wonder if your gynecologist learned his trade there?" Dr. Abrahams murmured thoughtfully, shaking his head and rubbing his eyes at the same time.

"Then he talked about puncturing the liver."

"Madness, sheer madness," he babbled, growing more and

more distressed and sinking down into his chair. "What am I to do with you?" he cried. "Outside, there's a famous writer who comes every day. He's perfectly healthy and can't wait to get sick. You're sick and want to get healthy. I can give you the medicines to take along with you, but you'll have to inject them yourself."

"I can't do that."

"Why not? The biggest dumbclucks do it here. You have to aim at the upper buttock muscle, or the outside of the thigh. Here—" He started to draw on my thigh with a felt-tipped pen. "Do you think doctors want to be called in to give you a vitamin shot? And think of all the money you'll save. O.K. One shot three times a week. When are you flying home?"

"This evening."

"Not if there's a snowstorm, you won't. And write to me." He tried to get up, decided against it, and held my hand gently. "I admire your songs," he said with a disarming smile.

"How do you know them?"

"I'm still not old enough to be above the occasional attack of homesickness," Dr. Abrahams answered. "And don't try to 'bear' pain any more, your nerves won't stand it. —Do you know what we need? More cortisone. Just look at the pregnant women. They'd never dare to show themselves on the street without the additional supply of cortisone the body produces in pregnancy. Cortisone gives us a lift, takes our inhibitions away." He said this like someone who had had it at the back of his mind for a long while and had suddenly remembered it was there. Then he looked tired again and said, "Ah well, what the hell. Ask three doctors and you'll get three different answers, that's what we call science."

In the way he sat there, crumpled up, wizened-wise, ironical and full of sympathy, dominant, alert, and resigned, a bundle of opposites, he reminded me of a great many other friends I'd had in California and New York, and who have nearly all died, one after the other, within a very short space of time. They were friends who had taken me in when I had arrived from the ruins of the land that had evicted them, or caused them to leave all their possessions and flee; they had admitted me to their circle and taught me about a world that had already been destroyed by the time I was old enough to look about me. I bent down and kissed him on both his badly shaven cheeks, then on the mouth, a little ashamed of this melodramatic way of saying goodbye, and very glad that I'd obeyed my emotional instincts. Caught up in a web of doubts, memories, and sadness, I said, "Your patients'll probably lynch me." He grinned as he sidestepped a vicious wallop from the window and said, "I've got a back door." He raised one hand, added, "Don't let them operate on you again," and turned away quickly, replacing his Velázquez on the shelf.

Two years later I went back to New York and learned that Dr. Abrahams had died of cancer. The list of friends whose death certificates have borne the word "cancer" seems as long as the number of fallen recorded on a town's war memorial.

Three hours after I had left Dr. Abrahams's office, the Lufthansa Boeing took off from Kennedy airport. It was the last plane to leave before the airport was closed for a week owing to constant snowstorms.

Our daughter Christina was already used to flying; still, she was thrilled to bits to be able to sit in the monster's belly and watch movies, hear music coming out of the armrests, pronouncing it the best toy yet. Perhaps it was a little too colossal, at all events she was fast asleep by the time we peeled away from the East Coast and headed out over the Atlantic. She lay snoring softly in one of the wide seats, and, as so often, I had the irresistible urge to protect her, physically, with my body, to annul her defenselessness and dependence.

The stewardess came and asked me whether she should put my packages up in the net. I said I'd be grateful if she'd put them on ice. Until my conversation with Dr. Abrahams, I hadn't realized the full meaning of the cartons I'd been handed so casually in the Hollywood hospital: for the first time in my career as a patient I'd been entrusted with a responsibility and treated like an adult.

Until now my position had always been that of a turtle on

its back, with small chance of finding someone to turn him over again; helpless, left to his suffering and pain. The fact that it's impossible to gauge another's pain allows us all too easily to become inhumane, inhuman; and even a person who has suffered excruciating toothache or migraine will laugh about it an hour later, when it's gone, because now it can only be assessed as a ratio, not really felt any more. This alone makes us unsuitable as feeling beings, and the title "fellow human being" bears witness to our gigantic simplicity or vast cynicism. My friend Henry Miller says, "For the person who feels, life's a tragedy, for the thinker it's a comedy." But how to apply the intellect, a taste for the unusual, when pain is gnawing at you like a pack of hungry rats? We weren't brought up to defend ourselves, we were trained to nod and duck and let it happen, as it always has happened and always will. We were taught not to ask questions and be thankful for one heroic, humane deed, forget the thousand atrocities.

The pilot switched on his intercom and told us his and his co-pilot's name, asked us to forgive him the delay in taking off, told us how high and how fast we were flying, what time it was now and what time it would be when we got to Frankfurt. Snow swirled by the windows and the plane rolled like a trawler in a fair-to-average high sea. Pilots have to undergo a thorough checkup every six months, I thought to myself. I've known a few and know too that they spend restless nights before these tests; they worry about the meticulousness with which they are held up to the light and tested: the heart, the kidneys—their physical and psychological health checked out to the last degree, to ascertain whether they're still capable of carrying the responsibility for human life. Who checks up on doctors? After the one qualifying examination, taken usually in their mid-twenties, they are established for life; in spite of stress and overwork, and regardless of whether they keep up with the constant flow of literature, information on new breakthroughs in every field of medicine, they will never have to submit to a test again. Pilots yes, but doctors no? Doctors, by and large, are almost childishly proud of their "science," and will defend this title fanatically, although the qualities that distinguish good doctors from bad ones belong in the realm of suspect parapsychology: the good ones have a "sixth sense" and obey an unerring "instinct," whereas the bad ones go by the book.

Three doctors, three different opinions.

But should there not be checkups on their continuing competence?

As opposed to the procedure for establishing guilt when a plane crashes, no indestructible little black box can be taken from the wreck of a human being.